"Weina Dai Randel's *The Master Jeweler* is a perfect, glittering, gorgeous jewel of a novel. You will be more than riveted; you will be transported. You will be utterly and wholly consumed. Delicious, decadent, and dripping with detail, this book is historical fiction at its best, at its most powerful and heartbreaking and beautiful, telling the story of one astounding young woman's ascent in a profession both unspeakably elite and punishingly difficult. It is a stunning tale of yearning, passion, betrayal, and sacrifice, spanning Shanghai's golden age to the turbulent years of the Japanese occupation and beyond. Reading *The Master Jeweler* felt like holding a Fabergé egg in my hands; I was in such awe. I absolutely loved it."

—Kristen Loesch, author of *The Last Russian Doll*

"*The Master Jeweler* is a brilliant tale of resistance and courage set against the glittering backdrop of the world of jewelry making and all its lurking dangers. Weina Dai Randel's meticulous research and vivid storytelling leap off every page, from Harbin to Shanghai to Japanese-occupied Hong Kong, immersing readers in a rich, evocative world. Anyu's bravery and determination will have you cheering for her with every twist and turn. A masterful novel that sparkles with depth, heart, and unforgettable suspense."

—Madeline Martin, *New York Times* bestselling author of
The Booklover's Library

"*The Master Jeweler* is Weina Dai Randel's best book yet. An unforgettable heroine, a relentless plot among the criminal rings of 1920s Shanghai, and prose that shines like a cut gem make this novel impossible to put down."

—Olivia Hawker, bestselling author of *October in the Earth*

"From 1920s Shanghai to 1940s Japanese-occupied Hong Kong, this extraordinary and immersive story of an orphaned girl with a preternatural gift for crafting masterpieces left me holding my breath until the last page. Blending untamed hope and bold female ambition with fascinating little-known details of war, Randel has penned a glittering tale, with writing as dazzling and opulent as the jewels her characters strive to create."

—Lynda Cohen Loigman, author of *The Love Elixir of Augusta Stern*

PRAISE FOR *NIGHT ANGELS*

"*Night Angels* offers a fresh non-Western-centric perspective on the rise of Nazism and Jewish persecution. Recommended."

—*Historical Novels Review*

"This powerful tale of resistance and everyday heroism will resonate with fans of Pam Jenoff and Martha Hall Kelly."

—*Booklist*

"*Schindler's List* takes an Eastern twist in *Night Angels*, the incredible true story of the Chinese diplomat who saved thousands of Jews in WWII Vienna. Quiet, scholarly Ho Fengshan has just been made consul general in Vienna, preoccupied with his troubled American wife, Grace, and disquieted by the new anti-Semitic laws sweeping Austria. Grace's friendship with Jewish musician Lola forces both Fengshan and his wife to the breaking point: How much can one sacrifice to save innocent lives? Weina Dai Randel pens an unforgettable tale of quiet heroism and blazing defiance in the face of evil."

—Kate Quinn, *New York Times* bestselling author of
The Diamond Eye

"An illuminating look at a little-known, inspiring piece of history we should never forget."

—Kristin Harmel, *New York Times* bestselling author of
The Forest of Vanishing Stars

"Weina Dai Randel's *Night Angels* is a gorgeous WWII historical tale of daring diplomatic pursuits that had me turning the pages way past my bedtime. Based on the true heroic story of Dr. Ho Fengshan, Randel's prose is rich and powerfully layered. By day, Fengshan is a warrior for his country and a fighter for humanity while secretly issuing thousands of visas to Jews to Shanghai to escape Nazi persecution. It is a sweeping novel filled with love, loss, high stakes, sacrifice, and redemption that will break your heart and fuel your soul."

—Lisa Barr, *New York Times* bestselling author of *Woman on Fire*

"An exquisitely delivered tale of three souls—a Chinese diplomat who risks everything, his benevolent wife, and a Jewish language tutor—all caught up in the hell that was Nazi-occupied Vienna, and of the resulting quest to hold on to hope and their humanity. Hauntingly beautiful."

—Susan Meissner, *USA Today* bestselling author of
The Nature of Fragile Things

Praise for *The Last Rose of Shanghai*

"Fans of sweeping, dramatic WWII epics that are rich in historical detail, such as Lisa See's *Shanghai Girls* or Paullina Simons's *The Bronze Horseman*, will be enthralled."

—*Booklist*

"Weina Dai Randel's novel deserves a place of distinction among WWII fiction."

—*Historical Novel Review*

"*The Last Rose of Shanghai* is a powerful story of the relationship between a Shanghai heiress and a Jewish refugee, set against the backdrop of a nightclub in China on the eve of the Second World War. Weina Dai Randel skillfully shines a light on a little-known moment in history through the lens of two vividly drawn characters whose unique and unexpected relationship is one readers will never forget."

—Pam Jenoff, *New York Times* bestselling author of
The Woman with the Blue Star

"Set in Japanese-occupied Shanghai, this is an unforgettable, page-turning tale of an impossible affair between lovers from two cultures. Randel casts an unflinching eye at the horrors of wartime Shanghai, where refugees starve while the wealthy and privileged continue to drink and dance, and where daily threats of danger and death only serve to fan forbidden passions to a blazing climax."

—Janie Chang, bestselling author of *Dragon Springs Road* and *The Library of Legends*

"*The Last Rose of Shanghai* vividly depicts the clash of East and West as Jewish refugees flee Hitler's Berlin for faraway Shanghai, where they struggle to survive amid the uneasy coexistence of Chinese magnates and Japanese invaders. Sophisticated heiress Aiyi knows she is taking a risk when she hires Jewish pianist Ernest to play jazz in her nightclub, but she has no idea she will be risking her heart, her family, and everything she holds dear as forbidden love blossoms and Japan's hold on her beloved home city tightens. Weina Dai Randel's poignant, sweeping love story paints a vibrant portrait of a little-known slice of World War II history. Not to be missed!"

—Kate Quinn, *New York Times* bestselling author of *The Rose Code* and *The Huntress*

"A sweeping novel that transports readers to 1940s Shanghai, *The Last Rose of Shanghai* is a must-read for historical fiction lovers. Filled with page-turning suspense and a poignant and unforgettable love story, Weina Dai Randel wholly immerses the reader in this richly detailed and powerfully drawn story."

—Chanel Cleeton, *New York Times* and *USA Today* bestselling author

"Set against a panorama so vivid you can almost hear the jazz in Aiyi Shao's nightclub, Weina Dai Randel brings to life fascinating WWII history new to me and, I imagine, countless other readers. The story of a well-born entrepreneur and the German Jewish refugee she loves will stay with you long after *The Last Rose of Shanghai* ends."

—Sally Koslow, author of *Another Side of Paradise*

"In a novel that spans time, space, and culture, *The Last Rose of Shanghai* is a riveting story of love, heartbreak, and redemption. The smoky night clubs, jazz bars, luxury hotels, family compounds, and refugee settlements of Japanese-occupied Shanghai provide a fascinating background to the lives of those caught in the crossfires of war. Weina Dai Randel is a skilled artist, giving the reader well-drawn characters of great depth, complexity, and heart. In the WWII genre, within the genre of historical fiction, *The Last Rose of Shanghai* stands out for its boldness and originality."

—Erika Robuck, bestselling author of *The Invisible Woman*

Praise for
The Empress of Bright Moon

"The author's talent for dramatic, well-timed dialogue, and portrayal of women's friendships and emotions—especially dislikes, jealousy, and fear—intensifies the reader's understanding of palace intrigue . . . A full-immersion, compulsively readable tale that rivals both Anchee Min's *Empress Orchid* (2004), about the Dowager Empress Cixi, and the multilayered biographical novel *Empress* (2006), by Shan Sa, which also features Empress Wu."

—*Booklist* (starred review)

"A must-read for fans of historical fiction set in ancient China, this novel offers a compelling look at a woman's unprecedented rise to power."

—*Library Journal* (starred review)

"Randel (*The Moon in the Palace*) offers a rich conclusion to her historical fiction duology about the woman who would become China's only ruling empress, in this work filled with sorrow and pain . . . Randel has done much to breathe life into the life of Empress Wu."

—*Publishers Weekly*

"Once again, Randel's gift for evoking the atmosphere of the palace shines. Readers are immersed in a world where vengeance is a way of life. Though accurate, the reality and brutality of some incidents may disturb gentle readers. Truly a fascinating read!"

—RT Book Reviews (4 stars)

"A fascinating vision of ancient China concludes far too soon in this suspenseful, romantic finale."

—*Shelf Awareness*

"Along with its predecessor, *The Empress of Bright Moon* is one of the most beautifully written, impeccably researched, and well-constructed historical fiction novels released this year."

—BookReporter

"As in her first novel, Randel is tremendously successful at portraying the world of seventh-century China while developing a forward-moving and engrossing drama."

—*Historical Novels Review*, Editors' Choice

"Historical fiction fans will appreciate this book. Well researched and smoothly crafted, and with a sincere and winning style, it seamlessly transports the reader into the seventh-century Tang Dynasty to experience, firsthand, a woman's grueling and sometimes humiliating path to power."

—*Washington Independent Review of Books*

Praise for *The Moon in the Palace*

"A must for historical fiction fans, especially those fascinated by China's glorious past."

—*Library Journal* (starred review)

"A very successful and transporting novel that beautifully captures the sounds, smells, and social mores of seventh-century China."

—*Historical Novels Review*, Editors' Choice

"*The Moon in the Palace* depicts Empress Wu's sharp, persistent spirit but does not neglect to make her believably naive and vulnerable, an untried girl among ruthless women. The intrigue and machinations of the imperial court come to life under her hand, a vast and dangerous engine with each piece moving for its own reasons."

—*Shelf Awareness* (starred review)

THE
MASTER
JEWELER

OTHER TITLES BY WEINA DAI RANDEL

Night Angels
The Last Rose of Shanghai

The Empress of Bright Moon series

The Empress of Bright Moon
The Moon in the Palace

THE
MASTER
JEWELER

A NOVEL

WEINA DAI RANDEL

LAKE UNION
PUBLISHING

Published by Lake Union Publishing, Seattle

www.apub.com

Amazon, the Amazon logo, and Lake Union Publishing are trademarks of Amazon.com, Inc., or its affiliates.

EU product safety contact:
Amazon Media EU S. à r.l.
38, avenue John F. Kennedy, L-1855 Luxembourg
amazonpublishing-gpsr@amazon.com

ISBN-13: 9781662525308 (hardcover)
ISBN-13: 9781662522536 (paperback)
ISBN-13: 9781662522543 (digital)

Cover design by Mumtaz Mustafa
Cover image: © Jenson, © Takoyaki Tech, © venimo / Shutterstock

Printed in the United States of America

First edition

In loving memory of my mother-in-law, Sheila Randel
(November 1, 1942–March 8, 2023)

CHAPTER 1

June 1945
Japanese-occupied Hong Kong

She was simply called the Jeweler. No one knew her name, her age, how long she had been incarcerated on the island, or why she had only nine fingers. A reed of a figure, she sat on a bench, hunching over a wooden block covered with an array of hand tools, metal plates, and precious gemstones. Her head bald, her fingers calloused and cracked, she worked—measuring, cutting, soldering—oblivious to the ripples of voices coming from outside her cell, the prismatic lights straggling onto the ceiling, and the cloud of stifling heat pooling in the room. After she finished crafting—an Art Deco ring, an Edwardian necklace, or an *en tremblant* brooch—she carved on each piece a minuscule image of a double-headed eagle and four cryptic letters: IMAM.

Rumors about the inscription swirled. Some prisoners whispered they indicated her name, for it was said that the Jeweler was once a world-renowned master designer, her jewelry had been desired and gifted to warlords, tycoons, and royal families around the world, and she was later appointed as the personal jeweler for a wicked princess.

But some prisoners believed the letters were linked to the names of the Jeweler's lovers. And it was said that she had two lovers: one who had tried to kill her and the other who was murdered by her.

Still, others on the island said that the gossip was all wrong and the engraving was, in fact, a clue to a hidden cache of Romanov treasures and a legendary diamond, which the Jeweler had stolen and secreted away before the war. Whoever deciphered the carving would be able to pinpoint the location and unearth the priceless hoard.

The Jeweler said nothing; her lips were sealed, her shell-shaped face as mysterious as dawn. She was silent when the black-uniformed officer who paid her a monthly visit warned and wheedled. She was mute when the sadistic guard stomped and shouted, the butt of his rifle crashing down onto her back. She stood still when her food was conveniently slipped into other people's mouths—a rice ball wrapped in a thin sheet of seaweed, a desiccated fish with withered guts, or occasionally, a hard-boiled egg that would have energized any starving prisoner.

Then, one day, as the flaming sun sank into the vast water and the misty island descended into the night's deep, despotic shadows, down the muddy lane lined with bones and stones, behind the female prisoners heading toward the rugged valley that would be their grave, the Jeweler heard the familiar echoes in the moaning wind, the whip of snowstorms, and the quiet promise of eternity.

She remembered.

CHAPTER 2

1925
Harbin, China, near Siberia

It was late August, and it had already started snowing. Anyu, the daughter of an outcast mother, sat on the bottom of a broken ladder near the train station, drawing on a sheaf of crumpled papers. Alone in a corner, Anyu had been working on the straight lines of tracks with rail joints and fasteners for hours. She was fifteen years old, a skilled artist, adept at her craft. Drawing was her favorite pastime, and she would sit there and sketch all day if she could. It wasn't that she had something else to do, or other specific places to go. The station, noisy as it was, was better than the windowless hovel she lived in, so after she finished her chores at home, she often came here, her very own public studio. Today, she wanted to draw the snow-swept train tracks, their dark iron grooves, and their long stretches into the emptiness.

A train arrived, driving a flurry of ice and snow toward her, rending the silence she treasured. She pulled her woolen cap lower and looked up. In the far distance, the platform was packed with throngs of suitcase-toting travelers, rifle-bearing soldiers, and vendors peddling sugar-coated crab apples. She watched their stabbing fingers, the frantic scurry of their feet, the sweeping arcs of their arms, and wished they would all vanish. She was drawn to the hulking buildings and whirring machines, the shapes and angles of still objects, and the fading shadows of the sunset; people, not so much.

Her fingers grew cold; Anyu put down her pencil and rubbed her hands together for warmth. As she shifted around, her pencil rolled off the paper and fell into the pile of snow at her feet. Bending to pick it up, she spotted a strip of purple fabric. Curious, she pulled it out and dusted off the snow. It was a heavy velvet bag, tied with a shining black silk drawstring.

Loosening the drawstring, Anyu reached in and took out a golden box embossed with the image of a double-headed eagle. The box was ornate and luxurious, fitting perfectly in her hand. When she opened it, she saw inside was an exquisite egg-shaped ornament crafted from smooth crystalline shells, their surface engraved with luminescent, feathery filaments that sparkled despite the bleak wintry air. Supporting the egg was a translucent rock-like gemstone, carved to resemble a glacier overflowing with rivulets of diamonds. Awestruck, Anyu touched the diamonds and traced along the delicate tendrils on the eggshell. Her fingers found a seam, imperceptible, and to her surprise, the egg unfolded to reveal an elegant trellis basket holding a bouquet of white flowers with gold stamens inlaid with gemstones.

Anyu gasped—this was an imperial Russian egg, one of the Romanov treasures. She had seen them in paintings sold in the stalls in the Dali District, where many Russians lived. She had never seen one of the actual eggs, let alone held it in her hand. *How did such a treasure end up in a snowdrift by the train station in Harbin, thousands of miles away from the imperial palace in Russia?* she wondered. It was undoubtedly priceless, encrusted with numerous diamonds and lustrous gems, but what enthralled her most was the egg's ethereal beauty. She had never imagined seeing something so vividly spectacular and ingeniously engineered. She wished to know who had designed such an artifact and had the skill to craft it.

Anyu looked around. No one was nearby; on the main road to the station, not far away, a procession of carriages passed by carrying

Japanese businessmen in suits who had just disembarked from the train. Across the street, swarms of beggars and starving migrants with shifty eyes huddled around a caravan of carriages and horses, and her greedy landlord—who had raised the rent again—was picking at roasted sweet potatoes from a vendor's barrel. He mumbled something, turned his head toward her, and cast her a baleful look.

Anyu wondered what to do with the egg. She could keep it for herself—it was the most valuable object she had ever touched. But the mere thought pierced her with shame. Only a dishonest, dishonorable person would do such a thing; Anyu considered herself a person of unwavering morality and integrity. She would return it to the owner, who must be desperate. She looked at the platform again, crowded with people she tried to avoid. It would be daunting to investigate who, among the mass of the crowd, might have lost this treasure.

She placed the egg back inside the velvet bag and tightened the drawstring. With the bag in her hand and her pencil and paper safely in her pocket, she wiped the snowflakes from her face and headed to the platform. She had only taken three steps when she heard a faint voice coming from a distance. A man, carrying a black suitcase, was hurrying in her direction from behind the caravan of carriages, shouting something.

He was very tall, with a slightly stooped back, and was dressed in a black turtleneck sweater and a black trench coat that reached his knees. He didn't have a hat; his golden hair, the color of fried rice, was tousled and speckled with snowflakes, and his eyes were gray, the shade of steel. He halted in front of her, gasping for air—a figure sculpted by winds, drenched in snow, a man, paradoxically, of refinement and misery, of strength and fear. A Russian man.

Anyu didn't feel like talking to him, a foreigner. She had seen many Russians in her city, who arrived via China Eastern Railway, part of the Trans-Siberian Railway, a monstrous five-thousand-mile stretch that began in Moscow in the west and ended in Vladivostok in the east. They ensconced themselves along the Songhua River and stamped Harbin with the seal of their exotic culture, building towering cathedrals with onion domes, erecting statues in the vast squares, and lining streets with opulent Baroque buildings. Anyu didn't know any Russians personally. She had heard some were good bakers, who filled the city with the tantalizing aroma of their delicious bread, *khleb*, sold in the corners of the city's major thoroughfares, a rare treat for children, but she had also heard they were a churlish bunch who showed no care or respect for Chinese customs and often shamelessly sunbathed on the beach of the Songhua River.

The man was blocking her, his gaze fixed on her bag. It was too late to hide it.

"Are you lost? The train station is that way," Anyu said.

"Train station? Oh no, no . . ." He babbled in his poor Chinese laced with a thick Russian accent. "Young lady. I hope it's not too rude of me to speak to you in such an impetuous manner. The bag you're holding, it's mine. I have been looking for it everywhere. I'm not sure how I lost it. I was here this morning . . . May I please have it back?"

Anyu would have gladly tossed the bag to him and told him to get lost, but the egg was too valuable to give away without verifying. "It depends. You'll have to answer my questions first. If this is yours, will you tell me what's inside the bag?"

The man stiffened, the light of caution swimming in his gray eyes, but he didn't reply.

"Do you understand what I'm saying?" Anyu asked again in Chinese. She should have spoken Russian, she realized, or English. Her knowledge of these foreign languages was decent, as a result of Mother's diligent teaching.

The man nodded but said nothing. He was in his forties, his stubble graying around his jaw.

"Who are you?" Anyu stared at him.

The man raised his right hand to wipe his face, and Anyu couldn't help but notice that his hand, bejeweled with a gold ring set with an opaque stone, was shaking.

"Do you know what's inside or not?"

"I do, young lady. It's an egg."

"What does it look like?"

"I wish I could describe it to you, young lady. But I'm afraid I can't. It's a very special egg."

His accent was terrible, but he had used polite phrasing in Chinese at least. "How did you get it?" Anyu asked.

From the platform came the train's whistle, people calling out for their families. The man switched his suitcase to his right hand. "Please. My train is leaving. I have to go."

"I can't give it to you. You haven't answered me." She stepped away.

The man lurched forward as if he wanted to wrest the bag from her hands. "No! Please don't run. Please. I'll tell you. The tsarina bestowed it on me."

"The empress of Russia?" At the train station, Anyu had seen incidents of robbery, kidnapping, and human trafficking and heard of many frightening, strange tales. This sounded unreal even compared to all that.

"Indeed. It was gifted to me by our tsarina, Alexandra Feodorovna."

She knew, as everyone did, what had happened to the empress of Russia. Mother still talked about the bloody massacre in the cellar where the entire imperial family was executed, including the tsar, the empress, and their children. It had happened years ago during the violent revolution that had gutted Russia. "But she's dead."

"She gave it to me before she was killed."

"Why would the empress of Russia give such a treasure to you?"

The man was perspiring despite the snowflakes that fell on his pale face. Once again, he had a difficult time bringing himself to speak. His hand trembling, he glanced at the train station and then the caravan and vendors across the street.

"If you're not going to tell me, I'm going home. It's cold here." Clutching the bag, Anyu veered toward the road. In a short distance, her landlord, wolfing down a purple sweet potato, cocked his head and then looked at the Russian man behind her.

"Wait, young lady. Don't go. I'll tell you all you need to know. Please don't go." The man caught up with her.

Anyu stopped. "Where are you from?"

"St. Petersburg."

"Why did the empress give you the egg?"

"It's a long story. I am a jeweler."

She had never come across a jeweler before. For all she knew, a jeweler in Harbin could mean an artisan who crafted jewelry or a trader selling jewelry; in any case, it was an obscure profession, almost secretive, and exclusive. The man in front of her didn't look like a typical craftsman or a dealer. She couldn't help but think that he was trying to deceive her, yet he appeared earnest. Despite his evasiveness, there was something sophisticated about the way he spoke, and his manners were different from the people she knew. Maybe he was indeed a jeweler from Russia, but what was he doing in Harbin?

The man spoke again, his voice composed but raspy. "Young lady, I was one of forty-two workmasters working under the direction of Mr. Peter Karl Fabergé, the greatest goldsmith in Russia. Perhaps you've heard of him?"

She shook her head. The name Fabergé was unfamiliar; Mother would have known.

"Then it's my privilege to tell you that Master Fabergé was commissioned to craft eggs for the imperial family, the Romanovs, for decades. He made eggs for the dowager mother and the empress, our eminent royal patrons, before the revolution. Our dowager mother adored the egg held in your hands, the Winter Egg. It was her favorite, crafted by one of my colleagues, with my assistance. When the treacherous Bolsheviks threatened to break into the palace, the imperial family, worried their gifts and treasures would be stolen, gave some of their keepsakes to the workmasters. I was entrusted with this egg and told to guard it and never to let it fall into the rebels' hands. It's my duty, and my honor, to safeguard the egg . . . I'm sorry. I'm afraid it is not at my liberty to divulge more. Does this answer your question?"

Anyu studied his face.

"May I have my bag?"

"There's one more thing. Are you on the run?"

The man froze.

"You were not forthcoming about who you are, and then you have this." She pointed at him—there was a trail of dark red on his right ear, running down his neck and into the collar of his turtleneck sweater.

The man's gray eyes glittered; he glanced around him—the carriages, the peddlers, the travelers. "If I may—"

"What do you have there? Let me see." Her landlord, who had been sidling close, reached out, startling her.

Anyu hid the bag behind her back. "Not your business."

"You're a good girl. Show me your bag. I just want to take a look. What's inside? Is it worth a lot of money?" her landlord said.

"Nothing valuable," Anyu said.

"Let me see. Give it to me."

"No."

"I said give it to me!"

Knowing what her landlord was capable of, Anyu had to be decisive. She stuffed the bag into the jeweler's hand and pulled him along. "Take your bag. You must run now. Hurry. Now. Quick!"

"Oh . . . thank you!" The jeweler took off, rushing along with her, holding the bag.

Behind them, her landlord cursed, *Bitch, bitch, bitch.* A poor runner, he shuffled his feet, gasping, struggling to catch up. The distance between them widened; the train station, sitting in the curtain of drifting snow, appeared closer with each of her steps.

When they reached the platform, the jeweler turned to her, his eyes flooded with gratitude. "You're an incredibly honest child. I truly admire your integrity. May I ask, what's your name?"

"I am Anyu," she said. Peaceful jade, Mother had named her, despite all that she had gone through.

The jeweler murmured her name in his barely passable Chinese, mispronouncing it as something that meant "dark fish" instead of "peaceful jade." Then he rummaged in his pocket. "Let me give you something. I'm indebted to you."

"You don't have to give me anything. It's your egg, mister."

"Isaac. Call me Isaac . . . I'm Isaac Mandelburg. How about this, take this."

She looked down at her hand—it was a silk handkerchief, large, clean, with crosshatched blue lines. One corner was embroidered with the letter M in a sweeping, elegant curve and an address in Chinese.

The train's whistle sounded again. The conductor's voice rang out. It was the last call for boarding.

The jeweler said hurriedly, "I'm on my way to my uncle's shop in Shanghai. This is the address. If you ever come to Shanghai, Anyu. Anyu? Please find me. I'll look after you."

Anyu had heard of Shanghai, a lucrative market for fur trade, a distant city in the south that she had never visited and perhaps would never visit. And the handkerchief, a man's token. She wasn't supposed to take it. What would Mother say?

But the jeweler had dashed forward, fading into the crowd on the platform, carrying his suitcase and his egg.

"You idiot!" A sharp slap. Her landlord appeared, panting.

Anyu held her face, burning. But the man was just getting started, his arm swinging up again. Before it slammed down, Anyu ran.

CHAPTER 3

In the stuffy, dim wooden shed she lived in with Mother, Anyu lit the kerosene lamp with a match and then paced, holding her stinging face. She was furious at herself, at the landlord. She should have talked back or pushed him; instead, she had run away like a coward. This was not the first time the man had attacked her. Whenever Mother was late paying the rent, he would burst into a paroxysm of rage, screaming and striking them with a broomstick.

Mother came home. She looked tired. Her braid was loose, and a tuft of hair fell in her eyes. Her expression was triumphant, though, as she raised a basket. "Look! Dinner!"

Hard-boiled quail eggs tonight. A rare treat. Mother must have sold more pelts than she had expected. With winter approaching, the demand for furs had picked up. Mother was pleased. She had devoted herself to selling and sorting fox pelts and sable skins; when she came home, her hair gave off the strong smell of animal fur.

"Mother," Anyu said, tearful, in spite of herself. The sting had reduced to a throbbing pain, but her face was swollen, and the mark of her attacker's fingers was visible.

"What happened?" Mother held Anyu's chin.

"The landlord."

"Oh no." Mother's expression, as usual, was a helpless look with an apologetic smile. A woman of mild temperament, she seldom got angry. Not even now. The depth of Mother's mellowness astounded Anyu. "Does it hurt?"

"You ask that. Every time."

Mother sighed. She turned to a chipped cabinet they'd bargained for at a secondhand store, took out a tin can of Tiger Balm, and smoothed the pungent gel on Anyu's cheek. "You'll feel better, I promise."

"Can we live somewhere else, Mother?" It must have been the hundredth time she had asked that question.

"We can't afford another apartment right now."

Anyu pushed away Mother's hand and walked to her *kang*. It was cold. The fire hadn't been lit.

"Maybe you can apologize to the landlord. Try to make peace. Don't be a troublemaker, all right, daughter?"

That was all Mother would say—don't be a troublemaker.

Mother was never a troublemaker, never confrontational, not even when the neighbors called her a whore behind her back. She heard them, but she never said anything. Mother rarely mentioned her past, but the landlord and neighbors wouldn't stop talking about it: how Mother, one of those educated women from a good family in Beijing, had been involved in an affair with the powerful warlord Zhang before he seized control of Manchuria during the warring years in China, after the collapse of the Qing Dynasty, and effectively defied the Nationalist government's order. At twenty, Mother dropped out of college to live with him in a villa in Shenyang. But the warlord soon grew tired of her and discarded her, and she was warned never to come near him again. When she found out she was pregnant, her father, a renowned scholar, could not bear the shame of having a promiscuous daughter. He had her lashed with a bamboo stick, threw her a bag, and ordered her never to enter their home again. Disowned by her family, Mother took a train to Harbin, the warlord's domain, and a few months later, gave birth to Anyu, sealing her unfortunate fate for good. For a single woman saddled with an infant, the prospect of marriage was out of the question, and she was doomed to be an outcast, an unwanted woman. Everything was a challenge, from renting an apartment and finding a job to even walking around unescorted at night. With her higher education, Mother had tried to be a governess for wealthy Chinese and Manchu families, but they heard of her scandalous past and dismissed her after a few months. She had taken sundry jobs over the years, making a few pennies here and there as a domestic servant and a laundrywoman, then selling furs and pelts and working as an interpreter for Russians who conducted business with Chinese merchants.

Mother never saw the warlord again, even though his mansion was within an hour's walk. The man was a womanizer with seven wives and didn't care about Anyu, his illegitimate daughter. He only left Mother a gold necklace with the pendant of Guandi, the god of war he worshipped. Mother cherished it, looping the jewelry around Anyu's neck and instructing her never to part with it.

Anyu felt sorry for Mother. With one mistake, she was cast out by her family, her life ruined, and turned herself, once a jade leaf growing on a gold branch, into a pariah. Did she have regrets? Had she loved the warlord? Did she hate the warlord? Anyu never asked, but sometimes she'd be troubled by the wistful look that escaped Mother's eyes.

"Are you listening, daughter?"

Anyu opened the firebox beneath the *kang* and lit the coal with a match. "We need more coal."

"Will you apologize to the landlord?"

"Why?"

"He's not a good man, I know, but he's our landlord. I just want us to be on good terms."

Anyu stabbed at the coal with a pair of iron tongs.

"Don't be so headstrong, daughter. If you apologize—"

"Never." Anyu shut the firebox door with a bang.

This was all Mother's fault—the landlord, this miserable existence by the train station. All of it a cruel punishment. For her entire life, Anyu had been lonely, growing up by the station with her mother in this hovel, with no one else to talk to, no siblings, no cousins, no relatives, no friends. For her entire life, she'd been treated poorly by the decent families who disparaged her for not having bound feet, berated by the mean-spirited neighbors who mocked her for her looks. They warned that she had peach blossom–shaped eyes and she would grow up to be a pestilence to men and women, a disaster to families, and a seducer like Mother. This confused Anyu and made her ashamed of her appearance, but she was helpless—she didn't know what to say to defend her own, or Mother's, reputation.

She had wanted to go to school but couldn't, because that privilege was reserved for children from wealthy families, and Mother couldn't afford to hire tutors. In the end, Anyu stayed at home and learned everything from Mother: mathematics, Russian literature, English, and how to draw snowflakes, gray herons, black-headed gulls, and white fish from the Songhua River. Unable to afford paper and pencils much of the time, she had sketched those images with a stick on the muddy shore.

Anyu wondered whether she'd spend her whole life like this. She was fifteen years old. *Old enough to marry,* as Mother had said. Ironically, she still wanted a marriage for Anyu, even though she had raised her out of wedlock, without binding her feet, without a family. But to Anyu, marriage felt like another trap. What if she met the wrong man, like Mother had? She'd rather do something—be a painter or a teacher. But a painter would be better.

Mother sighed, scuffing toward the coal stove with the basket. "So tell me, why did he hit you this time?"

"I found a bag. The landlord wanted it. But I returned it to the owner instead." Anyu climbed on the *kang* and emptied her pocket onto the small four-legged table on the platform. Pencils. Papers. And the handkerchief.

"You did the right thing. Don't worry. I'll deal with him. That's a fine-quality handkerchief. Where did you get it?" Mother came over.

"The jeweler gave it to me."

"The jeweler?"

"The man who lost the bag." Anyu told Mother about the Russian man from St. Petersburg and the egg he had lost.

"A Russian egg," Mother muttered, fingering the fine embroidered letters on the handkerchief, a spark of wonder in her eyes. "I've never seen one."

"He's gone now. You can throw the handkerchief away."

"But it's made of silk. It looks expensive." Mother folded it and handed it to her.

Anyu tucked it in her pocket, picked up her pencil, and began to draw. But she couldn't concentrate. The air was acrid, stifling without a window; the inky streaks of kerosene fumes hung low under the ceiling; there was no sound of the train coming from outside; silence, a ghostly shape, swelled. Suddenly, she was irritated at Mother—the way she stood, the way she talked, and even the mere presence of her in the room.

Anyu couldn't understand why she felt this way, didn't know what was happening to her. When she was a child, she was afraid of silence and had held Mother's legs and begged her to stay whenever she needed to leave, fearful that she would never come back; when she awoke in the morning, she would feel Mother by her side and watch her sleep, comforted by their togetherness. Now that Anyu was older, she no longer fretted that Mother would disappear, and she had grown accustomed to the silence of a room without her. Sometimes Anyu was even startled to discover that she wanted to be away from her, to leave her. Like the train. Gone. Such wild thoughts bubbled in her head, bewildering her, yet she didn't know how to quench them.

She would never tell Mother that, and she would never leave her, not now, not ever. She loved her mother. They would be each other's companion in this room for another year, another ten years, and it would be just them, the two of them, as it had always been, as it would always be. Which, Anyu tried to convince herself, was all that she wanted.

As Mother boiled the quail eggs in a pot, she said that she would work overnight from now on, as she needed to earn money to prepare for the brutal winter. She had found a job moonlighting as an interpreter at the night market at the back of the cemetery behind the St. Sophia cathedral. It was a secret market where exiled Russians sold jewelry rumored to have come from the imperial vault in St. Petersburg. For her interpreting, Mother would be paid a good sum, a financial lifeline for them.

"I want to go with you," Anyu said, excited. She had never heard of the night market before.

Mother shook her head. "They don't like to have spectators."

"I'll be careful. They won't know I'm there."

"I'll be busy. I won't have time to look after you."

"I'll look after myself."

Mother hesitated.

"If you don't take me, I'll go there myself."

"Don't be stubborn, daughter."

"You'll let me go?"

She sighed. "If you agree to stay out of sight."

On market day, two hours past sundown, Anyu arrived at the back of the cathedral with Mother. After repeatedly promising she'd be invisible, Anyu wove through the cemetery and crouched behind a tall tombstone shaped like a stallion. From here, she was close enough to see the sellers and hear the conversations but far enough not to be detected. She blew some warm air into her mittens and pulled her coat around her. A short distance away, Mother melted into the darkness.

For an hour, there was no light, no movement, no voices, no footsteps. The faint smell of damp earth and musty weeds permeated the cemetery, and a sheet of dark gloom blanketed the cathedral and the area behind it. Then snow began to fall.

Near midnight, pricks of golden light penetrated the darkness, and the lot at the edge of the cemetery was illuminated with kerosene lamps and paper lanterns. One by one, the jewelry hunters sauntered in the drifting snow, glistening eyes belying the mask of aloofness they wore. There were young Chinese men with cropped hair accompanied by their bodyguards, former Manchu dignitaries wearing ankle-length brocade skirts trailed by their servants, short Japanese officials carrying samurai swords, and some gray-haired Russian babushkas speaking fluent Chinese. They leaned over the sellers, twenty-three of them, who sat by a row of tombstones, their arms around their suitcases, their eyes shifting in alert. The sellers were more of a unified group: the former White Russian guards in red cloaks pinned with medals and epaulets indicating their previous ranks, pale-faced aristocratic men in black *ushankas*, and copper-bearded Cossacks reeking of vodka.

Mother stood beside the sellers, bowing slightly, her head wrapped with a brown scarf. She was the only woman among the group, the only Chinese woman the Russians trusted to speak for them, Anyu learned later. Mother's honesty, discretion, and refusal to accept bribes had helped her build strong relationships with her clients, and she was often hired through word of mouth—something that mattered greatly to her. She often made a point of reminding Anyu that a woman's reputation was like a porcelain vase: once cracked, it could never be fully repaired.

There were murmurs of the purity of a gem's color and the luster of diamonds and talks of dispersion and fluorescence and the fire and the cat's eye. Mother, in her composed manner, spoke softly and patiently, alternating between Chinese and Russian. Intently, Anyu listened, memorizing every word. Once or twice, through the flurries of snow, by the stark reflection of lamps in men's hands, Anyu caught glimpses of the contents of the suitcases: tiaras with button-sized diamonds, necklaces with thick gold links, cane handles in translucent green jadeite, trophy cups of pure gold, ruby bracelets, and sapphire rings.

The sellers claimed the pieces of jewelry were their heirlooms, and they were selling them to buy furs to get through the winter.

There were no Russian eggs.

༄

Winter in Harbin was both a dream and a nightmare but for the most part, a nightmare. The daylight was fleeting, the night endless. Anyu grew restless; her mood swung wildly like the gusts that roiled the waters of the Songhua River.

Some days, Anyu went dogsledding with Mother, her favorite winter activity and a rare moment of joy. The two, bundled in layers of coats and parkas, sat in Musher Wang's bamboo carriage pulled by his twelve ferocious Siberian huskies with their enigmatic pale-blue eyes. Then the joy of the treacherous ride began: flying and bouncing through tunnels of snow, sailing over the vast frozen Songhua River, soaring through squalls of freezing air sizzling with her frantic screams and the huskies' fierce barks, her heart suspended in awe of the speed, her mind penetrated by the fear of flying high, the fear of dying, of being dead.

But then there were days when the temperature plunged to –35°C, when ice palaces were haunts of nothing but blizzards, and songs and festivals were merely husks of memories. Then the land blended into a bewitching fable of frost and snow, and two minutes of breathing in the arctic air threatened to hurt Anyu's lungs and freeze her naked eyeballs.

For months, the icy spells of winter gripped the entire city. Like two hibernating animals, Anyu and Mother holed up in their room. In her mellow voice, Mother told Anyu the stories of animals on this land—the loyal phoenix, the black tortoise warrior, the azure dragon god, the white Siberian tiger called Nian, who terrorized an ancient village, and the noble heron cursed to search for a home in an eternal marshland. All animals had characters, like us, she'd say. Anyu would nod, feeding on the revelries of folklore and fantasies, nursing her toes and knuckles swollen from frostbite. Then she drew the bamboo, the tiger, the heron, and always now, ornamental eggs.

Spring, a belated guest, finally arrived. The sky shimmered like a polished silver dome; the sunlight spun gold strands on the barren field near the train station. One day, Mother returned home with a basket of shriveled carrots and yellowed chives, looking distraught. The market had been disrupted by a skirmish between some Japanese soldiers and the warlord Zhang's men, and two men were killed, she told Anyu. Mother had a deep mistrust of the Japanese, who had crushed the Russians in a naval battle, announced to the world their superior power, and then vanquished the armies in Korea and colonized the peninsula. She believed the ambitious Japanese militants were making excuses to provoke the warlord, intending to seize his territory and conquer Manchuria.

"But Warlord Zhang commands hundreds and thousands of troops. His men know how to resolve conflicts," Mother said.

For a split second, Anyu thought that despite being abandoned, despite all Mother's suffering and humiliation caused by her relationship with Zhang, she was still in love with the warlord.

But Mother proved to be overly optimistic, for the tension between the two groups kept escalating for the next few days. There was another loud brawl erupting in the streets, and then the Japanese soldiers ran into the warlord's men in a restaurant, and a bloody fight ensued. The train station was shut down, and the square was blockaded. Rumors said a large-scale conflict was imminent.

"We're running out of food. Let me see if I can find some quail eggs at the market. I'll be right back," Mother said one day and told Anyu to lock the door.

Anyu didn't give it much thought and went back to her painting, a white iridescent egg. Many years later, she would wish she had stopped Mother. She would wish she had told her not to go.

When it happened, it was sudden—a torrent of heat burst through the seams of the apartment door, the air seemed to crackle, a thunderous thud echoed in the distance, and the walls of the room shuddered. Confused, Anyu put down her ink brush.

The *kang* grew cold; the room darkened.

Mother never came back.

Anyu went out looking for her. She passed the wailing women and groaning men, passed the fallen walls and collapsed platform and blazing carts, passed the carcasses of Mongolian ponies and a pyre of metal and flesh. In the chilly night pierced by blades of lights and heartrending howls, she stumbled through the crowd, spinning around, around, choked by the pungent smell of oil and scorched fur. Near a pile of scattered coal, red like blisters, she caught sight of a shape and dropped to her knees. Someone asked if she was looking for her mother; someone else asked if she was sure this was Mother.

After Mother's burial, Anyu, feeling catatonic, sat on the cold *kang* without coal. She was freezing, her teeth chattering, as if she were gliding on a block of ice on the Songhua River, drifting and drifting. They said the Japanese had dropped bombs on the barracks near the train station, killing legions of the warlord's men and innocent people in their wake. But she refused to believe it, her gaze on the door. Mother was still alive; she'd come in very soon, holding a basket of quail eggs.

She slept for a while, then woke and ate some dried yam slices that Mother had wrapped in a newspaper. When she was tired, she fell asleep again. Many days and nights must have passed when the landlord came with a broomstick. He had given her enough time to grieve, he said, but Anyu was twenty days behind on the rent. Fumbling in the cabinet,

Anyu only found twenty cents at the back of the drawer. Eight silver dollars short for rent.

Growling, the landlord said he would take all that was in the room for payment and ordered her to leave. Her mouth dry, Anyu looked around: the rattan chair, the cabinet, the two bowls, the blue vase Mother had cherished, the kerosene lamp, and the warm cotton bedding. She struggled for words but found none. Eventually, she packed up her clothes, her drawings, and her pencil and stuffed them inside the pillowcase Mother had embroidered. Then she stumbled out.

On the street, she held tight to her sack. The blurry sun looked like a melting ice cube; the neighbors were scattered in the distance, indistinct, their shadows dark as wolves. A wave of panic raced through her body. It couldn't be; she was motherless, homeless.

She felt faint, her legs weak, her stomach grumbling. Down the muddy track, she passed the potato barrels, the haggling vendors, the hawkers gripping bills. At nightfall, she slept near a statue in the vast square in front of the St. Sophia cathedral. A few nights later, she awoke to three drunken ruffians pulling at her pants and unbuttoning her coat; she quickly fled. The next few days, she got some rest behind a gravestone in the cemetery until a homeless woman holding a bundle and a tattered blanket drove her out. Then, temporary respite in a dark alley reeking of urine and, later, a corner behind a sand dune at the shores of the Songhua River. Ice had thawed, water rushed, and the area was busy with women collecting their fish, fishermen cleaning their nets, and the Russian bathers who staked out the beach, brazenly baring their fat bellies.

Holding her sack, Anyu wasn't sure where else to look for shelter. Her grandparents' names and address were unknown to her, nor did she know any other relatives. The last person she could turn to was the warlord, who lived an hour away. The thought of him filled her heart with longing and fear. She had never met this man, only seen his serious face in the newspapers and heard about his insatiable appetite for deep-fried silkworm pupae and his capricious and cruel nature. However, she had thought of the warlord, sensed acutely his absence, and felt envy upon seeing a father-and-daughter pair passing by, and she was even haunted, at times, by an unspeakable desire to meet the man, to be simply in the same room with him.

What if she revealed herself to him? Would he nod at her and smile? Unlikely. But he couldn't have her executed for being his daughter, either.

Anyu slung the sack over her shoulder and walked to the warlord's mansion, the building she had known since childhood. For hours, she waited outside the gates. They remained closed, and eventually one guard began interrogating her. Her heart pounding nervously, she explained the relationship between her mother and the warlord and showed the guard the necklace with the Guandi pendant around her neck, hoping it would mean something. *Where did you get that? Give it to me,* the guard demanded. She fled but stayed stubbornly at the far end of the road. When the enormous gates finally swung open, she held her breath, searching, as an army of foot soldiers carrying rifles marched out, followed by cavalry, then eight black automobiles—the warlord, always concerned about assassination attempts, was fond of decoys. She tried to get closer but was held back by the multitude of foot soldiers. When one black automobile passed her, for a fleeting moment, she caught sight of a man's sharp face inside, the face of the father she had never met.

In the corner near the train station that had been her sanctuary, Anyu slumped to the ground and burst into tears. Harbin was vast, but there was no place for her; her blood relatives were out there, but no one wanted her.

Her sleeves drenched, she fumbled for something to wipe her tears, and there, in her pocket, was the handkerchief the jeweler had gifted her. She stared at the elegant letters and the jewelry shop address on the soft fabric. It had been eight months and two weeks since she came across the Russian jeweler. She could no longer recall his face, but she remembered he had promised to look after her. And his magnificent egg. She would like to see it again.

It was an impulsive decision, a decision that would lead her down lightless alleys and to a secret world, but as was often the case when an idea latched on to her, it was hard to shake it off.

Anyu wiped off her tears and rose. In a pawn shop near the Modern Hotel's pink stone building, she unfastened her necklace with the pendant of the lord of war and exchanged it for one fifty-Chinese-dollar bill, too low for the necklace's worth in her opinion, but enough to purchase a one-way train ticket to Shanghai.

Later, holding her sack, she climbed over the collapsed platform at the train station, boarded the train, and sat between a stocky businessman with a mustache and an old man hugging a cage of hens in his lap. As the train lunged forward, gathering speed, a shiver ran through her. She was riding a train for the first time; her life was racing forward. The rhythmic clatter of wheels rang in her ears in a thrilling cadence, the air infused with coal smoke from the engine. Outside, the area where she was born, where she grew up, and where Mother was buried rapidly faded away, and she pressed against the glass window, cold as a diamond; her face revealed no trace of fear.

CHAPTER 4

May 1926
Shanghai

After two days on the train, Anyu had misgivings about going to Shanghai. Her legs cramped, her bottom sore, she wished she had thought it through before spending a good portion of her money on a train ticket. The journey was an excruciating test of strength and patience. She couldn't walk in the aisle crammed with piles of luggage, nor could she draw with the train's incessant rocking and jolting. Once, she awoke at midnight to find a hand fumbling in her shirt. Panicked, she screamed. Luckily, a man with a missing front tooth took pity on her and changed seats with her. As the train continued to chug along the tracks, her ears filled with people's voices, and she was tormented by erratic thoughts that had never occurred to her before: What would happen after she found the shop? What if the jeweler told her to get lost? What if he wasn't there? What if he had forgotten about her?

Fifteen days later, Anyu arrived in Shanghai.

It was raining when she stepped out onto the crowded train station. Following the flow of people disembarking the train, she came to the street, where an army of rickshaw pullers waited in the misty rain. On the train, she had asked about Shanghai, and some well-wishers had told her directions to the jewelry shop. The easiest and fastest way, they had said, was by rickshaw, and it cost two cents. But she had never ridden a rickshaw, and she wanted to save money, so she decided to walk all the way to the shop.

She had just left the station when a group of men holding clubs ran down the sidewalk across the street from her. They shouted, grabbed a man with an umbrella, and struck him violently. Gangsters.

Anyu hesitated, holding tight to her sack. On the train, she had heard the Nationalist government had a tenuous hold on the city, which was overrun by gangsters. Between the chance of getting harassed and spending two pennies, she decided to stay safe, after all. She went up to a rickshaw puller, a skinny man wearing a vest, and told him the jeweler's address; the man looked at her curiously and nodded. Gingerly, she climbed into the vehicle, sat on the edge of the seat, and gripped the pole. The puller lifted the poles and raced down the street.

It was hard to stay on the slippery bamboo seat; the ride was bumpy, and the rickshaw was very fast and reckless, weaving between cars and carriages and ramming through the crowds on the sidewalk, narrowly missing people's shoulders. The traffic rules, obviously, didn't apply to rickshaws. After a while, Anyu grew accustomed to the turns and bumpiness and began to study her surroundings. She had not imagined Shanghai would be like this—very much like Harbin. Clusters of idle men squatted on the side of the street, legless beggars scooted along on the dirty ground, and suntanned laborers scurried around, carrying baskets with bamboo sticks. The city was different in some ways, though; there were no piles of snow on the street, no Kokoshnik Russian cathedrals. She sat silently as the rickshaw puller shot her one question after another—*Where are you from? How old are you? What are you doing in Shanghai? Why are you alone?*—in a strange lilt. It hit her. She was not in Harbin anymore; people here spoke Chinese with a song in it, and she with gunfire.

The ride felt endless, and the rain felt good on her face, soft like a stream. Anyu was hot, so hot, as if she were inside an oven—it was much warmer, and more humid, in Shanghai. She was wearing four layers: a coat, a cotton jacket, and two shirts for the nippy spring weather in

Harbin. She could take off her coat, but it would be indecent to disrobe in a rickshaw in public. She squirmed on the seat, then nearly slipped off as the rickshaw dipped into a groove, muddy water splashing on her shoes.

After they crossed a bridge, the scenery began to change. There were sleek, towering Art Deco buildings, palatial yellow Buddhist temples, colorful Taoist gardens with pink and purple columns, narrow-lane houses linked with clotheslines, and shops selling jars of coiled vipers and ropes of ox penises. And cars. So many cars. They honked and roared, belching clouds of fumes in the air. Inside sat young men dressed in fine Western-style suits, stylish women in fancy gowns adorned with plum blossoms, and middle-aged foreigners in top hats and tuxedos. Shanghai, like Harbin, was a destination for many people from around the world. And like Harbin, the city had areas governed by the Chinese authorities alongside districts controlled by foreign powers—a sad legacy of the Qing Dynasty's concessions after their defeat in the Opium Wars decades earlier. These foreign-controlled districts included the International Settlement, primarily administered by the British and Americans, and the French Concession, overseen by the French. The jewelry shop she was looking for was located in the French Concession.

The rickshaw slowed in front of a blockade—a checkpoint—where a guard in a black uniform stopped them. It seemed that the locals traveling between the districts were required to show their passes. The puller bowed and bowed, smiling obsequiously as he produced a pass from his pocket, and then they were waved through.

We are getting closer, the rickshaw puller announced in his strange accent, and finally, he stopped in front of a two-story building with a simple sign: "Jewelry," in Chinese and English, right next to a shop selling handbags.

Anyu paid the puller and walked up to the sidewalk, her shoes wet, her long braid dripping with rain. The thought of entering the shop and talking to strangers made her nervous, so she passed it deliberately. And then, because she knew she must, she turned around, pushed open the door, and entered the first jewelry shop she had ever visited, the place that would change her life.

The showroom was small, and quiet, but very bright. So bright that Anyu had to squint. She could make out a golden trapezoid light fixture on the ceiling, casting a blaze of incandescent light. Below it, an L-shaped glass counter with gleaming brass frames displayed rows of necklaces with geometric designs, sparkling bowknot and flower brooches, and gold rings set with colorful gemstones. There were also lustrous purple velour curtains, a round floor rug, a faint fragrance mixed with cigarettes, and neat shelves on the wall. Dazzled by the brilliance of electricity, which she had not had the privilege of growing up with, in awe of the luxury jewelry that she had never set her eyes on before, she didn't see the cheap chairs, the cracked windowsills, or the frayed edge of the floor rug.

"I'm sorry. We're closing." The young woman at the glass counter was scrutinizing her. Her tone was impatient, and her Chinese was barely comprehensible with her thick Russian accent. She looked to be in her early twenties, with large gray eyes and voluminous blond hair. She wore an elegant burgundy velvet dress fastened by a black belt with a cluster of keys; a gold necklace, delicately crafted with circles of varying sizes, hung around her neck. But the look that the woman gave her, the look that should have been reserved for the homeless at the train station, told Anyu she didn't belong in this place.

Anyu felt like turning around and fleeing the shop. But no. She stepped closer to the counter. "I'm not looking for jewelry . . . I came here to see Mr. Mandelburg," she said in Russian.

The woman looked surprised to hear Russian, but she frowned. "Who?"

"Mandelburg. The jeweler."

In her nervousness, Anyu had failed to recall the jeweler's first name.

"May I ask who you are?"

"I'm Anyu, Anyu from Harbin."

"I'm sorry. If you don't mind—"

"Wait. I can't leave. I have to find him. I won't leave until I see him. He knows me. He knows who I am. Look, I have his handkerchief. He gave it to me." She dug into her pocket and handed it to the young woman, realizing too late that it was wet.

The Russian woman held the handkerchief, but her frown deepened. "He gave it to you?"

"Yes. I found his egg and gave it back to him."

"His egg?"

"A Russian egg."

"You're not making sense. He doesn't have any Russian eggs."

"He does. He lost it in Harbin, but I found it. Maybe he didn't tell you."

The Russian woman raised her arm, and Anyu instinctively ducked. Then she realized the woman wasn't going to slap her like her landlord did—she was only pressing her own forehead with her middle finger, but the flaming anger in her eyes could have lit a match had she held one.

"Esther, why are you not packing up?" A man's voice came from behind Anyu. She turned around.

In the doorway were two men: one was elderly, stout, with a bald head, and the other was Isaac Mandelburg, the man for whom she had traveled across the country. Of course, this was what he looked like! Tall, reserved, with an elusive air. He wore a black apron covered with stains, a black turtleneck, a black shirt with a single pocket that held a loupe, a pencil, and some papers. There was no desperation on his face, nor any of the effusive gratitude she remembered; in fact, he appeared distinguished, aloof, with a look of tiredness as if he had trudged for ten thousand miles and longed for a place to sit. But the most disappointing thing about him was when he glanced at her, he didn't seem to recognize her.

"Father." The woman handed him the handkerchief and explained rapidly in Russian. "I have no idea where she got this. Is this yours?"

Anyu looked at Isaac, hoping, willing him.

"Indeed it is." The jeweler turned to her. "Greetings, young lady. I'm not sure where you got my handkerchief. I'm delighted that you returned it to me. Have we met?"

His Chinese was still the same, garbled and hard to understand, with a few Russian words slipping in; his voice was thick, metallic. Anyu asked, "Have you forgotten me? In Harbin? At the train station? I'm Anyu. I found your bag."

For a long moment, he stared at her without a sign of recognition, then his face changed. "Of course, that's you, young lady! Anyu? Anyu. From Harbin? At the train station. Yes. Of course. I remember you. It's wonderful to see you. It has been a while."

He remembered her!

"How long has it been? A year?"

Anyu beamed. "Nine months and two days."

He smiled with an air of genuine happiness that gave her great assurance. "Good memory. Time went by fast. I'm delighted that we meet again. Here in Shanghai. Do you have a moment? Would you like to come in?"

"Isaac," the other man with a bald head said and added something in a language she couldn't understand.

Isaac looked conflicted, glancing at the glass counter and her. "Esther, you can handle the packing. Right, Esther? Uncle David, you don't mind? I'd like to have a word with Anyu. Would you like to have some tea, Anyu? Do you like tea?"

"I like everything."

"Delightful! Come with me."

Anyu followed Isaac to a sitting area with two chairs at the end of the showroom. Behind her, Esther was grumbling, "Look, Uncle David. She's dripping water everywhere."

In the sitting area, Isaac pulled aside the curtain near a screen and revealed a small wooden door behind it. Smiling, he opened the door and gestured for her to enter.

Anyu stepped over the threshold and entered a dim narrow hallway crammed with cabinets. The air smelled of metal, acidity, and something pungent, a sharp contrast to the luminescent showroom packed with jewelry. She gripped her sack, trying not to crash into the wall.

Then she came to stand in front of a square table with six chairs in a small area that appeared to be a dining room; adjacent to it was the kitchen, with a coal stove. Near the stove were two elderly women, one in a black dress, the other in a white dress, busy preparing food on the counter. They had the same nose, same eyes, and same wrinkled skin. Twins. They gave her a glance, mumbling something Anyu couldn't catch. Then she smelled something delicious—food. Her stomach growled.

"They're my aunts, Aunt Hannah and Aunt Katya. Sit, sit." Isaac gestured, rummaging in a cabinet near the table. After a while, he gave up and sat across from her. "I'm sorry, it looks like we're out of tea."

"That's too bad. I'm thirsty," Anyu said.

Isaac chuckled. "We're having dinner soon. Perhaps you can join us. Would you like that?"

"Yes, I would." She was hungry, too; her last meal had been a cob of corn on the train. "You have a nice shop, Mr. Mandelburg."

"This is my uncle's shop. He was very kind to let me join when I arrived last year."

"Oh, you only came here last year? I thought you lived here when I met you in Harbin."

"Oh no. I was living in Harbin then."

"I'm confused. I thought you were from St. Petersburg?"

"Well, it's a long story." He had lived in many places across the world, he said. He was born in a backwater shtetl in Crimea, then migrated to a town on a hill in Kyiv, later settled in Warsaw, and then found a home in a bright apartment in St. Petersburg, where he thrived. But the Bolsheviks rebelled, and he was forced to flee. He first sought refuge in a barn in Moscow, then a fishing village in Vladivostok, and finally, an inn's cellar in Harbin. "I lived there for two years until the city became unsafe again. Fortunately, we got in touch with my uncle, who's been here for nine years, so I took the train to come here. That was when I met you at the station."

"I see. But you are a jeweler, aren't you?"

"I am, and so was my father and my father's father. I was the master jeweler, the lead designer of my family before the revolution." He continued. He had had many dreams in his life but found only one profession to be his true calling: jeweler. He had owned five stores and lost them all—one was ransacked by an angry mob, another set on fire by a jealous competitor, a third confiscated by the authorities, a fourth gone under, and the last he was forced to abandon after his colleagues were murdered in cold blood during the massacre that ended the tsar's reign.

Anyu thought for a moment. "You've been through a lot. Do you like it here?"

"I do. So, Anyu, how long have you been in Shanghai?"

Esther and Uncle David passed by, holding stacks of boxes. They didn't look in her direction, and Anyu noted, with surprise, that Esther walked with a limp.

"What? Oh." Anyu turned to face him. "I arrived today."

"Today. From Harbin?"

"Yes, by train."

"How was your journey?"

"Fine."

"If you don't mind my inquiry, what brought you to Shanghai?"

Anyu looked at him and looked away.

"Perhaps you are here visiting your relatives?"

A youth entered the kitchen; he had blond hair and gray eyes. He looked young, but the abundance of facial hair made him appear older. Samuel, Isaac said. His son. The young man plopped down in the chair across from Anyu, wiping beads of sweat from his forehead, glancing at her and then the sack in her lap.

"Isaac," Uncle David, the man with a bald head, said as he came in and sat at the table. Behind him followed Esther. "After dinner, perhaps we can continue our discussion."

"Yes, Uncle David." Isaac nodded; his tone was deferential.

"Have you finished with the tea?" Esther asked. It felt crowded in the small space, and Anyu wondered if it was normal for families to have so many men.

"It's my mistake. We are out of tea. I invited our friend to have dinner with us instead." Isaac introduced her to his family—a friend he had made in northern China, whom he had hoped to see again, he said. "She's here visiting her relatives."

"No. I'm not here to visit my relatives. I don't have relatives in Shanghai," Anyu said.

Esther and Uncle David exchanged looks—looks of alarm, of worry.

"I see. Did you come here by yourself? Where are your parents?" Isaac asked.

"I don't have parents." For weeks, Anyu had avoided thinking about Mother, and now that Isaac asked, it felt final—she was one of thousands of unfortunate orphans in this country. She had no one to rely on and no place to go. Briefly, she told them of Mother and her life by the train station.

"You're an orphan." Isaac's voice was soft.

"Mr. Mandelburg," she said. "I was hoping I could work for you."

"Work for me? How old are you?"

"I'm sixteen."

"You look like you are twelve," Esther said.

Anyu held her head up. "I don't lie. I will be seventeen in the fall."

"Fair enough. What can you do?" Isaac asked.

"I can draw."

"Good. What else?"

Anyu shook her head.

"Uncle David, how would you like an extra hand in the showroom?" Isaac asked.

"It's not necessary. Esther is doing a good job."

"I see." Isaac cleared his throat. "Anyu, you can stay with us for a few days if you haven't found a place."

"We don't have enough room, Father," Esther said.

Anyu glanced at Esther and then the other people at the table: Uncle David, the authority who had the final say, looked in her direction with a frown; the youth, Samuel, stared intently at her sack; and the two aunts glanced at her, whispering. If she couldn't stay here, where else would she go, then? She was about to speak when Isaac stood up and asked to have a minute with Esther and Uncle David in the hallway. The three left, talking in muffled voices. Isaac's voice was calm and steadfast, but Uncle David's reply was sharp, and Esther sounded bewildered. Anyu could hear them but couldn't understand their language.

Anyu sat on the chair, her back stiff. She had been hot in the rickshaw, but now she felt cold with her leaden, damp coat, and there was water in her shoes, worming between her toes when she wiggled them. She wished she could take off her waterlogged shoes and change and lie down for a nap—she was tired. And hungry. She was so hungry she couldn't focus.

"How much money do you have?" Samuel was leaning toward her; his Chinese was the best among all the Mandelburgs.

She lifted her head. "Why do you want to know?"

"I need ten dollars. Do you have ten dollars? I'll give it back when I win."

"Win what?"

"Forget it." Samuel got up and left the table, ignoring his aunt's call.

She only had nine dollars left after the trip. And even if she had more, she wouldn't lend it to Samuel, a gambler.

Isaac returned, smiling; the other two were frowning.

"Here's some good news that I'm happy to share, Anyu," he said. "We've had a discussion about a possible employment opportunity for you. My uncle has agreed we could use some help at the counter. You are Chinese, so you can communicate with the local customers and help them understand the jewelry before they make their purchase decisions. How does that sound to you?"

She smiled, elated. "This sounds wonderful."

"We'll provide you with food and lodging and ten pennies each month."

The offer was more than generous, beyond anything she had dreamed. She would have all she needed, food and lodging. And money—she would earn her own money for the first time in her life. Thanks to the jeweler who had promised to look after her.

"Have you sold jewelry before?" Esther asked, frowning.

Anyu shook her head.

"Do you know anything about jewelry?"

"No."

"Do you know how to sell jewelry?"

"I don't, and honestly, I don't like to talk to people." After she had told them the truth, it occurred to her that they might not let her keep the job.

Esther looked at her father, and Isaac raised his eyebrows. Then he squeezed out a smile. "At least she's honest about it, Esther. She is a very honest kid, you see."

"But honesty doesn't sell jewelry, Father."

"Well, Anyu, you'll try the counter?"

She nodded. It was only selling jewelry. It shouldn't be too hard.

"Then it's settled. Anyu, you'll work in the showroom with Esther."

"And where will she sleep? We don't have enough room."

"She can sleep in the attic with you."

"I certainly didn't think you'd give her the kitchen floor," Esther said.

The two aunts brought dinner to the table. Russian foods, it appeared. A basket of bread, dumplings in a soup, and a bowl of borscht. She was so hungry, she could have settled for just the crumbs in the basket.

But the rest of the people in the room didn't look like they were ready to eat. Isaac cleared his throat and began to sing, and they all joined, singing in the language she couldn't recognize. Awkwardly, Anyu sat there, listening, waiting for them to finish, wondering if this was a ritual they'd do for every meal; if so, how unnecessary!

At last, the singing ended, and Isaac passed a loaf of bread to her. Anyu took a fluffy piece with a golden crust and bit into it. It tasted wonderful, even better than the *khleb* she had tried as a child in Harbin.

Around her, people were eating with gusto and chatting loudly. They appeared to have forgotten about her. The aunts, Isaac, and the uncle conversed in a language she later learned was Yiddish, but Esther, who seemed to understand the language, only replied in Russian. Then Anyu heard Isaac mention Samuel; all of a sudden people stopped chewing, and Esther appeared as if she was choking. *He'll be back soon,* she said, not looking at her father's eyes.

Later, Esther took Anyu to the attic room she shared with her aunts. Carefully, Anyu followed her, climbing up a narrow staircase in the hallway. It was dark upstairs, and it took a moment for her vision to adjust. The attic space was smaller than the apartment Anyu had shared with Mother, and warmer, with a glass window. There were baskets filled with knitting needles and yarn, a tall shelf that held a few books in English, a beautiful table lamp with a beaded lampshade, a painted chest in cream, two small beds against the wall, and a dresser with a large oval mirror.

"This is nice," Anyu said, impressed by the variety of furniture. Her home in Harbin had been sparsely decorated.

Esther stood between the two beds, turning on the table lamp.

"What's wrong with your leg?" Anyu asked.

Esther's face reddened in the light. "None of your business."

"I mean, you're such a beauty. A pity you're a cripple."

Esther did not hit her like Anyu's landlord did, but it sure looked like she might. "It'll do you good if you keep your thoughts to yourself, little orphan from Harbin."

"Fine. Where should I sleep?"

Esther pulled out a trundle from beneath one of the beds, took out a rolled-up bamboo mattress, and stuffed it into Anyu's hands. "Over there."

Esther pointed at the corner of the floor near the other bed.

Anyu took the mattress and spread it. It was not bad, a corner for herself. She sat down, took off her wet coat, and wiped her face with it.

Then she unbuttoned her cotton jacket and removed another layer until she wore only a short-sleeved shirt. She felt lighter and more relaxed—she had never worn short sleeves in May, and it felt good. Rubbing her bare arms, she looked up. Esther's prying eyes were following her like a flashlight.

"If you're staying here, you'll have to hear some rules," she said.

"What rules?"

"Number One: Do not steal any jewelry."

"I don't steal anything."

"Rule Number Two: Do not enter the jewelry workshop."

Jewelry workshop. Of course, Isaac must make his jewelry here.

"Rule Number Three: You must sell at least one piece of jewelry in three months."

"Mr. Mandelburg didn't say three months."

"My father is too kind. He's doing a mitzvah because you're an orphan. He wants to feed you with the shop's income, but we don't have much. We have to pay taxes and rent and buy food. If you want to stay here, you must help with the sales and prove that you're not just a mouth to feed."

"What if I can't sell anything?"

Esther shrugged. "Then you'll find someone else's attic."

Three months to make a sale? She could try.

It was too early to go to sleep, but Anyu was utterly exhausted. She lay down. The cold, hard bamboo mattress pressed against her back, so different from the warm *kang* she was used to. But it felt good to lie down, to stretch out her limbs. Her head on her sack, she faced the wooden wall of the attic, listening to the rain dripping outside the window, watching a globe of golden light reflected from the table lamp. She had a corner to herself, a place to stay; she was no longer homeless. For the first time since her mother's death, after days and nights of jostling in the train, fearful, being on alert, she felt safe.

Drowsiness slipped over her like a silky cover. Her eyes fluttered; her breathing slowed. One last thought occurred to her: she had forgotten to ask Isaac about his treasure. Did he still have the egg? Could she see it?

CHAPTER 5

The next morning, Anyu awoke to the crisp chimes of bicycle bells on the street. She sat up, disoriented, surprised at the dark attic, the beds, and the warm air. Then she remembered finding Isaac in the jewelry shop and her job in the showroom. She sprang up. Esther, brushing her wavy golden hair, told her to change into a decent dress. She didn't have one, so she dug out her best summer tunic—one of only two she owned—and put it on.

In the kitchen, the aunts were brining cucumbers and carrots and cleaning. Anyu gobbled down two pieces of bread and was ready to sell jewelry.

When she entered the showroom, it was still early. The sun had just come out; the shop wasn't open yet. Near the empty shelves, Esther and Samuel were holding boxes with jewelry labels, watching Uncle David speak to a man wearing a green cloth cap. He was here to collect protection fees, he said in Chinese. Uncle David handed him a thick envelope and a bottle of vodka before ushering the man out.

Anyu would learn later that the Mandelburgs, denounced by the Bolsheviks, were no longer citizens of Russia and lived in Shanghai as stateless people. Their jewelry shop had no protection from the Russian consulate run by the Soviets, nor from law enforcement in the French Concession, the French police. They were obliged to obey the Chinese law, but with the Nationalists' shaky control of the city and lack of proper policing, the Mandelburgs were targeted by robbers and thieves in the crime-ridden city. To protect their valuables, they had submitted to the demands of the Green Gang, a massive gangster organization, who promised to provide safety for their shop on condition of monthly protection fees.

After the gangster's henchman left, Uncle David let out a long breath and locked the front door. Esther urged Samuel to hurry up, and the two began to open the jewelry boxes. Then came a knock on the shop door.

"I'll get it," Anyu said.

"Don't!" Esther said, leaning over the counter to see who was knocking. "Oh. It's Mr. Walters, Uncle David."

"Samuel, could you tell your father to come over?" Uncle David said and opened the door. In came a middle-aged man with closely set green eyes, a round face, and round glasses that made him appear like an owl, flanked by four tall Indian men wearing turbans—the Sikhs. A suitcase in hand, Mr. Walters scanned the showroom and gave Anyu an inscrutable look.

"Good morning, Mr. Walters. I hope I didn't keep you waiting." Isaac appeared from behind the curtain and led him to the meeting area.

Without a reply, Mr. Walters sat down, took out a small black pouch, and shook the contents onto a black velvet tray Isaac had provided— diamonds. White diamonds, yellow diamonds, already cut, at least a dozen of them, some with a high level of clarity and producing brilliant fluorescence in the shop's blazing light. Isaac studied them with a loupe and a flashlight and nodded. Mr. Walters presented another pouch, out of which tumbled rubies, emeralds, amethysts, and jade, gemstones in a spectacular show of color, which Isaac likewise examined. Then he reviewed and signed a notebook Mr. Walters handed to him. Finally, Mr. Walters buckled up his black suitcase, rose, and headed to the door, the four Sikhs following him. The entire process was conducted with no verbal interaction except Isaac's greeting.

"Is he the supplier?" Anyu asked Esther once the men left. Isaac, holding the pouches, went inside the house. The shop's front door was locked again; Esther, Samuel, and Uncle David continued unboxing and displaying jewelry inside the glass cases. It might be her imagination, but Anyu thought the gemstones' delivery had enlivened the showroom.

"None of your business," Esther said, limping toward a cabinet, holding a box.

"Is he deaf?"

Esther frowned.

"I knew it!" A deaf supplier. How unexpected.

"The shop will open soon, let's get to work."

"What can I do?" Anyu asked.

"Stay where you are," Esther said. They were efficient, placing the pieces on stands lined with black and red felt and tucking a slip of paper marked with a price underneath. It seemed there was a meticulous order about the setup. Some locations were for rings and necklaces, some for brooches and pins.

When all was ready, Uncle David and Samuel returned to the workshop, Samuel grumbling about his stomachache. The two aunts came in with their market bags; Esther opened a desk drawer near a shelf, withdrew a few bills, and handed the grocery money to one of the aunts. It appeared Esther was in charge of the family's finances.

Anyu leaned closer to the glass shelves; nestled inside were beauties of the finest designs, which she would come to learn in every detail: platinum brooches with crushed diamonds around sapphires and rubies, gold necklaces with pendants in rhombus, rectangular, and other geometric patterns, intricate earrings with thread-fine filigrees and gemstones, gold watches mounted with rose-cut diamonds, cigarette cases graced with ocean-blue enamel and flaming-red tinder cords, and silver-plated music boxes decorated with a brilliant-yellow sunburst.

"Do not touch anything." With a key from her belt, Esther locked the glass case Anyu was studying.

"I won't."

"I mean it. If you touch anything without my knowledge, you leave."

Anyu wondered why Esther had such an abrasive manner. She would have liked to befriend her. She had never made any friends. "I won't." Then she realized: "If I'm not allowed to touch anything, how do I show the jewelry to the customers if they want to see them?"

"You don't take them out of the case. You tell me. I'll take care of the customers."

Anyu nodded. "I plan to sell a piece of jewelry today."

Esther put her hand on her waist and tilted her head. She looked as though she was about to laugh. Her countenance was an envious image of symmetry and perfection, with large gray eyes, a smooth oval face, and a well-proportioned straight nose. Anyu, who loved to sketch scenery to illustrate a certain emotion, thought she could draw Esther's face right there, her visage inciting a feeling of awe and a deep sense of worship. She was the most beautiful girl Anyu had seen.

"Only one? How about two?" Esther said.

"We'll see," Anyu said. "I like all these pieces. They are beautiful. Who made them?"

"My father."

"All by himself?" She hadn't realized one man was capable of designing and crafting all of the jewelry.

"He's a dedicated man, and he's a master jeweler."

"How did he make them?" Those engravings, those designs, and those chains and clasps. It was a fine show of sophisticated craftsmanship.

Esther fixed her sharp eyes on her. "I wish I could answer your questions, but I'm busy. Could you move aside?"

Anyu retreated to the tall shelf along the wall, but then Esther came to open a cabinet and waved her away. She inched to the side to get out of her way. The space behind the counter was enough for six people, but apparently, it was too small for both of them.

At nine o'clock, when the golden sunlight poured onto the shop's window, and carts and pedestrians streamed past on the street outside, Esther unlatched the door and flipped over the wooden sign to "Open."

Then she stood beside Anyu behind the counter with an aggravated look that needed no more explanation.

Anyu held herself straight. If she could sell a piece of jewelry on her first day, then Esther would be friendly to her. Maybe she could even sell something without talking to anyone.

An hour passed, and not a single customer entered the shop. Esther glanced at the clock on the wall, frowning.

Finally, a fickle flow of customers arrived—two tall foreigners in suits and fedoras. Astoundingly, Esther greeted them with warmth and joy as if she had known them for ages. Her face bloomed, her eyes brightened, and her lips curved into a smile. Even her voice changed—it became as smooth as honey, intoning a mixture of Russian and Chinese. The way she talked was graceful, warm, and polite, complimenting the customers' taste; it was as though they were her friends or neighbors.

"What's the occasion? A birthday? Fabulous . . . Yes, this necklace has all the femininity and beauty, with the timeless charm of Edwardian jewelry. Is this something your wife loves? Not sure? Well, if you're looking for something modern, the Art Deco design is quite fashionable . . ." Esther went on to talk about the platinum ring with a sleek marquise-cut sapphire, the perennial appeal of filigree jewelry, the perpetually popular bowknot motifs, and the allure of black onyx earrings with enamel.

In the end, the two foreigners purchased the sapphire ring she'd recommended.

Anyu didn't say anything, but if this was the way to sell a piece of jewelry, she wouldn't be able to sell anything in three months, or three years. She had no idea about jewelry trends or what an Art Deco design meant, and she did not possess the charm, patience, or grace that Esther had. She had so much to learn.

"How much is this?" A Chinese man with glasses was pointing at a pair of earrings near her.

Anyu turned around. She had been watching Esther help an older man holding a cane and forgot about the customers entering the shop.

All of a sudden, her confidence in selling jewelry vanished, and she could feel her pulse quicken and her palms grow sweaty. She wiped her hands on her pants, over and over, willing the customer to go away. Then, composing herself, she peered at the jadeite earrings and the marked price inside the glass case and said, "Two hundred Chinese dollars."

The staggering sum was beyond her grasp of understanding. She had never laid an eye on a one-hundred-dollar bill.

"That's overpriced. It shouldn't be over one hundred."

"Yes."

"You agree?" The man looked surprised.

She nodded. "This price is out of line. This is not jadeite. It's a fake. One hundred is fair."

The man shook his head and walked away.

Later, Esther came over. "Did I hear it correctly? Did you tell a customer the jewelry was overpriced?"

"Two hundred is an exorbitant price for a pair of earrings."

"Exorbitant? Where did you get this idea?"

"This is fake jade."

Esther's face turned red, and her eyes glittered. "And you told the customer? Do you always speak without thinking?"

Anyu blinked. Did she?

"Use your brain! Keep your thoughts to yourself, would you? We need to make money."

Anyu blinked again. *Keep your thoughts to yourself.*

Later, when the customers came by, Anyu remained quiet and said nothing to contradict the marked prices. When the customers needed to hold the jewelry, she turned to Esther, who removed the trays and presented them with grace and patience, and when the viewing was over, she locked the pieces away. Anyu didn't touch the jewelry and made few remarks about the value of the gemstones or the craftsmanship.

At the end of the day, Anyu failed to make a sale. Standing in the corner of the showroom, she watched Esther and Samuel pack up the jewelry and carry the boxes to a jewelry safe inside the house.

They no longer needed her after closing. She picked up a damp rag Esther had left for her and began to wipe the glass counter, wondering whether she should explore the city in the evening. After being in the showroom all day, she wanted some fresh air and to walk the streets—in Harbin, despite the poverty and loneliness, seeing the sky and feeling the openness had always been her favorite thing. But she was tired, her legs sore after standing all day.

Isaac came into the showroom wearing his black apron. "How was your first day?"

"I didn't sell anything."

"That's all right. Would you mind me asking you something? Esther said you told the customer the jade was fake. How did you know?"

"I just know," she said and explained the night market where her mother had moonlighted, the conversations she had eavesdropped on, and the gemstones she had spied. From what she had heard, she could tell if it was real jade by inspecting its color, transparency, and luster. "Some jadeite has an oily luster, some doesn't. Another way is to click the jadeite and listen to the sound, but I haven't touched a real jadeite."

Isaac smiled. "What a surprise. Who would know an orphan growing up by the train station has a talent for discerning gemstones."

"I won't tell the customers," she said.

Isaac nodded and headed to the door behind the curtain.

"Mr. Mandelburg?" she called out.

He turned around at the door. "Yes?"

"Do you still have the egg?"

He froze, his mouth agape. "For your own safety and our best interest, I advise you not to mention it again, Anyu."

"Why?" The expression on his face, though, reminded her of the blood on his neck when they were at the train station, and his haste to leave. "What happened in Harbin?"

"I would rather not talk about it."

"But you have to, or I'll keep asking."

He shook his head, looking dismayed. "You're a stubborn kid."

That was what her mother had often said.

"You might want to take a seat." He came to the counter, and Anyu set aside the rag and listened.

When he received the egg from the tsarina's delegate, Isaac said, one of the White Russian guards from the Winter Palace, an unscrupulous man who had already stolen some of the imperial family's treasure, had demanded the keepsake from him, but he refused and fled. The guard had hunted him from St. Petersburg to Vladivostok and then to Harbin, where he had lived undisturbed in an inn's cellar with Esther and Samuel. Until one day, at the crack of dawn, the proprietor warned him of visitors. Climbing out of the cellar, he could see the White Russian guard and beside him a Japanese officer in the Japanese Imperial Army's overcoat uniform, a sword in his hand. He was short, slim, with narrow shoulders.

To keep his grown children from danger, Isaac instructed them to split up and meet at the train station, where they would travel to Shanghai. He opened the back door to let them out, hurried back to the cellar to gather his leather bag that contained the egg and portable valuables, and raced to the backyard. He was only a few feet away from the gate when the guard and officer came upon him. Holding the leather bag containing the egg, he trembled against the wall, next to the body of the proprietor who had warned him, as the deadly pair gestured and growled. It seemed an argument had broken out between the duo. The guard flew into a fit of rage, cursing, threatening, and whipping out his pistol. The officer simply watched, his head bowed, listening like an obedient daughter.

Then the unthinkable: with a blinding speed that Isaac almost believed was his imagination, the Russian guard stopped cursing, the pistol still grasped in his hand—a sword had pierced his heart.

Blood splattered on Isaac's face, and the yard roared with concerned guests clamoring, shouting, distracting the officer. Seizing the chance, Isaac slipped through the gate and ran for his life. When he was far away from the inn, with the killer out of sight, he washed the blood off his face with snow and went to the train station, trudging among the tide of Chinese, Russians, and Japanese soldiers. But he couldn't find his grown children at the station. He would discover later they had left on a different train, but he didn't know it then. Worried about their safety, searching for them among the crowds of people, fearful of the officer pursuing him, he didn't notice how he had lost his fedora and even the bag with the egg. Sinking into despair, he searched everywhere near the station until he saw Anyu, and to his greatest joy, she returned the bag to him.

"Are you sure it was a Japanese officer chasing you?" Anyu asked.

"I'm sure. His uniform was easy to identify; it had red collar patches and brass buttons set widely apart. Many officers in Harbin wore that type of overcoat to ward off the chill. He also had a crew cut, wore a military cap, and he was very young."

"And you said he carried a sword."

"A samurai sword."

"Do you think he's still after you?"

Isaac sighed. Anyu understood why he might stay silent. He was a cautious man; with a valuable egg like that, it was safer not to mention it at all.

Esther coughed in the doorway, folding her arms. Anyu had not noticed when she entered the showroom.

"I hope I didn't interrupt you two," Esther said.

Very soon, Anyu grew familiar with the routine in the two-story apartment the Mandelburgs lived in.

Each morning, Esther, Uncle David, and Samuel carried out jewelry boxes from inside the workshop that Anyu was forbidden to enter, unpacked them in the showroom, and displayed them in the glass cases. Isaac, busy creating new wares, rarely joined. Each evening, at closing, the three packed up, carried the boxes out of the showroom, and stored them in the safe in the workshop. Sometimes, when Anyu listened hard enough, she could hear the creak of the workshop's door opening and the metallic clang of the safe.

The apartment was small and musty, with damp walls, a muddy floor, an entrance to the showroom in the front, and a back door to an alley, where the women did their laundry and washed their dishes. There wasn't much free space to move around, and it felt cramped when all of them sat together. There were only two bedrooms on the top floor, the women's attic chamber and the men's room across from it. Being discreet, Anyu didn't set foot in the men's bedroom, but once when the door was left ajar, she peered into it. For someone with a priceless egg, Isaac lived a surprisingly humble lifestyle—the bedroom was sparsely furnished with two beds, two wardrobes, and a chest.

The workshop that Esther forbade her to enter was located at the end of the hallway on the first floor, secured by a brass padlock with a ring handle rather than a Chinese box-style padlock. On the doorpost was installed a piece of metal, a mezuzah, which the men touched before entering. Loud thumping and metallic striking sounds came from inside, sometimes even at night. The smoke from the furnace, the rust and the dust, the acrid scent of metal burning, and the sharp odor of chemicals wafted from the workshop to the kitchen and attic. Sometimes, when the workshop's door was left ajar, Anyu could hear Isaac's frustrated, muffled voice: *Samuel, wake up. Where is the chain I asked for?*

As promised, Anyu kept away from the workshop, even though her rising curiosity made her wonder how Isaac had crafted the jewelry. The Mandelburgs were Jewish, Anyu was told, which was something new to her; she had never heard of Judaism, only Buddhism. They didn't burn incense sticks like the Buddhists did, nor set up an altar in their kitchen for the Goddess of Compassion or the God of Fortune with an overflowing, enviable potbelly. In fact, they gave her the impression that they were discreet about their religion. The men rarely wore their yarmulkes in the showroom when there were customers, and they only conversed in Chinese and, occasionally, poor English. They worked every day during the week. On Fridays before sundown, they closed the shop, and the aunts set up a table with two candles, a glass of wine, and a loaf of bread. One of them lit the candles, covered her eyes with her hand, and recited by heart a blessing in a language Anyu couldn't understand. Then they all drank the wine and ate while Aunt Hannah, who always complained about something, grumbled that there was no place to attend services in the city and that finding kosher food was as hard as hunting for unicorns.

Two weeks passed. None of the customers Anyu talked to purchased anything. Selling jewelry was harder than she had thought. Conversing was a chore, and willing strangers to spend money was as challenging as sledding uphill in the dead of winter in Harbin. She learned to follow the customers as they browsed, pay compliments, and even smile, as Esther had demonstrated, but she felt like a sycophant and was bored to her bones.

But she would sell something; she still had plenty of time.

In the evening, after the shop was closed, when she was free, Anyu strolled down the street in front of the shop. She passed a handbag shop, an apothecary, and an emporium selling wooden puzzles, biscuits in tin containers, and cloth tiger toys. At a stall selling newspapers, she scanned for news about Harbin but found nothing. She remained in good spirits, enthralled by the vibrant street scenes. This was what she had been longing for, a different world from the train station. Her ears full of the squeaks of rickshaws and the honks of cars, she peeked at long-robed vendors selling pungent incense sticks, artists demonstrating paper-cutting skills, and men hawking mouth-watering steamy buns filled with minced meat. In front of a towering building, through a glass window, she saw some foreigners sitting at a café, sipping a brownish sludge that resembled sewer water—she wondered who would be so foolish to drink something like that.

A delicious smell wafted toward her, enticing her. Following it, she found stalls selling bowls of wontons and noodles and stands displaying skewers of barbecued squid sizzling with grease. She had never tasted squid before, and she would have liked to take a bite. But she had only nine dollars; she decided to pass to conserve money.

Then, looking at the fashionable women in long fitted dresses in rickshaws, Anyu felt a wave of sadness. Mother's joyous face appeared in her mind. She saw her waving the basket of quail eggs, shouting, *Dinner!* And her poised look while interpreting at the night market. And her warm body snuggling next to her on the *kang*, her rapturous voice spinning tales of animals while the snowstorm whipped the frozen land outside their room. *Oh, Mother.*

Anyu missed her—her face, her voice, her hands, her touches, her smiles, and her sighs. She missed the way Mother had held her face and asked, *Does it hurt?* She missed watching her cut her nails with the kitchen cleaver and wash her hair. She missed seeing her munch on juicy garlic cloves and slurp rich bone soups with radishes. Mother was the only person in the world who loved her, cared for her, tolerated her, and worried about her; she was her sky, her earth, her home. And now she was gone. Anyu felt like crying.

Isaac's shop was not a home; she didn't feel she belonged there. Isaac was warm to her, but the others found a way to build an invisible wall of alienation between them. Esther hardly spoke to her; the twin aunts, Aunt Hannah and Aunt Katya, held a united front to make her feel unwelcome at mealtime, chatting in a blast of Yiddish, giving no indication of their awareness of her existence; the uncle often growled at the sight of her; and Samuel hardly acknowledged her after she had refused to lend him money.

❧

"How's your day?" Isaac asked her while she was at the counter. Isaac usually stayed in his workshop, rarely entering the showroom during business hours. When he did visit, he kept a low profile, subdued and quiet. Today, he had come to meet the customers whose ring he had repaired, and in his patient voice, he had answered their questions and described to them the types of diamond cuts, the rose cut, calibre cut, pear-shaped cut, and marquise cut. At the end of the meeting, the customers placed an order for a necklace and matching earrings.

"I still haven't sold anything," she said.

"Don't worry. You'll make a sale." Isaac left.

Anyu stared at his back until he disappeared, and her mood lifted. Isaac was a kind man, and he cared about her. She wished he would stay, and she wanted to talk to him and listen to his voice. She scanned the jewelry in the glass cases, all the beauties he had crafted: Edwardian earrings with intricate filigree inlaid with sapphires and rubies, Art Deco rope necklaces strung with simple circles and triangles, flapper rings with asymmetrical designs, popular charms with Egyptian motifs such as enamel scarabs, pyramids, and sphinxes. An idea struck her.

In the attic, Anyu took out her pencil and sheets of paper she had brought from Harbin and began to draw bejeweled animals from her imagination: a ruby-eyed Siberian tiger set on an Edwardian pin, a platinum forest fox mounted with studs of diamonds, a necklace with a red-crowned crane encapsulated within a triangle, and a cornucopia brooch encrusted with a constellation of emeralds and sapphires. She drew fervently, fantasizing that one of them would turn into real jewelry someday.

She thought of Isaac's Fabergé egg again, its delicate image and its ethereal beauty. She was not supposed to mention it or ask, but now more than ever, she wished she could see it.

One month passed, and hard as she tried, Anyu failed to make a sale.

CHAPTER 6

"Customers have been complaining about her, Father," Esther said, standing beside the desk where she kept the cash.

The shop was closed, the jewelry packed, and the day was winding down. Isaac had just walked into the showroom to speak to Uncle David, and Anyu, who had taken the responsibility to keep the glass counter as spotless as possible, wiped the cases with a damp rag. She had taken her time cleaning, unwilling to leave, not glancing at Isaac but watching his every move out of the corner of her eye. Lately, she had been thinking about Isaac, anticipating his presence at dinner and in the hallway, thrilled at the sight of him. When he smiled at her, she felt her face flush and a flutter in her stomach. When he spoke to her, his words lingered in her mind like joyous tunes she played over and over before bed.

Anyu stopped cleaning. "I didn't hear any complaints."

"That's the problem. You don't hear anything," Esther said.

How could she make Esther like her? Anyu wondered. She still wanted to be her friend.

"What did they complain about?" Isaac peered at the tray Uncle David handed to him; it held some old rings in tarnished silver and gold, auctioned tchotchkes, and broken vintage jewelry. Isaac received diamonds from Mr. Walters, but he also looked for rare gems in clusters. When he found them, he recast them.

"There's no point in repeating their words. It's how she speaks and the look on her face. She can't smile, can't talk. She's as stiff as a newly excavated Egyptian mummy!"

"I can smile," Anyu said.

"And sales are down. She's driving away the customers."

"The sales are indeed down this month," Uncle David said.

"Summer is a slow sales season. Many wealthy clients are on vacation." Isaac, holding a ring with a pair of tweezers, studied it intently with a loupe.

"She's been here for a month!"

"A month and two days," Anyu said.

"Has it been that long? Have you paid her, Esther?"

He remembered her wage! She had been too embarrassed to remind Esther, having failed to sell a thing.

"For doing nothing?" Esther's gaze was like her beauty—sharp, blinding.

"Esther, Esther. Don't behave like a kid. Shall we take it inside?" Isaac took the tray and nodded at Uncle David. The two men went to the door behind the curtain, nearly crashing into Samuel, who was on his way out.

"Where are you going, Samuel?" Isaac asked.

"My stomach hurts. Going to see a doctor." He was holding something in his hands, which he quickly stuffed inside his pocket.

"Again?"

"I can't help it!"

Isaac shook his head and left the showroom with Uncle David.

"Can we talk?" Samuel, glancing at Anyu, whispered to Esther. "Outside?"

"Fine." Esther followed him out the door. They conversed on the street.

The showroom felt quiet and empty. Anyu scanned the gleaming glass cases and rinsed the rag. Next, she would sweep the floor, empty the wastebasket filled with cigarette butts and candy wrappers, and then go to the attic and draw. But she wished Isaac had stayed.

Esther returned to the showroom. She was trembling, biting her lip.

"How bad is Samuel's stomachache?" Anyu asked.

Esther ignored her and unlocked the desk drawer. With an exasperated look, she dropped some coins in Anyu's hands. "Here."

Ten pennies! Her wage. A large amount, enough to purchase bowls of noodles for both her mother and her. Anyu was giddy, her heart swelling with pride. How she wished her mother were alive so she could share her happiness.

"It's easy, isn't it?" Esther cocked her head.

"What do you mean?"

Esther put her hands on her hips. The cluster of keys clinked on her belt. "Getting paid for doing nothing."

Anyu enclosed the coins in her hand. Shouldn't her janitorial work merit a word of recognition? But fine. She wouldn't argue. "I'll make a sale. You'll see."

"You said that on the first day. What are you going to do with your money?"

She hadn't thought of it.

"You can make yourself look more attractive in front of the customers. Buy a dress. Plenty of shops on the street sell ready-made dresses."

Anyu scanned her plain gray long-sleeve tunic, long trousers, and cloth shoes with flat, worn soles.

"No."

"A pair of new shoes?"

"No."

"A lipstick?"

"Why would I waste money on that?"

Esther threw up her hands.

Grinning from ear to ear, Anyu pocketed the coins. She would put the money to good use, of course. She could buy a new pencil, some notebooks to draw on, or maybe a bowl of noodles.

She finished her cleaning tasks, made sure the shop's door and all the cases and drawers were locked, and turned off the lights. Then she went to the kitchen and left through the back door.

It was a pleasant evening, the heat dissipating. There was still abundant daylight, and the streets were teeming with pedestrians.

Anyu visited a few food stalls and then a stationery shop selling gilded paper and sets of the Four Treasures of a Study—a brush, ink, paper, and ink stone, all the refined scholarly stuff, not something she needed. It occurred to her that it might be a good idea to heed Esther's suggestion. Since she was earning wages, she could splurge on a ready-made pongee dress to make herself more presentable. Besides, summer was here; it was too hot to wear her tunic.

It didn't take her long to find a boutique displaying blouses and gowns. They looked beautiful, with soft fabric and bright floral designs. She played with a few short sleeves on the table, then moved to the rack holding ankle-length dresses. One by one, she scrutinized their elaborate frog buttons, seams, and lengths. She liked two dresses, a pink floral dress with peonies and a green pongee tunic with white lotus blossoms, each costing a whopping two dollars. She held both, unable to decide which one to buy. Then she put them back on the wooden frame.

A shout came from a grocery stall across the street. Three men, wearing distinctive green cloth caps identical to the one worn by the man who came to the shop for protection money, were harassing the shoppers. They sought a gangster who was hiding nearby, one of them said. The gangster had stolen the cash from Mr. Du's gambling house in the Old City and fled to this neighborhood.

A few customers near Anyu looked frightened and slid to the side. They whispered that these men were members of the Green Gang, the scourge of the city, a criminal organization that ran opium dens, gambling houses, and brothels throughout Shanghai. They were ruthless and violent; even the authorities in the French Concession left them alone.

Anyu stepped to the corner. She just wanted to get her shopping done and go back to her apartment. But the men's shouts began to unnerve her. She decided to purchase the pink floral dress and get out of there. She held the hanger, lifted the dress off the frame, and saw a pair of black eyes staring straight at her. She gasped. The man was young, almost her age, with shoulder-length hair, large eyes, and a pudgy nose.

Across the street, one of the gangsters holding a club sauntered toward her. "You. You over there. Did you see the gangster?"

She put the dress back to cover the face. "Yes. That way," she said, pointing to her left. "I saw him go that way."

The gangsters sprinted in the direction she pointed. The customers around her let out their long-held breath, and two women raced to the street to pick up the baskets of scattered vegetables the Green Gang had kicked aside.

Her heart pounding, Anyu peered at the rack. The youth slipped the floral dress off his head, winked at her, and slunk away. She wanted to kick herself. She had lied, for a gangster.

When Anyu returned to the shop, the apartment was dim and quiet. No one was in the kitchen; the aunts must have retired, and Esther was not around—perhaps she had left the shop with a male friend she had mentioned. The workshop's door was shut; from inside came clicks and the sound of a mallet hitting the metal. She hesitated. She itched to see Isaac and his workspace and how he crafted the jewelry pieces, but she had promised Esther not to enter. What if she stood nearby? Holding the dress, she crept close to the end of the hallway and stood at a good distance from the door. She could see a faint streak of light flickering through the narrow gap and hear Isaac's patient voice:

"When pricing rubies, you need to view them in different lights, as a direct incandescent beam makes the color intense, and weak daylight cools the color down.

"When assessing blue sapphires, look for those with purity and intense blue color. It is ideal if a stone has a violet overtone.

"When working with opals, extra attention to the type of background metal is needed. Because the setting will boost the stone's colors and affect the strength of the iridescence. Are you listening, Samuel? Samuel! Wake up!"

She had not heard these details at the night market. She would have loved to hear all the tips about gemstones. Fascinated, Anyu didn't leave until she heard footsteps come down the stairs.

Anyu thought she looked great in the new dress—she had always been self-conscious about her appearance because of her neighbors' criticisms, but the dress gave her an elegant, sophisticated look. It fitted her well at the chest and waist, and the color suited her. When she stood at the counter, she thought Esther's expression softened. But unfortunately, this wasn't enough to make customers, well dressed and overly decorated with pocket watches and gold necklaces, open their wallets. They sidled away the moment she approached, and sometimes, as if to confirm her ineptitude, they'd even purchase jewelry from Esther after a brief talk with her.

Near the end of the second month, she still hadn't made a sale.

Anyu dreaded entering the showroom, resigned to the fact that she was not good at persuading customers. She wished she could be somewhere other than at the counter, and frequently, she found her thoughts drifting to Isaac's workshop.

Her pace slowed when she smelled the acrid chemicals and the burning metal, and her ears perked up when voices echoed from inside. Whenever she could, she lingered outside the workshop, where the light escaped from the open door and winked on the mezuzah on the doorpost. Remembering Esther's warning, she didn't enter.

When Esther dropped another ten cents in her hands, Anyu grew anxious.

Only one month left.

She had to make a sale. She couldn't imagine leaving Isaac and the shop. She had grown accustomed to life under Isaac's roof, with the glass cases of jewelry, the tide of customers, and even mealtimes with the crowd of Mandelburgs. There was the rhythm of noisy chatter and animated liveliness in the daily routine that had eluded her in Harbin; there was comfort, security, and even moments of joy, which her life sequestered in the dank room with her mother had lacked. And when Anyu stood in the luminescent showroom, with Isaac close by, with the jewels glittering, she felt at home. She didn't want to leave.

She thought about having a word with Isaac. But what could she say to him, really? She was a failed saleswoman and a disappointment. She couldn't rely on Isaac's charity; she must contribute to the shop and prove her worth herself.

But what else could she do other than sell jewelry?

Once, when Anyu came downstairs, she saw the workshop's door was left ajar, and a sprig of golden light burst from the workshop and reflected on the wall of the quiet hallway. Since no one was around, she tiptoed closer, unable to resist, and leaned in.

The first thing she saw was a wall covered with drawings, drawings of rings, necklaces, and brooches, all colored with vivid hues. The one closest to her was a necklace featuring tricolored onyx, ruby, and emerald, set within irregularly shaped rectangles of varying sizes, all strung together to form a lush bouquet of elegance. With her perfect vision, Anyu could see the images were marked with notes about the scale and the sizes and types of gemstones. They looked exactly like the jewelry sold in the showroom. A jeweler's drawing, she realized, was not simply an image; it was a dance of light, an authentic vision of a craftsman, and a preview of the eloquent play of metals and gemstones.

She could do that—envision her designs, draw up the outlines, and mark them with metals and the sizes and types of gemstones, and not just one drawing but thousands.

Excited, she swung the door wide open and saw a table covered with an array of exotic tools: steel rulers, tweezers, knives, files, brushes, drills, hammers with round and flat faces, pliers with sharp tips and round noses.

Near the table, Isaac sat at a workbench with a curve and multiple drawers, holding a jeweler's saw, cutting through a piece of metal on a wooden block clamped to the desk. Then he put down his saw, discarded the remnants of the metal sheet, and produced the shape of a tree—he had transcribed the design onto a metal sheet by sawing it.

This was how a piece of jewelry was made; this was how a design, an idea, or an image transformed into reality. Here. In this room. By this man's hand.

A thought struck Anyu, bright like the beam of light on Isaac's workbench, golden, incandescent, glowing like the radiance of the Russian egg.

This was what she wanted to do—she wanted to hold the saw and the pliers, to cut metal sheets, forge plates, and twist wires. She wanted to craft beautiful jewelry—the necklaces, rings, brooches, and the Russian egg. She wanted to become a jeweler.

In the showroom, with the customers milling around, Anyu was distracted. Even as she urged herself to concentrate and work hard to make a sale, she couldn't stop thinking about the tools in the workshop, the drawings on the wall, and Isaac sitting at his workbench. At night, when she drew, she began to envision designs with an eye for the gemstones, the textures, the colors, the weight, the size, and the scale. When she wandered around the city, passing a garden with winding bridges, she'd imagine a bridge earring and its texture; when she saw an exotic French coffeehouse decorated with purple shutters and red tables, she'd dream up a pendant for a gold necklace and its color; and when she spotted the prancing horses and their jockeys on the enormous racecourse, she thought of a brooch and its movements.

Designing the jewelry was easy, but she wanted to know how to transcribe the design onto a metal sheet and learn to use tools to cut, engrave, and weld—all the metalsmithing techniques and skills. The only person who could teach her was Isaac.

If she asked, would he train her? Would he accept her as his apprentice so that she could help out in the workshop instead of selling the jewelry?

There was only one way to find out.

CHAPTER 7

Two weeks before the three-month deadline, Anyu cleaned the showroom, locked the front door, and gathered all her sketches from the attic. Then she went to the kitchen, where the family was eating dinner.

They had a simple meal today, some cabbage and bread and crackers, and the aunts were lamenting the food money they had lost. They had kept the bills in their pockets, but when they arrived at the market, they couldn't find them. How on earth had they lost them? They were bewildered.

Isaac was chewing a cracker with his mouth closed, listening to Esther, who was also bemoaning her money problems: the low sales and high expenses.

"The budget will be tight next month," Uncle David said.

"Mr. Mandelburg?" Anyu asked, holding her sketches.

Isaac dabbed at the corner of his mouth. "Yes?"

Anyu said, "I don't want to stand behind the counter, Mr. Mandelburg. I'd like to be a jeweler. I want to learn how to craft jewelry to help you with the shop. Will you train me?"

Everyone stared at her, Uncle David, Esther, and the aunts. Except Samuel, who yawned. He had the talent for releasing expertly formed yawns, loud and enduring, with deliberateness and powerful vocal capacity, filling the room with a spell of sleepiness that hovered in the air.

Isaac glanced at him and frowned. Samuel failed to notice, picked up a fork in slow motion, and stared as if it had become gold. He was twenty years old, four years older than Anyu, and he had grown a thick beard.

"Making jewelry is hard work, Anyu. It's manual work, hard labor, a tedious, dirty job," Isaac said.

"I don't mind. I'm good at drawing. I've been learning how to draw like a jewelry designer. Do you want to see?" She held out her papers.

"I'm sure they're fine drawings."

But he didn't look at them! "Here, here." She placed the stack near his crackers.

"Young lady, we're having dinner," Uncle David said.

"You won't regret it, Mr. Mandelburg," Anyu said.

Isaac sighed, took a pair of glasses from his pocket, and held the drawings. His eyes grazed over the Siberian tiger pin, the platinum forest fox, and the red-crowned crane. "These images are unique and refreshing. You're a talented artist, Anyu."

"You like them?"

"You have potential."

"I can be an excellent jewelry designer if you train me."

He chuckled, shaking his head. "I forget how young you are, Anyu."

"I'll be seventeen in two months, Mr. Mandelburg." She liked to see him laugh, and she wished he would laugh more often.

"Is this why you've been snooping around the workshop?" Esther asked.

Anyu opened her mouth.

"You are not allowed to enter the workshop," Uncle David said.

"I didn't enter it."

"Did you take anything from the workshop?"

"What? No!" Anyu was alarmed. *A woman's reputation was like a porcelain vase: once cracked, it could never be fully repaired,* Mother had said. "I didn't take anything!"

Isaac gave back her stack. "I can't train you, Anyu."

"Why not?"

"You're a girl. Women do not become jewelers in Russia," Esther said.

She was not wrong. The idea of a female jeweler was unimaginable to many. But she insisted. "We're in Shanghai."

"Well, tell me. Do you know any female jewelers in Shanghai?" Esther asked.

"Are you saying there are no female jewelers in the world?"

"Well," Isaac said. "Believe it or not, the jewelry industry has seen many fine female jewelers with astounding artistic talents. Esther might not know this, but Fabergé had two female master designers. One of them was the ingenious Alma Pihl, who designed the Mosaic Egg for Empress Alexandra Feodorovna, an egg inspired by needlework. She had an incredible gift, and she made her name with frosty snowflakes in a platinum-silver setting decorated with rose-cut diamonds."

"Still, jewelry making is not a woman's craft," Uncle David said.

"But Mr. Mandelburg said there were female jewelers," Anyu said.

Uncle David cleared his throat. "There were female jewelers— no argument there—but I wish to remind you that we do not train outsiders. We are a family of jewelers; goldsmithing has been our family's trade for centuries."

Anyu blinked. She had not forgotten; she was only a helper hired by Isaac. "But—"

"We're Jews. For hundreds of years, the sultans and emperors and tsars imposed brutal, restrictive policies to starve us, and many perished as a result. Our family has survived because of our goldsmithing skills. Isaac's father and his grandfather were jewelers, and I'm also from a jeweler's family. I worked together with Isaac's father since my sister married him. We've relied on our skills to make a living since we were in Crimea, when it was ruled by the Ottoman Empire. This is our family's trade."

Anyu had not realized their jewelry-making background. "But I can help with your family's business."

Uncle David shook his head. "We do not work with outsiders. Our means of survival have to be passed down from father to son; it has remained so for generations. It stays in our family. I'm not blessed to have children, but Isaac has Samuel."

Family legacy and the tradition of passing skills through sons. The Jews and the Chinese were very much alike, barring women from entering some professions. Anyu didn't like it at all; she looked at Samuel. "But he's not a jeweler, he's a gambler."

Silence fell in the room; Samuel's fork dropped to the floor.

Isaac put down his cracker. "I'm sorry, what did you say, Anyu?"

He didn't know.

"Is this true? Is this what you've been doing these days, Samuel? You had a stomachache and you needed to go see the doctor?"

Samuel turned his face away.

"Look at me, Samuel! When did this start?"

"What does it matter? What else can I do? I hate this. I hate my life!" He stormed off.

"Esther? You knew about this. Why didn't you tell me?" Isaac's voice was hoarse.

"Father, I wanted to tell you. I've tried—"

"Have you been giving him money?"

"No, Father."

"Then where did he get the money?"

"I gave him a few cents . . . but I won't do it again. I promise."

Isaac sagged in his seat; his shoulders dropped, his face slack. "My son, my only son." Then he pushed away his chair and rose, his eyes filled with tears.

Anyu's heart sank. She should have kept her mouth shut.

"You have two weeks," Esther said. She stood and left with Uncle David and the aunts. The house descended into a still gloom.

How had she managed to thoroughly alienate the family who sheltered her? She had not meant to cause pain for them. For Isaac, especially. She should have been working on learning some sales skills, and now she already had a foot out the door. What had she done?

Alone, Anyu sat.

CHAPTER 8

The apartment felt frosty for the next few days, even though it was summer. Anyu's untimely revelation of Samuel's gambling habit had made her an outcast. The aunts turned their backs on her, the men avoided her, and Esther was as cold as an ice statue.

"How did you know?" Esther asked at the counter, her face puffy, dark circles under her eyes. She had been sleepless, tossing and turning in her bed.

It was early morning; there were no customers yet.

"He asked to borrow money from me on the first day I arrived." Anyu stared at the glass case.

"He's a good boy. He's been following my father's orders his entire life, hiding in a fishing village and then a cellar, and working as a jeweler, but he's twenty years old. He can't live like a hermit; he wants to have a life outside the workshop. He likes Shanghai. He would like to see some girls, have a drink with them. Can you blame him? He tried so hard to stay away from the racecourse, believe me, he tried. But life is a joke for a man without a passport, a man without a future. Girls do not take him seriously. He's miserable."

Esther was a caring sister who loved her brother, Anyu realized. Were all siblings like Esther? Anyu wished Esther were her sister.

"He promised me the other day he'd never go near the racecourse again. But then you told Father. He's not going to forgive him, or me." Esther's voice cracked.

Isaac's tears, and now this. Anyu wished she could dig a hole and bury herself. If only she could take back her words, or reverse time. If only there were something she could do to alleviate their pain.

A moment later, the shop's door opened with a loud clash; Anyu raised her head, startled.

Five young Chinese men burst into the shop, a blur of long legs and out-flung arms. They all wore green cloth caps and were followed by a middle-aged Chinese man wearing a shimmering blue silk robe. He was clearly the leader, tall, with a layer of gold bands encircling his thick neck. He had a mean look, like a viper: his face was the shape of a triangle, and his ears stuck out like two small hands ready to grab.

Anyu didn't know who the middle-aged man was, but she recognized the men's green cloth caps. The notorious Green Gang that overran the city. Nervous, she looked at Esther.

Esther forced a smile. "Good morning, Mr. Du," she said to the man with a triangle face. "It's good to see you again."

The gangster leader? Anyu was surprised. But Mr. Du didn't seem to hear Esther's greeting. Folding his hands behind his back, he inspected the glass cases in the showroom and the license on the wall and paced to the necklace section of the display. He peered down. In an instant, his men swarmed around him, crowding in front of the glass counter near Anyu. They nodded and laughed, their gaze glued to the jewelry, their eyes intense with greed.

"How may I help you?" Esther squeezed close to her, to Anyu's relief.

"You're the daughter, aren't you? I remember," a man in a collarless black jacket said. "Well, Mr. Du is just in the neighborhood, making some purchases, so he thought to stop by."

"I'm honored to have Mr. Du in the shop."

"You have it ready?"

"The fees? Pardon me. I thought they were due in two days."

Usually, it was the job of the gang's representative, a man in a robe with a mild manner.

"Correct. But since we're here, we want to get our errands done and save another trip. Are you all right with it?"

"Of course . . . I'll get it for you right away."

But Esther didn't leave, and she looked at Anyu, hesitating. Esther would need to get the cash from the house; she didn't keep a large sum in the drawer at the beginning of the business day. Uncle David would have had the fees ready had he been home, but he had left the shop with Isaac to meet Mrs. Brown, a woman whose name Anyu had heard often. Samuel was nowhere to be found, and the two aunts were out shopping. Anyu and Esther were the only people in the building besides the Green Gang.

"Miss?" Mr. Du's man prompted.

Esther hesitated, torn between staying and leaving. She had never left Anyu alone in the showroom before. Eventually, she gestured to Anyu to stay put.

"I'll be right back," she said and then walked to the hallway.

Anyu felt outnumbered, watching the gang of five. They were loud, tramping around, knocking the glass cases, and commenting on gold and silver and gemstones in the Shanghai dialect with which she was not yet familiar. Mr. Du browsed the necklaces before her, humming a popular opera tune she had heard on the street. She was so close to the gang leader that she could smell his cigarette.

"This one. I want to see it." The man pointed at a gold snowflake necklace. It was an expensive piece, worth seven hundred Chinese dollars.

"Ah. You'll need to wait."

"Wait?"

"I can't take the necklace out of the case. I don't have permission to do so."

"Is it locked?"

It wasn't. Esther had not known she'd leave the counter. But Anyu held her ground. After months behind the counter, she had learned not to argue with a customer. But her instinct told her it would be trouble to obey Mr. Du, and she was not going to break her agreement with Esther and upset her further. It was as simple as that.

"There you go." Esther returned, panting. She must have run in and out as fast as her legs could carry her.

Mr. Du's man took the bills. "A monthly fee of two hundred Chinese dollars to keep the robbers and thieves away. What a deal. Without us, your shop would have been robbed shirtless."

"We're grateful," Esther said.

"That necklace, I'd like to see it," Mr. Du said again. "Are you going to show me? Your inept assistant is not cooperating."

Esther's face reddened. Mr. Du didn't offer to buy, but she couldn't offend him. Hesitant, she slid open the cabinet door, lifted the necklace with two hands, and placed it on a silver tray on the counter. "Everyone loves this snowflake necklace. It's so beautiful."

Mr. Du nodded, held it in his hand, weighing it, and then bit into a link to test the purity of the gold. He shook his head, unimpressed by the low grade of the metal, but he liked the necklace's design, Anyu could tell. Then his man in the collarless jacket asked to see a ring with a marquise-cut topaz. Esther opened that case and took out the ring; she was perspiring, smiling awkwardly.

Then another man asked to see a gold bracelet at the end of the L-shaped counter. Esther wiped at her face, nervous, limping from one side to another. It almost felt like the gang was taking advantage of her disability, but Anyu couldn't help; Esther had forbidden her to touch the jewelry.

Then, finally, the men seemed to have seen enough. They pushed the trays back to Esther and pulled open the door. "We'll be back next month."

The door shut behind them; Anyu felt like sitting down.

Esther was dabbing her face, putting the trays back. "Did you see that man? He's frightening. I didn't know what to do. I couldn't say no."

"I hope he'll never come here again," Anyu said, looking at the trays and stands inside a glass case, and then she noticed—the stand that had held the snowflake necklace was empty. "Where's the necklace?"

"It's somewhere." Esther bent lower to see the jewelry, lifting the trays and reaching out to every corner of the shelves. She couldn't find it.

"You showed it to Mr. Du," Anyu said. "Did he give it back to you?"

"I . . . don't remember. His men were demanding to see other pieces. They distracted me." She trembled. "Wait. I do remember . . . He didn't return it to me. He kept it."

Anyu swallowed. The snowflake necklace was worth seven hundred dollars.

Esther covered her face with her hands. "I can't believe this is happening. God! I'm so stupid! They tricked me. What am I going to do? Father is going to come back and he'll find out. He's going to be furious and he'll never forgive me. He's already angry with me."

Anyu swallowed again. "It's not your fault, Esther."

"It is. I gave it to that gangster. It's my fault." Her shoulders shuddered.

Oh, Esther's tears. Anyu had never thought she would cry, and she wished with all her heart she could comfort her. But she didn't know how. It was not something she had learned at home. She had never soothed anyone before, and words felt meaningless. Esther was right: Isaac would be furious at her, after she kept Samuel's secret from him, after losing the necklace. And there was nothing Anyu could do to help, unless she could put the necklace in Esther's hands.

"I'll get it for you."

Esther lifted her head, her face damp with tears.

"I'll get the necklace back. Then your father won't know it was lost and he won't blame you."

"How will you get it back?"

"I don't know. But trust me." Then she ran out of the shop.

CHAPTER 9

There was no sign of the men on the street. Stubbornly, Anyu searched, weaving between a fleet of cars and carriages and the crowd of pedestrians, and was nearly run over by a donkey pulling a cart loaded with bolts of silk. She peered into the clothes shops, the apothecary, and the barbershop—not a shadow of Mr. Du or his men. She couldn't tell how long she had searched when a young man in front of a teahouse with a gray tile roof waved at her. She ignored him; she wasn't feeling up to talking to a stranger.

Then she realized the youth looked familiar. He was the gangster she had helped escape. He was pushing a bicycle, wearing a white shirt and black pants. Out in the open, he looked decent, even friendly. She went back to the teahouse just as he mounted his bicycle.

"I knew we'd meet again. Remember me? I'm Confucius," he said, tossing his shoulder-length hair.

"Like the ancient teacher?" she blurted out. What kind of name was that?

"That's him! But I'm younger."

She would have laughed if she hadn't been so intent on finding Mr. Du.

"You peng zi yuan fang lai, bu yi yue hu?" he intoned.

"What?"

"It means 'Isn't it a happy thing that a friend from afar comes to visit?' It's from the old Confucius."

Anyu cleared her throat. "All right. I'm Anyu. Listen, I could use your help. I'm looking for Mr. Du. He might have passed here a moment ago with his men. Did you happen to see him?" She described Mr. Du's blue robe and his triangular face.

"Oh, you don't have to tell me what he looks like."

"You know him?"

"Everybody in Shanghai knows him. He is the leader of the Green Gang, the lord of the underworld. You didn't know?"

"He came to visit my shop." Then, hurriedly, she explained what had happened in the shop. "He took the necklace. Do you know where to find him?"

Confucius whistled. "You have terrible luck, you know. But find Mr. Du? Then what? Take the necklace back? No, no. No one takes anything back from Mr. Du."

"I need to know where he is. Can you help me?" It was ironic, but she was glad he was also a gangster.

"I wouldn't help you even if I could. And I can't!"

"I . . . I . . ."

"You haven't been in Shanghai for long, have you? Mr. Du is a powerful man, a dangerous man. He takes whatever he likes—gold, restaurants, houses, women, and men's lives. Anything. If he took your necklace, consider it a gift and let it go. It's just a necklace. It's not worth dying for." Confucius lifted the kickstand with his foot and began to pedal.

She lunged after him and grabbed a handlebar. He lost his balance and crashed to the ground.

"What are you doing!" He rose, rubbing his knee.

"I saved you! You have to help me."

He pulled up his bicycle and groaned. One of the spokes was bent.

"I need to get the necklace back, Confucius. It's important. The girl who I work for is very upset. I have to help her." She added in a demeaning, pleading tone that she hoped she wouldn't regret later: "Please."

"You really want to go? Mr. Du is everywhere."

"What do you mean?"

"Shanghai is Mr. Du's lair. He has many secret homes and offices. He also owns gambling houses, opium dens, and brothels. But you won't have a chance to step into any of those. They are heavily guarded. Even if you get in, you won't be able to get out."

"If you give me a location, I'll find him."

"I'm warning you. You'll lose your head. Don't blame me."

"I won't blame you."

He sighed. "Fine. Hop on."

Anyu looked at the bicycle; there was no seat. She would need to sit on the top frame. She had never ridden a bicycle before, and of course, any decent girl wouldn't publicly ride with a boy. What would people say? What about her reputation? "Is it far?"

"It's about two hours' walk. What? Are you too shy to ride with me?" Confucius said.

"I'm not shy."

"Then why are you standing there? Fine. You walk there. See you in two hours."

She looked around. A few people in the nearby shops were watching her curiously; it occurred to her that they'd gossip about her the moment she was out of sight. But why should she worry? She wasn't in Harbin anymore.

Anyu went to Confucius and sat on the top metal bar of the frame, her hands gripping the handlebars, her body maintaining a discreet distance from him. "Let's go."

"Hold on!"

If Anyu had been given other options, she wouldn't have ridden on the bicycle. It was a hazardous dive into a sea of cursing crowds, a blind sail through wet laundry hanging in narrow alleys, and a maddening race amid honking cars and speeding carriages. She gripped the bars for dear life, her bottom sore against the bare metal. She could have screamed and asked to slow down but held back for her dignity. When

Confucius finally stopped, she jumped off, her heart pounding, her legs stiff, her bottom aching.

"We're here," Confucius said.

Here?

They were in an alley lined with rows of rickshaws and fruit vendors with tarpaulin-covered carts. The building Confucius pointed at had a tall stone arch decorated with round medallion reliefs and a massive gate painted in a bold shade of red. In front of it paced back and forth a few burly men in green caps holding clubs. As she watched, the gate opened, a man in a long robe staggered out, cursing, and the men with clubs hoisted him into a rickshaw. "Come back when you have money," they mumbled.

A gambling house.

"I don't see Mr. Du's car or his men. I don't think he's here." Confucius sat on his bicycle with the kickstand down, squinting at the nearby buildings, the afternoon sun hanging over their gray rooftops. This narrow street was teeming with buzz-cut men holding placards printed with black characters saying "Play Slot Machines at the Six Nations!" "Win the Lottery Now!" "Place Your Bet on Dog Race, Free Drinks!"

"Where else could he be?"

"I don't know." Confucius shrugged. "You speak Chinese with a horrid Northerner's accent. Where are you from?"

"I need to know where Mr. Du is."

"So you're from Beijing?"

"No. Harbin."

"Where is that? Wait. Do you mean Harbin near Siberia? The place where your snot will freeze like a fossil? That's far! Why did you come to Shanghai?"

She glared at him. "Where can we find him, Confucius?"

"He could be in his favorite opium den."

"Do you know where it is?"

"Does the sun rise from the east?"

"How far is it?"

Confucius sighed.

༺❦༻

From a distance, the building resembled a palace hall, with its stately vermilion pillars, glazed orange roof tiles, and upturned flying eaves. When Anyu drew closer, she could see the red silky curtains and the four-poster daybeds. On the daybeds reclined robed men smoking long pipes.

A man wearing a black melon cap rushed out of the building and shooed her away—the den barred women from entering.

Night had fallen, and still, she didn't see Mr. Du, his car, or his men.

༺❦༻

At her insistence, Confucius agreed to take her to one final place.

"So why did you come to Shanghai? You haven't told me." He pedaled with ease, one hand steering.

"What's the place we are going?" She held on to the handlebars.

"You'll know when we get there. Are you going to tell me? Why?"

"Are we there yet?" She would have walked, but the daylight had vanished, and the streets were dark. She didn't want to get lost.

"Almost. I get it. You are a widow."

"I'm sixteen years old!"

"Many girls younger than you became widows. So you don't have a family? Is that it? Is that why you live with the Russians?"

He had been spying on her! "I work for them. They're good to me. They treat me well."

"But they're foreigners. They can't be good to you, and they stink. Didn't you smell them? They also carry diseases."

"That's absurd. You smell worse than them."

Confucius sighed. "I have a quote for you, but I won't say it. Anyway. Here we are."

The two-story building was beautiful, with a long corridor wrapping around the first floor and strings of red lanterns hung on the eaves. Some girls were pacing in the corridor, clad in tightly fitted colorful dresses that only reached their knees, their arms bare, their lips red in the glow of the lanterns. They swung something in their hands, handkerchiefs, fans, and swayed from one side of the corridor to another. Even though she was across the street, Anyu could hear laughter and a pleasant tune of lute and clappers dancing in the air.

A brothel.

Anyu slipped off the bicycle, her cheeks growing warm.

"There you are." Confucius got off but still had his hands on the handlebars.

"Are you sure he's inside?" Her mother would have forbidden her to be near the house of ill repute.

"Look." He thrust his head. "In the corridor near the tree."

It was too dim; she could only make out a few men's figures, but there was Mr. Du's car and two of his men leaning against it, smoking and talking. She recognized the man in the collarless jacket.

"They're going inside," she said.

"I bet Mr. Du is inside as well."

"I'll go in."

"You're kidding!"

"I have to. I need to get the necklace."

"Fine. You go in. I'm going home." He got on his bicycle.

He would abandon her! So be it. She would retrieve the necklace herself.

Anyu went to a cigarette vendor on the street and bought a packet of cigarettes with the money she had. Then she went up to the porch. No one stopped her—the girls, fanning their faces with their handkerchiefs, were busy chatting with their clients.

Once she entered the building, everyone seemed to try to get their hands on her. A sea of men—men with round faces, men with sweaty faces, men with shirts, men without shirts. Everyone was busy here, busy laughing, busy talking, busy yanking arms. Loudly, they shouted, *Wine! Here! More! Five dollars for ten minutes, twenty for an hour! You got yourself a deal. First door in the back!*

Anyu could feel the blood rushing to her head as she stood in an atrium painted the color of pomegranate, dodging this man and that man. A wave of an unbearable smell, a mixture of cigarette smoke and cheap perfume, engulfed her. And suddenly, a gong sounded, deafening, followed by a voice announcing the time.

Someone grabbed her arm. A drunken face thrust at her. "How much?"

She pushed him away.

"Don't be rude." The drunkard dared to squeeze her breast.

She slapped the hand. "Cigarettes for Mr. Du. Where is Mr. Du?"

The drunkard mumbled and staggered away.

"Where is Mr. Du?"

"Second floor on the left. The fifth room," someone answered.

She went up the staircase beside a painting of a pagoda hanging on the wall, dodging the customers buckling their belts on their way down. When she reached the second floor's landing, she heard something from a room nearby—they were cries, rhythmic, high-pitched, unlike anything she had heard before. Unable to resist, she pushed the door wider and peered in.

A woman, naked, spread on the bed draped with red silk curtains, and a man was charging at her, standing between her legs. The two cursed and mauled each other, the man slapping the woman's face, the woman thrusting her legs on the man's shoulders; they gritted their teeth, crouching, grunting; they seemed to want to beat each other to death, to tear each other apart, yet neither of them appeared to be in pain.

Anyu had never seen people couple before. This was how it was done, she realized, and it looked exhausting.

Then, suddenly, she saw the woman, depleted, sagging on the bed; a trickle of sweat, mixed with white powder and red rouge, ran down her face. The woman caught her gaze and widened her eyes. Embarrassed, Anyu turned around and raced down the hallway.

"She looked really pleased with the necklace. Did you see her face? That vamp."

Anyu stopped. The voice came from her right, around the corner.

"Don't let him hear you. Mr. Du loves that chick. Remember he just bought her a new villa."

"Where is it? I haven't been there."

"It's near the cinema on Fuxing Road. A fancy house with gray bricks and terra-cotta roof tiles. Miss Liao wanted something fitting her status because she's famous."

Miss Liao was a popular singer from a record company, Anyu recalled. Her sweet voice often graced the alleys.

"But that woman is greedy! She just got this necklace and she wants more. Mr. Du made an appointment for her with the French jeweler, what's his name . . ."

"I hate that Frenchman."

"Bellefeuille, right. That's his name."

"Right now, she can get anything she wants—"

"There! Were you looking for Mr. Du? Did you find him?" An old man without a shirt appeared beside Anyu.

"Go away." She staggered back, but too late; Mr. Du's men were coming to the hallway to see what was happening. Their eyes met; the gangsters dove toward her.

Anyu raced down the staircase, dodging the hedonist couples making their way up, the men shouting behind her. In a moment, she leaped into the atrium, which was even more crowded than before. Desperately, she fought her way out, pressed between women holding fans and men holding bills, their shrill laughter piercing her ears.

Someone shoved an elbow into her ribs; someone else stamped on her feet. Ducking lower, she used her shoulder to push through.

Once she made it to the porch, she looked behind. The gangsters were not in sight; she had escaped. Walking briskly past the simpering girls, Anyu came to the street and heaved a sigh. First time visiting a brothel, and it would be her last. But it wasn't entirely fruitless; she had learned what happened to the necklace—Mr. Du had given it to his mistress.

She wished Confucius were here and she could tell him all about the brothel, but true to his word, he had disappeared. It would be a long walk back to the shop.

She had started to walk when she felt the air shift behind her. Turning around, she saw Mr. Du's men lunge toward her from under the lanterns. She bolted, but they caught her in a swoop, lifted her, and carried her to a black car near the corridor. The car's window rolled down, and wisps of blue smoke twirled.

"Caught her spying, Mr. Du," the man in the collarless jacket said.

A beam of light flashed on her face. Anyu squinted, her heart pounding in fear. The man's grip was firm, like a vise.

"Well, look at this. A little slut." The man, reeking of alcohol, appeared in front of her, his triangular face stark white in the flashlight, his ears stretching out. "Search her."

Two hands fumbled on her breasts. On her waist and her thighs.

"She doesn't carry a weapon, Mr. Du," the man in the collarless jacket said.

"No weapons. Were you spying on me, little slut?"

Anyu's blood froze. "No."

"What are you doing here?"

"For . . . for work."

"You don't seem that type." He took out a cigarette and lit it with a lighter.

"I . . . I'm desperate."

"You're lying. Who sent you? The Nationalists? The Japanese?"

"No one. I'm here by myself."

Mr. Du blew out a stinky cloud of cigarette smoke.

She panicked; beads of sweat ran into her eyes. The men looked dangerous, and they were capable of doing anything. "I wanted to find work . . . but I changed my mind. I don't want to work there anymore. Let me go."

Mr. Du held his cigarette; the tip flickered. "You can't just come and go as you wish, little slut. And you know well, when you see me, you bring a gift. Where's your gift?"

"What, what gift?"

"No gift? That's too bad. Nobody visits me empty-handed. That's the law. You've broken my law. And that deserves a punishment." He tossed his head toward his men.

The man in the collarless jacket took out something from his pocket and flashed it before her. A pistol.

"No!" Anyu struggled but was unable to escape from the viselike grip. A thought occurred to her belatedly—she should have listened to Confucius.

"Your order, Mr. Du?" he asked.

"I'm feeling generous. Nothing major. A hand will be fine."

"Yes, Mr. Du."

"No, no!"

Someone threw her on the ground and shoved her head against the rough surface. A heavy weight slammed on her back and pinned her down. Her right hand, her dominant hand, was yanked to the side, flat on the pavement.

Then she heard a click.

Fear penetrated her as she realized what they were trying to do. "No, no, no!"

With all her might, she wrenched herself free, just as a loud bang erupted, followed by a flash of light, blinding, bewildering, and then came an excruciating pain.

She screamed as black blood spurted from her hand, and her pinkie exploded.

CHAPTER 10

Of what happened next, Anyu remembered little. She was screaming, rolling on the street where rickshaws and carriages squeaked by; no one approached her, no one except Confucius, who had mysteriously reappeared and carried her to his bicycle. He rode like a madman and took her to a place that smelled of choking herbs. In her dazed state, she heard an old man talking, then he fed her a spoonful of bitter liquid, and then he was cleaning her wound and bandaging her hand, and then the blissful fog of peace enveloped her. She was conscious, but then she wasn't. She struggled to stay awake, to make sense of what had happened, and she desperately wanted to ask—was this a nightmare?

Confucius said something, but she couldn't understand it. He didn't abandon her, after all, and for that, she was grateful. But her whole arm felt dead, and as hard as she tried, she couldn't see well. When she closed her eyes, she could envision, vividly, Mr. Du's big ears, the pistol, and her pinkie exploding. In utter disbelief, she looked at the stub covered with strips of white cloth, the stub where her finger should have been.

How could she still become a jeweler, with nine fingers?

Later, Confucius took her back to the shop and gave her a matchbox filled with pills, which contained opium, he said, very effective in alleviating pain. Aunt Katya, yawning, opened the door for her. Anyu shuffled across the dim showroom and entered the kitchen, her right arm stiff. The workshop was shut. Isaac was giving instructions, his voice indistinct. In the dark kitchen without a candle, she sat. Exhausted.

She needed to go to sleep, but she could hardly gather her strength to climb the stairs. Resting her head on the dining table, she closed her eyes and passed out.

When she awoke, she felt better, though she could still barely lift her arm, but there was no pain, thanks to Confucius's pill. Slowly, Anyu made her way to the stairs, climbed up, and entered the attic. The two aunts were snoring on their bed; Esther, wearing her cotton nightgown, was reading D. H. Lawrence's *Sons and Lovers*, a book she'd been reading since Anyu moved in.

"Where did you go?" Esther put down the book by the table lamp, her elongated shadow tracking across the termite-bitten floor.

"You don't want to know."

Anyu sat on the edge of her sleeping mat. Near her pillow was a sheaf of papers with her jewelry sketches. Would she be able to draw with nine fingers?

"Did you get it?"

"Not yet. I need a few more days. Does your father know it's missing?"

"No. I counted and packed everything. No one knows."

"That's good."

"What's wrong with your hand?"

Anyu gazed at her finger bandaged expertly with ointment and clean strips of cloth. "I got shot."

"You got shot?" Esther came over. Lifting Anyu's hand, she examined the bandages. "What happened?"

"I lost my pinkie."

Slowly, Anyu recounted her search, her capture.

Esther inhaled deeply. "I didn't know you'd risk your life like that. You really shouldn't have. You're lucky to be alive."

"I know where the necklace is. Mr. Du gave it to his mistress. I heard it from his men. I'm going to get it back."

Esther shook her head. "Look, I appreciate your help, but this is too dangerous."

"I have a plan."

"Forget your plan, Anyu."

"I have to. I promised."

"Are you always so stubborn?"

"Let me get the necklace, Esther, I'm sorry for what happened. I shouldn't have said anything about Samuel. I feel responsible. This is the least I can do. I'll get the necklace back so you'll forgive me."

Esther opened her mouth, and her perfectly symmetrical face was imbued with something Anyu had never seen before—a look of compassion, of affection, and she looked so lovely, like a goddess. Had she been drawing, she would have produced a memorable piece, but depleted of her strength, Anyu shut her eyes to get some sleep.

Anyu slept for two days. Sometimes, she awoke to Esther's voice. The young woman had placed some food and water by her side. Sometimes, Anyu awoke to silence, bathed in pain and sweat. *I must heal fast,* she willed herself. She had so much to do: retrieve the missing necklace, sell a piece of jewelry at the counter—her three-month deadline was approaching.

After four long days, Anyu could feel strength return to her body. She doubled the dose of the pills and began to work on her disguise— under no circumstances should she leave a trail for Mr. Du to trace back to the Mandelburgs' shop.

With some difficulty, she piled up her long braid on her head and put on a long cotton tunic. Then she slipped into the bedroom Isaac shared with Samuel and the uncle, searching for some men's accessories. She took Isaac's bowler hat, the brown leather bag that he often carried when he went out for meetings, and his work gloves, which she had seen him wear while hammering the metal plates—they were large enough to fit her bandaged hand.

In the showroom, Esther was speaking to two older women. Anyu slipped out, holding the bag with her good left hand, heading toward Mr. Du's mistress's house.

This time, she would retrieve the necklace alone.

࿇

There were four two-story gray-brick houses with terra-cotta tile roofs on Fuxing Road near the cinema, all lavish homes. Anyu knocked on each door until she finally found Miss Liao's home, the walled compound. A servant with rheumy eyes opened the door, looking at her suspiciously.

"Greetings." She tipped the bowler hat she'd borrowed from Isaac. "I'm a jeweler, sent by my master to work for Miss Liao. I'm here to take her measurement for her necklace."

"She doesn't expect a jeweler today."

"You want to ask her? I'm a jeweler," she said again.

The servant looked skeptical but ushered her in.

Anyu entered the courtyard, then an elegantly decorated reception room. It was late afternoon; the air vibrated with women's laughter and jazz music from a gramophone. Miss Liao was hosting a game in the back of the house, the servant explained. It would take a while.

Finally, Miss Liao came. She was beautiful, wearing a silk robe with poppies and long pants, a peony tucked in her hair. She had an egg-shaped face with a sharp chin, her black eyes flashing naughtiness.

"A jeweler, you said? Who's your master?"

Her voice was sweet like a child's, and the way she swayed her hips and undulated her arms reminded Anyu of folk dancers from a traveling troupe, but Miss Liao was more glamorous and attractive. "The House of Bellefeuille."

"Oh, that Frenchman. Why is he not coming himself?"

"He's under the weather. I'm new. I like to know the client's preferences and taste in jewelry before I create my design. It's my goal to elevate your stardom as a prominent singer in the city with my creation."

She giggled. "He knows how to talk, that Frenchman. You, too. I must have the days mixed up. I thought the appointment was next week. I'm in the middle of a mahjong game. Could you wait?"

Anyu hesitated. "I do have other clients to visit."

Miss Liao frowned. "Your other clients? Are they recommended by Mr. Du?"

"I can't discuss that, Miss Liao."

She pouted. "Mr. Du said he was going to come here today. Is he coming?"

Mr. Du was coming?

"Fine. I'll talk to him when he's here. What do you want to know? I need to go back to the mahjong game soon."

Staying calm, Anyu said, "In general, I'll ask some questions about your interests and get to know your taste. Since you need to get back to your game, we can save some time if you show me your favorite jewelry so I can get an idea about your preference. What do you say?"

"Fine with me." Miss Liao gestured to her servant to retrieve her jewelry box.

Out of the corner of her eye, Anyu watched the servant go down the hallway at the end of the room and then climb up a staircase; less than five minutes later, the servant returned with a lacquered jewelry box. The bedroom couldn't have been too far away, she deduced. When the mistress opened the box, on top of the cluster of gold and diamond accessories was the snowflake necklace. Calmly, Anyu asked her to put on each necklace and sketched them on her paper with her wounded hand, ignoring the ache. After a few drawings, Anyu said that was enough and Miss Liao's servant returned the jewelry box upstairs. To kill time, Anyu pretended to carefully study her sketches and finally, when the servant returned, she stood to take her leave. Remembering how Mother dealt with her clients, Anyu gave the mistress a bow. "I'll have your design ready for you shortly."

Miss Liao shrugged and went to play her game, and the servant ushered Anyu out to the courtyard. At the front door, Anyu said, "I'm sorry. It seems I must have forgotten my sketchbook in the reception room. Would you mind fetching it for me? It might have fallen behind the sofa. I'll wait here."

The servant was not pleased, but she turned around. Anyu gave her some time to get into the empty reception room and then dashed back and slunk into the hallway. At the end of the hallway with a moon-shaped entrance was a flight of stairs. She ran up and raced inside the mistress's bedroom.

The jewelry box was on the nightstand; she opened it, dug into the diamond rings and pins, and took only the snowflake necklace, nothing else. When she came downstairs, she could hear the voices of Mr. Du and his men in the reception room.

She panicked. She would not be able to leave through the front door. Turning around, she raced back to the bedroom, saw the balcony with a low, curved wall, and dashed toward it. Leaning over the wall, she looked down. The distance from the balcony to the ground was daunting. She had already lost her pinkie; did she wish to lose an arm or a leg?

Mr. Du's and Miss Liao's voices grew louder. They were coming up the stairs.

Holding her bag, Anyu climbed over the wall, took a deep breath, and jumped.

She landed on her feet. There was a crack as though her bones had snapped and pain shot through her legs like arrows, straight to her pelvis, up her spine, and to her neck. Flat on the ground, she panted, stifling a groan. Mustering her strength, she dug out the matchbox and took another pill.

When she felt the blissful ease coursing through her body, she picked up the bowler hat from the ground and got up on her shaking feet. Her good hand gripping the bag with the necklace, blood drenching her glove, she limped past a stand of cricket cages and an insect vendor who gaped at her.

It took her one hour of limping and lumbering down the lanes before she finally arrived at the Mandelburgs' shop. Daylight was slipping away. The shop was closed for the day, but inside she could see four Sikh guards with pistols and Isaac speaking to Mr. Walters. Not wanting to attract attention, Anyu went to the back door; it was locked. She knocked, but no one answered. Her head woozy from the debilitating walk, she leaned against the wall to rest and then went to the building's front door. Mr. Walters and his men had already left. So she knocked again; Esther answered, holding a cleaning rag.

"Why are you wearing my father's hat?" she asked.

"I'll tell you later. Here's your necklace." Anyu unbuckled the leather bag and took out the gold necklace. Her right arm was stiff; she nearly dropped the bag.

"You got it!" Esther's face, infused with joy, was so satisfying to see.

"I told you so. Now you have it, from my hand to yours."

"How did you do that?" Esther held the necklace, streaks of golden light reflecting on her face.

"I'll tell you someday. Where's your father?"

"In the workshop. Are you all right? You're so pale. You look like you're about to die."

"I'm tired, that's all. I'd rather go to our room." She took a step but stumbled. Esther reached out to steady her, inadvertently bumping into her hand. Anyu cried out. Trembling, she took off the glove; the bandage was soaked with blood.

Esther gasped. "You're bleeding."

"I have pills. I'll be fine. Can we go to the attic?"

"Yes. Come, take my arm. I'll help you up."

Esther looked different. Anyu had never seen her like this—it was almost as if she were trying to take care of her. Anyu took her arm.

"Let me take your bag and your hat. You're shaking. You must have lost much blood. You might want to watch your steps. Here. Take it easy, but my goodness! I still can't believe it!" Esther said, opening the door to the hallway.

The moment Anyu stepped inside, she could hear the angry voices of Isaac and the uncle and Samuel coming from the workshop, speaking Yiddish.

Anyu looked at Esther.

"Father says he needs a successor, and he can't be a gambler," Esther translated.

Before Anyu could speak, the workshop's door flung open, and Isaac came out, wiping his hands on his apron; his face, even in the gloomy hallway, looked dark with fury.

"What are you two up to?" he asked.

"We're going to our room, Father," Esther said, steering Anyu away.

"Stop right there. Why are you holding my hat and bag?"

"I'll put them back."

"I said stop right there. What's wrong with your hand, Anyu?"

Anyu flinched, unsettled by Isaac's anger. "I lost my pinkie."

"What did you say?"

Esther hurried to explain—Mr. Du's visit, the missing snowflake necklace that was worth seven hundred dollars, and Anyu's decision to retrieve it.

"Am I hearing it correctly that you got shot and you lost a pinkie for a necklace?" Isaac exclaimed.

"I can still be a jeweler."

Isaac threw up his hands. "What is going on? Samuel, Esther, and now you. Am I the last person in this family to know what happens? What else is being kept from me? You, Anyu, you have this fine, remarkable spirit. It's admirable. Why don't you put that to good use? I've explained it to you. I can't train you."

And then, as if he couldn't bear the sight of her, he broke away and went to the kitchen, where the aunts were emptying the ash from the coal stove.

"Let's go." Esther held her, helping her to the stairs.

Anyu felt dizzy. Leaning on Esther, she took one stair at a time and found her way to the attic. The short climb exhausted her, and she felt feverish. Dropping on her mattress, she fumbled for the matchbox, but it slipped from her grasp. Esther caught it, opened it, and handed her a pill.

"I think your father is angry with me," Anyu said.

"He's angry with all of us." Esther sat near her.

"He's heartbroken." A master jeweler without a successor. She could feel Isaac's sadness, and she wished there was something she could do for him.

"You might want to get some rest. It's going to take you at least six months to recover."

"One month."

"You have all the time you need."

"You'll let me stay? Without making a sale?"

"I'm not a charitable person, Anyu. I still believe you'll be better off staying with others. We're stateless Jews! But I think it's good for us if you stay. We need you. Get some rest, Anyu." Esther rose.

Anyu smiled. "No, don't go. Talk to me. Tell me about you and your family. Did your father have a jewelry shop in Russia?"

"It was more than a shop. It was an entire building near the Neva River. He was the lead designer of my family's brand."

"I've always wanted to know: Where's your mother?"

"She died when I was ten. Poisoned." Esther sat down. She remembered vividly the poisoning—the arsenic had been surreptitiously added to a spicy soup that was her father's favorite, she said. But that evening he was late from work and missed dinner, so the rest of the family ate the soup instead. Esther's grandmother and mother had ingested too much arsenic and took their last breath in the house. Esther and Samuel were very sick, too, but recovered. The culprit was never discovered, Esther said, but she believed it was one of her father's adversaries who had lost a commission to him.

Despite that, Esther had been happy in St. Petersburg. At fifteen, she had fallen in love with her neighbor Sal, but he was killed by a mob in the square and shrapnel had pierced her leg, leaving her wounded for life. During the revolution, her grandfather and the uncle on her father's side were killed. She lost touch with her cousins and her extended family. Then her father had to flee the country, and she followed him with her brother, stumbling from one city to another, living in the shadows, wasting away her youth in the wildland and backwoods. All the endless drudgery, selling jewelry, looking after her brother, putting food on the table.

"I have no future in Shanghai as a single, stateless woman," Esther said. "I want to get married. I'm twenty-three, but I feel ancient." Ideally, she'd marry a British man or an American so she could have a valuable passport, ending her stateless status, but her leg had turned her future bleak, and her long hours at the shop limited her social opportunities.

"British. Oh, that's why you always read D. H. Lawrence's novel at bedtime."

"I don't really understand it. My English is poor."

"I can teach you."

"You speak English, too? Anyway, I just want to find a husband, and it doesn't matter how old he is. I can't be too choosy. The pool of Jews is limited in Shanghai."

She had had only one suitor so far, a young British officer who had invited her to a party but never called again.

Anyu loved talking to Esther, loved hearing her thoughts, loved the feeling that there was no rancor between them.

"Do you want to get married, too, Anyu?" Esther asked.

She shook her head. That was what Mother had wanted. "I just want to be a jeweler."

"You are not going to change your mind, are you?"

No. Neither could she forget the beautiful egg that she wanted desperately to see but must not mention again. But Esther just reminded her of something most important—she had to do whatever it took to persuade Isaac to train her.

CHAPTER 11

Her wounded hand held her back; its healing a slow, frustrating process. One week passed, and she could barely curl her fingers. But lying in bed all day was not an option. Anyu bandaged her hand carefully and put on a pair of old-fashioned white gloves Aunt Katya gave her and returned to the counter. Trusting her now, Esther permitted her to take out the trays to show the customers, but Anyu couldn't focus, distracted by the pain in her finger. She was clumsy and slow, and she even occasionally dropped things.

When she held a fork, her pencil, or the broom to sweep the floor, she had trouble gripping it. When she slept, it was a shallow and uncomfortable doze interrupted by pain and discomfort—she was unable to roll over onto her right side. Her mood darkened. She had lost a finger, but it was as though she had lost the flexibility of her body.

Determined to regain her dexterity, Anyu began a series of exercises to strengthen her fingers. She flexed her right hand, tapping and running her fingers along the counter to ease their stiffness; she clenched her hand into a ball, then released it; she pinched repeatedly her thumb and forefinger to keep the blood flowing.

Isaac nodded at her when he saw her and occasionally asked how her hand was healing. His anger toward her had dissipated, and he looked calm and courteous, though a bit distant.

As long as he still cared about her, she could convince him to train her.

⌘

Days slipped by; the weather grew colder. The swift wind slashed through wilting magnolia and drooping gardenia bushes; the stands of myrtles shivered.

On the street, pedestrians hurried on, their backs hunched, their faces gloomy like the leaden autumn sky; even the loquacious street vendors selling barbecued squid and chicken hearts looked dispirited, their tongues tied. The newspapers said Generalissimo Chiang Kai-shek, the head of the Nationalists, was engaged to the youngest daughter of the Soong family. Another headline said that according to unconfirmed sources, several key members of the Japanese Kwantung Army, who were rumored to seek control of Manchuria from the warlord Zhang, had been invited to a banquet attended by the deposed Puyi (the last emperor of the Qing Dynasty, who was said to have every intention of reinstating his reign in Manchuria). The print of the news was large, sprawling like spiders.

Pulling tight her cotton-padded jacket, Anyu went to visit Confucius at the teahouse. She had not seen him since he brought her home after she was shot, but she had been thinking about him since, grateful for his help. Without him, she could have passed out on the street or died of blood loss. And she would have denied it if anyone asked, but she liked him, the first and only young Chinese man she had befriended.

Anyu didn't find Confucius at the teahouse—he had quit, the proprietor said. Confucius had not told her his home address, and she didn't know how to find him.

At dinner, Esther, Isaac, and Uncle David were discussing finances again. Esther recited all the numbers, taxes, rent, protection fees, utility bills, food costs, gold and silver plate costs, and gemstone payments to Mr. Walters. The list went on, and the uncle let out a long sigh.

"Father, will you consider joining the competition?" Esther asked. "If your design wins, it'll increase our shop's visibility in the city and move the sales along."

"What competition?" Anyu asked.

"The Annual Shanghai Jewelers Competition."

"Esther is right about this," Uncle David said. "What's holding you back?"

"It's too late to apply," Isaac said.

"How about next year?"

"We'll see."

"I understand your reluctance, Isaac, but you're in Shanghai. You're safe here. No one knows about your background. You can start a new career as a renowned jeweler again."

Isaac grimaced; his gaze fell to the ring on his hand.

"Isaac, I'm counting on you. The future of the House of Mandelburg is in your hands. You were the lead designer and your family's chief jeweler. You can rebuild your family's legacy in Shanghai."

Isaac didn't speak.

Anyu watched intently. There was something about Isaac she didn't know.

CHAPTER 12

October 1926

Lying on her mattress, Anyu listened to the wind sweeping over the roof. The house was quiet. Esther and the rest of the family had gone to attend a party. Outside, a car drove by; the loose windows clattered. Winter in Shanghai arrived late; Harbin would have already been buried in snow and frost before October.

Today, she turned seventeen. Anyu thought of her mother, who had always remembered her birthday but could not celebrate it with food or gifts. To console her, she would draw a bowl of noodles, a golden heap of delicious, twining noodles spiced with meat, red chili, and scallions. Once, to her surprise, her mother had brought home half a roasted duck to celebrate her birthday. How savory the duck was, with its thick, crispy skin; sweet, succulent meat; and rich, juicy fat. Mother ate the head, saying it was her favorite, and Anyu devoured the rest, chewing on the aromatic bones, sucking her greasy fingers, giggling, basking in Mother's loving gaze. It was the first time Anyu had tasted a roasted duck.

She was alone now, without a mother, without a home. She wondered if anyone would celebrate her birthday from now on, or bring her a roasted duck, or even remember her birthday. Tears trickled down her cheeks, hot on her skin, then cold, lingering on her chin, dripping to her chest, a tide of sorrow in a free fall. She had not thought of spending her birthday like this, the first birthday without Mother. Would all her birthdays in the future slip away in the dark, silent and alone? That was not what she had envisioned for herself, an orphan as she was. She would rather live well, live better than a nameless, lonely orphan; she would rather be known, and be celebrated.

A groan came from downstairs. Surprised, she wiped off her tears and went down the staircase. No one was in the kitchen; light gleamed in the hallway. The workshop's door was open; she leaned in. Near his workbench, Isaac knelt, searching for something on the floor, holding a lamp.

"Mr. Mandelburg?" She had thought Isaac was at the party with the rest of the family. "Are you all right? Why are you not at the party?"

"It's not for me." His head turned left and right, his hands fumbling. "I dropped a ring. Where could it be?"

She craned her neck, following the beam of light from his lamp. The floor was swept clean, and near his stool was a hide used to collect the shavings from metals. "There. Near the leg of the stool. Is that the ring you are looking for?"

"Where is it? Oh. Yes." Isaac rose, holding the ring. "Thank you. Good night, Anyu."

She didn't want to return to the attic yet. She had been waiting for an opportunity like this. "What's your real name, Mr. Mandelburg?"

He jerked his head toward her, the glare of his lamp blinding her. She held up her hand, squinting.

"I don't know what you are talking about, Anyu." His voice was calm.

"You use your uncle's last name, don't you? You are worried your identity could be discovered."

He was silent.

"What is your real name? I won't tell anyone, Mr. Mandelburg."

He turned around and sat on the stool. "Well, I don't know how you figured it out. My name is Isaac Umansky, son of the master jeweler Albert Umansky, who served as the court jeweler in the Winter Palace.

I was the master jeweler and lead designer of the House of Umansky in St. Petersburg."

"How does it feel to abandon the name that you spent your whole life building?"

"I'm grateful for this life I have, a quiet life, a life with family but no fame. This is all I wish for," he said. And no, he added, he rarely reminisced about the golden days of basking in admiration from eminent royal patrons, eccentric noblemen, and esteemed guests. In fact, he had prayed the history of the Fabergé eggs would be buried in dust and hoped that his name, once the lead designer of a prominent design house, once glittering like the jewelry he had designed, would be meaningless, unrecognized.

"But what about your skills and your superior craft?" she insisted. "Would you let them fade and be lost eventually?"

He looked at his ring on his right hand and stroked the opaque gemstone with his finger. It almost seemed he was recalling something important.

"Would you rather not have a successor?"

Isaac let out a long sigh.

"Teach me, Mr. Mandelburg. I just want to be a jeweler. I have to become a jeweler."

"Have to?"

"You've let me stay, but I can't sell anything. But I have the gift of a jeweler, as you said, and I love to draw. You've seen my drawings. I was born to be a jeweler. I want to learn metalsmithing skills and craft beautiful things that will last. I want to know all about gemstones and their qualities and learn how to set them. I want to be the greatest jeweler in Shanghai."

He looked amused. "The greatest jeweler?"

"You've given me a life here. You can give me a career." Then she added, "And through me, you can leave a lasting legacy."

He looked at her, his gaze softening. "How's your hand?"

"It's fine."

"Come in."

She stared.

"You said you want to learn metalsmithing skills."

He would train her! Grinning, she stepped inside the workshop for the first time since her arrival in this building, dazed, dazzled. Deeply, she inhaled the overwhelming smell of precious metals, pungent chemicals, pickling acid, and the odor of soldering flux. Her gaze fell on the drawings on the wall, the stack of envelopes, the tightly sealed jars that contained chunks of enamel, the array of tools, the anvil with a horn, the metal sheets, and the cabinets near the table. She wanted to touch them, to weigh them in her hands; she wanted to know all their names and purposes.

"I can train you, but no one else must know. At least for the time being."

She nodded.

"Sit at my workbench," Isaac said and opened a drawer in his jeweler's bench. "Can you hold a tool?"

"I can hold a tool."

He handed her a hammer with a round end and a flat head. "Take this chasing hammer. A versatile tool. It's good for decorating the surface of the metal without cutting it, but it also gives a gentle and firm blow."

Anyu weighed it in her hand. It was light, fitting her hand perfectly. Then she put it down and picked up other instruments—a jeweler's saw, a pair of pliers, drawplates, files, drill bits, soldering tools, forging tools, and a burnisher to polish the metal surfaces. Every tool had a purpose.

"Take some time to familiarize yourself with these, and eventually, you'll find your favorite tools. Now, you said you want to make jewelry. What would you say is the most important principle in crafting a piece of fine jewelry?"

If she gave a wrong answer, would he change his mind about training her? She studied these tools again, the marks on the ruler, the ring sizers, the block containing ball punchers in various sizes, the tweezer's fine tips, the sack containing pliers with different heads, and the compartments where they all belonged. The neatness, the orderliness. "Accuracy?"

"Precisely. Accuracy, exactness, precision. For a jeweler, this is an essential attitude. You begin with the design, the layout, the measurement, the thickness of the metal, the calculation in proportions, then you figure out the symmetry, the harmony, the beauty that captures people's hearts."

She nodded. Precision equaled beauty.

"If you don't mind, draw an apple."

She took a pencil from the desk and drew an apple measuring two centimeters in diameter on a sheet of easy-to-see-through tracing paper Isaac had given her.

"Good. Place the tracing paper on the metal sheet and try this jeweler's saw."

The jeweler's saw, a steel frame, was anchored to a bench pin on the table, and a blade was inserted on one end. The workbench was too high and too far. She scooted over to get closer and lifted her elbows.

"Use the proper posture. Like this. Support the frame against your chest and saw the apple out of the metal."

Following his direction, she leaned forward to keep the frame steady; positioning the saw frame vertically, she began to thread the blade and rotate the metal on the bench pin. When the apple was sawed out, Isaac gave her a file to polish the edges.

She stared at the apple critically. It was uneven on the edges; she could do better.

"You have a steady hand," Isaac said, glancing at her missing pinkie.

"It doesn't bother me," she said. *Only sometimes.*

He nodded. "Now let's hope you can bend wires with nine fingers. Ideally, jewelers use their fingers to form shapes of wires, so you see, we need strong fingers. The tools give you the leverage you need. You'll be more efficient when you're comfortable with them. Now I'll make an S-hook. These are the basic steps."

She watched him as he measured the length of a wire, filed the end to a taper, used a pair of pliers to bend the tip to form a tiny crescent, and then bent half of the wire in the opposite direction. Then he struck the apex of the curves with a planishing hammer, and there on the bench was a flat S shape, tapered at both ends. It could be used as a clasp or a link in a whole chain if there were more S-hooks.

Anyu took a bundle of wires of the same length and width and immediately began to make the hooks, remembering all the steps of tapering and bending. She had finished twenty of them, with only a few skewed shapes, when Isaac spoke again.

"Good work. That should be enough for today. They're coming home."

She heard Uncle David's, Samuel's, and Esther's voices in the showroom, the most disappointing sounds. "Mr. Mandelburg, what will I learn next time?"

"Metalworking basics. Cold connections, hot connections such as annealing, soldering, fusing, and pickling of three types of noble metals: silver, gold, and platinum."

"After that?"

"Cuttlefish casting, if you're interested. Have you heard of that?"

"No. Then?"

"Any serious metalsmiths need to learn the surface treatments such as repoussé and chasing and patina."

"After that?"

"The specialists' techniques of texturing and layering metals: inlay, filigree, reticulation, enameling, and perhaps etching."

"May I come back tomorrow?"

He glanced at the door, and she was about to protest when she detected a smile on his face.

CHAPTER 13

Icy rains engulfed the city, and the chilly, damp air slipped through the velvet curtains and wooden shutters and hung around the lamps like cobwebs. But there was no snow, unlike in Harbin, and there was no need to wear parkas or scarves.

Her pinkie had healed completely, and Anyu could hold a pencil and draw without feeling pain. During the day, she put on a black leather glove and stood at the counter with Esther, where Esther worked her charm selling earrings and necklaces. With the Chinese spring festival approaching, business picked up; many foreigners and locals browsed the jewelry in the glass cases.

Not wishing to let his uncle know, Isaac trained Anyu at midnight or hours before dawn, when people were sleeping. He gave her small tasks, making hooks for necklaces and simple bands for rings and earrings. He also demonstrated various techniques such as drilling, chasing, filing metal, cuttlefish casting, and lost-wax casting. To avoid making noise, he skipped forging on the horn-shaped anvil.

What Isaac said about metalsmithing requiring strong hands was no exaggeration. Her grip was strong with her exercise, but she grew tired while texturizing metal using roller printing, reticulation, and etching techniques. And soldering required careful heat maneuvering. A few times, she burned herself with the blowtorch and drops of melted solder fell on a metal plate. Wire riveting and tube riveting required firm insertion of her fingers, and very soon the tip of her fingers roughened and grew painful and then calloused.

"More," she said when she finished small tasks Isaac gave her—woven chains, a pendant with a locket, a ring with a crown setting.

In two weeks, she crafted bails for necklaces, chains, clasps, and closures, hinges for boxes, and all the small findings.

In four weeks, Anyu mastered the basics of metalworking: chasing, casting, stone setting, and fusing and soldering with the brass blowtorch.

In five weeks, she memorized the steps of filigree, the most beloved ornamental openwork, commonly seen in Edwardian jewelry. Time-consuming but rewarding, it required a strong hand to manipulate the wires, stretching, pulling, and twisting them into the desired shape, then mix flux in a mortar, and finally solder.

Occasionally, her fingers would lose the grip of the metal sheet while polishing, and the pickling acid burned her eyes, but nothing could describe her joy when she succeeded in making a bezel setting for a pendant or a pronged setting for a ring.

No matter the freezing rain, or the chilly air, or the numbed fingers, or the growing soreness of her muscles, Anyu came to the workshop the moment she was called.

Then the inevitable happened.

One evening, Anyu was making a bezel setting for a sapphire pendant when she heard a cough. Uncle David and Samuel were standing next to her. She put down the bezel pusher. She had been so absorbed in her work that she hadn't noticed their presence, and she was sitting on Samuel's stool.

"Isaac! What is this? Why is this girl here?" Uncle David looked exasperated, his gray beard shaking. Samuel came over. Anyu hesitated, but stood up.

Isaac put down his jeweler's saw. "Uncle, she has my permission to be here."

"What?"

"I truly believe she will be a fine jeweler."

"How long has this been happening? Two months? Three months?"

Three months and sixteen days. Anyu could feel the weight of Isaac's stress on her shoulders. Isaac revered his uncle greatly, but Anyu didn't feel the old man deserved it. It was not fair to chastise Isaac, the master jeweler who crafted all the jewelry and supported this household.

The uncle shouted, "Isaac, I don't know what's in your mind. You brought a stranger to our jewelry shop, and now you're training her. You have a great responsibility as the master jeweler and lead designer. How do you plan to run the House of Mandelburg?"

"Uncle, I assure you I am doing all I can to bring more business to the shop."

"Are you? Every day passes by; we pay the rent and taxes and daily expenses. The jewelry sales have been dismal. The shop can't sustain itself, Isaac. You've made some connections through Mrs. Brown, and I was looking forward to seeing you build your clientele in Shanghai. The last thing you should do is waste your time on someone unrelated to us."

"Uncle, allow me to explain—"

"What is there to explain about training a girl, an outsider, and giving away your family's legacy?"

Isaac took a deep breath. After a moment, he said, "She's one of us now, Uncle."

"I beg your pardon?"

"She has learned all the techniques of a jeweler. She'll refine the techniques and help in the workshop, if it's agreeable to you, Uncle."

"I can't believe it, Isaac. Your father would be rolling in his grave!" Uncle David stormed out; Samuel paced in the workshop, folding his arms.

She is one of us now.

Anyu gripped the handle of the bezel pusher, elated. After the loss of her finger, after nights of training, she had made it—she would be a jeweler.

Every day, Anyu came to the workshop after the shop's closing. All she wanted was to work, setting stones, sawing the metal sheets, soldering, and pickling to remove oxidation and flux. In this small room clustered with cabinets and tools, with the metallic clinks and whirs, she felt the calmness, this encompassing monotone rhythm of assurance—the same thing she had felt in the dank apartment she had shared with Mother. There was nowhere else she'd rather be; this workshop was her home.

She liked to be near Isaac, sharing the tools, breathing in the same pungent air of metal and chemicals. When she held the chasing hammer passed from his hands, she thought of how it felt to feel Isaac's hands, to touch him. Her face grew warm with these thoughts, her heart racing. Isaac was different from Confucius, yet she liked them both. She remembered Mother wanted a marriage for her and thought that she could imagine marrying Isaac or Confucius someday—if she would ever see him again.

One day in April, Anyu had just closed the shop with Esther and was ready to go to the workshop when she heard a knock on the window outside. Confucius. She put down the rag, wiped her hands, and told Esther she'd be right back. Esther gave her a look. "I didn't know you had a boyfriend," she said, but she didn't press further.

Smiling, Anyu opened the door to the street. By the dim shop lights and the taillights of the passing cars, she could see Confucius standing by his bicycle. She had been worried that she'd never see him again, and she was glad he came. But she didn't want him to talk to

Esther. "Confucius, you can't stay here. Let's take a walk. Where have you been?"

"Working." He handed her a paper bag and pushed his bicycle forward. "Chestnuts. Do you like them? I haven't seen you for a few months. You've been working hard, haven't you?"

"I'm a jeweler." She walked beside him. It was cold at night; there were few pedestrians around. The chestnut was warm, creamy, sweet; she loved it. She had never eaten roasted chestnuts before.

"A jeweler?"

"I've been in training, Confucius! Isaac is a master jeweler."

"The old Russian?" Isaac and his family might be stateless, but to the Chinese, they were still Russians because of where they came from.

"He's not that old."

"He's a foreigner."

"What do you have against foreigners?"

"Nothing. I'm surprised he'd train you, that's all. Will you make a lot of money?" They passed an alley where a few figures were smoking, their cigarettes flickering.

"Maybe." She nearly tripped over a pothole she didn't see, and he reached out to steady her. But he lost his balance, and his bicycle fell to the ground. When Anyu reached to pull it up, she bumped her head onto Confucius's. "Ouch." They rubbed their heads at the same time.

Then in unison, they said, "Sorry."

They looked at each other and laughed. And then, feeling strangely excited and happy, Anyu looked away.

Confucius pulled up his bicycle and they started to walk again. For a moment, neither of them spoke, staring straight ahead. Anyu liked the streets of Shanghai at night, the warm glow of the lanterns swaying under the eaves, the neon lights blinking through the shadows, and the peaceful stillness, with their soft footfalls and the faint clatter of horse-drawn carriages blending into the city's symphony. It seemed all the day's discontent had been erased, replaced by an unvoiced intimacy, an indulgent desire.

"Now, this is a sign," Confucius said, imitating the voice of an old scholar.

"What sign?" She glanced at him, the silhouette of his profile, the strands of his long hair bouncing on his shoulder. Warmth spread through her limbs.

"The world is going to end."

"What?"

"In two thousand years."

She giggled. "The chestnuts taste great."

"Glad you like them. What else would you like to eat?" he asked. And movies. Would she like to go to the movies? He liked *The Gold Rush*, which he had watched five times. Charlie Chaplin was a great English actor, he said.

She felt a strange excitement, enveloped by the night that echoed with the city's music. When Confucius's hand accidentally brushed hers, her heart raced, filled with anticipation. "I've never been to the movies."

"Movie tomorrow, then?"

"But where did you get money for the food and movie tickets? I heard you no longer work at the teahouse."

"Oh, I was offered a new job, and I got this." Confucius rang the bell of his bicycle, a new vehicle that he had acquired, the newest model, which she had not noticed earlier. He had been hired to make trouble in a bicycle shop, start a brawl, and then steal the bicycle, he said. The shop owner broke his nose, and he had a cut on his neck—he showed her the bandage.

Anyu stopped walking, dismayed. "You were hired to get in a fight, and you beat people up?"

He shrugged.

"Confucius, I don't like to see people get hurt."

"It's Shanghai. Everyone gets hurt, except the foreigners. But don't worry. We were disguised as Japanese."

"Why?"

"The Japanese want to stir up Chinese people's anti-Japanese sentiment so they can have an excuse to say their citizens were attacked and they needed to protect them, then they'll find a foothold in Shanghai. A trick they've been doing in Nanjing. But who cares? I got a new bicycle and was paid handsomely."

All her thoughts of going to the movies evaporated. Anyu stuffed the chestnut bag into his hand. "I'm going back. Don't come to the shop again, Confucius. I don't want to see you."

"Wait, wait. Why?"

"You're a criminal, you have no morals. I'm a jeweler. I don't want to be associated with you."

She walked fast, didn't look back, didn't answer Confucius's call. The night wind was picking up, sweeping through her thin tunic. She shivered, turning a corner. In front of a shop with two lanterns, a man was speaking in a low voice to a porter carrying a girl with bound feet on his shoulders. He handed him a few bills, and they went to an alley behind the shop. Anyu looked away, hurrying toward the Mandelburgs' shop.

She had meant it then, to never see Confucius again, convinced that his character and profession conflicted with hers. Many years later, when they did meet again, neither of them was the same as they had been, and she wondered how her life would have turned out had she not left Confucius that night.

CHAPTER 14

May 1927

Lessons on gemstones: Diamonds produced brilliance and dispersion and fluorescence; rubies and sapphires and spinels displayed asterism, also known as four-ray or six-ray stars; and aquamarine and obsidian and fire opals had chatoyance, the cat's eyes. Lessons on pricing gemstones: 50 percent for the purity of color, 50 percent for the clarity and treatment and cuts, size, and optical properties.

Isaac gave her a flashlight and a leather-bound notebook containing his notes about gemology. She had talent in discerning jade, but now she needed a solid understanding and practical knowledge of gemstones, which was vital for pricing and designing.

Lessons on the conventions of labeling a piece of jewelry: name, year, type of jewelry, size, metal, gemstones, and techniques used.

Then trips to the jewelry shops of Shanghai: renowned French jewelry shops, Italian boutiques, and American jewelry companies in the Concession and the Settlement—Cartier, Tiffany & Co., the House of Clemente, and Frost & Satin, and then the silver shops near Yu Garden in the Old City, the Chinese area. Isaac kept a low profile as they browsed the jewelry, only commenting on the prices and designs after they left. When they stopped at a shop named the House of Bellefeuille, neither of them entered. Anyu recalled the jeweler's name she'd used to trick Miss Liao, and Isaac said he'd had an unpleasant experience with the owner. He didn't elaborate.

Anyu couldn't help but notice that the styles and choices of precious metals and gemstones varied greatly between the foreign jewelers and the local ones—the foreign jewelers excelled in designing personal accessories and favored diamonds and gemstones, while the Chinese craftsmen preferred jade and silver, with designs focusing on household wares and home decor. The Chinese silver shops were restricted from using gold, she heard, which was used as currency and controlled by the Chinese government, but the same restriction didn't apply to foreigners.

"Perhaps you'd like to learn an important technique, Anyu, called enameling, which requires fusing layers of enamel onto a metal surface, a process similar to firing glazes on ceramics." Holding a silver pendant, Isaac explained wet-packing enamel, then an *en ronde-bosse*—in high relief—with a flower brooch, then painted enamel with another pendant.

"I've seen this technique before."

"You have?" He went to the second cabinet next to the tools and opened the drawers containing jars of enamels, boxes of silica and soda ash, and packets of chemicals for polishing the metals and platinum chloride for oxide finish.

"The surprise inside the Russian egg I found in your bag also used enamel," she said without thinking.

"You have a good memory. Fabergé eggs used over 144 enamel colors from mauve and lime green to scarlet. Alexander III's Coronation Egg, for instance, is noted for its velvety feel, a sophisticated technique that required engraving patterns on platinum before enameling, which we call *guilloché* enamel. The process also required lengthy hours of polishing with a special wooden wheel and wash leather. I'm not boasting, but few craftsmen today have the patience to accomplish such a feat."

"Fabergé eggs. We call them Russian eggs."

"I beg you to remember his name, Peter Karl Fabergé, an icon. Many metalsmiths, jewelers, and designers had the honor of working for him and enjoyed great creative latitude. He created this novel idea of producing *objets de fantaisie*, curios with high artistic value. His artifacts were so popular that he received the imperial commission every year. These days, his artful ornaments, especially those imperial eggs, have served as the models for goldsmiths and jewelers."

Anyu's heart raced faster. "I know I promised never to mention it again, but do you still have it?"

He paused for a moment. "Of course. It's my most precious treasure."

"May I see it?"

He looked at her.

"Mr. Mandelburg, I can't stop thinking about it. It brought me to you, from Harbin to Shanghai, and inspired me to be a jeweler. It is the most beautiful ornament I have ever seen."

"This is a common reaction for people when they see treasure—possession and obsession."

"I don't want to own it, I just want to see it. May I see it?" she persisted.

"I'm afraid not. Only a master jeweler is eligible to view it."

"Why?"

"It's a rule among workmasters. Previously, they agreed to show the eggs to collectors, but a few incidents happened, which led to violence and loss of life. To shield the eggs from the crude eyes of the greedy, they decided that only the master jewelers, the privileged ones, could lay their eyes on them."

"I want to become a master jeweler," she said.

He chuckled. "I don't want to dampen your enthusiasm. A master jeweler is a high, commendable honor, given only to a few exceptional artisans. He is generally believed to be a capable gemologist, an artist, and an engineer with social skills."

Anyu waved her hand. "How to become a master jeweler?"

"Traditionally, it requires a jeweler to produce an astounding body of work that earns universal recognition for its superiority and ingenuity in the pantheon of jewelry, establish a reliable clientele base, and build a stellar reputation in the industry. It takes decades to achieve that status."

"What is the nontraditional way?"

Isaac laughed. "The nontraditional path for those geniuses will be to win a prestigious jewelry award. You reminded me of Georges Mauboussin, a Parisian jeweler, who won a grand prize at the Paris Decorative Arts Exhibition and earned international acclaim. He's now lauded as a master jeweler."

"Is the award given by the Annual Shanghai Jewelers Competition considered prestigious?" She recalled that Esther had mentioned it last year.

"I can't imagine another award that'll claim this status. This is the only competition in Shanghai."

He had not competed. Anyu recalled his reluctance when Uncle David urged him to try.

"When is the competition, Mr. Mandelburg?"

"In mid-October. It's designed to meet the demands of the end-of-year gift-purchase season."

"That's in five months."

"Most houses start to work on their designs in spring."

She leaned in. "If I won the award, would you show me the egg?"

He raised his eyebrows. "Keep in mind there are strict rules for the competition, and many designers are master jewelers."

"Will you?"

"Very well. I shall show you the Fabergé egg if you win the competition and become a master jeweler."

"I better not waste time."

A few days later, while Anyu was crafting a baguette bracelet, Isaac told her that he had inquired about the application process for the competition and heard that the window to submit designs to the competition had closed. She would have to wait for next year. Anyu was disappointed. She couldn't wait a full year to see the egg.

Isaac had a peculiar schedule, Anyu noticed. He worked every day, but every Wednesday evening, he took off his apron, washed his hands with soap, and put on his black suit and hat. When he went out of the shop, a black Rolls-Royce sedan waited for him. Then, late at night, Isaac would return.

Once Anyu followed him out. Through the showroom's window, she could see the outline of a woman wearing a huge black hat inside the car.

"That's Mrs. Brown," Esther said when Anyu asked. "She's a powerful purveyor of diamonds and gemstones in Shanghai, also my father's client. She's from Britain."

"Why doesn't she come inside?"

"I don't know. She's always accompanied by her bodyguards."

A mysterious woman, and powerful.

"She's also the chair and the sponsor of the Annual Shanghai Jewelers Competition."

"Is she?"

"You've heard of it, haven't you? It's the most important event in Shanghai. The best design is chosen as the winner, and the winner enjoys extensive publicity and a substantial monetary reward, as well as an enviable number of orders from the elite clients in Shanghai."

Anyu was interested. "Does she make the rules?"

"That's what they say."

Anyu nodded.

The next day, Anyu declared she'd like to design and craft her own pieces.

"You have all the material you need." Isaac unlocked a cabinet drawer near his workbench, which stored gold sheets, silver tubing, wires, beryls, and several rubies and topazes, all the material Uncle David had locked up.

"Maybe not all," Uncle David grumbled. Next to him, Samuel was yawning.

Anyu ignored them and picked out some silver tubing. "Mr. Mandelburg, if I sell my first jewelry in a month, will you introduce me to Mrs. Brown?"

There was an exchange of looks between Isaac and Uncle David, and Isaac said, "Why do you wish to meet Mrs. Brown?"

"I hear she makes the rules for the competition. I saw her automobile a few times."

"Why are you interested in the competition?" Uncle David asked.

"She makes the rules, but the buyer chooses the winner," Isaac said.

"You'll introduce me to her?"

"I will, if your first design sells in a few months."

"No, not a few months. In one month," Anyu said.

It took her two weeks of working feverishly at the workbench and dreaming in her sleep before she finally finished her first piece—a gold necklace with faceted rubies and luminescent pearls set in a six-petal frame to form an intricate floral design. Flower pendant, 42 x 32 mm, fourteen-karat gold, polished, chased. She presented it to Isaac, watching him holding his 10x loupe, studying her creation. Then Isaac placed it on the necklace stand and gave it to Esther to display in the showroom.

Anyu bit her lip, deflated. Why hadn't Isaac commented on the necklace? What if no one purchased it?

The next few days, she stood at the counter, eyeing the glass case; then, one day, she was away from the counter, and when she returned, the pendant was not inside.

"The new flower pendant Father made? It's sold," Esther said.

That was her first piece of jewelry. Sold in a week!

Anyu burst into the workshop. "My pendant!"

The clack of the tools ceased. Uncle David and Samuel raised their heads, and Isaac rubbed his face. "What is it?"

"It sold in a week!"

Isaac sat up, and the placid visage that had been etched in her mind and visited her in her dreams countless times changed. His lips curved and the skin at the corners of his eyes crinkled to form a breathtaking smile, a smile of pride, a smile of deep affection. "That was quick."

"Will you introduce me to Mrs. Brown?"

Isaac leaned over the lamp and picked up a black envelope from a stack of papers. "Her soiree is next Friday. By invitation only."

CHAPTER 15

On the day of Mrs. Brown's party, Isaac and Anyu took a taxi to her mansion. When it stopped at two stone sculptures of prancing dogs, Anyu got out. In front of her was a palatial two-story English neoclassical building with a wrought-iron gate, where four policemen stood. Isaac showed them his invitation, and they were waved in. Walking down the meandering path in the garden with Isaac, Anyu studied the crescent balcony on the second floor, the massive lawn with lush foliage and flowers, the glimmering electric garden lamps, and the black Rolls-Royce sedans with chauffeurs in double-breasted ocher liveries. They stopped in front of a towering black metal door, where a white-haired doorman dressed in a sleek coat and leather boots ushered them in. Anyu had been prepared to see the grandeur of Mrs. Brown's mansion, but still, she was amazed. In her plain shirt and pants, she looked like a maid.

The spacious ballroom bloomed like a verdant summer from a fantasy land: the floor was covered with jade-shaded carpet in a pattern of floating white clouds, the walls were painted in soft emerald green, the pastel wainscoting was brushed with gold, and a massive chandelier sparkled with crystal leaf-shaped lampshades.

Under the chandelier, the men were clad in black top hats and tails, their lapels gleaming with gold pins, their wrists flashing diamond watches. Women wore long evening dresses adorned with lush sable wraps to ward off the late-spring chill. They all seemed at ease, gliding between white marble columns, their jewelry glowing in the light.

"Why would people wear snake jewelry, Mr. Mandelburg?" Anyu studied the women's adornments with interest. A panther brooch, a parrot barrette, a snake bracelet, filigree earrings set in platinum, Art Deco necklaces with bejeweled pendants.

"The snake represented everlasting, undying love in the Victorian era. Prince Albert gifted Queen Victoria an emerald snake ring and started a trend. It's a popular motif in Europe."

Anyu shook her head. "I wouldn't associate the snake with romantic passions. Snakes don't evoke auspicious sentiments in Chinese culture." But she understood. Symbolism.

A man wearing round black-rimmed glasses, Mrs. Brown's secretary, told Isaac she would see him once she finished her meeting. Isaac thanked him.

"Where's Mrs. Brown?" Anyu asked.

"There." Isaac gestured to a plump lady in a shimmering ivy-green dress sitting on a velvet sofa across from them.

Anyu gave her a good look. The woman appeared to be in her thirties. The most impressive feature about her was not her round cheeks, her bluish-green eyes with the saturated colors of highly prized emeralds, or her cloud-shaped blond hair, but rather her Edwardian diamond tiara. Anyu had never seen a tiara crafted to such perfection, with intricate branches and leaves adorned with numerous large, high-quality diamonds; she could identify at least thirty rose-cut diamonds in high brilliance. Even at a distance, the radiance of the tiara, bursting with dispersion and fluorescence, glowed in the room.

Mrs. Brown was thirty-seven years old, a widow who had lived in Shanghai since 1915, when her then-husband established his business in China. After his fatal fall from a mountain during an expedition, Mrs. Brown had taken over his business. She was knowledgeable in Russian, French, and Chinese, which she learned so her lapidaries wouldn't cheat her, she had said. As Anyu and Isaac approached, she was speaking to a Chinese couple: a young woman in a black dress embroidered with orchids and a man in a military uniform decorated with pins and medals. They looked familiar. Anyu stared, and then she remembered she had seen them in the newspapers. Generalissimo Chiang Kai-shek and his fiancée, Soong Mei-ling.

Surrounding Mrs. Brown were eight men wearing black fedoras—bodyguards. In fact, as Anyu inspected the ballroom, she found more guards in black shirts and hats, scattered discreetly.

"Would you like to know the elite of Shanghai? There's Mr. Morris, the man who's smoking a cigar," Isaac said. Henry Morris, a good friend of Mrs. Brown's, was also the owner of a few newspapers in the French Concession and the Canidrome dog track; his home was located on a lot that measured sixty thousand square meters. "And there is the British diplomat, Mr. James, and an Italian consul, Mr. Romano."

"I would never be able to remember their names."

"You might want to. They could be your clients," Isaac said.

"Clients."

"A master jeweler has to establish a devoted client base who inspires and fosters his creation. And you'll know this: a good jeweler makes jewelry, but a master jeweler builds relationships." Isaac took two champagne flutes from a server's tray and gave one to her.

She hadn't tried alcohol before, but everyone was holding a flute, so she accepted it. *A good jeweler makes jewelry, but a master jeweler builds relationships.*

Isaac continued discreetly pointing out the men to her, diplomats, tycoons, successful businessmen, collectors, scions of wealthy families, and jewelers—Americans looking for job opportunities in Shanghai.

Then Anyu caught several English phrases among the noise of the conversation. She turned her head. Near her was an Italian man wearing a striking ring with a clear, faceted Pigeon's Blood ruby encircled by brilliant-cut diamonds; a Hungarian architect with a beard shaped like wings; a pink-faced British naval officer; and a man standing with legs spread apart like a pair of pliers—the president of an American oil company. They were talking about Fabergé eggs.

"I'll pay one hundred thousand US dollars for a piece. Where are they?" the American said.

"Spirited out of the storeroom . . . No one knows . . . Eight. Yes. I hear eight of them are missing, but I could be wrong, and the report could also be deliberately misleading," the British naval officer said.

She took a few steps closer to listen better.

"Dead? No, not dead . . . The workmaster fled . . . with his eggs . . . Yes, someone saw him . . ." Their voices were swallowed by a bout of women's laughter.

"Yes, yes. I do know his name. Isaac Umansky . . . I'm sure of it."

"A Jew? Did anyone get him?"

"Jews. I hear they amassed many treasures . . ."

"No . . . I don't have his photo. I don't know what he looks like . . ."

Isaac returned his flute and took another one, his hands shaking. He must have heard, too.

"How did they know?" Anyu whispered.

Isaac shot her a look that made her instantly regret what she had said. She glanced at the well-dressed people, hoping no one had overheard her. Had her landlord gossiped about the egg? Who else had he talked to?

Isaac looked unperturbed, but he didn't speak a word after that.

Finally, the Chinese couple stood and left Mrs. Brown's sofa, and Anyu wove through the crowd with Isaac. Before they came any closer, one of the bodyguards asked Isaac to turn over his pockets.

"There's no need to search him. It's Isaac. Come, Isaac." Mrs. Brown extended her ungloved right hand for Isaac to kiss. The British woman had a pleasant, husky voice and the bearing of eminence that made people lean over and heed every word she uttered. "I'm pleased to see you, darling. It's not often that you come to my party. How are you?"

"I'm well. Thank you, Mrs. Brown," Isaac said. "It's so kind of you to meet us. I'm grateful for your time."

"You're my distinguished guest. I shall always have time for you, darling."

"Mrs. Brown, you are too kind. Please allow me to introduce my apprentice to you. Anyu." Isaac smiled—perhaps it was an illusion, but Anyu thought he looked nervous.

The British woman turned to her, the brilliance of the tiara lighting up her bluish-green eyes. She didn't speak, studying Anyu's face, her clothing, and her gloved hands.

"It's my honor to meet you, Mrs. Brown," Anyu said.

"If you don't mind, Isaac," the lady said. "Could we speak in private?"

That was it? She had only had one sentence to exchange with her. After all these weeks' expectations, Anyu was not willing to leave yet. "Excuse me, Mrs. Brown. Is the generalissimo looking for a wedding ring?"

Both Mrs. Brown and Isaac looked startled.

"Yes, but how did you know?" the lady studied her, more carefully this time.

"I read the newspaper. It said he had been engaged to Miss Soong. I assumed they'd be married soon."

Mrs. Brown handed her champagne flute to one of her bodyguards. "You are rather perceptive. Your assumption is accurate. He is looking for a wedding ring for his fiancée, and I made some suggestions to him. He'll find one that appeals to his taste."

"I'm sure he will," Anyu said.

"Now, here's something else you might wish to know, Isaac. The generalissimo also plans to pamper his fiancée with a brooch as a wedding gift."

"A brooch," Isaac said.

"I proposed that they serve as the judges of our annual jewelry competition. They've agreed to take on the duty of viewing the submissions and choosing the winner."

"This is fantastic news."

Anyu seized the chance. "Mrs. Brown, if you don't mind, may I ask for a favor? I hear the deadline for submitting designs for the competition has passed. Will you make an exception to accept one more submission? This is still at the early stage of preparation."

The lady raised her eyebrows. "No one has dared ask me for a favor before. Little girl, on whose behalf are you requesting?"

"The House of Mandelburg."

"So you decided to compete, after all, Isaac?"

He nodded. "If it's agreeable to you."

"Very well, Isaac. For you, I'd make an exception. Your house will be added to the list of competitors. However, I hope you can forgive me, one submission is all I will accept." She raised her hand.

Their time was up. Anyu rose with Isaac and went to stand by a marble column near a staircase as other guests took their seats.

"She's a frigid woman," Anyu said.

"Perhaps."

"I don't think she likes me."

"That's because she's British."

"Why is that?"

"I might be wrong. The Brits have mastered many skills, but expressing affection is not one of them. Something to do with their weather."

"Like the Russians?"

Isaac chuckled. "Like the Russians."

"I'd like to compete."

"I figured. Wasn't this the reason you requested to see Mrs. Brown? Now you have your wish."

"You remember your promise?" Anyu said in a low voice.

"I do. But as your mentor, Anyu, I'd like to warn you: The prospect of winning is, sadly, very slim, for a novice designer. It will be a fierce competition."

"I know."

"I think you might also want to know that the House of Bellefeuille has been the winner for five consecutive years, and the House of Clemente and House of Frost and Satin also have famed jewelers. These three houses possess enormous wealth and a high level of sophistication in crafting jewelry. To beat their creation would take ingenuity, skill, and luck."

"Monsieur Bellefeuille was the winner? Is he here?"

Isaac shook his head. "He and Mrs. Brown are sworn enemies."

"I didn't know that."

"If you insist on competing, then go ahead. Craft your piece."

"Would you craft a piece, too?"

"Mrs. Brown said one design from us. Her wish must be respected."

"We can create two and choose one. If my design is better than yours, you'll submit mine."

Isaac laughed. He finished the champagne in one gulp. "If your design is better than mine."

The soiree was in full swing, but Anyu, her heart soaring with joy, couldn't waste a minute more at the ballroom.

"We have to go home," she said.

When she left Mrs. Brown's mansion, she had already visualized a dozen designs featuring animals and birds that were meaningful to Chinese culture.

CHAPTER 16

Anyu started to draw the moment she arrived at the shop. Crouching at the kitchen counter, she sketched an image of a rising phoenix clutching a fireball and marked it with the exact measurements for its head, body, wings, tail, and talons. She would use three specially cut spinels for the body, gold granules in various sizes for the head, rose-cut diamonds mounted on platinum for the eyes, red enameling on the tail, and filigree to create openwork gold wings for the feathers.

Afterward, she filled out the description of the brooch on the jewelry slip Isaac used in the workshop: Rising Phoenix, 100 x 32 mm, eighteen diamonds, three spinels, platinum, granulation, filigree. Then, recalling what her mother had said about the bird, she wrote on a separate slip the symbolism of the Chinese phoenix, "*feng*: in the context of marriage, the phoenix is an equal partner to the dragon." Anyu was sure this would intrigue the bride.

When she finished, it was well past midnight.

The next day, she presented the design to Isaac and Uncle David, who had learned of the competition and appeared energized. But with one look at the design, Uncle David's jaw dropped. Isaac responded, "Bold design. Well done. However, the granulation on the head will require you to make a large number of granules, which will take hours of placing and fusing them."

"I can do that."

"The openwork of the wings is quite a challenge since the torch's heat might not be strong enough to melt the metal, but it can be achieved through chiseling and shaping."

"I can get it started now."

"You only have four months," Uncle David said. "There's not enough time. You won't be able to complete a design like this."

"I can do it."

Isaac nodded. "I'll request a loan of the diamonds from Mr. Walters. Uncle, given that she has four months to complete the design, would you free her from her duty at the counter to allow her to work in the workshop during the day?"

Uncle David declined initially, but at Isaac's insistence, he gave in. Isaac even moved a dresser from his bedroom and turned it into a workbench for her.

Anyu hardly had time to eat or sleep; all she could think of was the bird. When she was in the workshop, she worked on the design, washing the metal sheet with a scrub pad, forging the gold sheet, and shaping gold into beads, balls, delicate swirls, curls, and wires. Then, weeks later, she began fusing, enameling, and engraving. Halfway through crafting, she put down her chisel, scrutinizing her work.

She took a chasing hammer and smashed the whole piece.

"What's the matter?" Isaac asked from his desk. He was working on an elaborate Edwardian design for the competition.

"It's not good enough."

She started over.

Measuring. Cutting out the design. Forging. Fusing the granules. Pickling. Polishing. Finally, the beads were set on the round head, precisely as she had drawn. But the openwork of the wings was indeed most demanding to execute. Her eyes burned from intense concentration; the skin on her fingers was rubbed raw and then bled from polishing. She wrapped a clean cloth around her hand and fell asleep at the table after finishing one wing, and when she awoke, she began to bend and form the metal wires again. When the two wings were finally forged, she scrutinized them.

Again, she picked up the hammer and struck the creation.

"What's the matter now?" Isaac asked.

"I don't know what is wrong with it. It doesn't have movement." She was going to fail; she could never be a master jeweler.

"It's not easy, is it?" Samuel grumbled from his desk.

"Take a break," Isaac said.

"No." She sniffed, holding back the tears that threatened to escape, and gathered up the smashed piece. She would not stop or rest until the filigree openwork of the wings and the entire piece looked exactly like the drawing.

Only one month left before the deadline for submission.

She started anew with the bird. Then granules. Pickling. Polishing. Filigrees. Then claw-setting the diamonds and spinels. Tirelessly, she worked.

She ate two hard-boiled eggs for her meals and slept in the workshop. The moment she awoke, she continued. She worked for twenty-two hours a day and rested only for two hours.

Eight days before the competition, she completed her brooch, a soaring *en tremblant* bird.

She watched Isaac hold the brooch, studying it. His face looked like a stretched sheet of metal, untainted, smooth without a frown or smile, his gaze intense.

"How much should we price it?" Isaac asked.

"One thousand dollars."

He took the pricing chart she had filled out, reviewed the metal types, the gemstones' cut and color, their corresponding prices per carat, labor costs, designing costs, and the markup percentage, then jotted down the price.

"Which one should we use for the competition?" Uncle David asked. Isaac's design was a round medallion with thousands of fine filigrees that resembled a nest, fourteen-karat gold, chased. Five hundred dollars.

Anyu bit her lip. Her mentor's design was more sophisticated and stylish. If she were him, she would choose his. But Isaac picked up the bird, laid it inside a box lined with velvet, and said he'd bring it to Mrs. Brown.

"You're making a mistake, Isaac," Uncle David said with a heavy sigh.

For the first time, Anyu agreed with the old man.

The days after the submission of the phoenix were agonizingly slow; the hours dragged, the shop's door opened and closed, and she stood at the counter, her mind elsewhere. There was still one week left before the award ceremony, during which the winner would be announced.

"Look, Anyu." Esther waved a stack of newspapers at her. It was the *North China Daily News*, published in English. The newspaper printed an enthusiastic article about the ceremony and the accompanying exhibition and described in detail Miss Soong's reputation for her visionary jewelry style. The competition had attracted sixty-two entries of brooches, the article said.

Sixty-two.

Then, two days later, the newspaper printed: "A preliminary review was set up and ten entries were chosen as the finalists."

This was followed by an in-depth discussion of the jewelers in Shanghai, all but the House of Mandelburg. It predicted a winner—the House of Bellefeuille, the perennial winner of the award.

Then: "The top three most impressive brooches are now under consideration for the future Madame Chiang Kai-shek!"

Then, the day before the ceremony: "The winner has been chosen!"

Anyu felt sick. No one had mentioned her phoenix.

꘎

The day of the ceremony arrived. In the morning, Isaac, Uncle David, and Samuel went to the exhibition hall to set up their stand with a selection of wares from their shop. Anyu didn't go, making the excuse to mind the shop.

When it was time to leave for the ceremony in the late afternoon, Anyu told Esther she had decided to stay home.

"Why?" Esther asked.

"I don't have a decent dress," Anyu said.

"Do you want to wear mine?" Esther said.

"I can't."

"Come on, before I change my mind." Esther pulled her to the attic. She unfolded a white muslin dress with an empire waist, helped her put it on, buttoning up her back and tucking the folds around her hips—she had been sewing this at night, and she had hoped this would be her wedding dress, she said.

"Your wedding dress?"

"It looks good on you." They were seven years apart, but Esther had only a few more pounds than she had.

Anyu looked into the mirror Esther held up. A woman stared back at her—how much her body had changed. Her bosom was full and her hips had widened. She was almost as tall as Esther, a grown woman. She had turned eighteen, she realized.

"You're a pretty girl," Esther said.

"Are you sure?" She thought of what her neighbors had said: *You have peach blossom–shaped eyes. You'll grow up like your mother, seducing other men and ruining their families.*

"Are you trying to be modest?"

Modest?

"Now, don't forget this. A jeweler must wear something that glitters." Esther looped a gold Edwardian necklace around her neck. That had been her mother's, she said.

Anyu burst into tears. The stress and anxiety from the past few months had taken a toll on her, and she felt she was going to fall apart. She had been naive. She was only a novice jeweler. She shouldn't have asked to compete; she would be publicly humiliated.

"What's wrong, Anyu?"

"Esther, I'm not going to win."

"How do you know?"

"Have you read the predictions in the newspaper?"

Esther took out her handkerchief and dabbed at Anyu's face. "They're just predictions. No one knows the result yet except the judges."

"Will you go to the ceremony with me?"

"I can't, Anyu, I have to keep an eye on the shop. But go. No matter what happens, you're a fine, fine jeweler."

"If I win, I'll buy you a new dress."

"You promise! I want a new dress."

Anyu pulled on a long white glove that conveniently concealed her missing finger. She felt better.

CHAPTER 17

The moment she entered the grand ballroom in the hotel that hosted the ceremony, submerged in a cloud of cigars and cologne and champagne, Anyu felt like a fish jumping into boiling water. She could feel the heat from the golden chandelier burning like the midday sun while the tide of men and women rushing by pulled her in and pushed her out. Violin music wafted in the air; heels clicked on the marble floor. Everyone was talking—men gathering in groups, women in elegant dresses, and journalists holding cameras.

Journalists! Imagine a loss, in public. Anyu couldn't breathe, sweat pooling on her skin. Esther's dress was getting tight.

When she found Isaac at his stand, he mentioned a few designs that had enraptured the attendees. An American jeweler at the House of Clemente had crafted a snow leopard brooch with colored diamonds, gray moonstones, black star sapphires, and white gold. Another jeweler at Frost & Satin had presented a new, fascinating take on an ouroboros with seventy-six diamonds for scales. Anyu wondered if she had heard correctly. A snake, again? And then Isaac went on to talk about the generalissimo, Miss Soong, and Mrs. Brown.

And there she was, Mrs. Brown, standing near a stage at the end of the ballroom, wearing her Edwardian tiara with branches and leaves encrusted with diamonds, surrounded by women wearing memory wire–style bracelets, men flashing their unique gold cuff links, and still more journalists holding cameras. She was speaking passionately about something, and the crowd around her listened attentively. There was a thunderous wave of applause when she stopped, and she laughed, her tiara radiating.

"I'm going to see other jewelers' stands," Anyu told Isaac.

So nervous, she stumbled into the smoke-filled House of Clemente room, humming with soft greetings and whispers, luminescent with golden rays from the jewelry in vitrines. The crowd surrounded the five glass cases in the center; inside were pieces beyond her imagination: bejeweled giraffe bangles, jadeite butterfly brooches, lion's head pins, and salamander hair clips. The stunning gemstones were set in etched, hand-textured, and fabricated metal and embellished with diamonds, lapis lazuli, gold, coral, and any kind of gemstones she could imagine. She saw, too, the enthralled looks of the men and women, their intense want, their naked desire. That was the power of jewelry, its beauty and wealth provoking bright eyes, a frisson of excitement, an acute appreciation of wonder, and a primal instinct to possess.

She felt miserable.

The House of Clemente could win.

She dragged her feet to the House of Bellefeuille room, which was decorated with banners of awards and recognitions—Bellefeuille, after all, had been the winner of the competition for the previous five years. The house's collection was confidently unified and artistically stylized. All the bracelets, pendants, and even rings touted a single theme of a plant that resembled an iris, etched, granulated, inlaid, and enameled in a dazzling variety of gold, mauve, and grass green. She paused at a glass case that showed off two platinum bracelets with aquamarine irises, a simple design of a three-petal flower transformed into elegance. It was awe striking that a single flower could be idolized and envisioned in such a variety of forms.

She fanned herself. She was going to faint. The reputation for artistry and sophistication of Bellefeuille was in plain sight. The House of Bellefeuille could win again.

A man said something to her. She looked up. Beside her was a man in his forties, about Isaac's age, with a chiseled face, a dainty mustache, and lustrous brown eyes. He was strikingly handsome and brought a wave of spicy scent with notes of lime, nutmeg, and lavender.

"Ah, you don't speak French. A pity. French is the most beautiful language in the world, mademoiselle, and you're looking at the finest jewelry—French jewelry, known for its exquisite craftsmanship and superior artistry."

"It's beautiful." Anyu stopped fanning herself, but sweat was pooling in her gloves, and she worried it might drip onto the floor.

"In French, we call it *fleur-de-lis*. The three-petal beauty is France's national flower, a symbol of royalty, an icon associated with the king of France. And many designs here feature leaves. Bellefeuille, as you know, means 'beautiful leaf' in French."

"Do you think the House of Bellefeuille will win the competition?"

He studied her. "Bellefeuille has won for the past five years."

"I know that."

"What kind of jewelry do you prefer, mademoiselle?"

"Russian jewelry." To defend Isaac. She had learned everything from him.

"Russian jewelry? You must know it's notorious among jewelers, with its barbaric colors and the obscene sizes of gemstones that require a chainsaw. The Russian jewelry, some have joked, is another form of mineralogy."

Had she heard another man say this, she would have pointed out his arrogance, but this man had a way of expressing his confidence so even the insult sounded charismatic.

"You look familiar. Have we met?" he asked.

"I don't think so."

"Let me guess. You are a princess of a Shanghai tycoon and you order diamond necklaces and rings like men buy cigars. I have many clients like you, young and beautiful. And your dress, it's most exquisite."

"I borrowed it from a friend. It's not mine."

"Is that so? How honest of you. You look lovely. I'm Pierre Bellefeuille, a *bijoutier-artiste*, the owner of the House of Bellefeuille."

"Oh."

"You haven't told me your name."

"I am Anyu, from Harbin. I'm trained as a jeweler, too."

"Are you? And which house do you work for?"

"The House of Mandelburg."

He raised his eyebrows. "David Mandelburg is your mentor?"

"No. Isaac Mandelburg."

"I see. The newcomer. I haven't had a chance to meet him. He's quite shifty, isn't he? How does he treat you?" There was something in his tone that Anyu couldn't figure out.

"Very well."

He leaned over, his cologne a thick mist enveloping her. "You have a smudge on you. May I?"

His fingers touched her chin—they were clean, soft. A strange sensation ran through her. No man had ever touched her face in her eighteen years of life.

"Excuse me."

Anyu squeezed past the crowd and rushed out. At the door, she looked back. Bellefeuille, his arm on the glass case, was watching her as if she were a newly discovered diamond.

At the end of the exhibition, Anyu thought she had something figured out. The wealthy in Shanghai loved wealth but resented carrying it like a rock. It was all about glamour and glory. And the jewelry on display all shared a common theme, featuring exotic animals such as panthers, salamanders, lions, giraffes, and the ubiquitous snakes, except the flowers from the House of Bellefeuille. None of the jewelry besides hers hinted at Chinese legends or myth.

Her phoenix design was unique, rich with cultural connotations, refreshing among the Western concepts, and perfectly crafted. Would Miss Soong, a woman born in China and about to marry a Chinese leader, appreciate her reference?

"Anyu, there you are! I was looking for you."

Isaac appeared by her side. He looked hot, his face glittering; near him was Mrs. Brown, followed by another group of journalists with cameras.

"Mrs. Brown—"

"Come, darling. I'm dying to take a picture with you." The lady leaned over, the edge of her tiara grazing Anyu's ear.

Anyu barely had time to say anything else before the cameras flashed, and a chorus of voices exploded.

"Miss Anyu, where did you receive your inspiration for the bird?"

"Miss Anyu? Miss Anyu, what's your surname?"

"Miss Anyu, you're not from Shanghai, I can tell. Where are you from?"

"Miss Anyu, you look so young. How old are you?"

She looked at Isaac, caught off guard, unsure about the attention and questions.

"It'll be an honor, Mrs. Brown, if you could tell her personally," Isaac said.

Mrs. Brown's eyes widened. "Darling, I just made the announcement. Perhaps you missed it. You're the winner of the competition."

"I beg your pardon?"

"I'll be in touch with Isaac about the details, but yes, darling. I've been notified by the generalissimo's assistant. The generalissimo and Miss Soong have chosen your rising phoenix as their wedding gift. They have offered to purchase your brooch."

A wave of blazing flashes blinded her. All Anyu could see were the curious looks in women's eyes and the disbelieving stares from men. Anyu turned to Isaac, his figure a strip of polished metal. She began to tremble, and she wanted to ask Isaac again if this was true or if she was dreaming. Her second design had won the top prize. How was this real? But Mrs. Brown was still standing next to her, and the journalists were still asking her questions, and there, she saw her phoenix, displayed in a vitrine near the stage.

A round of thunderous applause burst around her, the cameras, diamonds, and colorful dresses fusing together; she felt dizzy in the spotlight. This was not what she had imagined—it was better than she had imagined. It was wonderful to be seen, to be recognized, to have accomplished something akin to a dream.

She couldn't remember how she came to stand beside the vitrine, how many people congratulated her, or what she replied. For hours, she stood in front of the cameras, facing people, smiling at the renowned jewelers whose designs she had defeated. She thought she had seen so much, yet so little. She felt like a fraud. Did they believe she was the jeweler? A master jeweler?

"Congratulations, master jeweler," Isaac said.

Anyu smiled. She would have kissed him, if it weren't for the crowd around her, the journalists, and the cameras. She was euphoric, drunk with success.

It was a moment that would change her life, a moment that cemented her new status in the city as a rising star craftsman, a moment that she'd relish and revisit countless times for many days and months. And rightly so. But she would have felt differently had she known what was ahead of her: a new life.

CHAPTER 18

That evening, when Anyu arrived home, she was engulfed again by the wave of euphoria. Everyone was elated; the small kitchen was crammed—Esther hugging her, Uncle David grinning, agog at the phoenix's sale for one thousand dollars, Isaac beaming, and the two aunts clapping their hands like children. Even Samuel, in a magnanimous way, smiled at her warmly and patted her on the back.

The entire family celebrated, sharing a lavish meal of roasted chicken, garlic bread, and borscht with heaps of cabbage. Uncle David produced a bottle of whiskey, poured it into the bowls since they didn't have glasses, and shouted, *"L'chayim!"*

Anyu finished the alcohol in three gulps; it rushed down her throat and made her giddy. She began to cough, but she liked it, all of it, the taste of alcohol, the chicken, the toast, and the Mandelburgs, their eyes brimming with joy. She had brought this to them, this happiness, this turn of fortune, and she was glad and proud. And she realized this was what she had wished for all along: to be accepted, to make them happy, and to genuinely be a part of their lives.

When she came to this apartment at sixteen, lost, drifting like snow, she had wondered if she could ever find a place to stay. And now she knew where she belonged.

୵ஂ

The next day, more good news arrived. Esther woke Anyu and showed her a stack of newspapers printed with huge photos of her and Mrs. Brown. Still half-asleep, Anyu read the headlines announcing her as the winner of the prestigious jewelry competition. The articles lauded her talent, awed at her young age—eighteen—empathetic that she was an orphan, and predicted, without reservation, that as the youngest jeweler, a girl who had won a major award, a Chinese jeweler who had designed the brooch for the generalissimo and his fiancée, she would have the Midas touch and everything she designed would sell.

She laughed. Fame—to be known, to be praised and worshipped. It was such a wonderful feeling. She was no longer a nameless orphan.

And then the newspaper's prediction came true—for the next five days, the showroom was packed with customers looking for the jewelry she designed and customers eager to place commissions: a commission from Liza Hardoon to make twenty-two Buddha pendant necklaces for her twenty-two adopted children, a commission from a Chinese diplomat's wife, a movie star, a British consul, an Italian naval officer, and even the head of the French Concession, who Isaac said had been Bellefeuille's client.

All the jewelry pieces Isaac designed were sold, too. The orders were accepted with a completion date six months out.

Then the payment of the brooch arrived. One thousand dollars! The profit lifted everyone's spirits. Isaac bought her a new workbench, believing that as a master jeweler, she should have her own workstation, and placed it right next to his. Uncle David said she was no longer required to work at the counter and promptly paid her a wage as a jeweler—ten dollars.

Ten dollars a month! How would she be able to spend it all! She sat at her workbench that was the right height for her. She could work and sleep here and never leave the workshop again.

With a whopping nineteen dollars in her pocket, Anyu took Esther to a tailor's shop in the Settlement and asked her to pick out any dress she liked. Esther's face lit up. They spent four hours in that shop, and afterward Anyu stopped at a bookstore, where she bought a Webster's dictionary and put it in Esther's hands.

Then, one afternoon, Anyu was crafting one of the Buddha pendants when Isaac asked her to accompany him.

"Where are we going?"

His voice was low. "The Vault of Gems and Treasures."

Her heart stopped for a few beats at the thought of what he would show her.

They took a taxi to the riverfront of the Huangpu River, passed a checkpoint, and got out at a wharf across from the nearly completed, towering Sassoon House, an immense nine-story Art Deco complex, its unique emerald-green rooftop glowing in the fading afternoon sunlight. Walking along the Huangpu River, they went down to an underpass and climbed a flight of stone steps to ground level.

The sun had gone down; darkness was descending rapidly. The towering elms and oaks swayed in the wind.

"This way." Isaac directed her to a pebble path lined with red brick buildings—a shopping center, it seemed—and then they arrived at a two-story shop selling cutlery with a "Closed" sign.

Isaac knocked; an Indian man wearing a brown turban opened the door just a crack.

"Which type of quartz is most valuable, rose quartz or smoky quartz?" he asked.

"Neither. Amethyst is known to be the most valuable and most popular quartz," Isaac replied.

The man glanced at her, hesitated, and opened the door to let them in. The shop was faintly lit by a lamp on the counter; there were rows of knives with curved edges like daggers lined on the wall, and silverware, serving trays, and candleholders displayed on the shelves. No chopsticks. This shop only served foreign customers, it appeared, but Anyu had a hunch it didn't serve anyone at all.

"Would you prefer knives of gold, platinum, sterling silver, or stainless steel, sir?" the man asked, his hands folded behind his back. He was armed with a pistol.

"Platinum."

The man stepped aside, and Isaac walked toward the wall with knives. He took hold of a knife's ivory hilt and turned. The wall swung to the side, revealing a hidden space behind it. Surprised, Anyu looked at Isaac, who smiled and gestured for her to enter. The moment she walked in, the wall slid shut behind them.

She was standing in a garden encircled by four walls draped with vines. In the fading light, she could see a bronze statue standing on an ivory pedestal in the center.

"The Goddess of Peace, designed by a well-known architect," Isaac said.

The Goddess had a long, slender body, a double-headed eagle perched on her right arm. "It's beautiful. But where's the vault?"

"Just a minute." Isaac raised his right hand with his moonstone cabochon ring and pressed the side of the ring with his other hand, and to Anyu's amazement, the cabochon lifted to reveal an image of a double-headed eagle, similar to the one on the Goddess's arm. He placed the eagle against the hollow of the Goddess's hand, fitting it like a key in a lock, and the hand lifted. The ivory pedestal glided to the side, showing a flight of dark stairs underneath.

Anyu gasped.

"Come in." Isaac waved and went down the stairs.

Anyu followed inside. She could see a long, dark passage in front of her, with two electric lamps flickering at the other end. "Where are we?"

"You'll see." Isaac's voice echoed.

Eventually, she arrived at a tall atrium illuminated by some electric sconces on the wall. Isaac came to a door and placed his ring on a brass plaque on the doorpost. The door slid open.

A secret room.

"Welcome to the Vault of Gems and Treasures," Isaac said.

Anyu blinked and entered the room, which was shaped like a narrow train, with sculptures in four corners and hexagon-shaped crystal boxes on shelves built into the walls. Bathed in the sconces' light, they glowed like a golden beehive. Awed by the sight, she stared at the boxes as if in a trance.

The crystal box near her held an enormous diamond rondelle, which must have weighed two hundred carats, multifaceted, with flawless clarity, dazzling with a bluish-greenish hue. A placard under the rondelle said that this diamond bore a striking resemblance to the Orlov Diamond, the diamond the Russian count Grigory Orlov gave to his lover, Empress Catherine the Great.

Next to it was a lavish filigree gold crown worn by Mumtaz Mahal, a Persian princess, the beloved wife of Mughal emperor Shah Jahān, who built one of the wonders of the world to honor her after her death, the white marble Taj Mahal.

Then an Edwardian necklace with a huge rose-cut diamond that was said to have belonged to Queen Elizabeth I. And a platinum necklace with the Maximilian Diamond, a thirty-three-carat lime-yellow cushion cut with astounding fluorescence, one of the two diamonds owned by Archduke Ferdinand Maximilian Joseph.

And more: an antique Tiffany necklace made in 1870, featuring intricate filigree work and granulation; a diamond canopy that was said to be part of the Peacock Throne created for the Mughal court in India; a Māori jadeite amulet from the seventeenth century; a seahorse in precious yellow jade hand-carved by a sixteen-year-old girl in Thailand.

And there, the splendid Alexander III Commemorative Egg, encrusted with rows of rose-cut diamonds strung together like beads.

Anyu had a hard time believing her eyes. "Are these treasures real?"

"Yes."

"What is this place?"

"I told you, the Vault of Gems and Treasures."

"I can't believe such a vault exists. Who owns it?"

"The one and only Workmasters Guild."

"The Guild?"

"When Fabergé hired the workmasters to create the eggs in the late nineteenth century, they faced fierce competition among themselves. Some were accused of greed, and some plots were carried out to harm our families. To avoid more loss and to protect their craft and gemstones, they founded a guild. They forged a strong bond over the years and built a vast influential network in Russia and Europe. With their access to diamonds and gold deposits, they developed ties with diamond cutters, gemologists, collectors, and even royalty from various countries."

The Workmasters Guild.

"How did they have access to the diamonds in Russia?"

"It is complicated. Many jewelers are aware of the diamond mines in South Africa; few people know that Russia has a number of diamond mines and gold deposits in the Urals and Siberia. As a matter of fact, one of the diamond mines in the Urals is known as the largest precious gemstone mine in the world. The workmasters had direct access to the mines, and they used these stones to craft jewelry for the imperial family. They also built a great reputation and established many channels and back doors to dealers, suppliers, and diamond magnates across the world. At the height of the Guild, we controlled ninety percent of the diamonds sold in Russia and Europe."

Diamond mines and gold deposits. Anyu had to take a moment to digest what she heard. "How did all the treasure end up here?"

"After the revolution, the workmasters were targeted by the rebels. Many were imprisoned or murdered. Some fled to Finland and England, and a few to Asia. We brought whatever we could carry."

Isaac was a member of the secret Workmasters Guild, Anyu realized. She scanned the treasures again, each worth the price of a small kingdom, encased in a crystal box, hidden underground. "Where's your egg?"

"Here." Isaac walked to a crystal box to her left and pressed his moonstone ring to reveal the eagle again.

"Why the double-headed eagle?" she asked.

"It came from the Romanov family's coat of arms, adopted by the imperial family in the fifteenth century. The workmasters revered the tsar but didn't want to violate the crest. They designed a simpler version of the two-headed eagle without the crown and religious connotations."

"Do all members of the Guild wear the ring?"

Isaac nodded. "There were forty-two rings for forty-two workmasters. The signet ring was designed to be inconspicuous but also identifiable. I received this from my father."

He held the ring and fitted it into the brass plaque that said "The Winter Egg." The box collapsed; in front of Anyu was the beauty that she had dreamed of seeing since she had first laid eyes on it. With his gloved hand, Isaac delicately lifted the egg. "Ready?"

She hastened to dig out her handkerchief and opened her palms as Isaac placed the egg in her hands. It felt heavier than she remembered, and the egg's surface, through her handkerchief, was smooth. She admired the rivulets of brilliant diamonds, the surprise inside—an exquisite basket of flowers. She cradled it gently, afraid that she'd drop it or tarnish it with her breath.

The egg that had inspired her, the egg that she had worked hard for all these months, the egg that had brought her to Isaac, the egg that had changed her life.

"Well?" Isaac asked.

"It's magnificent."

"But?"

"I can make something like that."

He laughed.

Giving the egg one last look, she handed it to him.

He shook his head. "It's yours now."

She stared at him. "Mine?"

"Yes."

"You're giving me this priceless egg? Why?"

"Years ago, I told myself I would give my successor the egg. I've been looking for a successor for ten years. I think I've found her."

He would honor her, naming her as his successor. Anyu's heart fluttered. "I don't know what to say . . . Does that mean I'll keep making jewelry for you? The egg . . . I don't know if I am worthy . . . What about Samuel?"

"You've proven yourself, Anyu. You are God's special gift to me."

Did she imagine this—his soft tone, the adoration in his eyes? Her heart pounded in a strange rhythm of happiness. "Isaac . . ."

"You asked me once how I felt about relinquishing my name. I think I told you fame means little to me. I only want to craft jewelry in peace."

But still. This was a huge sacrifice.

"When this egg was placed in my hands years ago, I swore I'd protect it with my life. It's time to find a new owner. But I'd be remiss if I didn't disclose the risk that comes with the ownership of the egg. Men have the natural tendency to possess a treasure, and those with more means have fewer scruples. It is dangerous to possess a prize everyone covets. You're probably aware of that, too. I understand if you decline my proposition."

"Decline? No."

He smiled.

"I'm not afraid." She gazed at him, thinking of how they met, the blood on his neck, and the gossip they had overheard at Mrs. Brown's party. "I give you my word. I will protect the egg and the reputation of your family with my life."

"Then my mission is accomplished."

"You won't be disappointed. This egg will be as safe as it can be."

"Now what would you like to do? You can take it with you or store it elsewhere to keep it safe."

She looked around her again. "How safe is this vault?"

"Very safe. You saw the man in the store, one of a team of twelve men who guard this place day and night. The crystal box is nearly indestructible and is only operable by the owner's signet ring."

She returned the egg to the box and slid the box back into the wall. "Then I'll keep it here. I'll come to see it when I need to."

"Well then, you'll need the key." He removed his ring and slid it onto the middle finger of her right hand. It was loose, but it stayed.

Anyu lifted her head, shocked. "You said this ring was for members of the Guild."

"Yes, and now you're one of them."

"What about you?"

"I'll cease to be a member. The Guild has strict rules. Its membership is only transferable from one master jeweler to another. My father gave it to me, and now I give it to you. From now on, you'll be the member, not me."

She smoothed her finger over the moonstone and found the narrow swath built inside the ring's band that concealed the double-headed eagle. She marveled at the mechanism. "It's a cleverly crafted piece."

"It is."

"As your successor, I am honored to wear this ring." She leaned forward and locked the box.

"There's one more thing. My appointing you to be a member of the Guild is the first step. You'll still have to earn the approval of other members."

"Other members?"

"Yes. There are four of them who currently live in Shanghai. Including one original member who fled from St. Petersburg."

"I'll talk to them. Where are they?"

"As a matter of fact, they are attending their monthly meeting here."

"I'd like to meet them."

CHAPTER 19

Who were the members of the Guild? Anyu wondered, walking beside Isaac down the train-shaped hall. They arrived at a dark oak door, and she stopped and fitted her ring into another brass plaque as Isaac instructed. It opened, and she stepped into what looked to be a lounge furnished with sofas and tables. Four people sat there, studying a tray of diamonds on a coffee table. She recognized one of them.

Mrs. Brown. She was not wearing her tiara or her gloves, and Anyu noticed her signet ring, a plain gold ring with a moonstone cabochon on her middle finger, identical to Isaac's. "Miss Anyu, I see you made it here. Please come and join us."

"Mrs. Brown," Anyu said. "I didn't realize you were a member. I thought Mr. Walters was a member."

"He works for the Guild." Mrs. Brown introduced her to the three men at the table: Mr. Petrov, a man in his sixties, dressed in a black tuxedo and a top hat; Mr. Lebedev, a middle-aged man wearing a suit in a fire opal color, a matching hat, and matching leather shoes; and Mr. Tang, an old man with his arm in a sling.

Mr. Petrov, Isaac added, was an original member of the Guild, the oldest surviving workmaster as far as they knew. The rest of the Guild were presumed dead, their rings lost.

Anyu remembered their faces. She had met them at Mrs. Brown's soiree. They looked rather haughty, studying her in silence.

Finally, Mr. Tang said, "She's only a kid."

"She's eighteen," Isaac said.

"And she thinks she deserves to be here," Mr. Tang said.

"Yes, I do," Anyu said.

Mrs. Brown raised her eyebrows.

"I do, too," Isaac said. "I wouldn't have chosen her as my successor otherwise."

"We've already had one woman, our leader, no less," Mr. Petrov, the oldest member, said in Russian. "Must we accept another one? The original Workmasters Guild only had men, who were required to be master jewelers."

"Must we bring this up again, Mr. Petrov?" Mr. Lebedev, the man in the matching fire opal outfit, sighed. "Mrs. Brown may not be a jeweler, or a master jeweler, for that matter, but she's a capable leader. Thanks to her, we're doing well in Shanghai."

"I didn't say Mrs. Brown shouldn't lead us because she's not a master jeweler."

"You've been implying that for four years, Mr. Petrov," Mr. Lebedev said.

"All I mean is that the rule of the Guild was broken when Mr. Brown died, and it's our responsibility to honor it moving forward. Are we going to?"

"I kindly request you, gentlemen, to save small talk for later and make a decision." Mrs. Brown looked unfazed. "Isaac has appointed his successor and asked to transfer his membership. Do you accept his appointee or object? Raise your hand if you accept."

"Before you object," Anyu said. "I just want to gently remind you that the Workmasters Guild, despite their best intentions, never predicted the exit from Russia. And yet, here you are, in a different country—such are the unpredictable turns of life. As for me, I am young, yes, but I'm also a talented master jeweler. I hope my age doesn't count against me."

There was a long silence; Mr. Petrov was frowning, and so was Mr. Tang. Mr. Lebedev looked at her curiously.

"You heard her. And?" Mrs. Brown asked.

A hand was raised—Mr. Lebedev's, and then Mr. Tang's. Everyone turned to Mr. Petrov.

"What are we getting here? She's not going to give up, is she?" Mr. Petrov sighed and raised his hand.

"Very well, then. I appreciate your vote. We're all grateful for Isaac's dedication to this Guild, and we're sorry we won't see him in this place again. Miss Anyu, welcome to the Guild. We're delighted to have you as one of our members," Mrs. Brown said.

Mr. Lebedev said, "Did Isaac tell you about our Guild? As a member, you'll learn the code for meetings and the ethics of the Guild. You are entitled to borrow the gemstones and gold and other minerals at a discount. So you see, you join the Guild as a jeweler, but you'll be backed by a huge network linked to the collectors, dealers, diamond mine owners, and the elite of society."

Anyu nodded. "What is my responsibility to the Guild?"

"There are no responsibilities; there are only benefits. However, there's one binding oath we'd like to request from you."

"What is it?"

Mrs. Brown said, "You must never tell anyone it exists."

Anyu looked at the ring on her finger. "You have my oath."

Later, Anyu and Isaac stepped out of the tunnel and into the garden with the Goddess of Peace. The garden was submerged in darkness; by the faint moonlight, she could see the walls of the courtyard and the shop, lit by a single lamp near the window.

The wind blew in her face. She sat on the plinth of the statue and felt the statue's hard ivory press against the small of her back. It was late, but she didn't want to go anywhere, fueled by something inexplicable. She couldn't help thinking that she had been only a girl living by a train station and an orphan when she came to Shanghai, and now she was a master jeweler, the protector of a priceless egg, a member of a secret group. She would never have imagined such a life; she felt as if reborn.

"When we return to the workshop, you can resize your ring." Isaac sat next to her.

In the dark, she couldn't see his face. "Does anyone else know about the vault?"

"No."

"Not even Esther, Uncle David, or Samuel?"

"They know about the egg but not the Guild."

"What will you do now that you're no longer a member?"

"I won't attend any more meetings or come to this place, but the Guild will have my loyalty until my last breath."

She chuckled. "What guild? It doesn't exist."

"Indeed." He laughed.

"I still can't believe you'd give me the treasure."

"But my dear Anyu, you are the most precious treasure of all."

She turned to him and did something she had never done before, something she had longed for during all these months—she reached out to hold his hand. For a brief and thrilling moment, she felt his skin, warm, dry, calloused, his strong fingers lingering, encircling hers. Her heart swelled with happiness. Now she was holding his hand. Would he kiss her? She was a master jeweler of the House of Mandelburg, but she was his.

There was a moment of silence. "Are you cold, Anyu?"

"No, yes, no. No."

He struggled for words, his silhouette a dark muse, and then he said, "I want you to know you're an extraordinary girl, Anyu. I've never met someone like you, and I'm proud of your accomplishment."

"I love you."

There. She said it. And she was glad. She had loved his smile, loved the way he looked at her, the way he took out his loupe and studied the designs. She loved him, for no one had loved her the way he loved her, and no one else would.

"Let's go home, shall we?"

His fingers slipped away, and for a long, cold moment, she held nothing. Confused, she didn't ask, but for the next two years, waiting with hope, her eyes tracing his arched back, her lips waiting for the kisses that never came, she wished she had asked: *Do you love me?*

CHAPTER 20

November 1929

At twenty, Anyu had won the annual jewelry competition for three consecutive years; she was the youngest female jeweler in Shanghai and had designed and delivered many pieces of jewelry for the cream of high society in the city. Her clientele increased at a steady pace, including compradors who made vast fortunes at the Bank of Shanghai, wives of Chinese diplomats, daughters of real estate moguls, and mistresses of American, French, and British entrepreneurs. She had well-known local clients as well—the famed opera singer Mei Lanfang, the rising movie star Ruan Lingyu, and many more.

She asked to meet all her clients in person in the shop, where she took the measurements of their necks and hands and sketched the pieces before finalizing a design. The purpose of jewelry, she believed, was to express a woman's taste, to highlight her fine features, and to accentuate her beauty. A woman's jewelry was personal.

And her attention to detail was praised all over Shanghai; she was extolled for her talent and unique creations, and with her fame came more commissions. In two years, the jewelry made by the House of Mandelburg became a desired commodity in Shanghai.

With the rising profits the House made, Uncle David considered moving into a bigger, more comfortable apartment, but he quickly realized it was risky as Mr. Du sent word that extra men had to be sent to watch his shop due to heavy traffic, and the protection fees increased tenfold. Realizing their relocation would be perceived as flaunting their wealth, Uncle David decided to stay where they were. As an alternative, Uncle David offered to renovate the attic and partition it to improve Anyu's living conditions and give her more privacy, but Anyu declined. She was used to the company of the women, and she liked the attic the way it was. She did accept a new bed for herself next to Esther's.

The Guild kept its word; Mr. Walters delivered a generous selection of gemstones, agate, garnet, lapis lazuli, and opal at her request. Sometimes, she visited the vault to admire the Winter Egg. Being in its close vicinity calmed her; sometimes, wearing a glove, she lifted the egg and studied its fine features. She could replicate it, but there would always be one singular Winter Egg.

Her social life became busy. Mr. Morris requested an interview for his newspaper. Organizations invited her to attend fashion shows, opera debuts, movie premieres, anniversary parties, and jubilees. There was even a flower delivery with a note from Pierre Bellefeuille, who requested dinner with her.

She chose to attend several parties and always invited Esther, who bemoaned her lack of a social life, to accompany her. Esther was twenty-seven, rapidly turning into a spinster, so she said. With these parties, Anyu hoped Esther could cast a wider net and find an ideal husband.

Dressed in long gowns handpicked by Esther, who prided herself on her good taste, Anyu and Esther visited the peculiar British clients in teahouses where white-powdered Japanese geishas performed their dances. They went to a two-story casino in the Settlement and sat at the roulette table while the gray-haired tycoons gambled; they waited in a drawing room with black walls in a mansion rumored to be haunted by vengeful ghosts; they drank gin and soda in a nightclub where wealthy young men paid ten pennies to dance the Charleston with lace-jabot-wearing White Russian women who were said to be former viscountesses and countesses.

Anyu learned to smoke cigarettes, which helped her concentrate, and she often chain-smoked packets of cigarettes in order to work for ten hours straight.

She also befriended her fans, some wealthy Chinese youths with Western educations who shunned the traditional, restrictive Chinese culture. They had drinking bouts to test their alcohol tolerance, and once, when she took off her glove to clean spilled wine, exposing her hand by mistake, they examined her hand with admiration—the scars from cuts, the thick welts from a blowtorch, the calluses on her fingertips, and the blackened stub where her pinkie used to be.

One of the youths, whose father was a wealthy silk merchant in Shanghai, invited her to his private chambers covered with cushions and pillows and offered long wooden pipes to smoke high-quality opium—the Great Smoke. She was curious to try and was appeased by the calming sensation that coursed through her veins. When she awoke, it was five days later.

She learned to decline those opium trips, but the talks with the *taitais*, the wealthy wives of the tycoons, were difficult to avoid. Meandering along the narrow paths in their private gardens with half-moon-shaped bridges, sitting with a gaggle of children playing on wooden horses, and watching silk-clad girls bowing and pouring tea for their elders in a shockingly pious manner, she realized the inadequacy of her grace and refinement and her utter lack of social aptitude and obedience.

Some of the women probed her about her parentage. *An orphan,* they'd respond with a dramatic intake of breath. *You poor thing.*

Then, *Are you married? No? You're twenty years old. Shouldn't you start a family?*

Sometimes, these talks exhausted her, and she grew bad-tempered—convinced that her mother, by choosing to live apart from her family, had robbed her of the companionship, the noisy messiness of an extended family, and the teachings of tradition and values upheld by many; sometimes, she wished her mother had found a way to reunite with the warlord.

Then, at a high-profile party attended by some Nationalist officials and their wives, she came across the Young Marshal, the son of the warlord Zhang from Manchuria, in a cigar room at a party. It had been eighteen months since Warlord Zhang's assassination, which the newspapers said was engineered by the Japanese Kwantung Army. The Young Marshal had inherited his father's armies and vowed to avenge his father's death.

He was a tall man with a long face and a straight nose. But they had the same eyes—the peach blossom–shaped eyes.

"I'm also from Harbin," Anyu said. She was only chatting with a military man, not a blood relative, and she wasn't expecting anything else, she told herself.

The Young Marshal, who was eight years older than her, nodded. "Your homeland is proud of you, Miss Anyu."

"Do you like to eat silkworm pupae, too? Warlord Zhang was very fond of them," she said casually. But if the Young Marshal was aware of her eyes, he would be intrigued.

"It's a delicacy."

"I wonder if this sounds strange to you. A girl I used to know kept a necklace with a Guandi pendant. She said your father bestowed that on her mother."

The Young Marshal puffed out some smoke. "Does she still have the necklace?"

"I don't believe so. She pawned it. Was the necklace special?"

"It's my father's folly. Whenever he was involved with a woman, he gave her a necklace with our family's god-of-war emblem and told her to go away. Those women were attracted to my father's power like a moth to candlelight. Who knows how many were only too happy to sleep with him, bear him children, and try to extort him. They are nothing to my family."

They are nothing to my family. The sentence rang in her ears long after she left the party. She might be the warlord's illegitimate child, but she was the Young Marshal's threat. Her existence was taboo, a mockery; she would never be part of the Zhang family.

Her mother was not given a choice, she realized, and her childhood had been a gift, after all—her sequestered life at the train station had allowed her to become a woman of her own without the fetters of tradition or the ties of family. From now on, her life was hers, hers alone; she would build her future, and her own family.

As always, she thought of Isaac.

CHAPTER 21

July 1930

She barely saw him anymore, only in the workshop where they could have some companionship, him striking the anvil and her grinding the dry flux in the mortar. As usual, they seldom talked, passing the gold wires and silver sheets without the need for a word; it was all comforting and assuring, but something was missing, something she couldn't identify, only a feeling—it was as if they were separate wires that couldn't be joined.

And when she invited him to parties and banquets, Isaac declined. These social calls were vital for Esther to make eligible matches, and he would be an unwelcome chaperone. Besides, his time for socializing was limited, given his commitment to design and jewelry making.

Isaac was, indeed, busy; with the flood of commissions, the House of Mandelburg had ascended to be one of the top jewelers in Shanghai, and he rarely left the workshop. But she couldn't help noticing that even though his relationship with the Guild had ended, he kept in close touch with the tiara-wearing Mrs. Brown. Without fail, Mrs. Brown, in her extravagant dress, came to pick up Isaac in her black Rolls-Royce with leather seats. They seemed compatible, a decent couple, and it made Anyu feel queasy.

❧

One evening, Isaac left the workshop after the store closed. Anyu couldn't concentrate on her work. She went out to the showroom. On the street, Mrs. Brown's black Rolls-Royce was just leaving.

Anyu went back to the workshop, where Samuel and Uncle David crouched at their workbenches. She picked up the tweezers but realized what she needed was a pair of pliers. Then she let the gemstones slip from her grip, misaligned, and even lost track of the next step. She felt utterly despondent. She couldn't recall the last time she had talked to Isaac alone; she missed him.

She went to the attic. Esther was peeling off her working dress and changing into her new dress, a pink sequined gown.

"Are you going out?"

"Yes, I have a dinner with Mr. Dearborn." Mr. Dearborn was an American merchant from Boston whom Esther had met at a party. Anyu vaguely recalled a heavyset man with a chivalric air. "Will you join us?"

Anyu shook her head and looked at the stack of invitations on the desk near the lamp. They were all from Pierre Bellefeuille, the owner of the House of Bellefeuille, the man who had chatted with her at the competition. Anyu remembered his handsome face, his flirtatious manner, and his sophisticated *fleur-de-lis* jewelry designs.

"He's a persistent man, Monsieur Bellefeuille," Esther said. "Are you going to reply?"

"No. Not interested. Do you know where your father is going?"

"He didn't tell me."

"I think he's out with Mrs. Brown again."

"They do spend a lot of time together." Esther turned to her. "How do I look?"

Esther's face was powdered, her cherry-red lips full, and the pink dress hugged her hips and breasts. By the light from the window, Esther's beauty was stunning. "You are beautiful."

"You like it? Good. Well, I don't know. What do you think about the white dress?"

"You look great in this one, Esther."

"I'm nervous. I really like him. I've been thinking about him all day at the counter! Silly me. I think he likes me, too. He might ask me to marry him, you never know," Esther said, examining her hair, and went on to say Mr. Dearborn had rented an apartment and opened a tobacco shop near the racecourse. He planned to stay in Shanghai.

It looked promising that this romance would have a happy ending, and Esther would find a husband who would give her security. "That's wonderful, Esther. Your father will love it."

"No, he won't. Patrick is a gentile."

"A gentile?"

"He's not Jewish, but I don't care. He's a true gentleman. I'd like you to have dinner with us and get to know him. Will you come?"

"Next time. I need to work tonight."

Esther studied her. "Are you sick, Anyu?"

"I'm fine. I'm going to work now."

Anyu went down the staircase; from the workshop came the heavy thud of a hammer striking the anvil and Samuel's voice. She turned back to the attic. "All right. I'll meet your man. Where are you having dinner?"

"At the Majestic Hotel," Esther said and ran her hands through her long blond curls again. She was rapidly becoming an old woman, as she said, but looked girlish, and nervous.

This was how love and marriage could change a woman, Anyu thought. She wanted to get married, too. She had met many men at parties and meetings, but still, the only person she had feelings for was Isaac.

Mr. Dearborn greeted them at the grand entrance to the Majestic Hotel, a luxurious hotel in Shanghai. He was a man in his thirties, wearing a fedora and a blue suit. He had a round face, blue eyes, and a nose shaped like a cigar. He nodded politely, took Esther's gloved hand, kissed it, and wouldn't let it go. And Esther leaned over him, giggling.

Neither of them paid Anyu attention after that, and Anyu walked behind them, passing the lavish flower bouquets, wicker chairs, and leather chesterfields, foreign women wearing summer dresses and sequined gowns, and men holding champagne flutes and smoking cigarettes. After two years of banquets and parties, she had learned to dress better, wearing a long silk gown embroidered with pink primroses, but she still didn't feel accustomed to this life of leisure and luxury. Designing and crafting was all she wanted to do.

Suddenly, Anyu felt lonely. She had never dined in a hotel with the man she loved and had never had a chance to kiss him. What would it be like to dine with Isaac at a fine hotel? Would Isaac ever kiss her?

Esther and Mr. Dearborn were glued together on a sofa in the grand ballroom that could host more than one thousand guests, and Anyu sat on a tufted chair with nothing to do. The hotel was a property of Horace Kadoorie, one of her clients, and it was enormous. The air was intoxicatingly sweet, scented with fragrance, and alight with mellow musical notes. Esther and Mr. Dearborn whispered in each other's ears, immersed in their mutual adoration. Anyu opted to attack the food instead—Mr. Dearborn had generously ordered enough food for one hundred people—golden pastries glistening with jam, sliced beef, a whole roasted chicken, a mountain of greens, apples, and bananas. And drinks! The hotel offered free gin and whiskey, Mr. Dearborn had said.

"What do you think?" Esther asked, her face flushed, when Mr. Dearborn took his leave to use the men's room.

"You're right. He seems like a true gentleman."

"He is! He doesn't smile that much, but he does smile! And Patrick is very smart. He loves whiskey and a special type of food called pie. Boston cream pie, or is it American pie? Boston cream pie, yes. I think that's the name. He said he'd install an oven if I learn to bake."

"Is he going to propose to you today?"

"Today?" Esther held a glass of whiskey and gulped it down. "From your lips to God's ears!"

When Mr. Dearborn returned, Anyu made an excuse to leave to give the couple space. She walked down a corridor decorated with fresh azaleas and daisies and passed a garden with a menagerie of statues in ivory and brass. Soft music came from the back of the hotel; she stopped to observe. Under an arbor festooned with lights and flowers, many guests dined at tables draped in white cloths. Near a trellis with white daylilies, a couple looked familiar; the man wore a black shirt, and he was facing a woman in a golden dress, her hair adorned with a diamond tiara. A few steps behind her were her shadow bodyguards in suits.

Isaac and Mrs. Brown were deep in conversation, unaware of the people around them. The sight prickled her. Anyu was rooted to the ground, livid. It was too much. It should be her sitting there with him in this beautiful garden, listening to music, her, not Mrs. Brown. Isaac loved her. Even though he didn't say it, he had given her the Guild's ring, the egg! He chose her to be his successor! What was he doing with Mrs. Brown?

Her eyes on Isaac, Anyu rushed to the magnolia tree on a terrace near them, ready to confront them both. Then she heard Mrs. Brown's voice:

"You've done enough, Isaac."

"I don't know," Isaac said.

"How old is she? Nineteen? Twenty? She's very popular; many people like her."

"She doesn't notice."

"You don't need me to tell you what's going on, Isaac. We both know where her heart is."

Isaac rubbed his face and raised his head. His gaze met Anyu's.

Anyu froze, then turned around and quickly walked away. Isaac followed her; she could hear him. Near a marble statue, she stopped. She could hardly find words to say, choked with anger.

"Anyu, I didn't know you were here." He walked to her.

"I came with Esther," she said.

"What a coincidence."

She glanced at Mrs. Brown, who sat at the table and watched them. She didn't smile; the diamonds on her hair blazed. There was this placidness on her face under the light, and she seemed to say, *Who do you think you are?*

"Will you have dinner with me, Isaac?"

He cleared his throat.

"Why not? Why Mrs. Brown and not me?"

"Mrs. Brown and I are complicated. We have a long relationship. We met before you arrived in Shanghai."

"But I told you. I love you."

He looked down. "I'm very proud of you, Anyu, for your brilliant work. You revived the shop's business. You're young, talented, hardworking. You love your clients and are loved by your clients. I'm lucky to have you as my successor."

There. Plain. Businesslike. Just as he had told her last time. But she couldn't live with that. This was not good enough. "That's it?"

"It's better this way."

"What do you mean 'better this way'?"

"A man must not be greedy."

She shook her head. "I don't understand riddles. Why don't you tell me what's on your mind?"

His eyes glittered in the light. "Anyu, a romantic affair between us will not end well, for you and me."

She didn't want to hear any more. She turned around; the sleeve of her dress snagged on something and ripped. The sharp sound reverberated in the air, and the guests turned to look at her.

Anyu kept her head up and picked her way out of the tables; at the edge of the garden, she looked behind. Isaac was not pursuing her.

In the grand ballroom, the band was playing loudly, and Esther and Mr. Dearborn were not at their table. Anyu sank into a divan, shaking in fury. She had to do something or she would scream. She waved a waiter over, ordered a bottle of whiskey, and began to drink.

The sharp note nearly choked her; she coughed. She was not a good drinker, and her anger rose with each swallow. She couldn't understand it. Isaac had trained her and chosen her as his successor, but why not marriage? She had elevated his shop's reputation, and she would have done anything she could to be with him, to be his. Why would he turn his back on her? Did she mean anything to him? Did he care about her at all? How could he do this to her?

One glass and another. Her vision blurred, her head pounded with alcohol, with fury, and she ordered another bottle of whiskey as a thought jumped into her mind. She would not accept this humiliation. If she couldn't be his wife, then she wouldn't be his successor either.

There was a man standing beside her, and she didn't know who it was or how long he had been there. Too blurry. She willed him to walk away so she could be left alone, but he was speaking to her. She blinked, unable to think coherently through the alcohol.

"There, there. Why are you crying, princess?" A hand held her face, a napkin pressed to her cheek. Gently, it dabbed.

She closed her eyes. "I'm not crying."

And then something loosened inside her, and tears fell in a free fall. She leaned against the man's shoulder and wept and wept, until all her anger, jealousy, feelings of abandonment, and sadness poured out.

"Whoever broke your heart is a fool, princess," the man said, stroking her back.

His English had an accent, and he smelled of a spicy scent. She had smelled that before. She blinked to see him better, but her vision was still blurry.

"You don't remember me."

"You are?"

"Monsieur Bellefeuille!" his companion, a woman in a strappy sequined golden dress, complained. He whispered something in her ear, and the woman sashayed away.

"Ah. It's you." She couldn't think straight, but she still remembered how he had flirted with her. He was a talented jeweler, very charismatic. She couldn't say she liked him, but she couldn't say she disliked him either. However, since her winning the awards, Bellefeuille had made some disparaging remarks about Isaac but still flooded the shop with his invitations. He was perhaps the last person she should have a conversation with.

"I have sent you many invitations in hopes that you'd grace my party. But I never received a reply." He inched closer and pressed his body to her.

"I've been busy."

"It appears so. Have you given any thought to my proposal, princess?"

"Pardon me. What proposal?"

"How would you like to work for me?"

"I can't."

"You're a very talented jeweler. The best in Shanghai, as people say. If you work for me, I have no doubt one day you can start your own jewelry brand."

He didn't understand. She was drawn to jewelry making because of Isaac and his egg. Starting her own business had never come to her mind.

"Are you here all by yourself?"

"No. I came here with a friend."

"Isaac Mandelburg?"

It hurt to hear his name. Pierre Bellefeuille had a talent for driving her mad. She rose, splattering the whiskey, searching. "I have to go."

"Where are you going?"

Her head throbbing, she blinked. The annoying French jeweler had asked something most painful. Yes. Where was she going? Where could she go? She had lived with Isaac and his family for more than four years and thought they were her family, yet it had all come down to this: She was wrong. They couldn't be her family, and the shop was not her home.

"I don't know." She rubbed her head. Esther was probably enjoying herself with her lover. She could wait for her to return, and then they could go back to the shop together. But she'd rather not go back.

"If you need a place to stay, I have a guest room. In fact, my chauffeur is waiting outside, and I'm ready to leave. I can give you a ride if you need it."

Anyu held the glass and peered at Monsieur Bellefeuille by the glow of the amber. He knew who she was, so he should have known better that she was not a woman in the notorious Blood Alley. Inebriated, she still had a good head for making sensible decisions. She was still a virgin, and as a child who knew too well of her mother's shame, she had vowed to spend her first night with the man who would be her husband, who, as she had longed for these years, was to be Isaac. And she remembered well, too: *A woman's reputation was like a porcelain vase: once cracked, it could never be fully repaired.*

Shaking her head, Anyu stumbled to the closest table, holding a whiskey bottle to get away from Bellefeuille. She refilled her glass, drained it, and watched the dancers on the parquet floor. The music was loud, her head pounding. Then, through the figures swimming in the light, she spotted Esther holding Mr. Dearborn's hand, turning her head to look for her. She was ready to go to Esther when the trumpet blared and a group of dancers swarmed the floor. Among them were two familiar people, Isaac and Mrs. Brown in the crook of his arm, a compatible, decent couple, smiling, their bodies close to each other.

Anyu felt as though a bucket of cold water had doused her. Isaac had said a romantic affair between them wouldn't end well; it was simply an excuse. He didn't want her. He wanted Mrs. Brown, the tiara-wearing Mrs. Brown, the diamond purveyor, the wealthiest woman in Shanghai.

Anyu stumbled back to the divan, where the French jeweler had sprawled. He stood up and reached out to hold her steady. "You're back, princess."

"Did you say you were about to leave?" she asked.

In Bellefeuille's Citroën, Anyu burst into tears again, drowned in the violent downpour of misery and self-pity and abandonment. She had never thought she was worthless, even as an orphan, but now she thought she might be. Through her tears, she could hear Bellefeuille comforting her—praising her beauty, her talent—and his vow: "I'll never treat you like this. I would never let you cry."

Her tears had dried when Bellefeuille's car stopped in front of a two-story neoclassical building on a street where massive trees loomed. In the bright headlights, Anyu could make out the wine-red French shutters and an arched wrought-iron front door. There would be gossip once she entered a foreign man's house unchaperoned at this hour, she realized, but she was too tired to care. Bellefeuille's arm around hers, her steps unsteady, she wound her way through the marble entryway lined with servants in black livery and stumbled into a grand room at the end of the hallway.

"Here we are," Bellefeuille said.

The bedroom was vast, furnished with elaborate Louis XV furniture and golden silk curtains and a crystal chandelier. There was a four-poster bed with a large nude portrait above the headboard: a young woman, all gold, including her skin, her hair, and her eyelids, lying upside down on a bed of glossy red leaves. The woman was vivid and seductive—her round breasts, her plump thighs, and the faint smile on her face.

"I'd like to be alone," Anyu said, sinking onto a sofa near the paneled wall. She could still barely walk, but she could see the desire in the jeweler's eyes, and it frightened her.

"Of course, but should you need company, I'll be in the living room," Bellefeuille said, but he didn't let her go, his arm encircling her waist, holding her against his body.

"I'm fine, Monsieur Bellefeuille."

"Call me Pierre." Finally, he left the room.

Alone, Anyu sat, holding her head, staring at the nude woman on the wall, her faint smile something like a mockery. She looked like Mrs. Brown, Anyu realized. What was she doing now with Isaac? Dancing? Laughing at her?

Anyu closed her eyes and listened to her breathing. Heavy. Loud. Frantic. Desolate. She wished there were someone to talk to, to complain to; she felt so lonely.

"Oh, my princess. Will this make you feel better?" Bellefeuille appeared, holding a red evening gown. "It's a beautiful dress. I purchased it in Paris. You must put it on. It'll improve your mood."

"I feel better now." She tried to sit up but tripped on the hem of her dress.

He caught her. "Your dress is ripped. Perhaps you'd like to change?"

"There's no need. I need to go."

"Stay, and you can stay for as long as you wish. Come, try it on."

She held the gown, tracing her fingers over the soft fabric. Even through her glove, she could feel its exquisite texture. "It's all right. I don't need—"

He held her hand and took off her glove. Her moonstone ring didn't seem to interest him, but he made a careful examination of her missing finger.

"It's true, you lost your pinkie," he said.

"It was a long time ago."

"A distant memory, then. I hope you've forgotten about it. Let me." He took off her other glove and untied the bow at the back of her dress, which slipped off soundlessly, and then he removed her bra, underwear, stockings, and shoes. He worked in a casual yet focused manner, his hands—soft like an artist's, not a jeweler's—sweeping over her body, and it almost seemed rude to protest, until she finally stood in front of him, naked like the woman in the painting. She couldn't quite understand what was happening and wondered if she should put her clothes back on and leave. But there didn't seem to be a reason to do so. Bellefeuille was kind to her, and Isaac had chosen Mrs. Brown, not her.

"You are beautiful."

She covered her breasts, trembling. What was she doing, she wondered, and there was a voice in her head. *You'll grow up like your mother, a seducer . . .*

"Don't be afraid," he said.

"I'm not." But she was—what was she afraid of? She didn't want to be here, she realized; she didn't want to be with Bellefeuille, a man she hardly knew. But what else could she do?

Bellefeuille fondled her naked shoulders. "I fell in love with you the moment I met you. Did you know? It was three years ago, when you first won the competition and ascended to stardom."

The evening when her world had changed.

"I've been thinking about you ever since. I sent you countless invitations and went to the banquets and parties you attended. I couldn't find you. You tormented me." He kissed her neck, her shoulder, and her arm, his lips soft and full of heat.

She shuddered, frightened but glad—here was a man who wanted her, who loved her at least. "Tormented you?"

"You are so young. You don't know what love is."

For all she could tell, love didn't exist.

"May I take you to the bed?"

She turned to the Louis XV bed; it was enormous, covered with a sea of golden comforters embroidered with starfish and conches and lush pillows decorated with silky frills. It was close, within six or seven steps perhaps. How did she get herself so close to his bed?

He lifted her instead, his arms firm around her body. Then he put her down on the bed. She sat on the edge, feeling the cool silk under her. Did she want this? Did she want to walk away? She didn't know. But she understood if she lay down, she wouldn't be able to get up again.

Should she get up?

"I'm in love with you, *ma chérie*." He was kissing her again, caressing her face, her breasts, and her thighs. "You're beautiful, my beautiful princess. Would you like to lie down?"

Could she afford this? After this, she was going to fall apart, vanish, and change into another woman. Yet she was lost and no longer wanted to know who she was.

She lay down.

CHAPTER 22

Many years later, Anyu wondered what would have happened to her life had she simply done this: What if she had drunk less? What if she had swallowed her pride, forgotten about Isaac's rejection, and returned to the shop with Esther, pretending nothing had happened? What if she had known love was not about revenge, nor about possession, nor about dignity? Love, as she would learn later, was about letting it go.

But these thoughts were not on her mind when she awoke the following day, engulfed in a blaze of silver sunlight permeated with a clotting smell of fragrance. There was no rhythmic breathing from Esther, or the whir of gnats and flies in the attic, or bustling bicycle bells ringing from the street. She lay there, unable to move, panicking, tormented by the splitting headache threatening to tear her apart. She had trouble gathering her thoughts or processing what had happened, although she recalled a few moments in the hotel, her conversation with Isaac, her disenchantment, and her anger.

"Bonjour, *ma chérie*. It's a beautiful day today. Shall we have breakfast?"

She turned around, startled. Near the bed stood Bellefeuille, wearing a silk robe with fur trim. His short hair was not yet combed; two tufts of silver-speckled hair stuck up from the sides of his head. His lustrous brown eyes twinkled; his face glowed with something like a sheen of smugness.

The memory of Bellefeuille dabbing at her tears and the ride to his mansion returned to her. Anyu almost groaned. What had she done? In her drunken state, she had allowed herself to be vulnerable and become the kind of loose woman she despised. Or was Bellefeuille to be blamed, too, seducing her with his kindness and taking advantage of her? She couldn't believe she was so stupid. She sat up, saw her bare shoulders, and sank lower. "Where are my clothes?"

"Your dress was torn. Now don't get up. I have something for you." Bellefeuille turned to a carved walnut Louis XV armoire and opened a drawer. When he turned around, he held a small velvet jewelry box. He opened it.

Inside was a brilliant butterfly with two rose-cut diamonds for the antennae, multicolored sapphires for the forewings, and blue beryls, amethysts, and emeralds for the hind wings; there was also a large hexagonal yellow diamond on the thorax and a rope of twisted gold on the abdomen. The wings were made of brilliant gold, which appeared to be more than twenty-two karats. She picked it up, recognizing its brilliance, bold design, and daring use of high-grade gold.

"Who made this?"

"A jeweler in Paris. Suzanne Belperron."

A woman.

"She's a novice designer, in my opinion. Her style is flamboyant, unconventional, and some say if you stare at her butterflies long enough, they could pierce your eyes."

But gold at this level of purity was highly malleable, and manipulating it required skill and vision. "Very impressive."

"You like it." He held her hand with the butterfly brooch. "Keep it. It's my gift, *ma chérie*."

"You'll give it to me?"

"A gift fitting for a designer like you. I'll introduce you to more sophisticated French jewelry. Van Cleef and Arpels, Boucheron, Mauboussin, Chanel, and more unique designs you won't be able to find in Shanghai if you work for me."

"I can't work for you." She shook her head.

"Why not?"

Anyu put the butterfly back in the box. "I thought of that in the hotel. I don't want to be a jeweler anymore. In fact, I won't touch the tools or design a single piece of jewelry from now on."

"Well, this is unexpected. Why?"

"I want to have nothing to do with Isaac Mandelburg."

"I understand the Russian jeweler is the tsar of pain, but to cut short your promising jeweler's career because of him? That's rather dramatic."

Dramatic? Maybe. But it would be her declaration. She would sever her ties with Isaac and eliminate his influence from her life. "This is what's going to be, Monsieur Bellefeuille."

"It would be a devastating loss to the jewelry world in Shanghai. You'll give it another thought, *ma chérie?*"

"I have to leave now."

"All right, all right. We don't have to talk about this. But please. Stay." He held her hand. "Don't go. Marry me."

Anyu wondered where Bellefeuille got this idea that she would marry him. She had only seen him twice as far as she could remember, and she barely knew him—yes, he had been crowned repeatedly at the annual competition in Shanghai, but that was before her arrival.

"You don't know anything about me."

"I do! I read all about you. You're an orphan from Harbin in the north, lost your parents at a young age. You're beautiful, talented, and the most popular jeweler in Shanghai. I want to marry you. I'm in love with you."

She shook her head. "I can't. May I have my clothes?"

He sighed. "Of course. I have something just for you." He sprinted across the thick blue Persian carpet and returned. "Try it. I think you'll love it."

He held a long, elegant cream gown made of fine silk; it had an empire waist, gracefully embroidered. Anyu had never cared for dresses as much as Esther did, yet she had never seen one as beautiful as this.

She slid her arms into the dress. It fell on her skin like water; the plunging neckline showed off her neck and breasts, and near the waist, it narrowed to hug her curves. In awe, she stared at the youthful, bold, luxurious image in the full-length mirror near the bed.

"Do you like it, princess?" he asked.

She studied herself again. "It's all right."

"I have more." He took her arm, crossed the grand gilded room with gold molding and silver wood panels, and then arrived in front of two giant wardrobes reaching the ceiling. With a dramatic wave of his hand, he flung open the first wardrobe and then the second: inside were red, violet, black, ivory dresses, hats with veils, gloves in delicate snakeskins and goatskins, and leather shoes with buckles. This, and this, and this. All hers. If she stayed.

There was no denying their beauty, and she could tell each piece was high fashion and cost a fortune.

"I'm not sure if they'll fit me."

"I know they'll fit you." He winked. "Are you hungry? Shall we eat breakfast before you leave?"

She hesitated. She was hungry. A few bites wouldn't hurt. She nodded and walked out with Bellefeuille. In the hallway covered with a lush black carpet printed with triangles and circles, a young man with a nose thin as a chopstick bowed to them. Butler Huang, Bellefeuille said, and introduced her to his servants in black livery, thirty-three of them, all locals: six cooks in aprons, five laundrymen, five housekeepers, five coolies, and ten gardeners, then two of Bellefeuille's personal assistants. They gave her a bow in courtesy.

Anyu felt foolish, standing in front of them. Who did they think she was? she wondered.

"You can pick your own amah, *ma chérie*, if you stay."

The way he said it, as if a personal servant was a dress. "I'm starving."

"All right. Is our breakfast ready, Butler Huang?"

"It is, master," the butler said.

"I'll have it on the patio in the garden. Come, this way, *ma chérie*."

They passed a few more bedrooms, a swimming pool, a music room, and a banquet room with a parquet floor. Each room seemed grander than the last, decorated with white wainscoting and high ceilings painted with murals. In one elongated room, all the walls were plastered with mirrors in different geometric shapes—the Hall of Mirrors, he said.

"Here we are." Bellefeuille steered her to double French doors, which two servants opened for them.

Before her was a vista like none she had ever seen before. There were shining bronze statues of chariots and gods, white marble fountains spraying streams of water, clay planters holding huge red blossoms, and a copse of willows and maples. Near a wrought-iron fence was a pond, where a dozen female servants in gray pants, kneeling on the ground, were trimming the lawn with shears. Now and then, they paused to measure the length of the grass they had cut.

"Great view," she said. Bellefeuille was trying hard to impress her and make her stay.

"As you can see, I'm a proud Frenchman. I have envisioned my own Garden of Versailles in my backyard. My clients at the *conseil d'administration municipal* of the French Concession adore this garden." He led her to a round table on the terrace and sat on a red chair with a cushion.

"Try the *éclair*, if you like, and *boudoirs*. Or *financiers*, made with sliced almonds. You like almonds? *Financiers* were created by nuns of the Visitandines order in Nancy. Try some." He gestured to the table filled with plates of fruits, cheeses, sliced meats, and a platter of pastries. Fine French food.

Anyu took a *financier*. "It tastes like beeswax."

"Beeswax? That's strange. It's very delicious. Have you had it before? Of course, the real French food is much tastier. I shall happily treat you with a lavish French dinner if you allow me. You haven't had an authentic French meal, I reckon. What do you say?"

Bellefeuille had a grand dramatic style, a hyperbole of a man, unlike Isaac. "I have to go after this."

"You're going back to Isaac Mandelburg." He sighed.

"Absolutely not."

"No? That's good to hear. I don't mean to pry. Was he the person who made you cry?"

She put down the *financier* and didn't meet his eyes.

"I knew it. That Russian jeweler is a man of dubious character. Few people in Shanghai know him, his background, or even when he arrived in Shanghai. He barely shows up at any social events, fails to win awards, manages a two-bit shop with his uncle, and if it weren't for you, they would have been out of business years ago."

Anyu said, "You resent him because his jewelry store took your business."

Bellefeuille waved his hand. "I won't deny that I have lost clients since you came along. I'm an honest man. But if you must know, Isaac Mandelburg was my *bête noire* before you brought his family brand to fame. *He* resents *me, ma chérie.* You might not want to tell him you're here, or he'd be livid."

"Livid?" Anyu listened intently.

"Of course! How do you think he'd feel if you, his famous successor, slept with his rival? He'd be devastated."

It had not occurred to her that Isaac would be hurt. But to her surprise, the thought of seeing him in pain and breaking his heart pleased her. Shouldn't it be his turn to suffer?

"Stay here and marry me, *ma chérie.* You won't regret it. I'll treat you well, and I can give you anything you want. You'll be happy here."

The almond flavor of the *financier* grew on her. Bellefeuille was right. It was delicious. "Monsieur Bellefeuille—"

"Call me Pierre."

"Pierre." Would she be happy, marrying a man she had only met twice? She doubted it, but she said, "I'll marry you."

"You will?"

"Yes."

"You make me a happy man!" He hugged her so tight that she felt as though her bones were about to be crushed. "I must announce this wonderful news to the world."

Anyu took a grape from the plate; she hardly paid attention as Bellefeuille showered his praise on her, hardly paid attention as he envisaged their future, an engagement party in a month and a wedding ceremony in six months, hardly paid attention as his butler promised to organize a grand engagement party fit for the union of him and the most popular jeweler in Shanghai.

Only one thought filled her mind at that moment: once Isaac heard of her engagement, he would regret he had rejected her, and he would find her and ask her to marry her.

CHAPTER 23

Later, Anyu told Bellefeuille that she needed to get her things at the Mandelburgs' shop. Bellefeuille discouraged it. *You have everything you need here,* he said, but at her insistence, he took her to the shop in his car. Anyu got out; he waited in the car with his chauffeur.

Esther would not approve of her decision, Anyu thought as she walked up to the shop and knocked on the window.

Esther saw her and came out. "Anyu! Where have you been? I've been worried about you. I was looking for you all over the hotel but couldn't find you. Come in!"

"I can't. I came to get my things, my dresses, and some money."

"Why?"

"I'm leaving," she said. "I'm going to marry Pierre Bellefeuille."

Esther jerked, stumbling on her bad leg. "You're joking. Do you even know him? You don't care about him. You declined all his invitations . . ."

Anyu might have explained—Isaac's rejection, last night at Bellefeuille's mansion—but there was not enough time. "Could you get my things for me? You know where they are."

"What about Father? Do you want to speak to him?"

"No. I don't want to see him."

"What about your commissions?"

"I've finished them all. The new designs haven't started yet. Your father should refund the customers. Can you get my things?"

Esther nodded. When she came back, she carried a black suitcase, frowning. "I don't understand why you're doing this, but you'll come back, won't you?"

Anyu didn't reply. She took the suitcase from Esther and got in the car. She didn't turn to see her friend, but she knew Esther was looking at her, and she knew, at this hour, Isaac must be working in the workshop.

Pierre Bellefeuille wasted no time putting together a guest list. All were his acquaintances; Anyu only invited Esther. And the party planning by Butler Huang proceeded at blinding speed. He reserved a band, installed festive lights in the hallway and the atrium, and meticulously produced a menu that consisted of rich soup, beef, mutton, fowl, and game, and finished with pudding, pastry, jelly, custard, cheese, and salad. The drink list went on for ten pages, including sherry, champagne, beer, and port wine.

Pierre Bellefeuille was forty-seven years old, Anyu learned. He was a fastidious man, adamant that his taste, food, clothing, and jewelry must reflect his fine cultural heritage. He requested his coffee to be piping hot, his nightgown pressed, and his slippers brushed. A stickler for routine and habits, he guarded his schedule with the same zeal as he did his wardrobe, which was filled with tailored suits, Napoleon costumes, and other attire.

He was a proud Frenchman, even though he had never visited Paris, which, to the best of his knowledge, no one in Shanghai was aware of. What people did know was what Bellefeuille gladly announced: his father was a diamond cutter from Saint-Amond-Montrond, the town famous for gold, and his father had lost his family's jewelry factory during the Great War. When an opportunity arrived, Bellefeuille ventured overseas and arrived in Shanghai.

He had been in Shanghai since 1919; one of the wealthiest foreigners in Shanghai, he owned five jewelry stores and a private mansion set on a fifteen-acre lot in the French Concession.

⚜

Anyu was given an amah (Bellefeuille insisted), a middle-aged woman wearing a lace hair band and a shirt with a bow. She appeared timid, never lifting her gaze to meet Anyu's eye. Speaking Chinese with a mix of a local dialect, she tidied up all her clothing and magazines quietly and efficiently.

To prepare her, as Bellefeuille put it, to "finesse the art of entertainment," Anyu began etiquette training to become a hostess.

In the salon that smelled of fragrance imported from Paris, Anyu watched a team of personal assistants demonstrate the rules of drinking wine, cutting steaks with forks and knives, sipping soup with a spoon, folding napkins, and setting the table. The sharp cutlery alarmed her. Every Chinese person would understand it was taboo to lay knives in front of guests, but the tutors pinched their lips and said she was to learn the French way.

After that, she was greeted by a stream of fashion stylists, four women and two men, standing beside carts loaded with garments said to be designed by the fashion icons of Paris. They lectured her on fabrics, styles, designers and their trademark dresses, and how to pair them with crochet or wide-brimmed hats. There were stacks of magazines to read, photos of fashionable women to peruse, and catalogs of accessories to choose. Then a gaggle of seamstresses arrived to measure her and offer a vast selection of silk, pongee, and brocades.

Then followed a makeup artist and his assistant, who instructed her to sit in front of a large mirror with a golden frame as her face turned into a canvas.

It was tiresome and confusing to speak to the people who frowned on her churlish behavior, and she felt like a doll practicing its movements and even learning to speak and smile. This was a different life from hammering a strip of gold under a lamp. Carefully, she sampled the scrumptious pastries and tasted the pungent red wines imported from Bordeaux; she browsed the catalogs of the newest fashion and jewelry designs in cryptic French; she even learned to savor what was said to be a cultural staple of Western civilization, the ungodly bitter coffee.

The day of her engagement party arrived.

She had not invited Isaac, but he would have heard of her engagement by now. Would he be sad?

In the morning, she took a bath scented with rose petals and began to get dressed in the guest room. A team of five hairstylists and makeup artists worked on her. Before dusk, she donned a red Chanel gown and a strap bracelet with sapphires and diamonds, her hair elegantly piled up.

The party started.

Standing next to Bellefeuille, Anyu greeted the guests at the entrance to the high-ceilinged ballroom. There were two hundred people, including many French Concession officials, the head of the French Concession, the chief of the police department, American bankers, and tycoons and their wives whom Anyu had not heard of.

Anyu was nervous despite her calm composure, and she smiled courteously and hugged and kissed the guests as the etiquette required.

None of the people she cared about attended her engagement party—Esther was not in sight, and Isaac had not been invited. Anyu thought of Confucius, whom she had stopped seeing. She wished she had not been so impulsive and cut ties with him. She had liked riding his bicycle with him, and he had been kind to her, even though he was a criminal. And her mother. How she wished she were here. She realized, with a pang of sorrow, that the most heartbreaking part of being an orphan was not living a rootless life, but rather a loveless one.

Congratulations, congratulations, congratulations.

The voices rose and fell, and Bellefeuille's laughter rose and fell.

Later, he gave an eloquent toast filled with pride and elation. Then the rich meal the butler had arranged was served. At the end, cups of coffee and boxes of cigars were handed out by the hired help from the Majestic Hotel.

Anyu did not touch a single dish. Her dress was too tight around her arms, restricting her movement, and her heart raced. She had never felt so nervous. Was she making a mistake with the engagement?

The music started. Some guests were dancing. Anyu felt dizzy, sitting on a sofa against the wall. Then she got up to use the restroom. She had already passed the cigar room when she heard Bellefeuille's voice from inside. She retraced her steps. The cigar room was draped with smoke, masking the men's faces.

"What about your mistress?" a man with a French accent asked.

"Which one?" another quipped.

There was a riotous guffaw.

Anyu took a champagne flute from a passing server and returned to the ballroom. It was not lost on her that Bellefeuille had a promiscuous selection of partners.

Near the ballroom's door, she saw Esther, beautiful, golden-haired Esther, dressed in a fine blue gown reaching her heels and a wide silk hat, regal like a dawn goddess, holding Mr. Dearborn's hand.

"Esther!" Anyu jumped, waving at her friend. "You came. I'm so glad. I thought you decided not to come. Where were you?"

"We were seated in another room." Esther's limp looked like a dance; she was smiling. "I wouldn't miss your engagement party for the world, Anyu. Look at you. I love your dress. You look splendid! Doesn't she look splendid, honey?" She nudged Mr. Dearborn.

"She looks like Mary Pickford." Mr. Dearborn held his cigar.

"Mary Pickford is a famous actress," Esther said, leaning toward Mr. Dearborn.

"I have a lot of dresses like this. I can show you, Esther. You'll love them."

"I'm sure I will. You'll forgive me for asking, but why would you choose him?"

"It's complicated."

"We've missed you."

We? Including Isaac?

"Father misses you, too."

Anyu's throat tightened. "How—"

"Who is this beautiful lady?" Bellefeuille came over.

"My friend Esther Mandelburg." Anyu introduced her to him.

"Isaac Mandelburg's daughter. I see. It's a pleasure." Bellefeuille grasped Anyu's arm. "*Ma chérie*, Mr. Morris is waiting to speak to you."

She didn't want to leave yet. She had only exchanged a few words with Esther! There was so much she wanted to ask her. How did she know Isaac missed her? Did he mention her?

"*Ma chérie?*"

"I'll catch up with you later, Esther."

"I'll be here, Anyu."

"Soon she'll be Mrs. Bellefeuille, Miss Mandelburg." Bellefeuille chuckled.

Esther was looking at her. "But, Anyu, you'll always be a member of the Mandelburg family."

Oh, Esther.

"This way." Bellefeuille steered her away to some jewelers who worked for him and a cluster of men in suits and their wives.

"Congratulations, Miss Anyu," Mr. Morris, the owner of the *North China Daily News*, said. "This is a beautiful engagement party."

She forced a smile. Esther was whispering with Mr. Dearborn in the corner.

"Miss Anyu, I'm thankful for the cuff links you designed. I need a few more. Should I visit the House of Bellefeuille to see your latest designs?"

"Unfortunately, Mr. Morris, I've decided to quit my jeweler's career."

"Quit your career? Why?"

"Pause her career," Bellefeuille said. "Temporarily. She's getting married! Mr. Morris, you can find any jewelry you like at the House of

Bellefeuille. Anyu will always be there. Could we have a few words in private?" He directed her to a corner where they were out of the earshot of guests. "*Ma chérie*, you don't mean to quit your career, do you?"

"Of course I do."

He sighed. "I'm devastated. I was going to ask you to design a piece for the annual competition."

"Pierre, I can't. I don't want to compete."

He sighed again. "Would you at least postpone announcing your decision to quit your career for the moment? Our engagement calls for a celebration, and I don't want to ruin it."

"Fine." Anyu drained the champagne and searched among the crowd. She couldn't find Esther and Mr. Dearborn.

You'll always be a member of the Mandelburg family.

That night, after the party ended, as the ballroom descended into emptiness and the music faded into the dark, with Bellefeuille thrusting inside her, all Anyu could think was: Did Isaac regret he had rejected her? Did he miss her like Esther said? Would he come to see her?

Two weeks after her engagement party, no visits from Isaac.

She was busy. Each day, fine dresses appeared in her bedroom: a lilac-and-black draped-back evening gown designed by Madeleine Vionnet, an embroidered silk chiffon dress by Coco Chanel, and sensationally soft and body-shaping two-piece garments by the legendary Jeanne Margaine-Lacroix. On the dresser were boxes of jewelry: an elegant Edwardian-style necklace with filigree and silky gold threads, an Art Deco gold-and-onyx necklace, and the newest emerald starfish brooch from the House of Boivin in Paris.

There were cocktail parties, noisy turf meets at the racecourse, and lavish balls in the hotels, and everywhere, her fiancé introduced her, the most popular jeweler in Shanghai. She conversed with the Italian officials, the Shanghai tycoons, the British diplomats, the Hungarian architects, the French police chief, and their charming companions.

In October, a few days after the jewelry competition that announced the House of Clemente as the winner, Anyu came across Mrs. Brown encircled by her bodyguards. When the crowd around her thinned and a moment presented itself, Anyu stood within the periphery of her vision.

Mrs. Brown waved her over. She studied her face, Madeleine Vionnet's evening gown, and then her hand, ungloved, wearing the signet ring and an engagement ring. "So it's true. You have switched houses."

"I'm getting married," she said.

Mrs. Brown straightened; her eyes looked wary. "When is the wedding?"

"In January."

"I suppose you've made up your mind?"

She nodded.

"I imagine this decision was made after careful deliberation. It is, of course, your personal life. Did Isaac give you his blessings?"

"Like you said, it's my personal affair." Then Anyu caught sight of Bellefeuille standing by, held back by the lady's bodyguards, unable to approach. "There he is. Mrs. Brown, I assume you're acquainted with my fiancé since he won the competition a few times. May I reintroduce you to him?"

She was not sure whether Bellefeuille could hear her, but he watched Mrs. Brown with an intense look.

"You may not," the British lady said. Then she left without saying congratulations.

Mrs. Brown hadn't changed, that frosty woman. And condescending. How dare she treat her as if she were Isaac's extension?

In the car back home with Bellefeuille, Anyu's mood darkened further. She had attended so many parties and the whole of Shanghai knew about her engagement with Bellefeuille, but she had not once come across Isaac. Admittedly, he was not a social butterfly, but if he wanted to see her, he would have showed up at some venues. It seemed Isaac was indifferent to her engagement, or maybe his heart was made of iron, impervious to sadness.

She took a Lucky Strike from the cigarette box, struck a match, and began to smoke. She had finished three cigarettes when she realized Bellefeuille was speaking to her.

"Yes?" It was smoky in the car, so she rolled down the window.

"I shouldn't feel surprised that you and Mrs. Brown are on friendly terms, yet I confess I am very much surprised that she would give you a moment of sole attention."

"Well, I did win her competition every year I entered. We have a history."

Bellefeuille let out a groan.

"Why are you so upset?"

There was silence.

Anyu sat upright. "I can't believe I just realized it now. She was your lover. She tried to avoid you. That's why. What happened? Why did you break up?"

"It's all in the past. No need to bring it up." Bellefeuille's tone was dark.

Anyu took a long drag of her cigarette. "I'll find out eventually, either from you or someone else."

"We had a falling-out. She believed I cheated on her, so she snubbed me and crawled in other men's beds, and then she found a new lapdog in your old master."

"When did her relationship with Isaac start?"

"A year or two before you won the award. How else was Isaac Mandelburg, a penurious workman from a two-bit shop, who had no clientele nor capital, able to run a jewelry shop?"

Anyu lit another cigarette.

"She could have slept with any man for all I care, but Isaac Mandelburg? The man is a nobody. And she was never honest with me, hiding her secrets from me when we were together. She's a powerful woman, of course, you know. She has a vast network and is well connected to the elite in Shanghai and even Queen Mary's royal representatives in Hong Kong. But she kept me in the dark about who she worked with and refused to introduce me to them. I suspect she also runs a smuggling business that deals with the Romanov treasure in Shanghai."

This was the first time Anyu had heard of the Romanov treasures from someone other than Isaac.

"She won't be running her smuggling business soon, mind you. Rumor has it that Mr. Du has gotten wind of her wealth. He's very interested in her."

"Mr. Du?"

"The gangster lord has unearthed some clues that she might work for a group related to Karl Fabergé, who crafted *objets d'art* for the Romanovs and wealthy men. Fabergé *objets d'art*, as you know, are rare treasures in history, given their superb design, historical significance, and artistic perfection."

Anyu was feeling dizzy after five cigarettes. She had trouble keeping her thoughts together. How much did Bellefeuille know? She couldn't say she liked Mrs. Brown, but she still cared about the egg, her egg, and she had sworn her allegiance to the Guild.

"Mr. Du said the group called themselves the Workmasters Guild, and they used to command the majority of diamonds sold to the tsars in Russia. It was an occult group in charge of the gemstone trade across the world, and at one time, they were closely associated with Thomas Cullinan, the man who discovered the Cullinan Diamond of Britain's crown jewels. Rumors say the workmasters are hiding in Shanghai."

"I hear they have been imprisoned or murdered by the Bolsheviks."

Bellefeuille turned to her. "How did you know that? Did your old master tell you?"

"Why would he tell me? I came from Harbin. Many Russians lived there."

He nodded. "That makes sense. But imagine, a guild with vast resources of diamonds and gemstones around the world."

There was something in his voice that chilled Anyu.

꩜

Three months had passed since Anyu left the Mandelburgs.

Bellefeuille was still a mystery, Anyu realized. She couldn't say she understood him. Sometimes, he'd shower her with affection and praise, convincing her that he was in love with her, but the next moment, he'd act distant and even mean, critical of her youth, her naivete, and her lack of cultural knowledge. His view of her artistry was also questionable.

One day, wearing a full-length dress with pink ruffles and a matching pillbox hat, Anyu was putting on a pair of gloves when she realized they were too tight. She had grown plump after attending banquets and parties, but she still hadn't seen or heard from Isaac. She wondered what was going on with him, and whether he cared for her at all.

Sometimes, when she looked at the signet ring, she thought of the priceless egg stored in the Vault of Gems and Treasures. When she examined her jewelry box gifted by Bellefeuille, she would think of the convention of labeling jewelry: *name, year, type of jewelry, size, metal, gemstones, and techniques used.* When she sprayed perfume on her arm, she thought she smelled the chemical odors in the workshop. When she slid a silk glove over the ugly stub of the missing finger, she thought of those wild days when she adamantly searched for the snowflake necklace. She recalled those evenings working beside Isaac, learning the techniques of soldering, sawing, and enameling; they felt so distant, yet so close.

She missed the pungent scent of acetone, the sensation of watching metal melt under the heat of a blowtorch, and the satisfaction of bending and twisting gold wires. She missed the Winter Egg, its delicate shape, its translucent beauty, and she missed most, even though she would never admit it, the face of Isaac, his smile, his polite way of turning to the side to cough, and the intense look in his eyes as he sawed.

CHAPTER 24

Then, one afternoon in November, her amah told her that a man named Isaac Mandelburg asked to speak to her outside the mansion.

Anyu's heart skipped a few beats. Finally.

It was a rare sunny day. The autumn air was cool, sparkling with golden sunlight that filtered through the canopy of plane trees on the street; leaves were falling, descending sluggishly. Outside the mansion, near a towering tree, stood Isaac, dressed in his usual black shirt and pants and fedora, his head drooping, his hand reaching to his hat as if to ascertain that he hadn't forgotten it.

She rushed to him. He regretted rejecting her; he would ask her to return to him. If he proposed to her, she would leave Bellefeuille this instant.

"Isaac," she said. *Isaac. Isaac.*

He raised his head. He was thinner. A ring of stubble had spread around his chin, a hint of exhaustion etched on his taut face; something in his eyes swam, a haunting shadow. He took out his handkerchief, coughed into it, and then folded it with the care she had often seen in the workshop. Her heart softened. He had indeed suffered. How foolish of them. Tormenting each other. All these months of worry, anxiety, and doubt.

"Oh, look at you! Beautiful, beautiful like a princess." He gestured—her pink taffeta dress with a bow, her matching hat with lace.

Anyu smiled. "I'm so glad you came."

"I have meant to visit you, but I heard you were very busy with parties. You're doing well, I hope?"

"Couldn't be better."

Isaac nodded, looking as if at a loss for words.

"How's Esther?"

She was doing well, working in the shop, Isaac said.

"And Samuel and Uncle David and the aunties?" Indeed, she had thought of them, too.

"They're well, too." Uncle David had suffered from a fall that hurt his ankle; Samuel spent time in the workshop whenever he wanted to; the aunties had a cold in the summer but had recovered, Isaac said, and then he dug out an envelope from his pocket. "I forgot to mention that Esther is marrying Mr. Dearborn. She wanted me to give you this invitation. She hopes you'll attend her wedding. It'll mean so much to her."

"Of course I will." Anyu tucked it into her pocket. "I'm happy for her. They deserve each other."

Isaac nodded, staring at a European building across the street with purple wooden shutters and a black wrought-iron balcony, where a pot of pink cosmos sat in the shade. Again, silence.

Why didn't Isaac ask her to leave Bellefeuille? Why didn't he tell her he wanted her back?

Isaac cleared his throat. "This is perhaps selfish of me to ask, Anyu, but I wonder if you'd return to our shop. We lost Mr. Walters's support since you left us, and the cost of purchasing diamonds and gems from other purveyors has been high. Besides, we've had to refund some clients who lost interest in us. We can't run the shop without you."

"As your successor?"

"Yes."

Her heart fell. She stared at a pile of leaves near her feet, a blend of orange, gold, crimson, and marigold, the colors of the gemstones, the amber, moonstones, and topaz. She remembered reading the unique elements described in Isaac's notebook and the tips on how to identify them by their color, luster, hardness, optical properties, and dispersion. "You won't marry me, will you? You choose Mrs. Brown."

"Mrs. Brown and I have a relationship, yes. It's a relationship I honor and feel grateful for. But we would not have the privilege to celebrate our holy matrimony. She doesn't wish for that."

"Then why wouldn't you choose me?"

"Believe me, I wish I could," he said, his voice hoarse. "Since your arrival, I've wanted to look out for you, and I wish to give you all that I have—to see you rise and succeed and to care for you. I love you, of course, God knows how much I love you."

Anyu's heart leaped in joy.

"But only in another world, in another lifetime, would I have the blessing to have you as my wife."

"Why?"

"I'm a simple man, a son of a jeweler, a father. I come from an old-fashioned family; I hold some principles as gold standard, principles that define who we are and what kind of life we lead. And I'm twenty-five years older than you. You're younger than my son and daughter. As a Jew bound by Halakah, I'm not allowed to marry a non-Jew."

"I don't care about the religious law, Isaac."

He smiled drily. "There. That's another thing I love about you: your fiery single-mindedness, your idea of living your life with abandon. And you make it appear simple, admirable. You humble me, Anyu. I wish I was twenty years younger, born in this country, and then I'd have the privilege of asking for your hand."

It would have been better had he said he didn't love her; what was she going to do with this fact that they could never be together despite his affection?

"I'll always love you, Anyu."

She hated it, his calm manner and his assurance. She jutted her chin. "Fine. I'm going to marry Pierre Bellefeuille."

"I assume you know him well enough."

"That's not your concern."

"You might know, Anyu, a Frenchman rarely marries a Chinese woman in Shanghai."

How dare he try to belittle her. To hint she was naive and would be a plaything? She was not a plaything; she knew what she was doing. Pierre Bellefeuille had dallied with other women; after all, he was a popular bachelor in Shanghai, but he loved her, pampering her with all the dresses and jewelry, throwing a lavish engagement party to show her off as his fiancée. Isaac would not marry her, and he wanted to destroy her relationship with the man who would give her a future. She would not let Isaac ruin her happiness.

"I don't want to see you again, Isaac Mandelburg."

He sighed.

"Here." She took off the signet ring and tossed it into his hands.

He stiffened as though he had been struck by a heavy blow, motionless.

"I decline to be your successor. You can keep your Fabergé egg. I'm no longer interested in it. From now on, I'm no longer associated with you."

"Wait, Anyu. Will you continue designing jewelry?"

"I haven't announced it yet, but if you'd like to know, I've decided to quit my jeweler's career."

"You don't want to be a jeweler." His voice was weak.

"I became a master jeweler at eighteen, I've seen the Fabergé egg and held it. What did it do for me? Nothing," she said deliberately.

"I hope you'll change your mind, Anyu, and continue your career, even if you decide to marry another man, even if you no longer work in my shop. It has been an honor to be your mentor."

Anyu turned around, walked down the path lined with flowerpots, and shut the door behind her.

❧

For the whole afternoon, a fire smoldered in her stomach, and she felt like striking the anvil and pounding on the wall. She flipped through magazines and kept tearing the pages. She smoked two packets of Lucky Strikes.

Unable to sleep, she left her bedroom, padding across the marble floor, out the French doors, and into the moonless replica Garden of Versailles. She sat on a cold bench, smoking, staring at the silhouette of gods and fountains, listening to the impetuous wind whipping the willow branches.

She had cut the final cord with Isaac; she would not see him again. Why had she done that? Why couldn't she forget how she felt about him and go back to his shop with him? And with the return of the signet ring, the sight of the egg, its spectacular image, would remain out of her reach. She looked at her finger, bare, without the ring, and it was as though a part of her was torn away. An emptiness, feverish, painful, raked her stomach. Why did it have to end up like this? Why was it so hard to love someone?

Her fingers grew cold, her feet chilled, and still, she sat there, trapped in the garden of madness. *You're going mad,* she said to herself. *You're going mad.*

She smoked and watched a sliver of smoke torch the fabric of darkness.

On the day of Esther's wedding, a wild animal invaded the garden. It overturned the flower beds, devoured the blossoms and leaves, and wreaked havoc in the mansion. The servants, holding brooms and frying pans, combed the entire garden, searching the nooks of the fountains and benches, but couldn't find it. They said it might have been a squirrel monkey, a wild cat, a rat, or a raccoon looking for loaches in the pond.

Anyu watched the chaos from behind the French doors. Bellefeuille was saying something, but she could hardly listen. Then she finally realized he was asking her to meet his jewelers.

"They admire you! Perhaps you'll pay them a visit in the workshop?"

"Why?"

"They're eager to meet you."

"I already met them. Twice." She wondered if Bellefeuille was trying to lure her back to jewelry making.

Bearing a gift—a bottle of French perfume imported from Paris—Anyu went to the restaurant where Esther had her wedding party.

It was a modest establishment, decorated with two red lanterns hanging on the front door, tucked among a row of unpretentious gray-roofed abodes. Inside, there was no live band, which Anyu had grown accustomed to, but it was crowded with many men and women, and there was a familiar tune from a gramophone—Esther's wedding song that she had hummed at bedtime—and Isaac was clapping and swaying in a brand-new satin suit, his face blooming with happiness.

And then there was Esther, magnificent in the white wedding gown Anyu had bought her three years ago, shrieking and laughing, holding on for dear life to the chair being carried by a group of men. All around her, people cheered and danced. An effervescent energy permeated the air, infused with the intimacy of family and the blind affection of those who loved one another.

Anyu remembered once when they were sitting inside a car to visit her clients, Esther had asked, if she had a choice, would she choose the life of a wife or the life of a master jeweler. Anyu had said resolutely that the ability to create jewelry was a woman's greatest asset, and to be recognized as a master jeweler was the meaning of her life.

Anyu was not so sure now, watching Esther, a daughter, a sister, and now a wife, living a life she couldn't have. And it occurred to her that she had been wrong. A woman's greatest asset, her proudest wealth, was not to be known but to be loved.

She gave her gift to a waiter at the door and left in tears.

CHAPTER 25

Bellefeuille was having a party in the mansion.

"Ma chérie." He waved at her when she entered the ballroom. "Come meet the esteemed Mr. Moller, a shipping business owner who controls the ships and shipyards on the east coast of China, the chair of the Shanghai Horse Racing Club, and his daughter, Miss Irena."

Anyu smiled and walked to them. On her way home, she had done some thinking. She had to start her life with Pierre somehow. He was a generous man, charismatic, wealthy, and he loved her. Their wedding was in two months; she would soon be his wife, and she was willing to play her role. Socializing with his clients was an inevitable obligation, even though she no longer wished to be a jeweler. "Delighted to meet you."

The father-and-daughter pair were each other's reflections; they stood shoulder to shoulder, at the same height; they had the same onyx-shaded hair gleaming with luster; and both were adorned with gold-rimmed eyeglasses. They looked deeply in love, a father-and-daughter duo, holding each other's arms, chattering about an acrobatic show they had watched in the Great World amusement center, oblivious to Bellefeuille and her and the people around them. Now and then, they leaned over and planted a kiss on each other's cheek.

Bellefeuille winked at her. "Mr. Moller is a doting father. He wants to give his daughter a gift for her eighteenth birthday. An extraordinary gift for this momentous occasion. Naturally, he thought of you. What would you say?"

She couldn't believe Bellefeuille would put her on the spot. Hadn't they discussed this?

"I—"

"A set," Mr. Moller said. "I'd like a necklace, earrings, a brooch, and a ring for my precious daughter. It must have at least eighteen rose-cut diamonds and eighteen types of precious gemstones to celebrate her eighteenth birthday."

"Eighteen diamonds!" Bellefeuille exclaimed.

"Do not be concerned about the cost. Do you have a design in mind? I'm eager to take a look." Moller kissed his daughter's cheek. The daughter giggled and kissed him back.

"Of course. It will be Anyu's honor to design such a unique gift for your daughter."

Moller laughed. To start with, he said, he'd be happy to make a deposit of one thousand dollars. Bellefeuille nodded, assuring him a most beautiful birthday gift for his daughter would be crafted.

Anyu pulled him aside. "Pierre, we've had this talk before. I've sworn not to design jewelry or make any jewelry again. I can't design a birthday gift for Mr. Moller's daughter."

"Would you make an exception? Just one exception. It's one thousand dollars, just the deposit. And more to come!"

"I can't."

"You will turn down such a lucrative commission?"

"Perhaps you could give this commission to someone in your shop?"

"Mr. Moller made a specific request that you design the gift. I can't renege on that."

"But I didn't agree to it."

"You have to help me, *ma chérie*. You're the most famous jeweler in this city!"

That was why he had proposed to marry her in the first place—he wanted to use her for his business, she realized. "Pierre, listen to me. I can't accept the commission."

He turned his back on her and chatted with his guests. For the rest of the evening, he sulked; he didn't speak to her.

⚜

But the following evening, when he came to their bedroom, he was all smiles. "I've found a perfect solution, *ma chérie*, that makes good business sense and respects your wishes."

She put down the fashion magazine she'd been reading. "What's the solution?"

"I'll have one of my jewelers design the gift for Mr. Moller's daughter and inform him it's your creation. You might take a look if you wish, but you do not need to move a finger."

She sat up. "You can't do that. That's dishonest."

"Dishonest?"

"I simply can't allow other people to use my name for jewelry I don't create."

"Oh, you won't design it, and you won't allow others to design it? Don't be selfish."

"I'm not being selfish. It's my name you want to use." Her name, her reputation.

"And you'd refuse a large commission from a reputable businessman?" He stormed out.

⚜

Bellefeuille was in a bad mood for the next few days. He complained about the food and threw the tray at the amah's face—Mr. Moller had commissioned the House of Clemente, he said.

Anyu felt bad about losing his business and tried to comfort him. In a Chanel nightgown with nothing underneath, she waited for him, flipping through pages of fashion magazines, and pouring wine in a glass—Bellefeuille liked to drink before bed. But he didn't come to the bedroom that day, or the next day.

She phoned the Shanghai Club, which Bellefeuille frequented. The man on the other end hung up when he heard her voice. For a month, Bellefeuille didn't come to her bed.

At her insistent inquiries, her amah, wringing her hands, whispered with halted breath that Bellefeuille had brought another lady home and slept in the guest room.

Stunned, Anyu went to the hallway outside the room. There was a woman's laughter and Bellefeuille's cheering from inside; Anyu listened, balling her hands, trembling.

A cigarette in her hand, she looked for the suitcase she had brought in her bedroom, but her amah said Bellefeuille had tossed it out, together with the contents inside, a long time ago. She couldn't find her savings either. She stuffed whatever she saw in a suitcase the amah gave her, packed up, stubbed her cigarette in the porcelain ashtray, and then went out of the room.

Her amah was wringing her hands at the door, her eyes asking, *Where are you going?*

She hesitated. After all these months, she was, again, facing a question for which she had no answer. She had no home, no money, no one to turn to.

Trembling, Anyu dropped the suitcase.

It made things easier that Bellefeuille didn't come to her bed for the next few days. When she heard the car's engine, she went to the atrium and looked out the window to see the couple who were now inseparable—Bellefeuille's new mistress wearing a black sable scarf and a hat shaped like a box. Anyu remembered seeing her at a party, Miss Lucy.

A few days later, Anyu woke up nauseous. In the bathroom, she threw up; when she called for the amah, she realized she had missed her period. Calculating the days, she had conceived the life about two months ago.

She slumped on the high-back chair, feeling cold. She was twenty-one years old; she had never considered becoming a mother or the idea of conceiving a child with Bellefeuille, especially at the moment they had drifted apart. He wouldn't like the idea. Or maybe he would? Maybe this would energize him and make him love her again?

She felt tired, a wave of lethargy overwhelming her. When she closed her eyes, she slept fitfully, falling in and out of a dream where she was wandering in a snowstorm. She felt her mother beside her, calling her name, asking her what was wrong and whether she had angered her landlord again. But she couldn't see her. Spinning, searching, she reached out for her, but all she saw were flakes of snow.

Anyu awoke, the image of Mother vivid in her mind. Was this a sign her mother would chastise her? Or a clue that Bellefeuille would love this child?

She would like to become a mother and have someone to look after. She could sing a lullaby to the little one, take him out for a walk in the garden, have him ride on her back, and teach him to draw, to make a ring or a necklace. And she would whisper to him about the beauty of the imperial Fabergé egg that had changed her life.

She wrapped a fur robe around herself and smiled. What would her child look like, she wondered. Would it be a boy? A girl? Would her child be gifted in drawing?

⌘

Two days later, she finally found Bellefeuille in the dining room, wearing his smoked silk pajamas and looking ill-tempered, berating the servants for his lukewarm coffee.

"Pierre, where have you been? I've been waiting for you. There's something exciting I need to tell you." She put his hand on her stomach.

He glanced at her stomach and then her face. His eyes glinted in the chandelier. "What is it, *ma chérie?*"

"I have good news. I'm with child."

He got up and went to pour some whiskey. Then he drained the glass. For a long moment, he paced before the ormolu clock.

She hated that she was right—he didn't care. But she was resolute. The child was hers, and she would take care of it, even if it had to be born out of wedlock. "I'm going to bed."

Later, Bellefeuille came. He looked like he had had too much to drink but spoke clearly. He was pleased with her pregnancy and hoped she would stay well for their impending wedding ceremony. He went on to suggest she eat a healthy diet rich in meat and cheese for every meal, and he had already scheduled a physician to examine her.

The physician came the next day, congratulated her, and ordered some pills to ensure an easy pregnancy. Bellefeuille was smiling, walking with her in the garden, his talk splashed with plans and promises. Once she gave birth to his child, he'd plan a trip to France and introduce her to his family, and the child would be raised in Paris. Would she agree to relocate? he asked. Anyu nodded. It was an easy decision—she would go wherever her child needed her.

Two days later, Anyu was tormented by a racking headache. The physician prescribed some herbal tea—a bowl of amber liquid; it smelled strongly of ginseng and star anise. "Will this hurt my baby?" She looked at the bowl, hesitant.

"It is for the health of the fetus," the physician replied. She drained it. She would drink anything for the health of her child.

To her dismay, she felt worse as the days went by. Her head pounded, her chest felt as if crushed by a brick, and she was too weak to get out of bed. One day, she awoke soaked with sweat and realized she was bleeding.

The amah fetched the physician again. It was only minor discomfort due to pregnancy, the physician said and advised her to keep drinking the herbal tea and have bed rest.

But two days later, she began to bleed profusely, and she could feel her body expel chunks of flesh or membrane. An intense pain shot through her abdomen; blood soaked the entire bed.

She must have passed out because when she came to, she was lying on a narrow bed in a hospital; echoes of groans and shrieks rang out from the hallway.

Bellefeuille was beside her, telling her to take care of herself and not to worry about anything else, then a Catholic nun in a black habit with a cross was saying, "Opium, opium," and another nun said, "Poor child, poor child," like a prayer.

Then there was no pain.

The days unfurled into an endless helix of fire and agony, the nights a starless, motherless sea. She turned away from the Catholic nuns who held out bits of opium to ease her pain, unable to open her mouth to speak, for if she did, she would scream and cry. She pulled the cotton cover over her head and mourned the unborn life lost before it had a chance to thrive. She had wanted it, the life that would make her someone, the life that would give her a family, the life that would make a difference for her. She would have fought for it and changed her whole world to protect it, just like her mother had done for her.

Had she asked for too much? What had she done wrong to deserve this despair?

Bellefeuille's voice came; she pulled down the cover, longing for him. The room was dark, smelling of alcohol, smoke, and cologne, and she was alone. She couldn't tell if she was hallucinating or if Bellefeuille was nearby.

"How many days will she need to recover? She's been here for two weeks." Bellefeuille's voice again—he was on the other side of the wall, outside the room. The door was left ajar; his voice slipped through.

"One more week at most."

A man's voice, but she couldn't figure out whose.

"How much did you give her?"

"One bowl at night, one in the morning, as you instructed, monsieur."

"Are you sure you didn't give her too much? Why is she so sick?"

"Her body might have had an adverse reaction to the herb, monsieur."

"See to it that she will survive. I don't want her to die."

"Give her some time. She's still young. She'll recover."

There was silence. "Does she know?"

"I doubt it."

"Good. She must never know. I have no intention of raising a bastard half-Chinese child."

Anyu shivered. She looked at the bowl that contained the herbal tea, the tea that had been said to strengthen her body, the tea that her amah had given her every day since she had revealed her pregnancy to Bellefeuille. All those days, she had drunk it and never suspected it.

Trembling, she picked up the bowl and threw it against the wall.

CHAPTER 26

February 1931

Nine days later, Anyu was discharged from the hospital.

Her amah came to fetch her—Master Bellefeuille was busy with a new line of jewelry that was set to roll out, she murmured. Anyu put on a long-sleeve black dress, a silk scarf, and a black coat and limped out of the hospital's hallway. Outside, the sky was a pallid face spotted with clouds shaped like colossal tears; the wind plunged down her throat, nearly choking her. She covered her mouth with her gloved hand and went down the stairs to the street, where a taxi waited.

In the car, Anyu had many questions for the amah but decided to ask nothing. She could tell that her servant knew about the herbal tea, but she wouldn't hold her to account. The old woman only did what she had been told. But Bellefeuille! He had drugged her and caused her to miscarry; he had deceived and lied to her all these months, and he had not had the nerve to face her. When she saw him at home, she would confront him, and she would not forgive him.

She looked out the window. For the thousandth time, she thought of the life she had conceived. Was it a boy or a girl? She would never know.

The taxi stopped; she held on to the door and stepped slowly out to ease the pain shooting from her abdomen. Then she blinked. In front of her was not Bellefeuille's grand mansion but a three-story apartment building with peeling plaster and rusted windows. And she was standing on a narrow pothole-filled street, not the tree-lined avenue. In her preoccupation, she had not even noticed the direction during the drive here.

She turned to the amah.

The woman stared at her black lace apron. This was a temporary residence Master Bellefeuille had found for her, she said.

It was then Anyu noticed the black suitcase her servant was carrying.

She wouldn't need to confront him, after all, she realized. Bellefeuille, who had talked her into marrying him, seduced her with his sugary words and silky dresses, kept her in his palatial home, forced her to miscarry, realized she was no longer of use to him and kicked her out.

The amah led her to a stone staircase. Anyu tottered past a gaggle of women washing laundry in a basin and climbed up, each step sending a shot of agony to her stomach. On the second floor, she entered a one-bedroom apartment with simple furniture. The amah set down the suitcase near her feet, murmured that the rent had been prepaid for six months, slipped a few coins into her hands, and left.

Anyu sat on the edge of the bed. Slowly, her eyes adjusted to the dimness of the room—cracked wood floor, soot-covered walls, and a cord dangling from a lightbulb, touching her shoulder, like a noose.

She stared at it, trembling. *Mother! Oh, Mother!*

When she was a child, she had thought her mother was gullible, stupid, to become a plaything for a man. She had never thought she would follow her path. But here she was, alone, used, scarred, miserable, in a dingy apartment, just like her mother, and she was worse; she had no fortune to keep a child, nor a home for herself. What would her mother have said if she were here?

She was twenty-one years old, but a fool. For six months and thirteen days, she had lived with a man she believed loved her. She had had some reservations about him the moment they met, yet she still drifted toward him and fell for him. How could she fail to see his mind, slippery and cold, a treacherous icy land?

Anyu awoke with a start. Bewildered, she sat up. Her face was wet, her hair soaked with tears. Somehow, she had fallen asleep. Her head ached, and she felt more miserable than she had earlier. The room was dim without light; there was the sound of water running downstairs and someone was having a fit of coughing. She had never felt this cold. She rubbed her arms and opened the suitcase the amah had left. Inside, packed evening gowns, shoes, hats, some jewelry, including Belperron's butterfly brooch. No blankets. She wrapped five dresses around her, still shivering.

There was a knock on her door. Bellefeuille? If it was him, she would slam the door in his face and tell him to get lost. There was nothing she could say to that man except hate, hate, hate. In a swoop that sent a crippling pain through her body, she ripped open the door.

In the hallway, an old man holding an *erhu*, a two-stringed instrument, stood in front of her neighbor's door; he turned to her.

She breathed hard, unsure of what to do. Then she took a deep breath and stepped toward the landing. At the top of the staircase, she stared down. The muscles of her abdomen screamed and her legs trembled. She forced herself to take another step, and then another, until she reached the cracked ground littered with trash.

On the street, she had to pause to catch her breath. It was cold, the wintery air pale like brine. Slowly, without a thought of where to go, she shuffled down the street, past barbers with shears in hand, earwax extractors holding thin metal scoops, marriage brokers brandishing zodiac signs, and fortune tellers clacking bamboo slats. She heard carriage drivers shouting at her, was shoved aside by businessmen wearing eyeglasses, spat on by phlegmy old men with poor vision, and stopped by smiling youths spinning knives in their hands.

She didn't see them; she kept shuffling.

How was it possible to feel so lonely when surrounded by people?

She must have walked for hours when she realized she was again in front of her apartment. Her head touched the bed and she was out.

For the next few days, she rose when the streets grew noisy, ate a few biscuits found in the suitcase, and walked and walked until it turned dark. This was what she would do, she realized: she'd walk until every tear of her misery left her, until her soul found peace.

The pain lodged in her abdomen, she plodded past the shops teeming with customers, the smoky bars, the Art Deco skyscrapers near the bund. She saw fashionable young women in fur hats and cloches, young girls wearing dresses with a slit near their thighs, prostitutes smoking cigarettes by the high walls of the fortresses around the Old City. She saw fur shops, clothing boutiques, automobile shops, hardware stores, soap shops, emporiums, temples, herb stores, brothels, opium dens, and jewelry shops. Once, she stood before a shop owned by Bellefeuille and stared inside. All the jewelry, all the beautiful golden brooches for sale, all the gold flowers that he had crafted. She couldn't bring herself to look at them.

How many days she walked in the city she couldn't remember, but soon, her stomach was no longer painful. She grew healthier, her legs strong with muscles, and she could walk from dawn to evening without feeling fatigued. She also lost some of her beauty in the sun, with dark speckles like sesames scattered across her cheekbones, her skin roughened like a peanut shell.

Her gaze found many people—the mothers holding children's hands, the young couples sharing a bowl at square tables, the actors with painted faces singing Beijing opera to a small crowd in the square.

She envied them, their companionship, their self-indulgence, and their dedication. She wished she were not alone. Then it struck her that she had been loved, too—there was Mother, who had died looking for food for her, and Confucius and Isaac, who had cared for her, too. Yet what had she done for them? She had thrown tempers and given her mother the cold shoulder, and she had pushed Confucius and Isaac away when she couldn't get what she wanted. She was not a good person, she realized; she had been willful, selfish, and ungrateful.

And Pierre Bellefeuille? Maybe he was her punishment.

One day, she came to an area with fallen walls and crumbled houses. Bricks, rafters, and furniture were piled on the streets; people were cooking rice in a corner where the roofs had caved in.

Anyu did not know what had happened to the area. A flood? A fire? But there they were, these people, after the destruction, after the loss of their homes, rebuilding their lives.

That evening, when she returned to her apartment, she took the few coins the amah had given her and bought a bowl of wonton soup on the street. Sitting on a bench, she savored every drop of the soup rich with minced meat and fragrant with scallions. It was her favorite food, and she had forgotten how delicious it was.

In her apartment, she opened her suitcase: the small purse she had purchased in a department store, the pillbox hats, the Chanel dresses, the fluffy pink gown that Bellefeuille had handpicked for her, and Belperron's butterfly brooch. She fingered the soft silk, thinking of those days of extravagance, those evenings of champagne, wearing the dresses that were not hers, picturing the wedding that was not meant to be, and she knew, for as long as she was alive, she'd mourn the child that could have been hers.

It was time to forget them all, the scars, the fantasies, and the scattered past.

She took the dresses and hats and the Belperron butterfly brooch to a shop and pawned them all.

CHAPTER 27

April 1931

Her cash was running low, and soon, she'd have to pay rent. She needed a job.

Anyu mulled over her options. Returning to the Mandelburgs was out of the question—it would hurt her pride—and working for other foreign houses was equally humiliating. She decided to look into the local Chinese stores. The city had nine jewelry stores, called silver shops, with which she had become familiar after walking in the city for many days. She still had the skills of a jeweler, and surely, the shops would hire her.

Anyu visited the Yang Qinghe Silver Shop on Nanjing Road, a stately two-story building painted in gold and adorned with calligraphy. She introduced herself simply as Anyu at the counter and asked if they needed a jeweler. She had no tools, or she would have demonstrated her skill to show her qualifications. The man at the counter looked surprised and told her to wait.

While waiting, she browsed the jewelry in the glass cases. Most of the objects were accessories for men, such as pendants, belt hooks, and belt rings; there were also enameled padlocks, decorative boxes, porcelain vessels, and vases with blue enamel glaze. Many designs, as she had expected, featured auspicious animal motifs, such as cranes, dragons, and phoenixes. Deities such as Buddha and the Goddess of

Compassion, who would provide protection to the wearer, were also popular, as were peonies and chrysanthemums.

There were few jewelry pieces for women. Anyu only saw some bangles, earrings, and hair accessories, their designs plain and simple, but all gleaming with an astounding sheen of yellow that could only come from twenty-four karat pure gold—a surprise. It seemed the shop had found a way to go around the government's decree. But she also understood the Chinese customers desired jewelry made of twenty-four karat gold, which was regarded as authentic gold; ornaments made of alloy, which Isaac and other jewelers had chosen, were looked down upon and considered fake. However, pure gold was too mellow to maneuver; even Belperron had opted for a lower grade of the metal.

The techniques of the jewelry mainly featured engraving, filigree, and inlay, and the designs were more realistic than stylistic. Most were made of jade in various colors and grades. Few used diamonds and gemstones.

"Miss Anyu?" The owner, Mr. Yang, a thin old man wearing a long gray robe, received her at the counter. He looked as though he had just awakened from his nap. He asked her about her training in his casual voice, scratching his chin and arms. When she replied she had learned her skills from a Russian jeweler, he appeared skeptical.

"We are a small family-owned silver shop, Miss Anyu, and we only hire reputable, trustworthy jewelers from local artisan families who have a history of designing jewelry for the Chinese imperial families." Mr. Yang stressed "trustworthy".

She took her leave, wondering if it would have been helpful if she had mentioned the House of Mandelburg.

Then she went to the Old Feng Xiang Silver Shop. This time, she gave her name as Anyu, from the House of Mandelburg.

She browsed the shop again while waiting. Old Feng Xiang sold items similar to what she had seen in Yang Qinghe's shop, but one hairpin caught her attention. It had striking blue enamel that appeared to be lapis lazuli from one angle and turquoise from another. The owner, a short man with glasses, explained that he had used the kingfisher's iridescent plumage as a pigment and laid feathers on hot metals shaped like stars and shells. Traditionally called *dian cui*, this was a technique he had learned from his grandfather, who had been an imperial metalsmith.

Even Fabergé's eggs, which used 144 enamel colors, couldn't produce two shades of blue with one pigment.

The owner's son, a youth wearing red suspenders, interviewed her. He had heard her name, read about her in the newspaper, and highly valued her designs. But sadly, he must honor the agreement held by the nine silver shops in Shanghai, which barred the Chinese shops from trading gold or silver with foreign dealers or employing foreigners.

She was unaware of the local businesses' agreement, which explained why the silver shops didn't feature jewelry with diamonds or other precious gemstones—they had no access to them.

"I'm not a foreigner," she said. "I'm from Harbin."

"You were trained by a foreigner. We don't work with artisans associated with them."

Anyu walked out of the silver shop, her head hung low. For the first time since she left the House of Mandelburg, she realized the immense luck she had had to have met Isaac, who had selflessly trained her, nurtured her, and elevated her career. It was foolish of her to have discarded it all.

Should she return to the Mandelburgs?

One morning, Anyu found a package wrapped in greasy newspaper left at her door. She opened it. Inside was half a roasted duck; its golden skin glistened, beads of fat dripping.

A man left it there, her neighbor, the old man who liked to play the *erhu*, told her.

Anyu brought the duck inside and devoured it. The meat brought memories of the duck Mother had bought when she was thirteen. How

Mother smiled, chewing on the bony head, while she stuffed her mouth with the succulent meat, and her heart was full, too, with her mother's love.

Whoever left the duck knew her taste.

Then, one day, she opened the door to see a man leaning against the railing. "Surprise!" he said cheerfully.

She recognized him instantly. "Confucius!"

The last time she saw him she had just turned seventeen. She had thought they'd never see each other again. "It was you! You left me the duck!"

He had grown taller, his face leaner, his eyes bigger, alert like a house mouse's. His hair was still the same shoulder length. "I thought you might like it. You look awfully thin."

Who would know they'd meet again. She smiled. "How did you find me?"

"You were sulking all over the city for months! My men had been following you. They were thinking about kidnapping you but held back because they believed you were crazy, a woman with nine fingers and a dead look in her eyes. You scared them."

"Your men?"

He gave five fingers. "We're a gang of five. We offer the best crimes in Shanghai: Kidnapping, coercion, burglary, bribery, gang fights, gun fights, spying. All except murder. For you, free of charge."

"I wonder if the great teacher Confucius offered advice on a code of conduct for criminals."

"Criminals? That depends on how you see it. But the great teacher's wisdom is free for all. Here's one: *An oppressive government is more to be feared than a tiger.*"

She shook her head. Still, it was good to see Confucius. "I thought I'd never see you again."

"I stayed away from you, as you said. But I've been following the news about you." He leaned on the balcony, brushing aside the laundry on a clothesline overhead. "I don't get it."

"Don't get what?"

"Mandelburg is twenty-five years older than you."

"I know how old he is."

"Bellefeuille is even older than Mandelburg."

"What are you trying to say?"

"Why do you like old men?"

Anyu's face grew hot. "They're not . . . old . . ."

"Is it because you don't have a father?"

What was that supposed to mean? Why would he say that? Yet it was true that sometimes she did perceive Isaac as a father figure, and for her entire life, she had felt the emptiness of not having a father—it was there, out of the corner of her eye and behind her back, where she couldn't see. Sometimes, this emptiness—wondering if and how and why—hung above her head like the sun.

Did she mistake Isaac's fatherly adoration for a lover's affection? Had Isaac known this all along and tried to tell her? He loved her, he had confessed, but he understood she was deep in her adolescent passion, and he had wanted to give her more time to mature, with an understanding that one day she'd realize how she truly felt about him.

She understood, finally.

"I knew it! You have a father complex!"

"Too bad. I was going to invite you in." She shut the door.

Confucius came over for a visit once a week and brought roasted duck and chestnuts and glutinous rice balls with sausage and egg yolks. Sometimes, they sat on the edge of the bed, feasting on the savory meat and licking their fingers; sometimes, they leaned on the windowsill, talking about the goings-on in the city and listening to the high-pitched operas carried by the wind; sometimes, he was a bit too close, his hand touching hers.

She didn't say anything. She liked Confucius, and she had thought of him in the lonely hours for the past four years. But love was a dangerous art that she had failed at time and time again. She wanted to take it slow.

One evening, they leaned against the windowsill, watching children play with fireworks in the street. The vendors had closed their stalls early, and the street was a children's playground. They held sparklers, their faces lit by the brilliant light.

"Why did you come, Confucius?"

"I can't stay away." He would like her to know him as a man, not a gangster, Confucius added. He had been born into a wealthy family, with his future planned out for him, he said. But his father died, and his mother got pneumonia, draining his family's wealth with each bowl of herbs. As a young man, he had once won a top scholarship at a university, but a magistrate bribed the school and the scholarship was given to the magistrate's son instead. When Confucius protested, he was dismissed for disobedience. He hadn't found a decent job since.

He was not a brave man, nor a good gangster who committed crimes like it was his calling. His motto was "It's better to be a living coward than a dead daredevil." Deep down, he felt guilty about robbing people of their money or possessions, and he swore to quit when he went to bed every night, but those oaths dissolved as quickly as the morning dew at sunrise.

"All I can say is that life is a thief who takes pleasure in showing off his sleight of hand. Most of us are incompetent players, and most of us are losers. But here we are, at the game table; we might as well pretend to win and have some fun, don't you agree?" Confucius said.

She considered. Who would have thought she'd end up in a dingy apartment like her mother?

"But you're still a gangster."

"If you think about it, you're more of a gangster than me," he said.

"Why is that?"

"Because you have nine fingers."

She held up her hand. The stump, where the missing finger had been, looked like a shriveled jujube date. She still remembered the shock and the pain when the gunshot tore through her finger. "If it weren't for you, I would have died."

"No doubt about that. But I would never let you die."

She didn't speak. Confucius was kind to her, but this might be another mistake. On the street, more children were running out of the buildings, shrieking, holding sparklers; her gaze followed them, those little sprites who reminded her of the child she had lost.

"Those stinkers," he said. "I want to have ten of them."

She turned to him.

"I assume you still want to get married?" he asked.

"Yes, in fifty years."

"I'll be there."

Deeply, she kissed him. What if she was an incompetent player? She would take a chance. And one day, she'd tell him about the child she lost.

They made plans: he'd take her to visit his mother, who lived in a modest room in the Hong Kou District, and when her apartment rental ended, she could choose to live with them or find another place. Anyu felt like smiling. Would she have a normal domestic life, with relatives and a home?

"I do hope you will find something decent to do," she said.

Confucius hesitated. "One last job tomorrow, then I'll quit."

But then, the next day, Confucius didn't come.

Anxious, Anyu searched for him. Restaurants. Gambling houses. Opium dens. And even a brothel. Outside a gambling house, she found his friend, Yong, his face bloody. The poor man's kneecaps were shattered, his ribs broken. There had been a gang fight, and the police arrested them. Confucius had fled.

Anyu hoped he was unharmed, somewhere safe, hiding and taking care of himself. And when the time came, he would find her and they would be together again. Maybe they wouldn't. Maybe they were not meant for each other.

The other Chinese jewelry stores declined to offer her a job as well, citing her background of being trained by a foreigner, and the only employment options left for her were as a maid or a washerwoman. Anyu couldn't believe this was her fate. Frequently, she thought of Isaac—she still cared about him. And his egg. And Esther—*You'll always be a member of the Mandelburg family.* Should she go back?

She studied her fingers; the tips were round, smooth, having not held tools for almost a year. She missed jewelry making—the joy of designing, sawing a gold plate, and watching a piece of metal transform in her hand. If only she were given another chance to be a jeweler.

One day in June, she passed a news stall. Glancing at the *North China Daily News*, she stopped. At the bottom, in large type, was the news: A Russian jewelry shop had been burglarized. The old man, the owner who fought hard, was wounded; the burglar had escaped.

It was Isaac's shop.

Anyu was worried. Was Uncle David wounded? How about Isaac? She wanted to know how they were doing and how much they lost, and above all, she wanted to apologize to Isaac for her stubbornness. She had made the mistake of leaving him. She should respect his wish—he couldn't marry her; that was all right. She just wanted to be a jeweler.

The next day, at the break of dawn, Anyu got out of bed. She picked up her suitcase, which contained her few belongings, and left the apartment. On the street, she began to walk, looking ahead, toward the only place she wanted to go, the only place where she truly belonged.

CHAPTER 28

It was still early; the dawn light poured over the gray tile roofs like a layer of pearly paint. The streets were quiet; here and there, a man emerged and vanished, a carriage rattled by, and a squeaking rickshaw raced past. Anyu passed the shops with lattice windows, the balconies with their hanging rattan birdcages, and the pavement damp with midnight rain, and for the first time, she felt at home in this city. She loved Shanghai even more than Harbin, Shanghai with its juxtaposed shabbiness and sophistication, its vanity and its gaucheness, its nakedness and its pretense. And she liked the city most at this hour, the moment before awakening, the moment before the world was ripped and redrawn again.

Anyu turned onto the street where the Mandelburgs' shop was located. The sun was rising; in the distance, the shop looked just as she had remembered—modest, masked in the pale fog, wedged between two red brick buildings. When she came in front of the shop, she could see the peeling paint around the store's elegant sign and the empty cigarette packets littering the ground. She paused momentarily before reaching out to the door, recalling her arrival more than five years ago. She had been sixteen then, a girl, scared and lonely, full of doubts, and now she was twenty-one, a woman, scarred and lonely, with no more doubts.

And she was ready to beg, ask for forgiveness, and do anything necessary to be part of the Mandelburg family again.

Anyu pushed the door open.

The showroom was lit; rows of jewelry filled the glass cases. Esther was cleaning the counter with a rag. She looked up, surprise dancing in her eyes, and a wide smile spread across her face. "Anyu!"

Anyu smiled back. "Good morning, Esther. You're early."

"I'm always the first in the shop."

Anyu switched her suitcase to her left hand. "I heard about the burglary. I was worried. So I came."

"Well, you know you can come anytime."

Her friend's words were more precious than gold. "Do you know who robbed you? What did you lose?"

"Some necklaces. Mr. Du claims he's investigating it. He said it was an insult that someone would undermine his authority and steal from a shop under his protection. We'll see." Esther came around the L-shaped counter.

Anyu gasped. "You're with child!"

Esther smiled and patted at the swell of her stomach under her oversized dress. "I'm seven months in. Soon, very soon, my baby will arrive, but I'll work until my baby tells me to stop."

Anyu couldn't take her eyes off Esther—oh, she looked beautiful. Her gray eyes, which used to be piercing, had softened; her face was glowing; and even her voice sounded melodic, without the sharp edge.

"Father is in the workshop. Should I go get him?"

Anyu switched her suitcase to her right hand, growing nervous.

"Why don't you go in?" Esther tipped her head to the door to the hallway. "He'll be delighted to see you."

Anyu gripped her suitcase with two hands and stepped into the hallway. It was damp, dark, and narrow as before. A sweet aroma wafted in the air. One of the aunts must be cooking rice.

The workshop door was left ajar; she pushed it open. Isaac, Samuel, and Uncle David sat at their jewelers' workbenches, holding their tools. Isaac was busy with a piece of metal on the jeweler's saw.

Anyu stepped in. The odor of metal, dust, and chemicals greeted her like an old friend. She put down her suitcase near the door. Her workbench was still there, covered with the metal tape measure, the hammers, the jeweler's saws, and the pliers.

"Good morning," she said.

They all turned to her. There was a moment of silence, awkward, as all the whirring and sawing of the tools paused. Then there was noise, chairs scraping the floor, throats clearing, and whispering. She could feel the heat rushing to her face, and her heart pounded.

Isaac was in front of her, and now she could see his right arm was suspended in a cloth sling—it was he, not Uncle David, who was wounded. There was a bandage on his forehead, and his lips were swollen. But his eyes were smiling.

"Why are you just standing there? Are you going to your bench?"

This was better than anything she had hoped for. "Yes," she said, grateful. "I'm going to my bench."

"Good. If you want to see the orders, you know where they are."

Relieved, she went to the wall near the safe and scanned the pouch that contained the sheets of order forms. There were only five. She took one. It was an order for a ring.

"You might wish to know that after the burglary, Father has decided to make changes to the business model. The merchandise in the showroom will be reduced. There are few orders from customers," Samuel said, holding his ruler.

"I see." She cleared her throat. "We'll find new clients."

She sat on her stool. The order was simple. It wouldn't take her long to complete.

She reached out for the jeweler's saw. The oak handle was cool, smooth, fitting snugly in her hand, just as before.

But it was cruel. Everything seemed to take longer, including sawing, making a bezel setting, and even polishing. She was clumsy, her fingers stiff, and the metal pieces were slippery. When she put the chasing hammer down to flex her fingers, she saw hours had passed and Uncle David and Samuel had gone for lunch.

Isaac came to her side.

Her heart raced faster; she couldn't help it, how she had missed him. But she composed herself. She could not afford to live in the old fancies and heartaches again. From now on, she'd bury her love and focus on her work. "I'll finish this in a few hours. I'm rather rusty."

"It'll come back to you."

"Thank you."

"I can't tell you how happy I am to have you back."

Anyu smiled. "I want to start over."

"I see." He went to his workbench, opened a drawer, and gave her a gold ring, the ring with the moonstone, the signet ring with the double-headed eagle emblem. "Then you'll need this."

She held it in her palm, trembling.

"The egg is yours. It's been waiting for your return."

She didn't know what to say, choked with tears.

He slid the ring on her finger. "You're my only successor, and I love you more than you can ever imagine. But life doesn't always give us what we want, does it? Maybe in good times, you might realize that some love is silent, some love is eternal, some love might not be seen, but it'll be felt."

Anyu wanted to cry. She would not speak of love in front of him again, but she would not stop loving him. "I want to create something new, something unique. But I have no inspiration. I can't draw."

"Draw whatever is in your heart. Draw what life has shown you along your path. Above all, draw the good things in life—you have your freedom."

Freedom.

That evening, Anyu lay on the bed Esther had prepared for her in the attic and listened to the aunts' soft snoring. Esther, who lived with Mr. Dearborn in their apartment, no longer stayed here at night; it was just the aunts and her. Anyu felt the smooth moonstone of the signet ring and unlocked the double-headed eagle beneath. She traced her finger over the heads, the wings, the talons. She could feel the egg close by, waiting for her—yes, she would visit it soon, very soon. It was hers, Isaac had said, or did she belong to the egg? She felt a flow of energy at the thought of the ornament with its superior artistry and beauty, revitalized by the stream of inspiration that had once nurtured her.

She thought of Isaac's words again. *You have your freedom.* Maybe freedom was knowing she had made mistakes in the past but she could do right in the future; freedom was living the life she desired, loving the man in the way she needed, and crafting jewelry as she envisioned.

She sprang from the bed and raced downstairs to the workshop. It was locked. She ran up to the attic, took out the sketchbook Isaac had returned to her, and sat at the breakfast table. By lamplight, she began to draw a butterfly brooch.

In the morning, when Isaac, Samuel, and Uncle David opened the workshop, she had already finished the drawing and was ready to saw. Isaac studied her drawing, counted the number of the gemstones she needed, and got in touch with Mr. Walters. Then she worked, using twenty-four karat gold instead of platinum, stretching it thin for the butterfly's veins, then one 1.5-carat pear-shaped yellow diamond for each forewing and hind wing, and two marquise-cut yellow diamonds for the thorax and abdomen.

For twenty straight hours, she didn't talk, didn't sleep; when her eyelids threatened to close, she went out of the workshop and chain-smoked in the kitchen and then returned, energized. When her stomach ached with hunger, she devoured a hard-boiled egg and a bowl of porridge.

Fifteen days later, using the lost-wax casting technique, she completed a set: a necklace, a ring, a brooch, a bracelet, and a pair of earrings.

Isaac held the brooch, his eyes filled with wonder. "Butterfly."

"There is a Chinese legend called 'Butterfly Lovers.' It tells the tragic story of a girl from the Zhu family and a boy from the Liang family. Zhu met Liang at school and fell in love. They swore an oath to each other, pledging their everlasting devotion. But Zhu's father arranged for her to marry another man. When Liang heard that, he died of grief. Zhu's wedding was interrupted by a storm, which brought the procession to Liang's grave, where Zhu wept and vowed that they'd never be apart again. At her words, a clap of thunder struck, opening the grave and engulfing Zhu. When it opened again, the couple had disappeared and out flew a pair of butterflies. So you see, the butterfly symbolizes eternal love in Chinese culture."

Isaac nodded. "A touching story. What will you call this set?"

"Eternal Love."

"I like it. I will bring these designs to Mrs. Brown. I believe she would like to see them. There's only one problem, Anyu," he said, holding the brooch with the inscription IM. "An artist's name is eternal; it outlives the artist, outshines an era, and outlasts an empire. As the designer of this set, I believe you are entitled to create your own maker's marks."

He offered her the chance to use her own signature, the signature every serious jeweler dreamed of. She thought for a moment. Holding the jeweler's saw, she carefully carved one letter on the brooch.

Now, she was part of his name. IMA.

Isaac kissed her forehead. Then, his right arm in a sling, the box of jewelry safely tucked inside his pocket, he left the shop with Uncle David to meet with Mrs. Brown, who had arranged a meeting with a group of private buyers, two compradors working for Shanghai Bank and some diplomats' wives. In the afternoon, they returned.

"How long will it take you to complete another set?" Isaac asked.

"Three weeks at most," she said.

"And a dozen sets?"

"Three months. Why?"

A diplomat's wife had placed an order for a dozen Eternal Love sets.

It had taken her two months, not three, when she set down the polishing cloth and wiped her smudged hands. A dozen sets of Eternal Love had been completed. In front of her were boxes of jewelry: necklaces with butterfly pendants, butterfly brooches, butterfly rings, butterfly bracelets, and butterfly earrings. She smiled. Her work had just started—more orders appeared on the rack as word got out that she had returned.

Then, one day, while Anyu was soldering one of her Eternal Love necklaces, Esther went into labor in the kitchen. The whole house jolted. Samuel went to fetch Mr. Dearborn from the couple's apartment but couldn't find him. He finally caught him at his shop in the Settlement. Isaac closed the showroom, the twin aunts boiled hot water, and Anyu carried a basin and towels, her mouth dry, her heart pounding in fear, waiting to help. Oh, poor Esther. Her heartrending screams could have ripped the apartment in half.

At midnight, Esther, bathed in sweat, gave birth to a baby boy—Matthew.

Anyu took a peek at the infant in Esther's arms—his eyes shut, his hands curled near his chin as if contemplating, and there were wrinkles on his forehead and white bumps and red pimples on his cheeks. He was so small, delicate, his face a fascinating wonder, his fingers and toes as tiny as peanuts. She thought of the life she had lost. Had she kept him, would he have been so small as well?

Esther gave Matthew to her to hold; Anyu was nervous. Carefully, she held her arms out and received the bundle. When she touched him, she started to tremble—it was as if the whole world were in her hands. She had to be careful, or she would drop him and break him. But he was weightless! Lighter than a hammer! And he was crying! Why did he cry? Anyu laughed, tears bursting out of her eyes.

Esther's baby, Esther's baby. He had captured her heart the moment he arrived, and he would have hers for as long as she lived. Anyu blinked back her tears.

After she handed him back to Esther to nurse, Anyu went to her workbench and began drawing a goldfish.

The next day, another set of designs, Pure Love, was created.

Isaac brought it to a jewelers' meeting. The head of a bank ordered two dozen of the Pure Love set, including rings, necklaces, and brooches.

❧

With the birth of her newborn, Esther took time off from the shop. The showroom was short-staffed. Whenever she could, Anyu helped with sales.

Unlike her previous experience at the counter, now talking to the customers felt like a relaxing and educational diversion. The younger generation came with a purpose, an engagement, a birthday, or a gift of forgiveness. The older customers were different. They shopped because they wanted to, and they didn't need prompts to dive into their past, their quarrels with their sons and their spats with their daughters-in-law. They went on and on, enumerating their ailments, from ankle pains to urinary tract infections. But they could also be emotional—one elderly Italian woman shared a heartwarming story about wanting a custom locket to keep the few gray hairs of her recently deceased husband, to whom she had been married for fifty-five years.

Patiently, Anyu listened, and patiently, she smiled, giving them suggestions.

A good jeweler makes jewelry, but a master jeweler builds relationships. She finally understood what Isaac had said.

A stubby man wearing a black fedora entered her shop one day. He wanted to talk about his mother. She was a spirited woman, he said, who enjoyed driving motorcars and shooting. A decade ago, their home caught fire; she dove into their home to rescue his Chinese governess. The governess was saved, but his mother perished in the fire.

He wondered if Anyu would design a necklace to honor his mother. He had come to her store personally, for he admired her designs. His mother's name was Laura, and he was Lawrence Kadoorie, the owner of the famous Marble Hall, son of Horace Kadoorie, one of her former clients.

The Kadoorie family were Jews transplanted to Shanghai years ago, Anyu had learned. They had arrived in Shanghai with nothing but rose to be successful business owners, and they were known for their generous charity toward the poor. She was touched by the mother's heroic story and the profound bond between the mother and the son and wanted to create a pendant to honor their special love as well as the family's resilient spirit as immigrants in Shanghai. For jewelry did not simply signify value for its diamonds and gold; it meant so much more—it was a token of hope, a gem of memory, and an emblem of conviction for eternity.

Two weeks later, she created her third set, Good Love, featuring a dragonfly with two *en tremblant* wings, their veins formed from diamonds shaped like an *L*, a cabochon sapphire for the thorax, and an elongated abdomen crafted from rectangular jadeite set in gold. Lawrence Kadoorie's eyes lit up when she put the pendant in his hands.

"A dragonfly," he said, smiling. A man well versed in Chinese culture, he understood that the dragonfly, revered for its ability to tread on water, trek on land, and fly through the air, was lauded as a good luck charm, a harbinger of positivity and prosperity, and a symbol of adaptability. But more than that, the dragonfly, as the folklore described, was a protector of children, a messenger from the beloved in the spiritual world.

When he displayed it at a party in his residence, the Marble Hall, the city exploded with excitement. Accolades poured in:

"A perfect marriage of Eastern whimsy and Western aesthetics."

"An exquisite conjury of gold and gemstones."

Good Love would become the most demanded jewelry line for the year of 1932.

Everything was going exactly as she had imagined—her creations brought the House of Mandelburg to new heights of popularity, and the brand, having taken a hit after her departure, reclaimed its iconic status to become the most favored in the city. This was precisely what she wanted for Isaac, for his family. Her family.

Then, one afternoon, in March 1933, Samuel came into the kitchen, where she had been smoking. His golden hair was combed neatly, parted in the middle, his gray eyes intense. He hadn't gambled again, Esther had told her, and as far as Anyu could tell, Samuel, at twenty-seven years old, had recommitted himself to the family business, working during the day. In the evenings, he'd go out, and when he came back, she could smell a whiff of fragrance on his suits.

But Samuel wasn't entirely warm to her since her return. He sometimes created minor inconveniences, hoarding the tools she needed.

"Smoking again?" he said.

"What do you want?" Anyu blew smoke through the open window in the kitchen, holding what must have been her thirtieth cigarette of the day. It was impossible to work without smoking. Tobacco gave her spurts of energy and kept her mind sharp, so sleeping was no longer a necessity. She only dozed off in the workshop for two to three hours a day, all that she needed. But smoking in the workshop was unsafe; as a solution, she took breaks smoking in the kitchen with the window open.

"Mr. Walters was scheduled to deliver diamonds, but he failed to show up."

"Your father knows about this, doesn't he?"

Samuel hesitated.

"Did Mr. Walters say when he'd come?"

"No."

"You look worried. Why are you worried?"

Samuel turned around to leave but stopped. "Did Father give you the Midnight Aurora?"

"What are you talking about?"

"You shouldn't have come back." He left the kitchen.

Samuel's displeasure was hard to understand, and so was his question. Anyu finished smoking and returned to the workshop to work on her commissions. Isaac, she realized, wasn't around.

Later, she was forging a ring when she felt a tap on her shoulder. She looked up.

"Isaac, where have you been?"

"I couldn't find Mr. Walters." His voice was weak.

"Oh."

"Mrs. Brown asked to see you in the vault."

⁌❧

The cutlery shop looked the same, subdued, with the "Closed" sign hanging on the door. Inside, Anyu gave the coded answer to the Sikh guards and went down the staircase under the Goddess of Peace statue. Isaac waited outside on the street.

This was the second time Anyu had visited the vault since her return. Her first visit to the secret place had been brief but necessary— she had longed to see the egg; after the viewing, she had returned to the workshop to work.

The vault was quiet. She walked through the safely guarded room and came to face Mrs. Brown, who held a suitcase with twelve compartments filled with jewelry pouches. The light was dim, and the air smelled of Mrs. Brown's fragrance, not cigarettes.

"I believe I have all you need here," the British lady said, handing her the ledger and suitcase.

Anyu inspected the diamonds, counted them, and signed the ledger with her name. The Guild had been kind to her; without its support, she never would have completed the sets in such a timely manner.

"You surprise me, Miss Anyu. I've been impressed with the jewelry lines you've created."

"I'll be happy to make something for you, too, if you like."

"Since when did you become so nice?"

It was a bristly question, but Anyu thought Mrs. Brown's tone was pacified. She still remembered what Bellefeuille had said about Mrs. Brown. He had bitterly accused her of withholding her secret and defamed her by implying she lived a promiscuous lifestyle, but Anyu could see, beneath her cold demeanor, that Mrs. Brown was, in fact, a dignified woman with a discerning eye, and a confident leader. "Why couldn't Mr. Walters come to the store?"

"Well, I was going to tell you. He disappeared."

"Disappeared?"

"We've been looking for him for a month. But I'm befuddled. He's deaf, he lives alone, he's a discreet man, and his social circle is small.

Only a few people in Shanghai are acquainted with him. Perhaps he got into trouble at the wrong time and the wrong place."

Bellefeuille had mentioned Mr. Du was interested in Mrs. Brown, Anyu recalled. "Do you think Mr. Du has something to do with it?"

"The gangster leader? He usually stays away from foreigners, and the police at the Settlement keep him at arm's length. But now that you mention it, I'll have them look into that. We'll find Mr. Walters."

Mr. Walters worked for the Guild, and he was a crucial person linked to Mrs. Brown and the Workmasters Guild. "Are you safe, Mrs. Brown?"

She tilted her head. "Darling, what a question. Is there something you have to say?"

Anyu stared hard at the lady, then turned around to look at the treasures and the vault—it had taken the master jewelers six months to build it, Isaac had said; this place was even more secure than the generalissimo's bedroom. "May I take a look at my egg?"

"Of course." Mrs. Brown walked toward it, her heels clicking on the marble floor.

Anyu arrived in front of the shelf that held the crystal box. She pressed the side of her signet ring to reveal the double-headed eagle and fitted it inside the crystal. The case unfolded, and she took out the box that contained her egg. "If you don't mind, Mrs. Brown, I'd like to take it home with me."

The lady was silent for a moment. "It's your egg."

Anyu tucked the box into her coat pocket, and with one hand holding the suitcase, she headed toward the exit.

When she came out of the cutlery shop, it was raining. Isaac was waiting on a park bench with an umbrella.

She ducked under his umbrella. "I have all the diamonds we need for the Good Love line. And the egg. We must find a safe place in our shop and hide it."

"What? Why did you take it?"

"I have to. She knows, but she didn't tell me."

"Knows what?"

"The Guild is compromised; there's a leak."

CHAPTER 29

But how could that be possible? Who was the leak? Isaac kept asking, astonished, and he looked on the verge of collapse, despite Anyu's assurance that Mrs. Brown appeared to have everything under control, the vault was safe, and her retrieval of the egg was only a precaution.

As soon as they reached the workshop, Anyu looked around for a hiding place. The safe was too obvious.

At night, while the house was asleep, Anyu used her knife to cut out two bricks from the wall near her workbench. With Isaac's help, she built a hidden niche and placed the box that contained the Fabergé egg inside. Then she slid the two bricks back into the wall, concealing the niche.

It was not the safest place, but it was the only viable option for the moment. And only two people in the world knew where the Winter Egg was. She and Isaac.

Two days later, Anyu was working in the workshop when Isaac told her Mrs. Brown had important messages for them and asked to see them at her mansion.

It was raining again. The taxi they took moved slowly, and it was difficult to see anything through the windows. Then the rain stopped, and the taxi honked at every turn. The driver, a young man with a cigarette in his mouth, cursed, muttering something about the Japanese soldiers flooding the streets.

"Where are they?" she asked. She had been working all day inside the workshop and rarely paid attention to the people outside.

"You don't see them? They're everywhere!" He took out his cigarette and pointed at some figures exiting a two-story restaurant with two women in flowery dresses. "They're dancing with our women and taking them to their beds, bribing them with money and dresses. They are a bad influence. Yesterday, they got into a fight with a few gangsters and shot them! They're going to take over Shanghai!"

She gazed out the window. It was true that among the pedestrians were many Japanese soldiers in uniforms. She thought of Confucius and hoped he was not entangled with the agitators. His absence had made her change course and return to Isaac, for which she was grateful, but she also longed to see him again.

"They can't take over Shanghai," she said. But she remembered what she had read in the newspaper. The Japanese Kwantung Army, which rumors said had assassinated the warlord Zhang, had invaded Manchuria last year, driven out the Young Marshal's army, and established a puppet state of Manchukuo, with the last emperor of the collapsed Qing Dynasty, Puyi, as the emperor.

"I wonder if Mrs. Brown has news about Mr. Walters," Anyu said, changing the subject.

"She might. Samuel was asking about Mr. Walters, too," Isaac said.

"Samuel is very concerned about him, isn't he?"

The driver grumbled and finally stopped at Mrs. Brown's mansion, guarded by four men wearing raincoats. They recognized Isaac and waved them in.

Mrs. Brown was waiting for them in her emerald living room. She had tea and biscuits ready, but she was pacing and deep in thought. After a brief exchange of pleasantries, she asked, "Anyu, Isaac said you believed there was a leak. How did you know?"

Anyu mentioned her conversation with Bellefeuille and said, "I confess it was only a hunch because you're a prudent woman, and you won't make an announcement until you are certain who the leak is."

Mrs. Brown sighed. "I still haven't discovered who."

Mr. Lebedev? Mr. Tang? Mr. Petrov?

"Did you find Mr. Walters?" Anyu asked.

"I did."

"Where was he?"

"In the river."

Isaac let out a sigh. He had been weighed down by stress since Anyu's visit to the vault.

"I received a phone call from the police this morning and identified him," Mrs. Brown said.

"Do the others know?" Isaac asked.

"I've phoned Mr. Lebedev, Mr. Tang, and Mr. Petrov and warned them of the leak. They were all in shock, as you can imagine. I'd like to reiterate that the police in the Settlement are investigating this case; they will leave no stone unturned. Whoever the perpetrator is, Mr. Du or his gangsters, I guarantee they'll be held responsible."

"I worry about your safety, Mrs. Brown," Anyu said quietly.

The British lady smiled and gestured to her bodyguards in the corners.

Anyu took a deep breath. "In an unthinkable event, Mrs. Brown, what is your plan for the vault?"

Mrs. Brown looked at her, and Anyu could see the lady had given careful thought to the Guild's treasures. "I have it on lockdown for the moment. You won't be able to enter. As soon as I find a safe place, I'll arrange a transfer. In the meantime, I apologize, but the Guild won't be able to fill your order of gemstones. You may have to make do with what you have for a while."

Anyu nodded. She had enough gemstones to work with for the next six months, but finding a safe place for all those diamond crowns and treasures . . . It was easier said than done.

When Anyu and Isaac left the gate of Mrs. Brown's mansion, the sun had come out. A flock of doves squawked and flew to the roof of another building on the street. Anyu looked up. Under the roof, near the window of the second floor, a man wearing a military uniform and a cap was holding a pair of binoculars, looking straight ahead of him—at Mrs. Brown's mansion.

She would bet that he was not watching birds.

For days, Anyu tried not to dwell on the Guild's crisis and immersed herself in jewelry making. One evening, she finished smoking and entered the workshop. She paused abruptly—Samuel, in front of her workbench, slipped something into his pocket. Startled, he bolted out. Frowning, Anyu went to the packaged stack of the Good Love sets to be delivered to her clients the next day and counted the boxes. One was missing. A box that contained a brooch.

She ran into the dim showroom. Samuel was already outside. "Samuel! Wait!"

He had ducked into a taxi.

Anyu debated about what to do. He had taken the brooch, and she had to get it back. Holding her purse, she hailed a car to follow him.

Ahead of her, Samuel stopped at a grand hotel, the Sassoon House, and entered the building.

Anyu had never come here before, but her clients admired it, saying it was more luxurious than the Majestic Hotel. It looked elegant with checkered marble floors, crystal chandeliers, and large blue porcelain vases holding bouquets of fresh flowers. Pleasant music played somewhere, and some guests sat on a rose-red chesterfield, smoking.

She found Samuel in a restaurant, leaning over a woman wearing a silver hair band. The woman looked familiar, but Anyu couldn't remember where she had seen her.

Samuel looked enthralled, holding her hand with one hand, and gave her the box that contained the brooch. He looked glorious, his eyes tender, eager, and his face lit golden by the light from the chandelier. He was smitten with this woman.

In the lobby, Anyu took a Lucky Strike from her purse and began to smoke. She was about to finish the packet when Samuel appeared.

"Samuel," she called out quietly.

He frowned but came over. "Did you follow me?"

"Who's the girl?"

"Which girl?"

"Samuel. I saw you with her."

"Miss Rose. If you really want to know. What are you doing here?"

"You took the brooch. I need it back."

"What brooch?"

"The one you gave her."

"I didn't give her anything!"

People were looking at them. Anyu thought, belatedly, that she should not have asked for the brooch. Samuel was twenty-seven years old, and he needed a girl more than anything. There were other ways she could help him. She stood up and left the hotel without a word.

In the workshop, Anyu worked until dawn to finish another brooch for her client. She would pay for the gold and diamonds from her own pocket. She didn't tell Isaac about Samuel or his clandestine meeting in the hotel.

A few days later, Isaac came into the workshop asking if she was prepared to participate in the annual jewelry competition. Mrs. Brown, still investigating Mr. Walters's murder, had received a message from the representatives of the queen of England, Queen Mary, a collector of jewelry, who asked for three brooches as gifts for the governor and his staff in Hong Kong. The winner would be chosen by the queen, and the commission was six thousand dollars.

Anyu no longer sought prestige or commissions, having already earned plenty of both, but she looked at Samuel. "Would you be interested in competing?"

Samuel glanced at her and his father. "I'll pass. I won't be able to win."

"What do you say we design the piece together? I'll be the chief designer, and you will be my assistant. If we win, you'll be recognized for your skill. You'll be a master jeweler."

"That's a wonderful idea!" Isaac exclaimed.

"But, Father—"

"By the way, Samuel, Mrs. Brown was at a party with Miss Rose the other day. She showed her a Good Love brooch and said it was a gift from you. How come you didn't tell me?" Isaac asked.

Samuel put down his chasing hammer, his face pale.

"He told me," Anyu said. "He asked me and I said yes. I forgot to list the item and report it to you. Sorry." If Isaac discovered Samuel's deceit, he would not forgive him.

"It's very generous of you. I didn't know you were acquainted with her." Isaac nodded.

She could feel Samuel's gaze drill into her. She got up to smoke. In the kitchen, the aunts were washing cabbages. Anyu opened the back door and went into the alley. She had just put a cigarette into her mouth when Samuel appeared beside her.

"Cigarette?" Anyu asked.

He took it from her, and Anyu struck a match to light it for him.

"You smoke too much. You're too thin. Do you sleep at all?" he said.

"Be nice to me, Samuel. If I don't smoke, I can't make jewelry, and I'll die."

Samuel inhaled. "Why did you lie for me?"

"I wouldn't use that word." Anyu tapped the ash off her cigarette. "You love Miss Rose, I can see. And she's a beautiful woman. How long has this been going on?"

"After you returned. I met her at a party. She broke her ankle in an accident, and I carried her to her apartment."

"Your chivalry must have impressed her."

"She's easy to talk to. We get along."

"What do you usually talk about?"

"Everything. My work. Her job. She's an accomplished ballet dancer; she dances at the nightclubs every evening, except on Mondays. She has many men courting her, many men with money, but she only likes me."

"So you gifted her the brooch."

"She declined it at first. She's not the type of girl you think she is, Anyu. When we met, she didn't know who I was."

Anyu didn't say anything.

He took a deep drag of his cigarette. "I didn't have luck with women. You know. Who wants to marry a stateless Jew? I want to marry her."

"Will she agree?"

"I don't know. I'm only a little-known jeweler."

"Once you win the competition, you'll be a master jeweler, and all of Shanghai will know you. You can choose any girl you like."

Samuel looked at her, his eyes ablaze. "When do you want to start?"

"Now. I'll need some kingfisher's feathers," Anyu said, remembering the technique of *dian cui* that she had glimpsed in the Chinese jewelry shop.

⁂

It took Anyu, Isaac, and Uncle David three days to finally purchase a handful of kingfisher feathers at a bird market—the kingfisher, as it turned out, was a mischievous bird and hard to capture. Carefully,

Anyu trimmed the plumage and, using tweezers, arranged it on a hot metal mold shaped like a petal and melted it with a blowtorch. Once the feathers turned into a pool of unblemished turquoise liquid, she placed the mold inside the kiln. Samuel watched her, following her steps, continuing with the rest of the plumage.

Eight days later, she rubbed her sore eyes and straightened. In front of her sat a stunning blue orchid brooch inlaid with kingfisher feathers, set on twenty-four karat gold filigree petals.

When she presented the brooch, she heard a collective intake of breath from Isaac, Uncle David, and Samuel.

On the day of the award ceremony that would announce the winner, Anyu went to the hotel with Isaac, Uncle David, and Samuel. She was late—Esther had come to the shop that evening with Matthew, and she had played with the toddler, the cutest angel, and forgot about the time.

Once inside the ballroom shrouded in a cloud of cigars and cologne and champagne, standing among the men in tuxedos embellished with gold cuff links and women wearing flapper-style dresses and long pearl necklaces and journalists holding cameras, she felt as though she had traveled back six years. She could afford a loss; but for Samuel's sake, she'd like to win.

A server in tails came by holding a tray of champagne. She took a flute. "Where is Mrs. Brown?" she asked Isaac.

"There she is," Isaac said, pointing at a figure under the chandelier.

Mrs. Brown, wearing her Edwardian tiara, was surrounded by a crowd, as usual. It was impossible to detect either stress or joy on her placid face. Anyu hoped she would announce the winner soon so she could go home and get some sleep.

She caught sight of Pierre Bellefeuille, whom she had not seen for more than two years, near an enormous oil painting. He had one hand in his pocket, one hand around a young woman's waist. They were speaking to a journalist holding a camera. Anyu felt her chest tighten; she turned around and walked toward the string quartet on the other side of the ballroom.

"You're avoiding me," Bellefeuille said, his voice rising above the music.

She couldn't believe it. There was no way to get around him.

"*Ma chérie*, what happened to your vow of quitting your jeweler's career?"

Went away with our wedding vows that we never got to say, perhaps? she wanted to retort. She thought better of it. "I was wrong. Making jewelry is my life. I could take a break from it but can't quit it."

"Didn't I tell you so? You should have listened to me. What do you say we leave this place and get a drink for old time's sake?"

She shook her head.

"Come on. Is this how you treat your old lover? I wouldn't ask to speak to you if it wasn't important. I wonder if you can help me."

"No, I can't."

"You haven't heard me yet! Listen. A client of mine is extremely fascinated with the Romanov treasure, especially Fabergé eggs. He's interested in purchasing them. He's willing to pay a steep price for them."

"Why did you ask me? How would I know?"

"*Ma chérie*! Your master is from Russia! He knows about the *objets d'art* better than anyone. Would you ask him?"

"No."

"Don't be cruel."

She laughed. "Pierre Bellefeuille, let me tell you this once and for all: Whatever happened between us is over. Stay away from me. I no longer wish to see you."

He raised his eyebrows. "You're angry. What's the matter? I went to the apartment to look for you, but you'd already left."

Or did he? But she didn't want a fight or entanglements of any sort. It was all in the past, and she didn't want to look back. "You should have told me if you didn't want the child."

"There must be some misunderstanding, *ma chérie*."

"I heard you in the hospital. I heard every word."

He pursed his lips. "Then you should understand. How many half-Chinese French children do you see in Shanghai? I can't jeopardize my business for a half-breed. You know this. You understand the Chinese way. And now you are sleeping with the arrogant Russian jeweler and taking my clients from me. Is this your revenge?"

How fast he changed his face. She put her glass back on a tray and walked away.

Near the staircase were Isaac, Samuel, and Uncle David. She went to them.

"Are you all right?" Isaac put his hand on her shoulder, eyeing Bellefeuille.

"I'm all right."

"Mrs. Brown is ready to announce the winner, Anyu," Samuel said.

"Good. Samuel? Can we talk?" She pulled him to a corner, out of people's earshot. "You're going to win. Can you promise me something after you win?"

"Yes, what is it, Anyu?"

"You'll not see Miss Rose again."

He looked at her. "Why?"

"She asked you about Mr. Walters, didn't she?"

"Yes."

"Did she ask you about Mrs. Brown, too?"

He swallowed.

"Mr. Walters is dead." She could feel Samuel trembling, and she held his hand and squeezed it to let him know she would keep it a secret. Isaac would be devastated if he knew his son had been used to betray the Guild.

On the stage, Mrs. Brown took her time to greet everyone and then opened the envelope that contained the name of the winner.

When Anyu heard it, she still couldn't believe it. She looked at Isaac, Samuel, and Uncle David—her people—and then the crowd erupted in a sea of cheers and applause, all the faces in front of her, her clients, the movie stars, the hoteliers, the bankers, the socialites, beamed.

Their design had been chosen by Queen Mary, who even enclosed a paragraph extolling the beauty of the orchid brooch.

Anyu waved at Samuel to go up to the stage. Samuel looked stunned, his eyes glazed, staring at the golden trophy in his hands. She felt a lump in her throat. The happiness of success, the rush of elation, and the overflowing drunken feeling racing through her veins—she had experienced that before. And yet. This time, it meant so much more.

She moved to stand with Isaac, Samuel, and Uncle David. There was nothing like celebrating success with those who stood by her side.

"You won," Samuel said.

"We won," she said.

With this honor and the popularity of her jewelry lines, the House of Mandelburg was catapulted to a new level of esteem, far surpassing the House of Bellefeuille and the House of Clemente. The House of Mandelburg would be a legend.

And Samuel would find his love, a girl he deserved.

CHAPTER 30

November 1933

The news of Mr. Lebedev's murder came a month after the award. Little was known about what had happened except that he was seen meeting with a Japanese officer in a restaurant before he was shot. Mr. Lebedev, Anyu remembered, was the middle-aged man in a fire opal suit, the one who had been first to speak up to support her admittance to the Guild.

Isaac was shocked, his face grave. He said lugubriously that he had a sense of foreboding; he was unable to work for days.

Samuel swore he didn't know about the murder, and he had stopped seeing Rose as promised. Anyu believed him. Samuel was a decent man; he was lured to talk about Mr. Walters and Mrs. Brown, but he didn't know about Mr. Lebedev or the Guild. Samuel vowed to find out whether Rose had used him, and a few days later, he broke down. He said he had gone to interrogate her, but she had disappeared.

When Anyu relayed to Mrs. Brown what Samuel had told her, the British woman pledged to investigate, just as she had promised after Mr. Walters's death. In her quavering voice, she also confessed that she still hadn't found a secure alternative to the vault.

Anyu could no longer concentrate on her work. Who did this? Who targeted Mr. Lebedev and Mr. Walters? Who did Miss Rose work for?

❧

One day, Isaac, his face pale, closed the door after Uncle David and Samuel left the workshop and asked Anyu to sit on the stool across from him.

"Anyu, I've been giving it much thought, and I fear our Guild is in grave danger, and you are in grave danger, too." His eyebrows were knotted, his eyes somber.

"You're overthinking it, Isaac," she said, trying to comfort him.

"I fear Mr. Lebedev is only the latest victim, and the Guild is exposed. We'll face the biggest challenge in our life. No matter what happens, I want to ensure you're safe."

Anyu kept her composure; she didn't look at the cache where they hid her egg.

"I have something to show you." Isaac unbuttoned the top of his shirt to reveal a necklace with a pendant. He unhooked it from his neck and held the pendant with two hands. "Tell me what you see."

Anyu took a loupe and studied the stone under a flashlight. It looked inconspicuous, weighed about ten carats, and was shaped in the earliest cut, a table cut, with a flat surface on top and a small flat surface at the bottom, its edges unpolished. To an untrained eye, it would be mistaken for a flawed blue aquamarine with weak opalescence. But when she examined it more carefully, she found her hand trembling with excitement. "This is an extremely rare blue diamond, not yet treated; it shows high brilliance in the color bands and a feathery line of inclusion, but it has clear purity of color and fluorescence. Where did you get it?"

"It's a diamond that belonged to my father, and his father, and his father's father. They were all jewelers, and the stone was passed on from generation to generation. It's called the Midnight Aurora."

"Midnight Aurora?" She remembered Samuel had mentioned that.

Isaac nodded. "We believe this stone is legendary, as ancient as civilization as we know it. My family's lore has it that this diamond traces back to prehistoric times and holds the essence of the creation of light. Some of my relatives even believed this was a *tzohar*."

"*Tzohar?*"

"A luminous gemstone God gave Noah when he needed light to construct the Ark. Now, I know it's hard to believe, and *tzohar* was only mentioned once in the Bible, and its reference was vague. Some would even argue it meant a skylight, not a luminous stone. But we know what we know."

"You believe the diamond I'm holding is the very stone that Noah used for illumination as he built the Ark?"

"Precisely."

Anyu wasn't convinced, but she could agree that it was, indeed, a rare diamond.

"What I want to tell you is this diamond is also called the Diamond of Life. It has a special power; it grants the wearer the ability to evade the claws of death."

"You mean it grants the wearer immortality?"

"Oh no. That would be a curse, wouldn't it?"

"Maybe. But isn't it true that some diamonds are cursed?" Anyu said, recalling whispers of maleficence associated with extraordinary diamonds such as the Hope Diamond, the Koh-i-Noor Diamond, and the Regent Diamond. These diamonds were said to be part of a divine body, and when they were stolen, the gods cursed the thieves, and thus all the owners of those diamonds met their disastrous ends, murdered, executed, ripped apart by dogs, or dead in penury.

"The curses, as you know, were invented to prevent greed."

"But it can't be denied that evil begets evil."

"Fair enough. So, if diamonds were cursed because of malicious intent, can a diamond with an auspicious origin and treasured by its rightful owner bestow blessings?"

"Ah. I can't argue with that. But how do we know the diamond grants the ability to evade death?"

"It has been intertwined with my family's survival for centuries. I can relate to you my father's narrow escapes from death, but you don't know him. I'll tell you what I know. In October 1917, a few years after I became the guardian of the egg, the revolution broke out in Russia. Hundreds of innocent men, Jews and aristocrats, were arrested, harassed, and murdered. My father and Uncle David were separated while they tried to flee the city. My father divided the jewelry for my brother and me and told us to go to the east and south, hoping to meet in another country someday. It was a desperate time, and the three of us dispersed in the dark. My father left first, and my brother and I followed behind. But eventually, the Bolsheviks caught all of us and forced us to embark on a prison barge where many Jews and aristocrats were confined. Soon after, the Bolsheviks threw a bomb onto the barge to kill us all. My father died instantly. My brother and I went to help him, kneeling by his side, but a second bomb exploded. My brother, along with many others, was killed. Only I, of all people on the barge, survived."

This was Anyu's first time hearing him recount his life and losses.

"And then there were attempts on my life by arsenic." Isaac held the diamond with two hands, and his eyes swam with grief.

Poison in the soup that killed his wife and his mother, Anyu remembered Esther telling her.

"Shall I recount more tragic incidents? For the past ten years, I have fled with my family from St. Petersburg to Moscow, Vladivostok, and Shanghai. I've escaped an accident on a ferry, witnessed many unspeakable deaths, and survived attempted assassinations. Many people in my vicinity have perished, yet I've lived."

Anyu looked at the diamond in his hands. Only with her trained eye could she see its special glow; for many people, it was only a cheap stone. "Do you truly believe a diamond could protect you and bring you luck, Isaac?"

"Do you, Anyu?"

She hesitated.

"You must believe it. In a world of murder and greed, a survivor must believe in blessings. Are you a survivor?"

She wanted to smile. Did she need to say more? After all these years, if there was one thing she had learned, it was this—she was only an orphan, and yet she had found a home, become a master jeweler, and owned a Fabergé egg. She was blessed indeed. "I am, and I believe in blessings."

"Very good." He walked behind her and looped the necklace around her neck. "From now on, you're the guardian of the Diamond of Life. It will protect you and bring you blessings and luck in the face of disaster and death. As the guardian of the Diamond of Life, you must promise you'll always wear it, never sell it for profit, and you must vow that the only moment it leaves your body is the moment you find the next guardian of the diamond."

She trembled. He would entrust a legendary diamond to her? "What about you, Isaac?"

"I've been wearing this for twenty-five years, since my father appointed me as the head of my family's jewelry house. But I do believe you need it more than I do. With the exposure of the Guild, the egg's future is precarious. You, my successor, the sole protector of the egg, must be safe."

She held the gemstone in her hand—it felt cool, its grayish-blue deep, unfathomable, like the stories of the past, like the sight of the future—and she understood he had given her not only a priceless diamond but also a life, a life of a jeweler, a protector, and a guardian.

The workshop's door opened. Uncle David and Samuel came in.

"I'm delighted to meet the new chief designer of the House of Mandelburg," Uncle David said.

"I don't understand," Anyu said.

"It's our family's tradition that the guardian of the Midnight Aurora becomes the chief designer of the house. You've been the most dedicated jeweler I've ever seen. We owe our success to you," Uncle David said.

"I'm honored." Anyu beamed.

"It looks good on you," Samuel said.

"Samuel." This should be his; he had wanted it.

"You don't need to say anything, Anyu. Did Father tell you an important thing regarding the Diamond of Life?"

"What?"

He gave an enigmatic smile. "It stays in the family."

CHAPTER 31

March 1934

Four months passed; the murders of Mr. Lebedev and Mr. Walters remained unsolved.

It was early in the morning. Anyu walked into the showroom holding a cigarette and an ashtray. She had been up since midnight, crafting the orders she had received after winning the award for her brooch design. She had grown thirsty, but the thermos in the kitchen was empty. The aunts were not in the kitchen.

Under the bright chandelier, Samuel and Esther were arranging the jewelry pieces in the shop. She was pleased to see Esther, who had started to help out in the mornings. But only in the morning, as she needed to look after Matthew at home. Motherhood suited Esther, who laughed more often and hummed lively tunes when not with customers. She was still a protective and caring sister to Samuel, however, asking Anyu about girls who could be Samuel's potential dates.

And Anyu, true to her promise to Samuel, had not told Esther about his relationship with Miss Rose or his role in Mr. Walters's murder.

"Where are the aunts?" Anyu asked, smoking her cigarette.

"They'll be back shortly. Don't smoke in the showroom, Anyu. Customers won't like it if the shop is too smoky." Leaning over the shelves, Esther adjusted a stand that held five rings.

There were knocks on the door.

Esther went to open it. She explained that the shop was not open, but the person at the door refused to leave.

Anyu went to the window. Near the door was a girl wearing a blue kimono printed with cranes, and behind her was a red palanquin carried by four men in long tunics, while the street, which should be bustling with carriages and carts at this hour, was unusually empty.

"If you don't mind, could you return in an hour?" Esther said.

"Sorry, I'm Chizuko." The girl had a plump face and eyes tilted upward at the end, reminding Anyu of the Japanese women in Harbin. "We can't wait for the shop to open. Please be prepared to receive Her Highness Yoshiko Kawashima, formerly known as Aisin Gioro Xianyu, the fourteenth daughter of Prince Su of the Aisin Gioro tribe, the ruling clan of the great Qing Dynasty, the cousin of Puyi, the emperor of the newly founded Manchukuo in northern China." The girl bowed, her hand extending to the palanquin.

The curtain of the palanquin was pulled up, and a woman in a white embroidered kimono emerged. She looked in her late twenties, had long hair that almost reached her waist, and a garland of chrysanthemums on her head. Her face was almond-shaped, her eyes black as midnight. A samurai sword hung on her belt, and she walked with a strange gait, soundless, like a deer padding through a forest. All the people around the palanquin prostrated themselves as she paced toward the shop.

Anyu forgot to smoke. The Qing Dynasty had ended decades ago, and she had never heard of the princess.

"My apologies. As you can see, we're in the middle of setting up for the day," Esther said.

Kawashima didn't seem to hear her. She looked around. Her gaze passed Samuel at the counter, and then she dipped her head. "I'd like to meet the owner of the shop."

Her Chinese had a Northerner's accent; her voice was soft. She had the submissive air that Anyu often saw on the faces of Japanese women in Harbin, but also the aloofness common to those high-ranking aristocrats.

Anyu stubbed her cigarette in the ashtray. She was about to speak when she heard a cough.

"I am the owner of the House of Mandelburg." Isaac appeared. "How may I help you, dear customer?" he said in Chinese.

"I'd like to place a very special order for a piece of jewelry in the shape of an egg."

"An egg?" Isaac asked.

Anyu frowned.

"It has to resemble one of the Fabergé eggs, with a surprise inside. Have you any knowledge of them?"

"I humbly confess such curios are not my specialized area."

"I read about your jewelry shop in the newspaper. Your shop was praised by Queen Mary, a high honor. I don't suppose you'll have trouble creating an egg. I request my egg, the Kawashima Egg, to be crafted with the same sophisticated ingenuity and perfection as Fabergé eggs." The princess waved, and behind her, her assistant, the Japanese girl, came up to the counter with a bag. From the bag, she took out gold ingots and counted them. Twenty gold ingots.

"This is the deposit of one thousand dollars. The rest of the money, another thousand, shall be paid when I receive the order."

Isaac didn't look at the bag. "This is a great honor for my house, dear customer. But if it makes any difference, many jewelers in Shanghai have excellent knowledge of Russian jewelry."

"I'd rather my egg come from your house." She turned to face Anyu. "You are my chosen jeweler for my Kawashima Egg. I expect the egg to be completed in six months."

Anyu cleared her throat. "I'm afraid I can't. I have other commissions in the queue. Six months doesn't give us sufficient time to design and craft."

"Would you agree to seven months?"

Anyu looked at her. "I'll do my best. Although, Your Highness, it is customary that I know about my clients' taste before I design their jewelry. Why are you interested in making an egg similar to a Fabergé egg?"

The princess said, "If you promise not to share my personal details with the journalists, I'll be glad to tell you. I do not fancy a life in the spotlight of the media."

Anyu nodded.

"I was five years old when my family's reign ended, the traitors of the country executed many of my relatives, and my entire family fought to survive. Fearing for my safety, my father gave me up to be adopted by his friend Samurai Kawashima in Japan. I was eight when I sailed to Japan, and I knew I was doomed to an exile's existence, and I would never see my parents again. In my adoptive father's home, I lived a lonely life. My only comfort was the imperial Fabergé egg my father gave me as a parting gift, a token to remember my birth. I cherished it. The artifact of ultimate perfection gave me something that nothing else could—happiness. When I was fifteen, my father died and my mother committed suicide to follow him to the afterlife. I became an orphan."

An orphan princess of a bygone imperial family.

"Then I lost my Fabergé egg. It was stolen, I'm sure. I never saw it again. I still dream of it. It is the only memory I have of my parents and my family. You would make one for me?"

Anyu nodded, staring at the sword she carried.

"If you don't mind, I'd like to see the design in three weeks." Kawashima walked out of the shop. On the street, she entered the palanquin, surrounded by people who remained prostrate.

"What's her name again?" Esther said.

"She's beautiful," Samuel said.

"I don't know how to say this. I feel like I've met her before." Isaac's face was pale.

"You have?" Anyu asked.

"But I don't know where we could possibly have met. She's a princess, and she grew up in Japan."

"If you're worried about it, we don't have to take the commission."

He wiped his face. "Never mind."

"We'll take the commission, then? How would you design the egg, Anyu?" Samuel asked.

She thought. "She has a Japanese name, even though she is a Manchu. What do you say we look at that angle?"

But she shared Isaac's unease. The princess was not telling the truth. The Qing Dynasty's reign ended in 1911, when she was five years old. If she left for Japan at eight, it was in 1914; that was before the revolution that overthrew the Romanovs in 1917. Her parents couldn't possibly have had access to the tsar's eggs.

Three weeks later, the princess's assistant, the girl Chizuko, came over to inspect the design.

Cautiously, Anyu presented an egg steeped in Japanese culture: two halves of eggshells made of moonstones, gold filigree of cherry blossoms inlaid with sapphire, a button-sized palace carved out of jadeite, and a round Pigeon's Blood ruby as a rising sun, peeking from a bed of opals shaped as clouds. The surprise was an orthorhombic sword made of diamonds with a high degree of fire and dispersion.

It was a work of art, but she knew little about Kawashima's taste. She might reject it.

"It's a beauty. I'll pick up the egg in six months and one week," the assistant said and left the showroom.

Six months later, Anyu put down her polish cloth and wiggled her stiff shoulders. Finally, the egg was finished. The past months, however, had been intense and full of pressure. Every day, she had carved, sawed, and polished, but she could feel an ominous cloud coalescing at the back of her head. This Kawashima Egg had been one of the most challenging ornaments she had completed.

Isaac looked as if he had drained all his energy; his mustache grayed, and his eyes were rimmed with red threads. When they were alone, he confessed that he was worried about the Guild and her Fabergé egg. Several times he had met Mrs. Brown, who said that she had found some suspicious men loitering around her estate. She didn't give details.

"Only you and I know about the Winter Egg; no one else knows," Anyu reminded him.

A few days later, the assistant sent word that Kawashima would come to pick up the egg tomorrow.

The next morning, Anyu waited in the showroom with Isaac. She was nervous, and so was Isaac, pacing, holding the briefcase with the egg. Would the princess accept the egg with grace? She couldn't wait to hand it over and be done with it.

The sun rose and crept to the top of the roof across the street; the customers came and went. The princess didn't show up.

"Does she still want the egg?" Esther asked, little Matthew chasing her around the counter. She had started to help out regularly in the showroom, and the little one was three years old and had grown up to be a fearless explorer. Wearing a plaid romper, he was chuckling, crying out, "Mama, Mama!" Then he tripped and fell on his bottom; his lips flattened to a line.

Anyu picked him up and brushed dirt off his pants. Little Matthew always got her attention, even now.

"Anyu, could you take him to the kitchen? He needs a change," Esther said.

"Do you have a stinky? Do you? Do you?" Anyu carried him to the kitchen, where the two aunts were making lunch. Little Matthew was giggling, his fist in his mouth. Anyu kissed him on each cheek, and little Matthew grabbed her fingers and stuffed them in his mouth.

It tickled.

Anyu laughed. She lifted his tiny fist and kissed his fingers one by one. The boy had grown, the fine down of his hair lengthening into strands of gold. She had been seeing little Matthew almost every day, but still, when Esther took him home with her, Anyu missed him. He was Esther's child, but he had wrapped his auntie Anyu around his finger.

When she returned to the showroom again, Isaac was standing by the counter, holding a piece of paper in his hand. "Anyu, Kawashima just sent word. She prefers that we deliver the egg to her residence, Maison Iwar."

"Why?"

The ornament, encrusted with diamonds and other precious gemstones, was worth two thousand dollars. Why would Kawashima ask them to deliver it at the last minute?

"She didn't say."

"I wish she would honor her word and come here," Uncle David said.

"I could deliver the egg for you, Father, but I have a doctor's appointment for Matthew." Esther took Matthew from Anyu's arms.

"I'll deliver it," Anyu said.

Isaac glanced at several customers who had just entered the showroom. "May I have a word with you in the workshop?"

"Of course." Anyu gave Matthew a squeeze and went in. She followed Isaac into the workshop and closed the door.

"Anyu, I've been thinking about this. Something is amiss. The princess is making excuses. Let me deliver the egg."

"I think it will be fine, Isaac."

He rubbed his face. "How about this: I'll go with you. Let's deliver Kawashima's egg together."

"Fine." She reached out to touch his face, a light touch, to remind him she cared about him, to let him know she respected his will and she wouldn't cross the line and give him grief.

Isaac smiled, a brilliant yet poignant smile that would haunt her in her dreams for many years to come.

CHAPTER 32

When they stepped onto the street outside the shop, the sun, which had spun glorious golden rays above the tiled roofs, had vanished. A vast cloud shaped like a claw hung above the buildings. The air looked gray like metal, noisy with a cacophony of wheels squeaking and cars honking, but the breeze was pleasant, with a hint of summer heat. Maison Iwar, located in the French Concession, was just a short ride away.

Anyu hailed a taxi and got in first, and Isaac, holding the briefcase with the Kawashima Egg wrapped inside a jewelry case, sat beside her in the back seat. The street near the shop was busy, as always, crowded with laborers carrying bamboo sticks and pedestrians and rickshaws and cars. And some Japanese military jeeps.

Anyu took out her cigarettes and lit one. It was no small responsibility to ride with two thousand dollars' worth of jewelry. And in a stranger's vehicle.

"Is it paranoid to say that the sight of the Japanese soldiers always brings me unpleasant memories of Harbin?" Isaac said.

Anyu knew what was in his mind—he had not forgotten the Japanese officer. The pressure of delivering the expensive egg must have caused him additional stress. "It'll be all right. We're almost there."

At the intersection near the apothecary, the car careened sideways and turned onto a narrow lane where the sky was sliced by long laundry sticks poking out of the windows from the building's second floor. Once they exited, they came to a wide avenue where a group of men in crew cuts were weighing sacks of rice on a massive scale. The laborers slid the weight on the scale, arguing and shouting.

There was not enough room to pass. The taxi stopped; the driver growled and slowly reversed.

Anyu looked behind her. Near the lane they had just left emerged men in long black mourning garments carrying banners, Buddhist monks holding wooden fish, and musicians playing cymbals, trumpets, and *suonas*—a funeral procession.

With paths blocked in both directions, the car turned onto the lane to their right and crawled forward and again came to an abrupt stop.

She craned her neck, looking behind, wondering if the rice sacks had been moved out of the way, but there, she saw two figures, in Western suits and hats, racing toward her car.

Maybe it was the way the men pulled their hats so low to cover their eyes, or maybe it was the way they swung their arms. Anyu was alarmed. "Look. Those men."

Isaac's eyes grew alert. "Who are they?"

"I don't know." Anyu knocked at the driver's seat. "Could you please drive?"

But it was too late. The two men were already beside them. One rapped on the window on Isaac's side.

Anyu was about to warn Isaac not to roll down the window when it shattered and a torrent of sharp glass burst into the taxi. Screaming, Anyu raised her arm to shield her face.

"What is this? Who are you?" Isaac shouted, his body twisting, fighting the hand that reached in to open the door. The other man had lunged to her side.

"Drive, drive!" Anyu cried out.

But the driver's door opened. The driver fled.

They were trapped.

Breath caught in Anyu's throat. They had no weapons to protect themselves, and Isaac was losing the fight.

Then the window on her side was smashed, and a hand shot out to grab her neck. She was lifted off the seat, her head knocking against the ceiling. She wanted to scream, but her throat was constricted. Through her blurred vision, she could see a hand near Isaac fling the door open. A pistol.

"Let her go! What do you want? Money? I'll give you the money. I have money. Let her go!"

She couldn't breathe with the man gripping her throat. She could hear the funeral music, pierced by a distant wailing, blasting, merciless, and mirthless, and a man's voice, barely audible, rose above the chaotic mania, saying, "Fabergé, Fabergé."

"I don't have it," Isaac said.

She kicked, fighting for air, but her head was thrust to the side, and a spear of sharp pain shot through her neck, paralyzing her.

"You let her go!"

The entire car rocked. She saw flames, scalding, bursting like the tip of a blowtorch. This was not how she envisioned death, and no, she couldn't die, and she wanted to keep making jewelry.

Suddenly, she could breathe. Fresh air sailed into her lungs, and she dropped to the seat, coughing, inhaling, sightless.

Isaac was calling her. "Anyu, Anyu, are you all right?"

She struggled to sit up, fumbling to find him, still unable to see, but she felt him embracing her, his body shuddering, his face wet with tears. He kissed her, her forehead, her eyes, her nose, her lips. "God, I almost lost you. I can't lose you."

It dawned on her. What he had done. "Oh no, Isaac."

"It's going to be fine. It'll be fine."

She wept, yet felt grateful. To have narrowly escaped the crazy hijacking, to be so close to Isaac, to see the depth of his love for her. He was right. It would be fine. She was still here with him; they were safe; they were alive.

A sudden crash of glass. Anyu looked up, and this time, her vision was as clear as crystal—like a diamond: outside the car, a pistol was aiming at her.

Bang.

A sharp pain pierced her chest, and the force threw her backward against the door. It crashed open, and she fell out of the car and crumpled to the ground. All she could hear was Isaac's angry cries and the fading music of *suonas*. And she cried out—seeing Isaac, his face bleeding, half lying on the back seat, his mouth moving and his hand raised in the air as if demanding this barbaric violence to stop.

Then came an explosion of another gunshot, and Isaac's chest bloomed.

CHAPTER 33

When she came to, Anyu heard some indistinct voices echoing from what felt like a dark, amorphous pit. A searing pain speared her chest, and she could barely breathe or lift her arms. Someone was tugging at her shoulder, dragging her, cursing. She shook off the hand and blinked. She was upside down, lying in a pile of broken glass on the pavement, and one of her feet was wedged under the seat of the taxi; blood spilled, dripping on her leg. She sat up and wiggled her foot out. But for a moment, she was bewildered. The bullet had shot her, and the diamond felt scalding on her chest, but she was not bleeding. Somehow, she was alive, unscathed.

A stranger was cursing, telling her to get out of his car. His car, his car. Ignoring him, she stood up. "Isaac? Isaac!"

He lay in the car's back seat, soaked in blood, without the briefcase. She climbed over and held him, feeling his face, calloused hands, and shoulders. He was gone, her mentor, her lover, her steadfast believer. He had kissed her and told her he couldn't lose her. And they had killed him. What was she going to do now?

She heard some noises, and the driver was shouting again, urging her to leave his cab.

"Take us back to our shop," she said, trembling. She needed help. She couldn't do this. She had lost Isaac. She must tell Esther, Samuel, and Uncle David. Everyone. She must explain to them, and—no, someone must explain to her what had happened.

The driver shook his head.

"Take us back to our shop!" she screamed.

Sometime later, the car moved; the rice sacks, the scales, and the crowd receded to the background. When they finally arrived at the shop, Anyu kissed Isaac and pushed open the car door. *I'll be right back,* she wanted to tell him.

How she left the car and came inside the shop, she couldn't remember. Standing before the translucent glass cases, in a state of near catatonia, she was speechless. What could she tell them? What would they say? Suddenly, she was afraid.

But no one came to her; no one asked her why she was back and alone.

She blinked. Everything felt off. The velvet curtains had been torn, the glass on the counter shattered, and the necklaces and brooches were missing. There were no customers, no Samuel, no Esther or Uncle David. It was so quiet in the showroom she could hear her own heavy breathing.

She dragged her feet toward a Good Love necklace near a broken glass case and picked it up. For a moment, she stared at the beautiful necklace she had crafted, unable to comprehend. She staggered toward the doorway behind the curtain and entered the hallway.

It looked endless, a dark tunnel. Her head hurting, she paused, her hand on the wall, her knees struggling to straighten. Then she saw them, the twin aunts lying on the floor, deep slashes in their chests; Samuel, near the threshold of the workshop; and Uncle David lying flat in a pool of blood at the foot of the safe.

The wall, where she had hidden the Fabergé egg, had crumbled; the box was gone.

Anyu shivered.

Isaac's murder in the taxi, the loss of the Kawashima Egg, and this bloody crime in the shop. This must be a nightmare. When she woke up, she would see everyone again. And Esther, too. Esther would tell her it was only an awful dream.

There was a creak of the door and some footsteps. Someone had entered the showroom.

Anyu shot up to her feet. She stumbled out of the workshop, to the hallway, and into the showroom, and there near the counter stood Esther, her face a river of tears.

"Anyu, do you know . . . what happened . . . My father . . . my father . . . he's on the street," Esther said. Her impeccable voice that had charmed many customers was quavering, and streams of tears cascaded down. "I don't understand. I don't understand what's happening, Anyu. Weren't you supposed to deliver the egg to Kawashima? Did you deliver it to her? Why . . . why is he—"

"I'll tell you," Anyu said. "I'll tell you."

But she couldn't speak another word. She just stood there, swaying, looking at everything but seeing nothing. And then Esther came beside her, and Anyu threw herself to her and wailed.

Anyu had little recollection of what she did over the next few days. But Esther was busy arranging the funerals and shivas. When Anyu finally had a moment to herself, she retreated to the workshop and didn't leave.

Inside, she paced from the door to the furnace, then from the furnace to the empty safe, and then to her workbench. A precise route. Ten steps here, twelve there, and ten again. The workshop smelled just as it always had, pungent with the oxide, the acetone, the smoke, and the odor of metal. She could find Isaac on everything: on the bamboo handle of the saw frame, on the tip of the cold blowtorch, on the gleaming surface of the cabinets. She could see his hunched frame, his intent eyes, his black shirt with a pocket holding pencils and a loupe, and his unreserved smile. She could still sense his gratification as he engraved the surface, polished the rings, and layered enamels. She could feel his calloused fingers, his strong grip, and his kisses on her lips.

Then all the chasing hammers, the jeweler's saws, the pliers swam before her, and her head hurt, and she saw it again—the image of Isaac bathed in his own blood in the car.

Rage burned inside her. Who did this?

Anyu smoked when she was awake, and smoked until she fell asleep. Days passed, or months.

"Shouldn't you get up from the floor now?" Esther's voice. When the attack on the shop happened, Esther had already left with Matthew for the doctor's appointment. Had they been in the shop, she would have lost them as well. But poor Esther. On one fateful day, she lost her father, her brother, her uncle, and her aunts.

"I'll get up." But Anyu remained where she was, leaning against the wall. She took out a cigarette and gave it to Esther.

Esther took the cigarette and sat on the floor with her. In silence, they smoked. The house was too quiet without the men's voices, the hammers striking the anvil, the aunts' quiet chattering.

"I want to find out who did this," Anyu said.

"Do you think the murder of my father and the slaughter in the shop are related?"

It couldn't possibly be a coincidence. The robbers had taken the Kawashima Egg and her signet ring—she hadn't realized it was missing until recently—but they had also wanted the Fabergé egg, and after Isaac had revealed the location to save her, they still shot him. What she didn't understand was whether these crimes were committed by the same people or two separate groups. And who were they?

"Did you see the car hijackers' faces?"

Anyu shook her head. "I only saw their legs and hands."

"My father cheated death so many times—bombing, shooting, ferry accidents, even diseases—before we escaped to Shanghai. He was the lucky one, always lucky." Esther wiped at her face.

"That's because he had the Diamond of Life."

"Had?"

"He gave it to me."

"What?"

She was wearing it. And now she understood—the scalding heat from the diamond after she was shot. The bullet must have hit the diamond instead. The diamond wearer had the power to evade death, Isaac had said.

"You took his diamond."

"I—"

"You slept with my father."

"What? No, no, Esther. It wasn't like that."

"I know what was going on between you two, of course I knew. But I thought you had integrity and honor, and you wouldn't go too far. He's twenty-five years older than you."

"We didn't . . . He promoted me to the chief designer of the House of Mandelburg."

Esther stood. "You shouldn't have accepted it. The diamond was his, and it had saved him many times. If he was still wearing it, he would still be alive."

Anyu wanted to weep.

"It should be Samuel's, not yours. Samuel, my brother!"

"I know . . . I know . . . I'll find out who did this, I promise."

"Will that bring him back? Bring my brother back?" Esther left.

Anyu heard the showroom door shut. For a long time, she sat. Then she rose from the floor and headed to the showroom. Locking the door behind her, she went out to the street. She didn't know where to go, but she needed time to think. Esther was overwhelmed with grief, and Anyu couldn't blame her. She needed to find out who killed the Mandelburgs and robbed them of the Fabergé egg and the Kawashima Egg.

It was a premeditated crime, and the robbers knew who they were and what they had. And then she stopped. How had the robbers known Isaac had the Fabergé egg? As far as she could tell, only the members of the Guild and Isaac's family knew about the egg.

But no. There was another person.

She shivered. "Rickshaw, rickshaw!"

❧

Anyu leaped out of the rickshaw and tossed a coin in the puller's hand. Then she flew toward Pierre Bellefeuille's mansion and pounded the door. Bang, bang, bang. The wrought-iron door with swirling leaves opened a crack, and she burst through, rushing down the granite path toward the immense building with the colonnade of marble columns. Some familiar faces—Butler Huang, the amah, the cook, and other servants. She ignored them, shouting for Bellefeuille.

In the garden, near a statue, she found him sampling cakes under the shade with two female companions wearing hats.

"How dare you!" She dashed forward to slap him but was held back by the butler.

"Look who is here. I don't recall inviting you, mademoiselle." Bellefeuille put down his cup.

"Isaac is dead. His family was murdered!"

He raised his eyebrows. "How? What happened? He was rising rapidly in the jewelry world. Only a few months ago, he had received a big commission."

"You know how!"

"I do not understand what you mean." He had the decency to smile and nod at his companions.

"You! You did this! You murdered them!" She trembled. She hated this man, his eyes, his voice, his hands. How could she have ever believed that she would have a life with him?

"Murder? No. That's outrageous. Why would I kill your lover?"

"It was you. I know it was you!"

Bellefeuille frowned. "Be careful, mademoiselle. Murder is a serious accusation in the French Concession. My tolerance is not boundless, despite our shared past."

"You asked me about the Fabergé eggs in the ballroom. You said your client wanted to purchase one, but I declined. So you hired the hitmen and robbed us. You killed him and his family. You bastard!"

He narrowed his eyes. "I recommend you leave. You're childish, overwhelmed, inconsolable with grief. You're hurling vicious, slanderous accusations. I won't tolerate that."

He denied it. Of course he'd deny it.

She couldn't think straight, filled with fury. "I believed in you, I went to bed with you, and I almost bore you a child. And yet you deceived me and aborted our baby. I let that go. But for this, this cruelty, this cold-blooded murder, I will never forgive you."

"Enough! I'm an honorable man, protected by the law in the French Concession, and I will by no means tolerate your pernicious invective."

The butler held her arms back and hauled her out of the garden. "Where's my egg? Give it back."

Bellefeuille crossed his legs and leaned back on the metal bench. And then she was lifted off the ground by two strong arms and carried out. She shut her eyes so she wouldn't see the smug smile on his face.

"I'm in a good mood today, so let me give you some advice, mademoiselle. You are so young. In time, you'll know that this is simply part of life. In Shanghai, there are crimes and there are victims, but you'll never know who is the mastermind."

He relished her pain; he was part of the horrendous scheme. But he didn't have the egg.

Who was his coconspirator? Who took her Fabergé egg? And the Kawashima Egg?

Stumbling away from the mansion, Anyu thought of another man.

CHAPTER 34

In a teahouse, Mr. Du's office on Nanjing Road, Anyu told his men that she had come to report a crime. They led her and Esther, who had insisted on coming, to Mr. Du on the second floor. Slowly, Anyu described the crime in the jewelry shop. Four dead. The shop ransacked. Isaac's death happened outside the shop, so the gangster refused to hear the story. The protection fees only covered them for the shop, not any of the owners or staff beyond the storefront.

The man looked at her and Esther. "The Russian shop on Julu Road. I remember. It is very unfortunate. My condolences."

"We were wondering if you have any suspects." Anyu watched him. The gangster leader, who had his minions collect the protection fees, had not stepped inside the shop since his pilferage of the necklace. He had grown older, his ears like wings, and he was meaner. It was said he had formed an alliance with Generalissimo Chiang Kai-shek, who desired the gangster's clout to fight the encroaching Japanese armies in the city.

"Suspects? Not yet."

She was tempted to ask whether he had directed his men to commit the crime himself. "Will you keep investigating?"

"Of course we will."

"We have lost much of our jewelry," Esther said, giving him an inventory of what was missing and the damages in the shop. They had been nearly cleaned out; all the jewelry in the showroom and the contents in the safe and gold wires and silver tubing and gemstones were taken.

"I shall inspect your shop to verify your account. I can't promise the items will be recovered, miss. Robberies like this are all over Shanghai, and we only have so many men."

"And an egg," Anyu said.

"An egg! Now that's curious. Why do you care about an egg?"

Anyu took Esther's arm and turned to leave. Mr. Du didn't appear to know anything about Fabergé eggs. It wasn't him.

On the street, Anyu felt faint. She had barely eaten anything for the past few days, and her head hurt.

"I'm going home," Esther said and walked away.

Anyu dug out a cigarette packet from her pocket. It was empty. She tossed it away in frustration. There was yet one more person who could help investigate, and Anyu was counting on her.

By the time she turned onto the street where Mrs. Brown's mansion was located, the daylight was fading, and the streetlights had been turned on. In the distance, Anyu could see the majestic neoclassical English building shielded by towering trees. She had no appointment, and she wondered if she would be turned away. But she hoped Mrs. Brown's bodyguards would recognize her and let her in.

As she drew nearer to the mansion, she could see a dark cloud mixed with sparks of flame surging above the trees. It came from Mrs. Brown's mansion or somewhere near it. Surprised, she picked up her pace. Many people crowded on the street, watching, pointing, and she could smell the acrid odor and hear the sputter of wood and the crashing of glass. When she reached the mansion, her knees grew weak. The garden gate was open, and a throng of men in long robes was rushing through holding wooden buckets filled with water. Under the mantle of darkness, spirals of smoke exploded through the windows with red frames, the fire crackled, and the entire balcony collapsed.

"What happened?" she asked a man rushing out, his face covered with soot.

"Biggest fire I've ever seen." He shoved her aside.

Anyu heard a shout—a fleet of men emerged from the sickening cloud, rushing toward the lawn near the entrance, carrying a stretcher. They were followed by a doctor with a medical kit, the British consul she had met at banquets, and his staff in double-breasted suits.

"Oh my God," a voice said.

Anyu shivered. The woman's blond hair had been incinerated, and her face was terribly burned. But Anyu could still make out who she was.

"There are more bodies inside the building," someone said.

Anyu looked at Mrs. Brown's fingers—they were bare. Fear gripping her heart, Anyu ran to the Vault of Gems and Treasures.

When Anyu finally reached the cutlery shop, she was exhausted and feeling sick. But just as she feared, the door was open, and the Sikh guard was nowhere to be seen. In the garden with the Goddess of Peace statue, the secret panel to the underground door was agape. She gasped for breath, then slipped through.

The air underground smelled stale. Her legs trembling, she forged ahead. There was a beam of light coming from the distance. She shielded her eyes with her hand. "Who's there?"

No one answered.

When she was closer, she could see a flashlight lying on the ground. She stood in front of it, afraid to pick it up.

She forced herself to walk into the vault, her heart hurting too much. On the ground lay the guards, Mr. Petrov, and Mr. Tang. The shelves that contained the crown worn by the wife of Mughal emperor Shah Jahān, the diamond necklace that belonged to Catherine the Great, the antique Tiffany necklace made in 1870, and the splendid Alexander III Commemorative Egg were empty.

CHAPTER 35

December 1934

Someone was knocking on the door.

Anyu paused sweeping the kitchen floor, the broom in her hands. She wondered who was outside. The shop had been closed for a month, or months, she couldn't remember, and her days were mere repetitions of cleaning, wiping the dust on the shelves, and sweeping the floor. She couldn't make any jewelry. When she sat down at her bench, she fiddled with the pliers and the hammers, her mind racing. Who killed Mrs. Brown? Who robbed the vault? Where were the treasures?

Then when she stood in the showroom, she felt as if in a trance, looking at the naked sockets in the ceiling, the bare windows without the velvety curtains, and the empty shelves without glass. All her means to find out the identities of the robbers and murderers had led her nowhere. She didn't know what else to do or how to reopen the shop. She was the chief designer of the house, and it was up to her to keep the business going. But she had lost Isaac and the Winter Egg that was entrusted to her, and she was lost, too, in the storm of grief, rage, and despair. She could barely feel anything, her hands wooden, her heart a rock, and she wanted nothing other than to sink in the dome of pain, to sleep in the spiral of sorrow, and to be drowned in the darkness that would be her salvation. If there was salvation.

She lowered her head and continued to sweep from the wall to the empty table, from the sink to the back door. The scratching of the broom echoed in the small space.

The knocking persisted.

Anyu went to the showroom and looked out the window.

It was Confucius, carrying a wreath of white chrysanthemums. His face looked thinner, his eyebrows thick. His shirt was torn near the collar, and his shoes were coated with mud.

"Come on in. Look who's here. I thought you were dead. Where have you been?" Anyu said, a glimmer of happiness rising from her chest. She had thought of him, and yes, she had missed him.

"On vacation." He looked apologetic.

"That must have been a terrible vacation. You didn't gain weight."

"You can say that again. The hotel had poor sanitation standards, and the staff liked to answer my call with a baton."

"I see. How long were you in jail?"

"Long enough to know you regained the crown of the best jeweler and then got robbed." Confucius handed her the wreath of flowers. "For your mentor. My condolences. You're lucky you survived."

"You've heard."

He scanned the empty showroom. "My men told me of the hijacking and the killing in the shop. The bloodiest thing I've ever heard of. All happened on the same day, to the Russian family. I asked around. I hear the taxi driver was scared to death, but he remembered the faces of those two robbers. It didn't take that long to find out who hired them."

"You know who hired them?"

"You're going to hate me if I say this. But what is done is done. You can't bring the dead back."

"You have to tell me. Who hired them?"

"If the rumor is right, the two thugs were seen talking to a Japanese man after the robbery. They met him at a restaurant nearby and gave him the box they took from the taxi."

A Japanese man. "What did he look like?"

"He was quite short, slim, and carrying a samurai sword. My men say he lives in a massive mansion that used to house Japanese soldiers. It's called Maison Iwar."

Kawashima's residence. Since Isaac's death, Anyu hadn't thought of her. But it didn't make sense. "She paid a deposit of one thousand dollars for the egg. Why would she rob me of her own egg on the day of the delivery? It doesn't seem logical."

"So she wouldn't have to pay the rest? Who knows." Confucius shrugged.

"I don't think so." The robbers had also demanded to know the hiding place of the Winter Egg.

"Well, that's what my men told me."

Anyu frowned.

"Look at me, Anyu. You have to let it go."

"No. I have to find out who did this."

"You want a professional opinion? The street robbery and what happened in the shop were organized by highly skilled criminals. They killed cleanly and left few traces. You are no match for them."

"Wait. You said they killed cleanly."

"Yes, the robbers had guns."

"But the uncle, Samuel, and the aunts were not shot. Their wounds were not gun wounds. They were killed by a knife." Or a sword.

Confucius sighed.

"Could that killer be a swordsman?"

"That's possible. I don't know. I'm starving. Are you hungry? We can go get some food."

"I'm not hungry."

"All right. You know I'm back and I'll be in the neighborhood. I'll see you around."

Anyu opened the door to let Confucius leave. Then she sat on the chair near the screen, took out a cigarette, and began to smoke. The robbery and the slaughter in the shop had to be connected, committed by the same criminal group or even the same criminal. If what Confucius said was true, then the robbers, who also snatched the Kawashima Egg in the car, must have been instructed by the Japanese man to kill Isaac and find out the information about the Winter Egg; the Japanese man must have also organized the slaughter of Uncle David, Samuel, and the aunts and the theft of the Winter Egg.

Who was the Japanese man? Did he know Isaac? Anyu forgot to smoke—didn't Isaac mention the Japanese officer in Harbin who pursued him? Could they be the same person?

And Kawashima. Did she rob her own egg to save money? Was she involved in the crime? She also carried a sword. Anyu had not seen her use the katana, but would a princess carry a sword purely for ceremony?

All the questions to which she had no answer. But she knew one thing—once she uncovered the identity of the Japanese man, she would be one step closer to the murderer and the robber who took her Winter Egg and the Kawashima Egg.

Anyu went up to the attic, changed into a gray tunic and pants, and tucked a wallet with some money into her pocket. Then she opened the shop's door.

Esther was outside with Matthew. He wiggled out of his mother's arms and raced to her, giggling, his hair shining like gold. A cute little thing.

"Matthew!" Anyu bent over and enfolded him into her arms—she could feel his heart pump against hers, his small frame, his smooth skin, and smell his sweet scent. She closed her eyes, branding him into her memory.

"You'll spoil him," Esther said.

Anyu let him go. "Esther, I'm going to Kawashima's residence. I'll be right back."

Esther folded her arms and frowned. "Why?"

"I'm looking for a man in her residence. I think he might be the killer."

Esther shook her head. "They're gone. You can't bring them back."

Oh, Esther. She was still grieving for her family, still angry at her. What could she say? She wished it had been her, not Isaac, or Samuel. Anyu put her right hand on her chest to feel the diamond under her cotton tunic, the stone's irregular shape, its inconspicuous size.

"I want to let you know your father was very important to me. He taught me the jewelry-making craft. He gave me a life and more. He made me who I am today. I loved him."

"What does it matter?"

Anyu wanted to give her a hug. Esther, her friend, her sister, her blessing. Would they ever feel close to each other again? "I just want you to hear it from me."

Esther lowered her head, sobbing.

"Goodbye, Esther." Anyu walked out of the shop and closed the door behind her.

On the street, Anyu hailed a rickshaw. It bounced past the banner-flying streets, the lattice-windowed storefronts, the bicycles parked under bare oak and hickory trees. It was nearly the end of the year, she realized. What a horrid year of 1934. The months had coalesced into a murky puddle of tears.

She wondered how she could find the Japanese man and what to do if she came across Kawashima. Did Kawashima have anything to do with the murders as well?

Finally, she arrived at Kawashima's residence. It was a traditional Chinese compound with high gray walls that extended all the way to the end of another street; on the street, a lush ginkgo tree leaned to the side like a wind-blown umbrella. The enormous front gate was guarded by two stone lions with wavy manes and a soldier in a Japanese Imperial

Army's khaki uniform. Above the gate, etched in the stone, were two words: Maison Iwar.

Anyu passed the front gate and heard a shout, guttural, almost angry, coming from inside the compound, followed by the sound of a bell. She frowned, unable to make out the significance of the sounds. From everything she could see, this was not an ordinary residence.

How could she enter the building with the high walls and a guarded gate?

She wandered to a side street and saw a broom abandoned near a restaurant. She took it and went back to Maison Iwar and began to sweep, gathering piles of golden fan-shaped leaves on the ground. She was dressed modestly in her tunic. She could pass as a sweeper.

She had been sweeping for two hours when she saw a fleet of trucks chug down the street. They stopped in front of the mansion, and the gate opened.

The guard waved, and the trucks, engines roaring, slowly pulled into the compound. Holding her broom, Anyu sidled beside the rear wheel of the last truck, hiding her legs from the guard on the other side, and snuck inside the compound. She didn't know what to expect once she entered; for all she knew, she'd be standing in front of an army of Japanese imperial soldiers who'd shoot her like a target.

But there was only one soldier, who shouted something, and she pointed at her ear, shook her head, and raised the broom in hand. The soldier frowned and waved her to the side.

Her heart pounding, she swept across a slab of stone on the landing near the wall; out of the corner of her eye, she could see more soldiers in a garden to the left, with winding paths and tall stone lanterns. When she moved along the trimmed bushes, she spotted in the distance a row of three-bay buildings with crimson pillars, a pond surrounded by a grove of willows, and an empty pavilion with a stone table in the center. In the air wafted a strong odor of manure and animals. When she peered through a stand of pines, she could see the stables along the wall, a brown horse grazing, and a group of men wearing leather overalls shoveling manure into wagons.

It occurred to her that Confucius had not described the Japanese man's appearance in detail, and she would have trouble identifying him.

Dusk came. Anyu swept around a stone lantern near a pine tree and stopped to wipe her face. She was tired and cold; her entire body had been so tense. Had any soldiers discovered who she truly was, she would have been dead in a second.

Then she heard a strange chorus of shouts again. Following them, she came to a courtyard with columns of soldiers holding broad swords. They were practicing some kind of swordplay, and leading the group was a man in a short crew cut, a yellow scarf tied around his head, wielding a samurai sword like a thunderbolt. His movements were smooth, his thrusts decisive, his footfalls light as autumn's fallen leaves.

Anyu stared, her heart jumping to her throat. There was something uncanny about the man's appearance. A thought came to her. She shouldn't have come here; this was a trap. Anyu had an urge to run. She had just turned around and taken three steps when she heard a voice behind her.

"Hello."

Anyu dropped her broom and found herself face-to-face with the person who was said to be a princess—Kawashima, dressed in a khaki uniform, with a yellow scarf around her shorn head and a sword in hand.

CHAPTER 36

"You," Kawashima said.

Anyu swallowed hard, not because of the sharpness of the princess's sword, nor her agility, but the look in her eyes—they were the eyes of a killer. "Who are you?"

Without the wig with long hair and the kimono, she had completely shed her captivating femininity. "I am Yoshiko Kawashima; I also go by Ryosuke Kawashima."

"Are you a woman? A man?"

"I am a woman."

"Then why the crew cut and the uniform? Is it a kind of disguise?"

"It doesn't matter what you call it. I prefer to wear men's uniforms."

"I knew you were not telling the truth when we met. Are you even a princess?"

"Why should I explain to you? But since you dare pay me a visit, you earned it. Everything I told you was true. I was born to Chinese nobility and adopted by a Japanese samurai. I am Japanese."

"Then why are you here in China?"

The princess laughed.

"You want to restore your family's power."

"China belongs to my family. It will bow before us soon. Manchukuo is only the beginning; my cousin is already sitting on the Dragon Throne. Emperor Puyi, the great ruler! It's his birthright."

"But the Qing Dynasty is long gone."

"We're restoring it. It has been a long, torturous journey. Had I been born a man, I would have taken over China years ago."

"Do you mean you or the Japanese Kwantung Army?"

Kawashima narrowed her eyes. "The army follows my command. But enough is enough. You and I have unfinished business, jeweler. You owe me the Kawashima Egg. Where's my egg?"

"We were robbed on the way to your residence."

"So I've heard. That's a pity."

"Why did you ask us to deliver the egg to you at the last minute?"

The princess shook her head. "That's my business. I don't need to tell you. Now, I commissioned an egg and gave you a deposit of one thousand dollars. But I didn't receive the order. How would you like to pay the debt?"

Anyu was at a loss as to what to reply. She could accuse Kawashima of the robbery, but she had no proof, and as a customer, Kawashima had the right to receive the egg she had commissioned. "I'll reimburse you the deposit, rightly. Would you be kind enough to accept the deposit in installments?" The safe, where the family's savings and the jewelry inventory had been kept, had also been robbed.

"I don't need the deposit. I commissioned an egg, and I expect to receive it. Is this not what your master agreed to do?" There was a subtle tinge of threat in her voice.

"Yes . . ."

"But he's dead. Will you honor his words?"

"I will, and as the chief designer of the house, I shall craft it for you."

"Good. I'm glad we've reached an understanding. I request you craft my Kawashima Egg here."

"Here?"

"I'm offering you a chance to repair your house's reputation, as well as an employment opportunity."

Anyu would rather die than work for a murder suspect. "Respectfully, I must decline."

Kawashima's eyes narrowed.

Anyu held her head up.

"You don't have a choice. Or I'll announce to the entirety of Shanghai that your house took the money and failed to honor our agreement."

The last thing she wanted, after Isaac's death, was to damage his name. "Very well. I'll work for you for six months to complete the egg."

"I offer you a contract of two years," Kawashima said.

"I don't need two years to craft an egg."

"It's the minimum required employment."

Kawashima wanted to use her, Anyu realized, but maybe she could use her, too—this was her chance to go deep into her lair, to find out if she was the real mastermind of the murders. And if she was, Anyu would take back her Winter Egg and avenge the Mandelburgs' deaths.

"Two years. Will you honor that and free me after that contract?"

"I'm a samurai. Honor is in my blood."

"I accept your offer."

"Chizuko!" the princess ordered. "Take her to the workshop."

Her assistant, the girl with the plump face, appeared beside her with a lantern.

"This way," she said to Anyu.

"Workshop?"

The assistant didn't reply, and Anyu followed her as she turned to a path on the left. For a fleeting moment, Anyu was pierced by regret. What was she doing? Slaving here for two years. She should have been thinking of restoring the Mandelburgs' shop. Without her, the House of Mandelburg would cease to exist. What would Esther think if she didn't return?

In the flickering lantern light, she trekked through a small bamboo grove, passed under a red wooden frame, and arrived at a five-bay one-story building decorated with traditional Chinese curved eaves and dragon gables.

A Japanese man in a black kimono came to greet her; he was the foreman, Mr. Tanaka, the assistant said and led Anyu to a nearby room where she was to strip off her clothing. It was routine, the assistant said, that her clothing would be inspected before entering the workshop and after leaving to prevent stealing. Anyu disrobed.

With nothing other than the necklace of the Diamond of Life on, Anyu waited; after a while, the assistant returned with her clothing. She got dressed and was led into the workshop.

Inside, the room was permeated with soldering fumes, thick kiln smoke, and pungent chemical odors; through the pale miasma, she could see there were about thirty men. Some sat at workbenches along the walls, some gathered at the kiln near shelves of enameled eggs at the far end of the room, and some were gathered at tables with irregular semicircles, measuring, carving, or sawing. No one turned their heads toward her or stopped the work at hand.

They were in their forties or fifties, with paper-white beards, rust-colored faces marred with grooves and welts, and soot-smudged fingers. Untidy, they looked like they hadn't bathed for a year. Some wheezed, clearly from inhaling too many noxious fumes from casting; some had strange red-rimmed eyes, and their movements were labored, lethargic. The room, vast like Mrs. Brown's ballroom, was loud with hammering and sawing, strangely devoid of human voices.

"I'll take you to your workbench," Mr. Tanaka said.

Frowning, Anyu wove her way through the clusters of tables to reach a workbench at the end of the room. Mr. Tanaka gave instructions: she would have her own measuring tape, a jeweler's saw, sheets of white paper, pliers, and a file and other small hand tools, but soldering equipment and casting machines were to be shared; she would need to fill out forms to request solder sheets, wires, tracing paper, polishing tools, gemstones, diamonds, copper, brass, or any other metal and scraps from the foreman.

The day's schedule was outlined: Six o'clock, at the sound of the bell, rise from bed, breakfast in the hall next to the workshop, exercise, work, lunch break, work, dinner, and work. At ten o'clock, bedtime.

Work, work, work.

"You may start to work tomorrow," Mr. Tanaka said.

"What are they making?" Anyu asked, looking around her.

"The treasures." He led her to a group of men at a corner, who craned their necks, scrutinizing the sketches on the pillar. One glance, and her jaw dropped. The sketches formed a collage of Fabergé egg drawings, ranging from the first Hen Egg, presented to Tsar Alexander III in 1885, to the Renaissance Egg in opaque agate, the Rosebud Egg in vibrant-red *guilloché* enamel adorned with rose-cut diamonds, and the Coronation Egg adorned in glossy yellow *guilloché* enamel accented by gold strips. It also included the last two eggs, created for the dowager empress and Empress Feodorovna: the Cross of Saint George Egg and the Steel Military Egg.

A total of forty eggs. Her egg, the Winter Egg, wasn't part of the collage.

"Why do you keep the illustrations of the Russian ornaments?"

"By the order of Her Highness Kawashima, the jewelers here are required to make them."

"All of them?"

Mr. Tanaka nodded.

Kawashima was obsessed with Fabergé eggs, Anyu realized, and by the look of the sketches, she knew their names, their workmasters, and their dates of production. It must have taken her years of research to unearth the details of the Romanov treasure. Would an obsessive collector of *objets d'art* like Kawashima go to extremes, scheme, and commit murders for an authentic Fabergé egg?

The bell rang, signaling the end of the work for the night. Mr. Tanaka led her to a room on the second floor of the adjacent building. It was small but clean, with a sliding door made of bamboo and paper. There was no furniture, no bed, only a lamp on the floor. Then Mr. Tanaka opened a closet and handed her rolled-up bedding—the floor was reserved for her fellow jewelers. She, a woman, would sleep in the closet for privacy.

If Kawashima had the Winter Egg, where would she keep it?

The next day, at the sound of a bell, Anyu awoke and slid open her closet.

Following the trickle of men out of the building, she trod down a covered corridor to a dining room, where she held a tray and accepted a hard-boiled egg, a block of fried tofu, porridge, and pickles from two servants holding ladles. She ate standing by the wall; the men either squatted or sat on the floor. Then the bell rang. They filed out to the space in front of the five-bay room and stretched their arms and legs to a Japanese song from the radio. When the bell rang again, Anyu filed into the workshop. The sounds of metal sawing, filing, hammers striking against anvils, filled the room.

From memory, Anyu drew the design of the Kawashima Egg. She remembered every detail, the straight lines, immaculate circles and triangles, and shadows and highlights. She remembered showing the design to Isaac, their ride in the taxi, his devastating cries—*I almost lost you*—and his kisses. The pencil slipped from her hands; tears welled in her eyes. Suddenly, she was overwhelmed with grief that had lodged in her heart for these months.

"Don't cry. They don't like that," the jeweler next to her, a man in his forties, whispered.

Anyu sniffed, dabbing her eyes on her sleeve.

"They'll take you, if they see you cry, and you'll be thrashed in the yard for everyone to see." The jeweler didn't stop working on his engraving, didn't lift his head.

Thrashed.

"Keep drawing. Don't let them see us talking."

Anyu nodded, but she couldn't focus, listening to her neighbor's low voice, barely audible under the filing. The workshop operated under strict rules: signs of laziness would result in a penalty of ten lashes; complaints, ten lashes; stealing, a beheading.

"How did you end up here?" her neighbor asked. "I recognize you. You're the master jeweler of the House of Mandelburg, aren't you?"

She nodded and explained her situation as briefly as she could, and her neighbor sighed. His family name was Cai. His family owned a small business in Hong Kong, making jewelry for British and Portuguese officials' wives. He came here because he was promised a good salary and was contracted for two years. But he had been confined in the workshop for two years and four months because he was unable to finish the eggs on time. Then Mr. Cai told her about the other jewelers: the jeweler with a missing ear, Mr. Cai said, was abducted from Qingdao when the city was attacked by the Japanese, and the jeweler three benches down had lost his entire family and needed a job. They had been here for a year.

At noon, Kawashima came to the building. Clad in a full Japanese Imperial Army officer's uniform and cap, a sheathed sword in hand, she paced the room, assessing every piece in the jewelers' hands. Then she came before Anyu, her black eyes expressionless like a dark pond.

"You'll have your egg soon," Anyu said.

"I want to see it when you finish."

"As you wish."

After Kawashima left the building, Anyu asked to have a cigarette break.

Mr. Tanaka didn't look pleased. "Five minutes. Outside the building."

Anyu took a packet of cigarettes and a matchbox and walked out to the porch. Standing by a red pillar, she lit a cigarette and watched Kawashima ascend a moon-shaped bridge near a bamboo grove on the hill.

Each day was a repetition of the previous day. Eat. Work. Sleep. Eat. Work. Sleep. The exercise was mandatory, the hours rigid, but the meals were nutritious, a bowl of cabbage soup and potatoes and peanuts and a chunk of meat or fish; occasionally, there were apples. Outside their sleeping quarters, there was always a guard who kept a close watch.

Eight days after she arrived in the workshop, Anyu witnessed a brutal beating of an enameler accused of careless handling of gemstones and destroying gold wires. The poor enameler was lashed and left with a broken leg.

Then, on the last day of January, five weeks after she had begun to work in the workshop, she was walking to her room with Mr. Cai, when he whispered there was a visitor asking about her at the gate. The guard told the woman to leave, but she insisted on standing under the ginkgo tree.

A visitor? "Does Kawashima allow visitors?"

Mr. Cai shook his head. "No. But the visitor has an American passport. She showed it to the guard. If she were Chinese, she would have been beaten. The guard couldn't drive her away."

"Where is she?"

"She's still by the ginkgo tree. You can see her from the window."

Anyu raced to her room shared with the other jewelers and looked out the window. Under the ginkgo tree was a sight she could never forget—Esther, wearing her long yellow cotton dress and a wide straw hat with a red silky band, fanning her face. She paced, her legs rising and falling, a beautiful dance in the afternoon sun.

How did Esther know she was locked inside? Anyu wondered. Did the guard tell her? Oh, Esther. She was not angry with her anymore; she had forgiven her. Anyu felt her eyes moisten.

Esther! Esther! She wanted to shout, to get her attention, but she was too far. Desperate, Anyu took a copper basin and angled it in the sun. She turned it around and around, spinning the light into the air, until finally Esther stopped and turned in her direction.

Anyu waved her hands. And there, Esther, standing by the ginkgo, raised her hands as well. Anyu laughed. Esther saw her. She knew she was alive.

February arrived; on the last day of the month, Esther appeared under the ginkgo tree again. She showed the guard a piece of card that must be a passport—her American passport—and was permitted to stay. Then she stood under the ginkgo tree for a good twenty minutes, pacing, waving her hands, and then left.

From then on, a pattern was established. Esther came to see her at sundown on the last day of every month.

⋇

Eight months passed. Anyu didn't find a chance to slip out of the workshop, nor was she able to see Kawashima. But she finished her Kawashima Egg, a brilliant egg inlaid with precious jadeite and diamonds, with the surprise inside, a samurai sword.

She asked to deliver it to Kawashima. "Would you mind? She told me to deliver it to her myself."

"Did she?" Mr. Tanaka said, boxing it in a velvet jewelry box.

"She mentioned that when I arrived last year," Anyu said. "I'm sure she has some questions. Or would you rather answer them on my behalf?"

"Fine. You can come along."

She untied her apron, took off her gloves, and followed Mr. Tanaka out. Several jewelers, their faces wan, stared at her curiously, wondering what gave her the privilege of leaving her workbench.

It was near noon, and the sunlight filtered through the crown of the trees in full bloom. Some pink blossoms unfolded their petals, a squirrel skittered along a trunk, and a cardinal stood on one leg at the tip of a twig, oblivious of a potential fall. This sight of life, an escape from the hammer and soldering, filled her heart with optimism.

Mr. Tanaka was not heading toward the bamboo grove, she noticed. Instead, he crossed the bridge and turned to a building with a blue roof. The doors were shut; a guard waved him off, speaking Japanese.

"She's seeing a guest," Mr. Tanaka said. "We should come back another day."

"Can we wait?"

"She doesn't like to be disturbed." Mr. Tanaka looked morose.

Anyu had no choice but to leave with Mr. Tanaka. "What's this building?"

"Her showroom."

Did Kawashima keep her Winter Egg there as a trophy?

As they crossed the bridge near the bamboo grove, she spotted a black Citroën parked on the gravel. She paused to stare. It was not a common car in Shanghai, and she only knew one man who owned one.

Later, Mr. Tanaka delivered the egg to Kawashima without Anyu. Her chance of confronting Kawashima slipped away.

⁓❦⁓

For the next ten months, Anyu was ordered to craft the imperial Coronation Egg, a gift presented to Tsarina Alexandra by Tsar Nicholas II for their 1896 coronation. Inside was a replica carriage perfectly engineered with turning wheels, a foldable step, and operable doors that would open and close. After the completion, Anyu requested to deliver the egg personally to Kawashima but was denied.

Then she was informed the Kawashima Egg had broken, and she must make another one.

"Broken?" She couldn't believe it. The egg was made of solid material and embellished with diamonds and other precious gemstones. Despite the poor conditions she had worked under, she knew her craftsmanship had been flawless. "I want to see Kawashima and ask her."

"She's not available," Mr. Tanaka said.

There were six months left in her contract. She had enough time to complete the egg, but her mood was gloomy. She still hadn't discovered her Winter Egg's whereabouts or had the opportunity to see Kawashima. And she missed Esther, who came monthly still but at such a distance, and she missed the shop and little Matthew; she missed Confucius. She missed them so much.

A few days later, Anyu fell ill. It had started with a minor burn on her hand when she lost hold of the blowtorch, and then the wound became infected, and for one month she lay in bed, shivering, running a high fever. When her fever eventually broke, she returned to the workshop. But the fumes and chemicals stung her eyes and gave her headaches; a dull pain in her chest tormented her. She had trouble concentrating. When she heated pieces of thin sterling on a firebrick, the metal shriveled into a ball—she had simply stood there and forgot she was fusing. She even overheated brass and didn't realize it until the noxious zinc fumes made her cough.

By November, two months before the end of her contracted time, she had only finished the moonstone eggshell, the first step of the crafting, and she had fainted three times and injured her head. Fatigued, unable to hold her saw, she was sent to her bed to recover.

"I cannot release you from the contract if you don't finish your egg," Mr. Tanaka warned tersely.

She was a prisoner; she might die here, she realized.

New Year's Eve arrived. Anyu made her way to the window, hoping to see Esther, who had come every month. A storm whipped outside, gusts lashed at the building, and rain pounded the walls; all the gates, the walls, and the trees blended into the storm. She couldn't see anything but the black nimbus clouds, the pouring rain, and the blinding lightning that shot piercing pains into her eyes.

Esther wouldn't come in the storm; she probably had given up seeing her now. It was New Year's Eve, after all. She should be celebrating with Matthew and Mr. Dearborn.

Pain stabbing behind her eyes, Anyu stared hard into the storm, searching for the yellow dress and the red hat. She didn't see anything at first and then straightened—she could make out a woman holding a red umbrella across the street. She limped under the ginkgo, one arm across her body as though cold; then the wind charged at her, and the umbrella snapped. The storm poured over her, and she was drenched instantly.

Esther had come, despite the storm; she had come each month, standing under the ginkgo tree, to let Anyu know she was not alone, to let her know she was not forgotten.

Silently, Anyu wept happy tears. She was loved—yes, she was loved.

The next day, Anyu sat at her workbench, determined to finish the last ornament in this prison.

CHAPTER 37

August 1937

Eight months later, after days and nights of slaving in the workshop and suffering a monthslong sickness, after two years, eight months, and twenty-five days at Kawashima's residence, Anyu finished her second Kawashima Egg. On the day she was to present it, she insisted on submitting it herself. It was her last chance to have a face-to-face meeting with the woman who had robbed her of her egg, and now years of her life. Mr. Tanaka, after a long pause, agreed.

Carefully, Anyu placed her ornament in a box lined with black velvet. The egg had taken her longer than usual to complete, with her headaches, increasing sensitivity to lights and noise, and devastatingly low vision. The long exposure to the chemicals in the workshop had wreaked havoc on her body, making her a victim to all types of ailments and aches.

Anyu picked up the box and wove her way out of the workshop. Since her arrival, the number of jewelers had dwindled. Some had left, some were thrashed again, and Mr. Cai, who had fallen ill, had died six months before.

Outside the building, Mr. Tanaka stood, looking at something far off. She followed his gaze. An encampment had been built near the stand of pines on the other side of the red gate. Japanese marines wearing khaki uniforms and peaked field caps were transporting rifles and guns from trucks.

Kawashima's ambition of taking over the country seemed to be coming to fruition. These days, Anyu had seen large contingents of soldiers appear in the yard in front of the workshop, and the food rations for the jewelers had diminished. Word was that the food for the jewelers was given to the marines, who transported bombs and firearms from a warship in the Huangpu River to the princess's residence. And very soon, the pilots for Japanese warplanes would arrive.

Rumors of a conflict between the Japanese militants and the Chinese ruling government, the Nationalists, had been swirling. But this was the first time she had seen the marines with her own eyes. She still had a hard time believing that the Japanese, who had invaded her hometown, were preparing to invade Shanghai.

"I'll need to inspect your clothing before you leave the building, then I'll take you to the princess's showroom," Mr. Tanaka said.

"I request a moment with her alone," Anyu said.

Mr. Tanaka nodded, crossed the bridge, and led her toward the building with the blue roof. She slowed down. Near the pear tree was the black Citroën again.

"She didn't tell me she had a visitor," Mr. Tanaka growled.

"I'll wait," Anyu said, holding the box with the Kawashima Egg. Going back to the workshop was not an option.

And that was when she heard a thunderous boom in the distance. There was a tremor on the ground; the building rattled.

"It has started! It has started!" Mr. Tanaka sprinted toward the marines' encampment, where the troops were looking up at the sky, grinning. *The bombing has started! Mobilize!*

Bombing Shanghai? Anyu's heart sank. She turned to the black Citroën; inside, Bellefeuille's chauffeur in his livery sat in the driver's seat, tapping on the steering wheel.

She ran up the stone staircase and entered the building with lattice windows. Kawashima was not inside. The room was quiet, spacious, lined with cabinets, tables, and glass shelves; encased inside the shelves were replicas of Fabergé eggs: the Hen Egg, the Mosaic Egg, and the Coronation Egg she had crafted. Kawashima's showroom. Anyone else would have been more discreet with the priceless eggs encrusted with diamonds, but Kawashima didn't seem concerned that her treasures would be a target of theft.

Holding her box, Anyu browsed the display with mixed feelings. There was no denying their beauty, their exceptional value, and their superb craftsmanship, but seeing their sparkling brilliance, she couldn't help but think of the endless hours of labor, the wan faces of the sickly jewelers, their stagnant looks, and their tired souls. What was the value of creating art if the artists were slaves?

A dizzy spell seized Anyu, and she lurched forward, nearly crashing into the shelves. Balancing herself, she stared at her own reflection in the glass. Nearly three years of imprisonment had taken a toll on her: her hair was thinning, graying near her ears; her skin was pallid, blotchy, and blackened, uneven like an etched silver sheet; and her back stooped. She was only twenty-seven.

A groan. Faint. Coming from the adjacent room on her left.

Slowly, she tiptoed to the room and peered in. Her jaw dropped.

Kawashima, clad in her uniform, was holding her stomach with one hand, a sword in the other, standing in a pool of blood. Facing her was a standing figure, a man in a purple suit, a man whom she wished she'd never known—Pierre Bellefeuille.

He didn't see her, with his back to her, but she could see what he was holding. A pistol.

"My patience is limited," Bellefeuille said.

"You won't get out of here alive," Kawashima said, raising her sword.

"Try me again."

"You weasel." Kawashima panted.

"We had a deal. You keep your egg, and I take the treasures. Let me ask you again. Where are my treasures?"

"I've told you many times in the past that I have no knowledge of them. When I arrived at the vault, all the treasures were gone."

"Gone? How could they all be gone?"

"The British woman must have relocated them."

"The same old rubbish. You liar. You took them for yourself. I know it."

The three-year mystery unraveled before Anyu. Bellefeuille had been working together with Kawashima, and Kawashima was his client who had asked to purchase the Romanov treasure. They had made the agreement that she'd seize the Fabergé egg from Isaac and raid the vault, and he'd keep the workmasters' loot. And now Bellefeuille had come, for he'd never received his share.

"Give me my treasures or I'll take your eggs," Bellefeuille said and turned to his right, where the glass shelves held four eggs—the Third Imperial Easter Egg, crafted by Peter Karl Fabergé, the Cherub with Chariot Egg, the Mauve Egg, and Anyu's egg, the Winter Egg. These imperial treasures had not been featured in the sketches in the workshop, and they appeared to be authentic Fabergé *objets d'art*.

"Stay where you are!" Kawashima shouted.

The gunshot rang out at the same time as an arc of white flashed in the air. And then the room fell silent. Anyu stood still, her heart in her throat.

A clunk. The pistol slipped from Bellefeuille's hand, and he fell sideways in a heap. Kawashima gasped, blood dripping from her sword and gushing from her thigh.

Anyu stepped into the room and walked to Bellefeuille. A pool of blood spread beneath him; his face was contorted, his eyes angry, eyelids fluttering, then he was finally still. He had been a poor lover, a malevolent jeweler, and a morally repugnant human, but seeing him lifeless, Anyu felt sorry for him, a man devoured by greed. At least his death had been quick and painless.

"You killed him," Anyu said.

Kawashima's face was twisted with pain. "He deserved it."

Anyu felt dizzy again. The room appeared to be blurry, and the pool of blood seemed to flow toward her. "You killed him before I had a chance to ask him. How did he know that Isaac had the Winter Egg?"

"He heard it from a woman who had an affair with your master's son."

Miss Rose worked for him. "I see. Then what kind of assistance did he offer you?"

"Without his help, I would not have known where your master was. I almost cornered him in Harbin, but he slipped out of my hands. He was cunning enough, changed his name in Shanghai. When I met the Frenchman, asking to purchase the eggs, he thought of your master but didn't tell me immediately. He had an eye on Mrs. Brown, it turned out. And he had been collecting secrets about her and following her and her cronies for years. Then he learned of the vault, but with her tight security, he was unable to break into it, until I showed him the British woman's signet ring."

Anyu felt a stab of pain in her heart. Bellefeuille had seen her with the ring before and had not suspected, but the same ring from Mrs. Brown would no doubt have roused his suspicion. It wouldn't have taken long for him to discover the double-headed eagle and unlock the vault.

"He also gave me good tips and advised that I'd have better odds of succeeding if I used you as leverage. He believed you mattered greatly to that old jeweler, and he was right."

"He plotted the robbery?"

"Never underestimate the blackened heart of a bitter lover who bleeds the bile of revenge."

Anyu closed her eyes. "And you did all the dirty work. You hired rogues to hijack us in the car, and you slaughtered Isaac's family and Mrs. Brown and the rest of the Guild members. You committed all these heinous crimes for an egg."

"It's mine! I had three real Fabergé eggs, and now I have four!" Her eyes were rimmed with blood, her lips twitching, as she held the sword for support. Had she not been shot, Kawashima would have slashed Anyu already.

Anyu stared at the ornaments on the shelf. "Four real Fabergé eggs, including my Winter Egg. Why are you obsessed with them?"

"I like them. I've been drawn to beautiful things since I was little, and I grew up with them: sapphires on my shoes, diamond bangles. I could have anything I asked for. I was born into the Aisin Gioro clan! My ancestors founded the great Qing Dynasty! Then everything was taken from me and I was a pauper, an orphan in another country."

"The eggs were never gifts from your parents, like you claimed."

"What does it matter? Those eggs were created for the Romanovs, and I am the daughter of the great Qing Dynasty. I have imperial blood, so they should belong to me. I sell the replicas for money when I'm bored, and I hunt the real ones. It's fun."

Fun? "Do you know what this egg means to me? It was created with the assistance of my mentor, and it was gifted to him by tsarists who were unwilling to see it fall into the rebels' hands. Since he was entrusted with it, my mentor was hunted by greedy people like you. He protected it with his life, only revealing its hiding place to save me when your robbers hijacked us." Anyu stopped to catch her breath.

The princess lifted her foot an inch.

"Do you understand? This egg is not simply an ornament; it's the essence of his legacy, his genius, and his sacrifice, and I promised to protect it for as long as I live, but still, if I could give you the egg in exchange for his life and his family's lives, I would."

"It's my egg!"

"You already have three. Isn't that enough?"

"Enough? I want more. I want to find all the imperial Fabergé eggs. I have to collect all of them. All fifty of them."

Anyu shook her head. "You're obsessed, and you're greedy. I've been your prisoner for two and a half years. It's over now. I'm going home. I need my egg back."

"Come take it." Kawashima put her hand on the sword's hilt.

Anyu knew what would have happened next, a lunge and a blow with deadly precision, had Kawashima not already been wounded twice. But she had Pierre to thank, in the end. "You can barely stand. I'm not afraid of you."

Kawashima raised her sword deliberately.

"All right, then." Anyu picked up the pistol that had slipped out of her former lover's hand. She had never used a gun before. But with one close look at it, the barrel, the bolt inside the receiver, the trigger mechanism, and the locking latch, she knew how it worked. She was a jeweler, after all.

"Put it down."

Anyu held the gun unwaveringly with two hands. "You murdered Isaac and his family. I'll kill you."

She pulled the trigger.

Bang. Kawashima stood still, then the sword slipped from her hands, and she dropped to the floor.

Was she dead? Anyu didn't have time to think. Her vision was blurring; her hands were trembling. She shook her head to steady herself. Then she turned to the glass shelf that contained the four eggs and fired. The glass shattered. She reached in and took the box that contained the Winter Egg.

With the ornament safely in her pocket, Anyu ran outside toward the Citroën. She knocked on the window. "Please get me out of here."

"Miss Anyu? Is that you?" The chauffeur looked stunned.

"Quick, quick." In the encampment, the marines and Mr. Tanaka had left, leaving bundles of rifles near their sleeping bags.

"Where's Monsieur Bellefeuille?" The chauffeur looked around frantically.

The ground was still quivering. Were the Japanese still bombing?

"He can't make it. Go now!"

Reluctantly, the chauffeur started the car and bounced down the road. Anyu looked behind. She could see, from the back window, Kawashima, drenched in blood, crawling over the threshold, brandishing her sword. Anyu's heart dropped. Kawashima was still alive. She would not let her egg go without a fight.

"Go, go!"

"The front gate is shut," the chauffeur said, slowing down.

"Just drive!"

"You're crazy!"

But then, as Anyu hoped, the chauffeur sped, and the car blasted through the gate. A great force slammed her, throwing her backward. She could feel her eyes bulging, and her head hit something hard. A shower of bricks rained down; debris stung her eyes. Then, finally, the car slowed to a stop.

The chauffeur groaned, but he was all right. Anyu crawled out of the car and stepped onto the street. It was eerily quiet. No rickshaws, no cars, no pedestrians. She had heard the bombing, but it seemed this area was spared. There was no hole in the ground or collapsed buildings, only some piles of broken shutters and roof tiles.

She coughed, wiped the blood dripping into her eyes, and felt her pocket to make sure the box was safely tucked inside. Then she began to walk in the direction of the Mandelburgs' shop, hoping to find Esther.

CHAPTER 38

The way to the shop took longer than expected. A few times, Anyu, exhausted, had to lean on the telephone poles to gather her strength; fortunately, for all her bloodstained face and tattered shirt, few people cast her a second glance. Many hurried on or peered at the sky. Vaguely, she heard some thuds echoing in the distance. The Japanese fighter planes were bombing the Zhabei District and the Old City, the areas where the Chinese lived, people said.

When she turned onto the familiar street, busy with commercial banners, she quickened her pace. The shop's door was unlocked, and she burst in.

It was no longer a jewelry store but a shop selling packets of cigarettes and bottles of imported whiskey and gin. Mr. Dearborn must have turned it into one of his shops. No one was behind the counter.

"Esther!" she shouted. "Esther!"

No one answered. She made her way to the hallway, the kitchen, then the workshop—it was locked. She went upstairs, found no one, and came down. Signs of human habitation were throughout, with utensils and photos in the living quarters—there was a portrait of Mr. Dearborn, Esther, and Matthew on the wall. They must have left temporarily.

Anyu wondered what to do. She was tired and wanted to rest for a while, but she couldn't linger, fearing Kawashima would pursue her.

For a moment, she sat on a chair near the shelf. Then, as if in a dream, she heard a noise and saw a shadow rush to her from the front door.

"Anyu? Anyu! It's you. Thank God! I can't believe you're here!"

It was Esther. She looked beautiful, with a red dress, a leather handbag, and an Art Deco gold necklace with round, faceted sapphires. Beside her was Matthew in his navy overalls and brown oxfords—a big boy now. How he had grown up!

Anyu wanted to laugh but cried instead. "Esther! It's so good to see you. I was wondering where you were. I saw you under the ginkgo tree. Every time. You always came."

Esther was crying, too. "I wished I could speak to you, but they wouldn't allow visitors. Look at you . . . Oh, Anyu."

"I look terrible, I know."

Esther laughed. "Oh my God. I'm so happy you're alive. You could have died. All the blood, and your face. Are you hurt?"

"I hit my head. I'll be fine." She wiped her eyes, but for all her determination to stand straight, she swayed.

Esther caught her. "There. I've got you. What do you need? What can I get for you? Some porridge? Some whiskey? A cigarette?"

"I don't need anything."

"I have missed you! I didn't know they were releasing you today." There was a honk coming from the street, and Esther said, "Oh, Anyu, I could talk to you forever, but we have to go. It's not safe here. The Japanese are bombing Shanghai. The Nationalists are fighting back in the sky."

"Where are you going?"

"We were ready to go to a shelter in the American consulate until Patrick returns from his business trip, but I forgot the passports, and we had to come back. Maybe you can come with us. Will you?"

"I can't."

Matthew, hiding behind his mother, peeped at her. If she could hold him, she would be so happy. Did he still remember her? For two and a half years, she had dreamed of uniting with Esther and Matthew, but who would have known that when the moment came, it would be time to say goodbye again.

"Why not?"

"I escaped from Kawashima's residence. She would have killed me. I worry she's not going to give up."

"What happened?"

"She was the one who killed your father and your family and robbed us."

"Kawashima?"

Anyu took the box from her shirt pocket. "Look. I got it back."

Esther took a deep breath. "The Winter Egg. I can't tell you how many times I've heard of it, but my father never showed it to me. You should take good care of it. You're the chief designer of the House of Mandelburg."

It was good to hear that—the chief designer of the House of Mandelburg. Her house. Her brand. She wanted nothing more than to keep crafting jewelry and restore the house's glory. "But I can't stay with you. I have to leave this city. Kawashima is alive. I fear I would put you in danger."

Esther hesitated. "I don't want you to leave."

If only Esther knew how much she wanted to be with her and Matthew.

"Where will you go?"

"I think I'll go to Harbin. That's the only place I know. I'll take the train."

"Now?"

Anyu nodded.

"You'll need a ride to the station. Come on, let me get our passports, and I'll take you. At least we can spend a few minutes together."

Anyu couldn't decline the offer. When Esther returned with their passports, they went outside. Darkness had fallen; a car was waiting for them. Anyu ducked inside after Esther, and with one look at the driver, she cried out.

"Confucius?" He was at the wheel! "What are you doing here?"

"Anyu, is that you?" His eyes were round with surprise. "When did you get out?"

"Today, just now. But why are you here?"

"Oh, Anyu, Confucius has been working for Patrick since you left. He's our chauffeur. He's looking after me since Patrick is in Hong Kong. He also informed us of the Japanese plans to attack a week ago, and that was why we were able to save our stock." Esther hoisted Matthew to her lap. "To the station, Confucius. Anyu wants to go to Harbin."

Anyu beamed. Confucius had learned how to drive; he had listened to her and found a respectable job. He had grown a beard, and he actually looked like a decent man in his brown fedora. It was impossible to confess how she felt, but while in Kawashima's residence, she had missed him.

"Harbin? Why?" Confucius started the engine.

"I can't stay in Shanghai. It's not safe for me or everyone if I stay," Anyu said. The car started to move, and she turned to Matthew. "Matthew? Do you remember me?"

He nodded, his blue eyes guileless, intent.

Anyu extended her arms; Matthew looked at her for about two seconds and then climbed closer to her. Her heart exploded with joy. He was six years old and still her little Matthew.

"Does it hurt?" He peered at her.

"Oh, my face?" She wiped her forehead. "It's just blood. It doesn't hurt at all."

He handed her something—a miniature red tractor, meticulously detailed, with wheels, a trailer, and a sleek, realistic design. "Do you like it?"

"It's very nice."

"You can play with it if you want. It'll make you feel better. You do it like this." He held the seated farmer figurine, turned the steering wheel, then snapped open the front engine compartment to show the engine and the cabin—his new famous Graham-Bradley toy. His fingers were dexterous. He would be a gifted jeweler.

"Shit." Confucius was reversing the car.

"What's wrong?" Anyu asked. The car swerved. In the dark, she could see they were turning onto a broad avenue near Avenue Joffre, but a double-decker bus, spewing smoke, had blocked the street.

"The Japanese Imperial Army is guarding the streets."

Was Kawashima trying to stop her from running?

Confucius swiftly turned the wheel and drove into a narrow alley where people carried sacks of sand to barricade the streets. All the buildings were dark to avoid attracting the bombers.

"Hold on!" He turned sharply onto another lane, and for an agonizing moment, the car bounced and belched, narrowly avoiding crashing against the white fences near the streets. Finally, he pulled out of the twisting lanes and came to a wide boulevard.

"We'll need to take a detour."

It was then she heard a loud noise. One of the tires had burst.

"Shit!" Confucius shouted again, winding through the street, willing the car to move forward, dodging the debris in his way. Eventually, the car slowed down and stopped moving. He turned off the engine and got out.

Anyu followed. In the dim light, she could make out the traditional Chinese compounds with walls and several two-story houses. She didn't know where she was, but she could tell they were far from the station and the consulate.

"Confucius, could you hail a taxi and take Esther and Matthew to the consulate?" Anyu said. With the flat tire, she couldn't reach the station, but Esther could still go to the consulate by taxi.

"That can certainly be done," Confucius said.

"What about you?" Esther climbed out of the car, holding Matthew's hand.

"I'll find a way to the train station."

"I've been thinking, Anyu. I don't want you to go to Harbin. You don't have a family there. Patrick is in Hong Kong; why don't you go there? He'll take care of you. There are ships at the wharf in the International Settlement that sail to Hong Kong every day, and the Settlement is spared from the bombardment."

"Hong Kong?"

"You'll be safe there. It's ruled by the British."

That could be a good idea. She would be away from Shanghai but remain in touch with Esther and Matthew. Anyu stroked Matthew's head. How wonderful it would be if she could watch him grow up. "I'll go to Hong Kong."

"I know a safe way to reach the wharf. I'll take you," Confucius said.

"Without a car?"

"Yes."

"I prefer going with you to the wharf if you don't mind me tagging along, Anyu. My bad leg might slow you down, but I'd rather not leave you, and it's hard to find a taxi with the bombing," Esther said.

I'd rather not leave you. Anyu felt a wave of warmth course through her. Esther, who had visited her every month, who had let her know she was not forgotten, whose love and constancy had nourished her during the darkest hours of her imprisonment. Esther, her friend, her sister, her blessing.

"Of course." Anyu kissed Esther's cheek and took Matthew's hand. "Let's go."

"Follow me." Confucius dove into a dark alley.

CHAPTER 39

In the dark, they hurried on. Anyu picked up Matthew when he grew tired, Esther was determined to keep up, and Confucius led them along. She could barely see what was before her or where they were headed, listening to the echo of their footsteps on narrow lanes. The bombing in the northern district and the Old City had quieted, but the street fights between the Nationalists and the Japanese had started. She could hear the firing of machine guns and the explosions of grenades in the distance. Stumbling and depleted of strength, she stopped now and then, holding Matthew, staying close to Esther.

They'd take a ferry in the Nantao District and sail north on the Huangpu River to the wharf in the Settlement, Confucius said. The water passage, a common transport for the poor locals, was unknown to foreigners, but it was a safe route.

They must have been running for hours when she felt the air change—there was the smell of a river, earthy, fishy, the sound of lapping water, and a strong odor of rotten clams and reeds, and she could see a few skiffs docked along the shore. The night in this corner was peaceful. There were no frightening warplanes in the sky, devastating surges of fire above roofs, or the awful screams of tires. They had entered a backland haven. Near the shore, Confucius went to negotiate with a ferryman wearing a pointy hat, and the three waited at the pier; when he waved, they came to the ferryboat.

The boat was narrow and tiny, just big enough for five people. Anyu helped Esther settle on a horizontal board near the stern and sat next to her, Matthew snuggled between them, and gripped the edge of the boat as it glided in the darkness. This was her first time riding a boat, and it felt different from being on a train or in a car. She felt as though she were leaving a land of troubles and being carried away on calm waters, with the night breeze sweeping her face, the starry sky, the silhouettes of skiffs swaying at the swamp, and the steady swing of the ferryman. Now and then, she could hear the squawks of ducks, the croaks of toads, and the flutters of night birds' wings. There was something spiritual, to be close to the water.

She let out a long sigh. It had been a long day since she escaped from Kawashima's workshop, and now all she wished was to stay safe and live a quiet life.

"I've never been to Hong Kong before," Esther said.

"Me neither," Anyu said.

"Will you be all right?"

"Mr. Dearborn is there. I'll be all right. Will you come for a visit?"

"I was just thinking about that. I've been wanting to go to Hong Kong for a while." Esther was quiet. "Confucius, when will we arrive at the wharf?"

"Very soon," he said.

In the dark, Anyu could only see an outline of Confucius and his hat. She hadn't had a chance to talk to him, and suddenly she hoped the boat ride would take longer. "Esther, how did you come to know Confucius?"

"He came to my shop looking for you. I recognized him. He asked if I needed help. Patrick happened to need a chauffeur so I hired him. He learned to drive," Esther said.

"He's a generous man," Confucius said.

A man from Boston, Anyu remembered. He had been good to Esther. "How have you been for the past three years, Confucius?"

He chuckled. "I'm a promising young man, you know that."

"How many children do you have now?"

"Children? Why would I have children?"

"Aren't you married?"

"I'm married to Mr. Dearborn's car."

Anyu smiled.

The scenery began to change—the harbor was visible ahead. A palisade of golden beams glittered along the shore; bulbs of lights illuminated the immense cruise ships and sailboats and junks. The wind carried pulsating jazz beats and faint laughter from afar.

When they arrived at the wharf, Anyu disembarked, looking around cautiously. It seemed business was going on as usual here: families were gathered at the gangway, saying farewell to the passengers; laborers, carrying bulky luggage, were crossing a plank to the ship; the air was punctuated by the sounds of horns and rushing water.

There were no Japanese soldiers in uniforms.

"Confucius," Esther called out when he headed toward the ticket booth. "Three tickets, please. Two adults, one child."

"Esther!" Anyu cried out.

"I might as well come visit now," she said. "It'll be a huge surprise to Patrick."

"Oh, I'm so happy. We'll be together again." Anyu almost burst into tears of joy. She leaned over Matthew and kissed his face, then Esther's.

When Confucius returned from the ticket booth, he gave a blue boat ticket to her and two tickets to Esther. "You'll be surprised to know that they have plenty of tickets available to Hong Kong. You're on the next boat; boarding has just started."

Anyu took the ticket and looked at the ship, where the sailor was waving a flag and whistling. "You can come with me," she said softly to Confucius. "If you want to."

Confucius's eyes twinkled in the light from the ticket window. He reached out to hold her hand. "I want to."

"You do?"

"Look." In his palm was another ticket. To Hong Kong. One-way. "I was just waiting for the right moment to tell you."

She laughed, embracing him. This was wonderful. He would go to Hong Kong with them. They would have a new life together. And this time he was no longer a gangster; this time they could live the life they had planned. They were indeed meant to be.

Esther smiled and whispered something in Matthew's ear. Matthew came over and held Anyu's hand. Together, the four went to the gangway, joining the crowd carrying suitcases.

There was a commotion from the street. Anyu jumped, looking behind.

Near the telephone pole across the street was Kawashima, her shoulder bound with a strip of white cloth, marching toward the wharf with four Japanese soldiers. And the crowd, panicking, rushed from the street to the wharf.

"Stay calm and we'll board quickly," Anyu said.

"I have a pistol," Confucius said.

"Don't use it, please. If you shoot, you'll attract her attention. Act normal."

The crowd surged fast; a multitude of people rushed around her. Anyu picked up Matthew, fearing she would lose him, and told Esther to stay close. They were only a few feet away from the stern of the ship. Once they boarded, the captain would fold up the ramp, and they'd sail away.

It took longer than she wanted, but finally, they set their feet on the ship, and Anyu felt the deck vibrating and people's suitcases stab her ribs. When the last passengers came aboard, a sailor lifted the ramp, and the ship pulled away from the shore. She let out a long breath.

"That was close," Esther said.

"We made it."

"Look." Confucius pointed at the wharf.

Anyu put Matthew down and held on to the railing. In the dim light, the wharf on the other side of the water was receding, dark like an abandoned island, but a figure stood, a sharp blade in her hand.

Anyu touched her pocket where the Winter Egg was safely tucked. She had escaped from Kawashima, at last.

Inside, the boat was humid, crammed with passengers. Anyu found four seats near a window and sat down. Until then, she hadn't realized how exhausted she was. Only this morning she was still in Kawashima's residence, and now she was going to Hong Kong with Matthew, Esther, and Confucius.

Matthew sat next to her. "What's in your pocket?"

"A toy."

"Can I see it?"

"Someday. I'll show you, someday."

The ship rocked; several bags slid to her feet. A wave of voices rose, people crashing their shoulders against each other and apologizing. Next to her, a man smoking a pipe was saying "Believe me, Shanghai has turned into a pile of rubble, and the war is going to last for a few years. The Nationalists can fight back, but they don't stand a chance. The Japanese will take everything they can and destroy anything they can't take. It's high time to get out of here."

Later, Anyu went out of the cabin to get some fresh air. There were only a few people out on the deck; the waves roared, rushing to her ears. She leaned over the railing, looking ahead.

The night was dark; the shore of Shanghai was aflame with golden lamp lights; they grew weaker as she watched, diminishing; the breeze was gentle, carrying a tune that sounded like a man's voice, barely audible.

She had a lump in her throat. She would not be able to return to this city again, nor could she work as a master jeweler for the rest of her life. This was a farewell to the city she had called home, a conclusion of the brilliant years of creating and crafting as a top designer of the world. Had she been given another chance, she would have stayed, to enthrall her clients with her creations, to rebuild her mentor's name. She would have lived as a jeweler of the House of Mandelburg and died as the chief designer of the House of Mandelburg in this city.

Yet she was also grateful, for she had the Winter Egg and the Diamond of Life, she had persisted and survived, and she had enjoyed fame, seen greed, and learned about love. She had come to this city as an orphan and left as a guardian. She had her beloved family, the people who cared for her, whom she would give her life to protect, who were her blessings.

She couldn't see Kawashima's face, nor did she want to think about her; but the princess was out there, searching for her. Except that she would not have her hands on the egg, never again, as long as Anyu was alive.

CHAPTER 40

October 1937
Hong Kong

Fifty-eight days later, Anyu arrived at the port of Hong Kong Island.

Sunlight, bright like pure gold, the air warm, damp, scented with musty algae and fresh fish. Seagulls skimmed over the water in Victoria Harbor, junks with black and brown sails breezed past the coral-edged shores lined with emerald palms, and monasteries with ruby-red roofs floated in clouds in the far distance across the green hills in Kowloon. *Kowloon*, they said, meant "nine dragons" in Chinese—it was named after the divine dragons sleeping under the mountains, who must not be disturbed, or they'd unleash accidents or disease or death as punishment.

Anyu held up her hand, shielding her eyes, gazing out. People on the ship had said that everything in Hong Kong was brought over by the early colonizers, the trees of the flame of the forest from South Asia, the five-petaled frangipani from Hawaii, and the feverishly pink bougainvillea from South America. They also said Hong Kong's stories could unfold in the cracks of the steep streets slithering through slums and saloons, that Hong Kong's love could be sought on the quiet echoes of wooden fish and the incense smoke that smelled of frankincense and pepper, that Hong Kong's tears could be seen in the flap of fork-tailed sunbirds, the specked shells of barnacles, and the jelly-tongued limpets.

They said all the people loved Hong Kong, ministers and mistresses, cooks and crooks, villagers and vagabonds, and they also said Hong Kong was like no other, for it was an island for refugees, an atoll for the faithful, and a harbor for all birds of passage.

With Confucius, Esther, and Matthew by her side, Anyu, wearing the Diamond of Life under her shirt, carrying her bag that contained the Winter Egg, walked down the ramp.

CHAPTER 41

December 1941

Holding a saw, Anyu sliced through a white cuttlebone. Fine powder spilled over her fingers and piled on the desk as she moved the saw back and forth. When the bone split into two halves, she put down the saw, took a knife, and began to carve the shape of a two-inch basket inside the soft interior.

She had heard about this direct casting method from Isaac and watched a few jewelers use this method in Kawashima's workshop. She liked this cuttlebone casting process, a convenient method since she had limited tools and funds. With seafood abounding in Hong Kong, cuttlefish bones were also affordable; a dozen could be purchased for one Hong Kong dollar. Using this method, she had crafted two halves of eggshells and a white five-petaled flower with gold stamens.

It had been four years since she arrived in Hong Kong. With the help of Mr. Dearborn and Esther, she had opened a jewelry shop in a crowded neighborhood in Causeway Bay. She didn't sell jewelry, only offered a jewelry repair service. Her drawers stored many broken pieces treasured by her customers: a rusty ring with a crushed claw setting, a silver necklace with a broken hook, and a brooch hollow without a gem. They belonged to a loud-voiced grandma with a hefty dowry, a flighty young widow making ends meet by selling grass jelly, and a deaf man who hoped to surprise his daughter, who would soon be a bride.

As always, she would carefully polish the pieces, straightening the angles and soldering the broken hooks. She charged small fees but treated the projects with the same care as a royal commission. In this crowded neighborhood, no one knew her background or past fame; they only knew her as Anyu, from Harbin.

She liked Hong Kong, the sea, the hills, the boats, and the warm air. Her life, as she had prayed, was serene. During the day, she repaired and crafted jewelry; at night, she unfolded the rattan mat and turned the area into their bedroom.

When she was not working, or her vision was too bleary to work with tweezers, she visited the streets downhill. She'd buy fish balls from street vendors, watch locals crack eggs in a glass with alcohol and gulp down the raw egg yolk mix, and bargain with betel nut sellers and paper fan vendors. She had turned thirty-two and gained some weight, although she walked with a stoop that made her appear much older, and she felt, at times, she was an addled old woman with violent spells of headaches and an energy-draining cough.

She was lonely, sometimes, and longed for Confucius at night. She had married him two months after they arrived in Hong Kong. They had a joyous ceremony with Mr. Dearborn, Esther, and Matthew in attendance, all the people she cared about. She wore a gold locket necklace gifted by Esther, the third piece of jewelry she owned, the only necklace she was free to show, and Confucius put on a tuxedo with tails. They feasted on plump whitefish seasoned with green onion, clams doused with black bean sauce, and fried prawns with minced garlic, and all had too much wine. After the ceremony, she hiked on a mountain to the Tsing Shan Monastery with Confucius, burned some incense, and wished for a happy and peaceful life together. Then, drawn to its serene atmosphere, they made a pilgrimage to the monastery once a year, renewing their devotion to each other.

They had lived happily for three years before Confucius was struck by a racing car last year. He died in the hospital with Anyu holding his hands. *Life is a thief who takes pleasure in showing off his sleight of hand,* he had said. How Anyu wished he had cheated and won so she could have spent her lifetime with him.

She stored Confucius's ashes in the same monastery, Tsing Shan. They didn't have children, but she had Matthew, who was all she cared about these days.

Every minute with Matthew filled her heart with joy. She walked him home from school, made him Chinese noodles, took him to the beach and markets, and taught him how to make jewelry. She had been right about Matthew being a gifted jeweler. He was a quick learner, had dexterous hands, and possessed a natural talent for drawing and spatial reasoning. The first time he soldered, she guided his fingers, melting the silver wire. Matthew laughed and insisted on doing it himself; he singed his eyebrows and hair but quickly learned to hold the torch like a seasoned jeweler. When he finished a chain at eight, she felt she had won a sizable commission.

Esther and Mr. Dearborn had been good to her. They supported her financially when they first arrived, but the biased racial law in Hong Kong prevented all of them from living together, so the Dearborns lived in Central.

Mr. Dearborn's exporting business had taken off in Hong Kong, and he only returned to Shanghai twice. Esther thrived in Hong Kong. She kept her Jewish identity under wraps and was happier to be called an American. Her striking beauty made her the center of every gathering; her limp gained many empathetic remarks. She socialized with many British women and expatriates from India and Australia, and her social circle included women of the wealthiest echelon in Hong Kong: Margaret Mak (the first wife of Robert Ho Tung), Hilda Selwyn-Clarke (the wife of Selwyn Selwyn-Clarke), and even Ursula Boxer (the wife of Maj. Charles Boxer).

A spate of coughs shook Anyu; she put down the saw and stood. Her workshop, a closed space without windows, lacked proper ventilation, but it was safe and necessary. This area was notorious for clever thieves who pilfered with long poles fitted with hooks; anything in a room with an open window was asking to be stolen. She reached for the radio on the desk and turned it on.

The two hosts, in their cultured British accents, were in a heated discussion:

"The new governor, Sir Mark Young, has reestablished the Gin Drinkers' Line in the New Territories. It's strong enough to withstand any assault."

"The Japanese would tear through that line in one day."

"Impossible. The Japanese soldiers are known for their poor eyesight, and they wouldn't be able to advance at night."

"Poor eyesight?"

"Everyone knows that! They are no match for our garrison. May I remind you that we have thousands of well-trained Royal Scots and Indian units and a superior artillery force, including heavy and long-range guns. Our air force possesses armed flying boats, torpedo bombers, and experienced pilots."

All the radio talked about these days was the imminent attack on the island by the Japanese and how to defend the colony. She couldn't remember when it had started. When she arrived in Hong Kong four years ago, the radio only publicized automobiles, the queen, and the horse racing clubs. She had been saddened to hear, after their departure, that the Japanese had seized complete control of the Old City in Shanghai, and since then, they had attacked more cities in the south. Japanese forces now occupied Guangzhou, a neighboring city of Hong Kong's New Territories. It was depressing. The Japanese had won every war, from Harbin to Shanghai to Guangzhou. When would this end?

She turned the radio off. The talk brought her nightmares of Kawashima, standing on the wharf, her sword a bolt ready to strike.

A plague. This poisonous time, this stench of war, this greed of the Japanese military.

The clock struck two; Anyu wiped her hands clean on a rag, went to the door, and stepped out.

The humid, warm air enveloped her; she shielded her eyes with her hand and peered at the street downhill. In a few minutes, Matthew would skip to her, out of breath, his golden hair a blazing fire opal that burned every passerby's eyes. She had prepared a delicious snack for him, lotus seeds soup mixed with petals of lily bulb sweetened with rock sugar, which had taken her most of the morning. She devoted all her attention to this golden boy, but would always want to do more.

"Matthew, Matthew! There you are. Are you hungry?" She saw him climbing uphill, wearing his school uniform of black pants and white shirt, his schoolbag flapping against his leg.

Matthew glanced up at her and pinched his lips.

He was ten years old, already as tall as her, fluent in Chinese and English. He attended a school for British and American children, and Anyu was his willing caretaker. He had been moody these days. Once he had told her not to pick him up at school, and when he had friends around, he addressed her as "amah."

Anyu took no offense. How Matthew treated her didn't affect how she thought of him, a special, gifted child.

"Matthew, look what I made for you today."

"I have to go." He threw his schoolbag into her arms and ran back down the street, where another boy in a school uniform waved at him.

"Wait, wait! Where are you going?" She locked the door behind her and followed him.

"I'm going to Henry's house. Don't follow me."

Henry's house was located on the Peak, the highest mountain in Hong Kong, which touted the best view of the island, but the neighborhood forbade her presence. Hong Kong was odd this way; the public spaces and venues were separated for the whites and the Chinese. The cable tram that ran to the Peak was off-limits to her, and so were the first class of the Star Ferry and even the public botanical parks. She was not used to being treated as less than others—in Shanghai, while certain clubs barred entry or membership to Chinese people, the racial division had been discreetly blurred, and as a famous jeweler, she had never been turned away from anywhere for her race. But this was how the lofty white British ruled Hong Kong, she had learned: by blatantly extolling their privilege, living apart from Chinese like her, whom they mocked as maggots.

But Matthew needed to eat his snack! He would be hungry.

Anyu raced downhill, keeping a distance from Matthew so he wouldn't be annoyed, but soon she lost sight of him. Distracted, Anyu almost ran into a hawker selling slippers—he was covered with them, a necklace of slippers and a stack of black cloth slippers atop his head. She halted, picked up the slippers he had dropped, skipped aside, and continued to run down the hill.

Then she saw Matthew surrounded by a group of local Chinese youths. They seemed to be taunting him and his friend Henry. One youngster in ripped beige pants yanked Henry's bag; another pushed Matthew. Henry, smartly, had found a chance and ran away, but Matthew staggered backward, lost his balance, and fell into a nullah. The youths laughed, kicking him in his shoulder.

"Stop!" Anyu raced down the street and lunged toward the rascals, her arms flinging out to strike them. "Stop! Stop that! You scoundrel! Don't you dare touch him. Stop. All of you!"

A few ran away, but the youth with ripped pants was still attacking Matthew. Anyu smacked his head and thrust him aside. "Leave him alone, bully!"

"White ghost! White British ghost! You'll all soon be gone!" he shouted at Matthew, shuffling back.

"Get lost! Or I'll call the sepoys to arrest you!" Anyu threatened. Most Chinese people thought Matthew was British, given his features and coloring. She reached out to pull him out of the nullah. His feet were submerged in the filth, and he had scratched his forehead and elbow. She picked some trash from his shoulder and hair and rubbed his arm.

"Who are those rascals? Do you know them?"

"No." Matthew groaned, his face pink with humiliation.

"How long have they been bullying you?"

Matthew shrugged. "They came out of nowhere."

"Shame on them!"

"Henry and I were going to play billiards at his house. No more school this year."

"So soon?"

"Some teachers have left the island. They said the British are done for, Auntie. All of them. Those in England will be killed by the Germans, and those in Hong Kong will be killed by the Japanese. Hong Kong won't belong to them anymore."

The Chinese on the island disliked the British as much as the British disliked *them*. Since the breakout of the war in Europe, people on the streets, even her clients, had been discussing the British struggle in the war against Germany. With every report of German victory came the gloating and questioning of the British's ability to rule this island. The consensus was that the mighty empire, where once the sun never set, would eventually sink to the bottom of the sea, and all their colonies would turn on their masters and drown them with stones.

"Nonsense. The Japanese can't touch the British. Let's go home. Are you hungry?"

Matthew walked backward ahead of her. "The sepoys are planning a mutiny, Auntie. You didn't know?"

"What?"

"The British authority ordered them to ditch their cloth turbans for steel helmets, and they revolted. They said it was against their religion. Henry said so."

"Oh." She couldn't believe Indian policemen who worked for the British government would risk that. They had long been praised for being faithful to the queen.

"Are the British done for?"

"Absolutely not. And you're an American. You're safe here. Let's go home. Your mother is coming for dinner."

Anyu put on an encouraging smile, but news like this unnerved her. There had been numerous disturbances as far as she could remember: the exodus of the British women and children last year, the strikes of workers in the Royal Navy's warship dockyards, and the disputes over immigration concerning those labeled as the "impure," whom the British looked down on.

But if the British were to sink to the bottom of the sea, then the froth of war would devour them all.

CHAPTER 42

In her apartment, Anyu cleaned up Matthew, watched him wolf down the lotus seed soup she had prepared, and kept asking if he wanted more. She enjoyed moments like this, feeding him. The room was hot and humid, enveloped in a thick cocoon of heat, even though it was December. Anyu fanned him with a large paper fan to keep him cool.

After eating, Matthew walked into the small space of her workshop and studied the cuttlebones she had sliced up.

He sat at her workbench, looking at ease. When he was younger, she had to warn him not to touch this or that, but now, she trusted him with every tool.

"What are you making?" he asked.

"A basket of flowers."

"Is it done?"

"It is."

He lifted the basket to the light; it was small, the size of a ring. "Why do you always carve *I-M-A* on your jewelry?"

"It's my maker's marks, my signature. It means 'I am Anyu,'" she said. "But wait for a minute." Holding the saw, she carved another letter.

"*I-M-A-M.*"

"The second *M* is you. You'll be a great jeweler someday. This will be our signature for the House of Mandelburg." She had often talked about Isaac with Matthew, the skills he taught her, and how he elevated her to being a master jeweler. "And this"—she drew the double-headed eagle symbol right next to it—"is from a secret organization I belonged to. I can't tell you more than that. I've taken a vow to protect it. But you know about the Midnight Aurora."

He stuck out his tongue. "You always talk about that, but I don't believe it. It's just a stone."

He used to believe, when he was younger. "It's not simply a stone. It's the Midnight Aurora."

"Why would Grandfather give it to you if it was so powerful?"

She patted his back. "Sometimes there are answers we can't understand; sometimes there are answers we refuse to understand. When you grow up, you'll know."

He shrugged. "Can I make my horseshoe crab pendant today?"

Horseshoe crabs were Matthew's favorite sea creatures. Whenever they went to the beach, Matthew liked to play with them.

Anyu picked out her pen and a sketchbook from the row of tools lined up on the wall. "There you go. Precision is the key, don't forget."

He sat, his feet firmly on the ground, his head leaning forward. Quickly, he was lost in his drawing. For a ten-year-old, his concentration was remarkable.

When Esther arrived, it was almost midnight. They had already finished dinner. These days, she worked at a counter at Lane Crawford selling jewelry. She also helped out at Mr. Dearborn's shop during the day; in the evenings she lounged at an exclusive club for upper-class women, which had marble staircases and polished teak-paneled rooms.

Esther took off her lace hat and sat on the small sofa, wearing a purple taffeta dress, looking apologetic but beautiful as always. She had been in a good mood these days, but not now. "Sorry I missed your dinner."

Anyu gave her a cigarette. "That's fine. Are you all right? Something is bothering you."

"I don't know how to tell you the news. I think I saw Kawashima."

She had never wanted to hear her name again. "Are you sure?"

Esther puffed out a torrent of smoke. "There were Japanese soldiers in the department store today. She was wearing a man's military uniform and carrying a sword. I will never forget her face."

Anyu's heart dropped. "Did she see you?"

"No."

She breathed out. "Good. What was she doing?"

"She was speaking to a few salesmen at the counter. She was asking about jewelry stores on this island."

She was still searching for her, for the Winter Egg. But Anyu had been careful, lying low, staying away from jewelry's limelight, doing only repair work. She should remain unidentifiable among the sea of people on this island. "I wonder, out of caution, if you'll stay out of sight. Maybe take a few days off from the store?"

"The thing is, Anyu, I've been worried about life in Hong Kong for a while. You've heard the news."

"But the radio says the British are well equipped and sufficiently armed."

Esther shook her head. "The public is kept in the dark, I'm afraid, and the government wants to keep it that way. The situation is dire. I've heard that, in the best-case scenario, the British are hoping to hold out for ninety days, and then they can't do anything other than wait for rescue from the American Navy sailing from Hawaii."

Anyu had yet to learn of the British reliance on the Americans. "You think the attack is inevitable."

Esther sighed. "Patrick says it's not a matter of if; it's a matter of when. Now, with the arrival of Kawashima, I think we need to look for a way out."

"What way out?"

"I've talked to Patrick. We've contacted a friend to arrange a boat trip to Macau. Once the details are set, we will pack and leave. What do you say?"

Leave Hong Kong? Anyu looked around: the coal stove, the wicker basket she used for groceries, the bamboo mat she unfurled at night to sleep on, and the workshop in the closed space where Matthew was drawing. She had not thought of leaving this nest, but wherever Esther went, she would follow. "Macau sounds nice."

"Good. I'll be back in ten days."

"He'll stay with me until you find the ferry. Sound good?" Anyu said.

Esther nodded. She held the cigarette between her fingers, watching the smoke slinking above the lamp. In the air hovered the smell of tobacco mixed with Esther's floral fragrance and the acetone from the workshop.

"Anyu, I don't know. I have a bad feeling about this war, about Hong Kong."

"It's going to be fine. We've been through worse."

Esther gave a dry smile. "I've been thinking that life for someone like me has been rather tragic. For my entire life, I've been running from war. The war in Russia, the war in Shanghai, and now the war in Hong Kong. I can't help but think my life is simply a sad interlude of an extended elegy."

"You left Shanghai for me."

"I'm glad we're here with you, glad I have you."

It was not often to hear words of affection from Esther. Anyu tapped her cigarette against Esther's in a gesture of fondness. "And I have you," Anyu said.

She could have said more, counting their miseries and sharing their victories. But there was no need. Esther knew too well how she felt. After all these years together, they were well attuned to each other's thoughts, and the love between them needed not to be counted, or compared, or boasted about. They were friends, sisters, family. Now and forever.

Esther smiled. "Do you remember I once told you not to stay with us because we were stateless Jews?"

"And I refused. All I wanted was to live with your family."

"You were stubborn. You're always so stubborn."

Anyu took a long drag from her cigarette. "Have you wondered what your life would be like without me?"

"Are you blaming yourself for what happened to my family? No. It's not you, Anyu. It's because Father was a jeweler, it's because of who we are. You have been our lucky charm. If it weren't for you, I wouldn't be here today. I would be dead in Shanghai, along with my father and Samuel."

Anyu's thoughts drifted. "I miss them."

"I miss them, too," Esther said quietly.

All of them. Isaac, Samuel, Uncle David, and the aunts. And Confucius. And Mother.

Later, they went to the workshop, leaning against the doorpost, watching Matthew, his head bent, a wisp of gray soldering fumes kissing his forehead and wandering to the ceiling.

"Don't worry. I'll look after him," Anyu said.

"I know you will."

"You come back in ten days," Anyu said.

Then they'd escape again. As they had done before.

After Esther left, Anyu kept Matthew busy. As soon as he awoke, she fed him fruit, porridge, and eggs and walked with him to the ferry terminal, where they took a two-hour ride to the Tsing Shan Monastery, where Confucius's ashes were enshrined. They hiked the steep stone steps meandering through towering ancient Indian rubber trees with spiral trunks and glossy leaves, passed through the mountain gates, and visited Confucius's grave.

"He's the keeper of my secrets," Anyu said. "Will you promise that you'll pay respects to Confucius when you grow up?"

Matthew nodded.

Later, they meditated in the worship hall, and Anyu told him the tale of Reverend Pui To, a Zen master who was said to reside inside a chalet near the pagoda, and, of course, the stories of the Diamond of Life.

After they left the monastery, they spent the afternoon at the beach, walking along the long, endless shoreline. Matthew hunted for horseshoe crabs, and his knowledge of the creature surprised her, as always. The horseshoe crabs were the cousins of spiders and scorpions, he said, and they looked ferocious, with a long swordlike tail, their entire bodies covered with a hard shell with sharp spines and pointy ridges, but unlike the venomous scorpions and predatory spiders, horseshoe crabs were harmless, had rare blue blood, and were often defenseless when attacked.

"They only eat worms, clams, and mollusks. They have not changed their diet for ages, and their appearance has remained the same for millions of years. They are the oldest creatures on earth, older than dinosaurs." He picked up a horseshoe crab and turned it upside down, its ten legs wiggling.

Some things were indeed eternal.

One day, they were playing at the beach again when Matthew looked up at the sky. "What's that?"

Beyond the turquoise waves, near the shores of Kowloon, far on the horizon, a few birds circled, leaving black specks in the gray air. A blaze shot up, plumes of smoke ascending.

Anyu frowned, shielding her eyes from the sun. She couldn't tell the precise location of the blaze, but it didn't look like a drill or an accident.

"Let's go home, Matthew."

On her way to her apartment, she asked the vendors, pedestrians, and anyone she encountered about the fire, but no one seemed to know. Matthew turned on the radio. There was only music.

The next day, a grave man's voice delivered the news that Kai Tak Airfield, which the Royal Air Force used, had been bombed; the Japanese had attacked Kowloon.

"I told you. It's happening," Matthew said. "What will happen to us?"

"You heard the news. The British in Kowloon will fight back, and there will be a bloody battle before they land on Hong Kong Island. But we'll be out of here by then. Mother and Father will come back, and then we'll leave for Macau."

"When will they be here?"

"Soon." Anyu didn't show her worries on her face. It had been a week since Esther left.

"Are the Japanese going to kill us all?"

"No, you're an American. They'll leave you alone."

"The radio said the Japanese were also at war with the United States, and we are also their enemies."

She had heard that, too, and hoped it was a rumor. "We'll stay in the apartment to be safe, Matthew."

Every day, there was news of looting on the streets in Kowloon, shop ransackings, and robberies of trucks driven by hospital employees. Anyu was glad she had saved enough rice and beans for several months.

Ten days passed; Esther didn't come.

Anxious, Anyu left the apartment to find Esther. Had she and Mr. Dearborn found a ferry to Macau? She should have heard about the bombing of Kai Tak Airfield by now, and if she had not found a boat, they needed to hurry. Once the Japanese crossed Victoria Harbor, they would be trapped. She went to Esther's apartment in Central, but no one was home, and Mr. Dearborn's shop was closed. Anyu decided to go to the department store where Esther worked. Matthew insisted on coming along.

Walking toward the department store, Anyu could hardly recognize the streets that she had crossed every day: the bombing of Kowloon had spooked people in Hong Kong. There were no street vendors or people pushing strollers, the buses and trams were not running, and the taxis were out of sight. She realized with a shiver—the Japanese were invading Hong Kong Island any minute.

"Stay with me, Matthew. You hear? Do not leave me."

She rushed to the stately Lane Crawford building and pushed through crowds of people holding bundles of clothing, lamps, and even bedding. They were not regular shoppers, she realized; they were looters, their faces glazed with hysteria.

And then she heard it—a faint whir like a mosquito buzzing. She looked up. A warplane. Then another. They cast long shadows ahead of her like two dark creatures under the sea.

"They're bombing the island, Auntie," Matthew said.

"Let's go find Mother. Go."

They dashed inside the department store; it was a scene of unspeakable frenzy. Men were smashing the glass counters, fighting for furs and bags and clothing, while others groaned on the floor, clutching their bleeding heads. Anyu found a clerk wearing the store's uniform sitting on the floor with a bleeding face.

"Esther Mandelburg?" he said, his voice barely audible. "She left the store to check on her husband a few days ago. I hear they were arrested by the Japanese."

Arrested? "Where are they?"

"I don't know."

A thunderous roar rocked the building. The roof collapsed; the second floor toppled. Bricks crashed down.

Anyu lunged to cover Matthew. "We have to go, Matthew. Let's go."

She grabbed Matthew's hand and dove out just as the balcony caved in. In a mad dash, hand clasping Matthew's, she rushed out of the building and raced down the street. She was only a few feet away from a church when another bomb struck, and the steeple collapsed with a groan. She stopped, heart pounding in her chest, looking around her. In desperation, she sped toward a café near a palm tree, holding Matthew's hand. She had just taken two steps when a stray bullet whizzed past her, and a man holding a heap of hats sagged beside her. She shivered; in a few short minutes, they had escaped death three times.

"I want Mother! I want Father!" Matthew shouted, his face streaked with tears.

"We must get out of here first." She pulled him along. The streets were shrouded in a dense fog of dust and smoke, deafening with the sound of shelling, and the ground trembled. It was hard to see where she should go, but her mind was clear. With the Diamond of Life, she would evade death, and as long as she held Matthew's hand in hers, he would survive, too.

"We need to find them, Auntie."

"We will. As soon as the bombing stops. Let's go back to our apartment. You stay with me, Matthew."

"You're crushing my hand."

"Sorry." She loosened her grip, just a bit, then sped up, racing down the street filled with the cacophonous noises of buildings exploding and people screaming. She tried hard not to glance at the warplanes roaring above her, tearing her gaze away from the people with bleeding faces and the bodies slumped over the stone stairs.

Hong Kong was descending into hell.

For six days, the sky exploded.

The trees lay flat, the hills shuddered, the buildings moaned. The screeches of humans blended into the shrill cries of gulls above the water. Clouds of charcoal smoke surged and surged across the sky, throttling a black sun.

On Christmas Day, the island was quiet, like an empty cage.

In the air, cinders from the fires floated, spinning like snowflakes, the bare hills the color of desert sand; in the harbor, hulls of junks drifted, and broken sails bobbed.

On the radio, a voice said that Governor Young had surrendered. He had taken a motorboat to Kowloon across from the harbor, where the Japanese had set up their headquarters inside the Peninsula Hotel, and signed an unconditional surrender document. The exchange had been friendly, and he was back at his governor's manor, holding his Malacca walking cane with a gold band. The radio didn't mention the treatment of the American hostages, who were declared the enemy of the Japanese.

All day, Anyu stood at the top of a hill near her apartment, hoping to see Esther's return, observing the activities on the streets. Then later in the afternoon, she saw a parade of officials on horseback and in jeeps, trundling along the shelled buildings, with soldiers carrying the Japanese flag heading toward the Wan Chai District, where a massive crowd had gathered in Statue Square.

The foreign civilians, the Royal Army Medical Corps, and the surrendered Royal Scots were taken to the square, waiting for orders, one of her neighbors said.

Orders?

She could imagine what orders they would be. The Japanese 23rd Army had won the war, and the moment of reckoning had come for the foreigners, who would likely be sent to internment camps.

"Quick, quick." Anyu took Matthew's hand and raced downhill.

They wove through the streets to the west, to Statue Square in Central. It was a short walk, but it took them a long time to climb over rubble and reach Chater Road. Then they couldn't go any farther, blocked by an army of Japanese soldiers. Standing on a stair, she could see the red canopy of the Queen Victoria statue but nothing else. After some searches, she finally found a ledge near a stone lion. She beckoned Matthew over and climbed onto the pedestal, craning her neck. Then she saw them—around the fence of the statue were the defeated British soldiers, the bleeding Indian policemen, and a bit farther, in front of the towering HSBC building, with their backs to the harbor, looking at the street, was a neat line of unkempt foreigners. There were so many of them, men in black silk coats, women in skirts.

"Do you see them?" Matthew's eyes were glazed.

Anyu shook her head, and then she was still. In front of the arrested foreigners was a figure in an officer's uniform, carrying a sword—Kawashima.

"Mother should be there. Do you see her?"

There. Anyu finally spotted Esther, her hair blooming like brilliant golden trumpet flowers. She was thirty-nine years old, Anyu remembered, a loving mother, a likable saleswoman, and a caring wife.

"I see her! There she is! Will they release her? Will they send her to a camp, Auntie?"

Anyu couldn't see anything through the crowd. Standing on tiptoe, she craned her neck and caught sight of the tips of the rifles in front of the neat row. She shivered.

There was a loud shout in Japanese and the rifles were lifted.

"What are they doing?"

Anyu felt her heart shatter into pieces. Tears gushing out, she turned Matthew toward her and held him tight. "Don't look, don't look."

And Esther was looking upward, to the sky, perhaps searching for Anyu, asking her to look after Matthew.

Then there was a blast and the golden trumpet flowers faltered. The entire row fell backward. The gunshots, deafening, shook the square, echoing above the statues.

The harbor bled blood.

CHAPTER 43

Later, it was known that about five hundred foreigners had been executed in the square. Anyu never knew if Mr. Dearborn was among them. He was not heard from again.

Ninety-six days after the execution of her friend, four months before Matthew turned eleven, Kawashima found Anyu.

From the top of her apartment's roof, Anyu watched the woman skulking up the hill, her left hand holding her sword. It was late afternoon; the sun had vanished behind the billow of smoke that incessantly rose these days. Near her, some local women in black shirts and pants, who had been scouring for food scraps, ran into their homes.

The moment to make a difficult choice had come.

"Matthew." Anyu tapped on his shoulder. "I'll go down to meet her."

They were sitting on the roof of their apartment, a hiding place from the gangster looters. The past few months had been brutal, with street looting, shooting, and harassment from the gangsters throughout the city. She showed Matthew the hidden stock she had saved over the years, the tinned beef, the canned peaches, the dried salted fish concealed under the floorboard near the door; she reminded him over and over of the monastery on the other shore, had him memorize his grandparents' names and address in America, and instructed him what to do in the foreseeable future if anything separated them. But she had hoped she would never have to face this moment.

Matthew shook his head, his face and hair smeared with mud she applied to disguise him. "I don't want you to go."

At his voice, Anyu was not so confident about her plan anymore. He was only a child. Would he be able to find his way to the ferry? She wanted to stay and protect him. "I can't let her see you or know who you are. She'll take you. She'll hurt you and use you as leverage. I won't let that happen."

"I don't care! Don't leave me—"

"Oh, my boy, my boy. I'll never forsake you. I care about you more than my own life. I've loved you since you were born. And I'll always love you, no matter where you are or what happens to me. Do you believe me?"

"I do, Auntie. But please don't go."

Kawashima had reached the top of the hill.

Anyu unhooked the necklace with the Diamond of Life around her neck. She gave it a final look and looped it around Matthew's neck. "There. You see? I'll never leave you."

He looked at the necklace, his eyes dull like stones.

"Remember what I told you? It's a legendary stone, a precious treasure, and it'll protect you as it has protected me. It'll keep you safe. It'll bring you good luck and blessings. Promise me you'll never take it off. You'll always wear it. It's very important."

"I don't want it—" He sobbed.

"Don't be scared, little Matthew. You must believe after all the smoke and bombs, there will be sunshine. You must believe that, in the river or in a tent, under the stars or on a rooftop, you will survive. And most importantly, you must believe, no matter how many years and months go by, we'll meet again."

Anyu leaned to kiss his forehead and slipped down from the roof.

The soil under her feet was dry, warm, like slowly burning amber. She could hear the voices coming from the hill and hurried to the back door. She opened it, padded across the floor to her workbench, and pried open a board inside the wall near it. She took out the box that contained the Winter Egg and stuffed it in her pants' pocket.

The front door opened. Daylight glared on her face.

"There you are." Kawashima's voice.

"You found me." She couldn't see the killer's face, only her glittering eyes. Behind her were two soldiers in uniform.

"You hid well. It took me four years."

"You don't give up."

Kawashima laughed.

"I'll take you to the egg." Anyu stood.

"Where is it?"

"We'll need a boat," she said.

In the harbor, there were no junks, no fishing boats, no steamships, no ferryboats with painted wooden roofs; the massive double-prowed cross-harbor ship looked like a distant toy parked at the pier in Kowloon. A thick mist swelled, swallowing a few white boats bobbing in the river, drifting like moths.

The motorboat rushed at an astonishing speed, and Anyu had to grip her leather seat to keep steady, aware the killer was watching her every move. If her plan worked, they would reach Lantau Island in twenty minutes.

"I'm going to vomit." Anyu crawled across the cabin and reached the stern. The motorboat was quite large, with a second deck and a main mast, but no handrail. She dug into her throat and leaned over the edge of the ship.

"Get back here," Kawashima warned.

Anyu stood up, took out the box, and held it with her right hand.

Kawashima came to stand before her, her eyes flashing in anger. "You deceived me. Why did you say it was on Lantau Island?"

"I never said it was on Lantau Island. I said we needed a boat."

Kawashima put her hand on her sword.

"If you kill me, I'll drop it in the harbor," Anyu warned.

"You wouldn't dare."

Anyu looked at the box. "You executed my friend. She was my family."

"She was American, the enemy of our country."

"Did you ever love someone?"

The fog drifted to the princess's face and then dissipated. "I was given up for adoption at eight. I'm an orphan."

"I'm an orphan, too."

"Do you know what it's like to be visited at midnight by your adoptive father when you're sixteen? Then married off to someone you never met? You don't know anything about me. The egg is mine. I must have it."

Anyu sighed. "I will give it to you since you want it so much. Come closer."

Kawashima clumped toward her; the boat swayed. Then she stopped when she was about five steps away.

"Closer." Anyu beckoned with her free hand, maintaining her balance as the ship tossed.

Kawashima took one more step.

"It's yours now." Anyu placed the egg in the killer's hands. Kawashima studied it, and then, the corner of her mouth tilting upward, she laughed triumphantly.

Anyu lunged forward like a spear and thrust her off the boat.

A shriek. Kawashima's arms flailing, her hand stretching to catch the egg in the air. Then she grew smaller, and with a splash, she hit the waves, almost at the exact moment when the egg reached the surface and sank into the white foam.

At last, the princess had the egg, as she had wished, and no one would ever take the treasure from her.

Some voices rose. The soldiers' guns pointed at her.

"Where's the princess?"

She recognized the man in command—Mr. Tanaka. "In her grave."

A blow came down on her back, and Anyu fell into the harbor.

CHAPTER 44

When she regained her senses, Anyu found herself lying on a pier, her clothes soaked, her hair dripping with water. She sat up, squinting, the hot sun burning her eyes. Her face was burning as well; when she wiped it, she could feel sunburned flakes of skin peeling off. She had no idea what she was doing on the pier, how long she had been out there, or why she was near the water.

Japanese soldiers surrounded her, their faces stern.

Anyu blinked. *What's going on?*

But so strange, she couldn't hear herself.

A soldier slapped her. *Where is the egg?*

She held her face. *What egg?*

Eventually, the men tied up her hands and threw her into a green six-wheeled truck. Her head hit the metal frame of the window and she tasted blood in her mouth.

Panic raced through her.

She had lost her voice; she had lost her memory; she couldn't remember her own name.

CHAPTER 45

April 1942

The island was called Lamma Island, they said. A menacing soldier came to interrogate her—always asking about the egg—and then a gaggle of doctors carrying briefcases came to examine her. Naked, she lay on a narrow bed, exposed in bright beams, helpless. She wondered what she had done and whether she'd die on the surgery table for an egg.

Then she was confined in a small cell with a bed, a bench, a chamber pot, and a table with jeweler's tools and pencils and gold and silver and gemstones. Fascinated, she picked up the tools one by one, feeling the weight in her hand and listening to the soft clinks. A familiar wave of thrill shot through her stomach. It was perhaps a trick of the light, but something seemed to shine through, and voices, hard to catch, like music, echoed in her brain.

As if guided by an unseen force, she began to make a hook, a link, a bezel setting for a ring, a chain. She could hear the footsteps of the Japanese guard with a rifle outside her cell, the whispers of the food delivery women who came and went, and the other voices of the island, of the prisoners' misery, of the waves and the wind; she didn't raise her head.

⸙

Days passed, then months and years. She made rings, necklaces with pineapple pendants, jade belt buckles, silver cigarette cases, and emerald incense burners.

Each object flickered, emitting an intense phosphorescence like a diamond in the dark, evoking something like a piece of lost memory. She remembered the sky of snow, the bone-piercing chill, a dingy apartment near the railway, and a woman with a soft voice, and then, as if in a mirror, she saw a solitary child by the railway, drawing with her freezing hands. And then her hands, holding a precious egg, surreal like a glacial kingdom. She, a piece of jade, an orphan.

She remembered her years in Shanghai, the city of gold and gangsters, the bewitching French jeweler with a charming face, and the most beautiful woman she had ever seen, wearing a yellow dress bright like the sun.

She remembered she had loved, deeply, two men, one by the name of Isaac, the other Confucius; one was old, the other was young; one bent the metal, the other broke the morals; one had given her a diamond, the other had made her feel like a diamond. Her love for them was like a tide, ebbing and flowing, full of mystery, full of regret. They had protected her, given their lives to her, and loved her back. Yes, she had loved them, and they had loved her back.

And then, one day, peering at a pea-sized sapphire through a loupe, she remembered the princess obsessed with the eggs, and she remembered Matthew, the golden boy she had loved since he was born, the boy with the Diamond of Life.

She remembered her name.

The door opened.

The Japanese guard shouted for her to leave. Anyu stood and wobbled toward the door, holding the blowtorch she was working with. Her legs felt weak, having been sitting for long hours, and she had to reach for the wall to support herself. The soldier from the pier had come again, collected all the jewelry she had made, and asked more questions about the egg. Anyu remained silent.

Outside her cell, the warm wind caressed her face. She closed her eyes. She had long lost track of the seasons, forgotten how the island looked or exactly how long she had been there. This moment of freedom, of returning to the real world, was unexpected. It was near sunset; the palm trees, the shoreline, and the sky appeared faint, like shadows. Many women were gathered near a tent, where they had slept; some trudged through the grassland to her left, their heads drooping like parched sunflowers.

"Go." The guard prodded her to join them.

Where were they going?

A shot startled her, distant but close; for a moment the women froze in their trancelike walk, and then a wave of shrieks washed over the quiet island. The women scattered like startled animals.

Someone fell beside her.

"Help me," a woman said.

The voice sounded familiar—the food delivery woman. Anyu took her hand, but as she pulled, she lost her footing and crashed over the woman. Together, they rolled and fell over a slope. The drop was steep, taking her breath away. Finally, she hit a log and stopped moving.

"Where are we?" the delivery woman asked, lying a few feet away.

Anyu shook her head. She couldn't see very well but could still hear the volley of gunshots and screams in the distance.

"I know you. You are the Jeweler."

Anyu sat up. Her body ached; she might have broken her rib.

"Are you mute?"

She cleared her throat, but then she began to cough, and the urge, as always, stormed inside her lungs like a tyrant.

"It's all right, you don't have to talk. I think we're safe here."

Anyu nodded.

"They are planning on killing us, do you know? Rumors said the American submarines torpedoed the Japanese, and the Japanese are losing the war. They're leaving the island. So they organized a massacre on this island to get rid of us. Don't move!"

Anyu looked around and saw what she meant—they were not alone. Around them, hanging on the branches and leaves, reflected by the fading daylight, were strange creatures: bright-colored Romer's tree frogs, fuzzy caterpillars, moths the size of a saucer, and spiders parading with their pencil-like legs.

Anyu sat still.

"Watch out for those caterpillars; they're poisonous," her companion said, groaning. Then she introduced herself—Rain. She looked to be in her twenties, much younger than Anyu. Originally from a village in Guangzhou, she had been in Hong Kong since she was ten, and she had been imprisoned here for three years. "I think I broke my leg. It hurts."

Anyu wished there was something she could do.

"We'll hide here. Just in case the soldiers are looking for us. Once we survive this, we can go home."

Home. To see Matthew again. Anyu no longer felt the stab in her rib or intimidated by the colossal insects lurking beside her. She found a cave nearby and crawled inside with Rain. For the entire evening, they listened to gunshots and heartrending cries coming from uphill.

At dawn, the screams died down; the forest sank into a mournful silence. They crawled out.

"Look." Rain nudged her.

Outside the cave, above them, where her cell had been, red flames flared, plumes of black smoke spiraling above the forest. The raging inferno went on for three days, the air hissing with heat and rent by the agonizing cries of trapped animals, the ground ablaze with kindled grass and branches. The odor of scorched flesh and burning tree bark hung on the island, and the smoldering smoke and heat drove Anyu to tears.

When the fire finally eased, the once-verdant forest had turned into a bleak cemetery of charred groves shrouded with ashes. Dizzy with hunger, Anyu went to hunt for food since Rain was immobile with her broken leg. But she was unable to go too far, deterred by the choking smoke and flickering embers on the path. After much foraging, she returned with three roasted frogs and a big-headed turtle—the best she could do.

They ate them all.

With food in her stomach, Anyu trekked across the warm forest ground and went to the prisoners' camp. There was not a single female prisoner left; the tents had been burned to the ground, her cell buried in a pile of rubble, and all the gold, gemstones, and tools had vanished. The Japanese guards were gone, and so were the boats.

Each day, Anyu climbed out of the cave and trekked down the hill to the shore, looking for the boats that would take them to Hong Kong, a distant island. Matthew should be fourteen years old by now, a big boy. She couldn't wait to see him.

They were hungry, always hungry. With animal carcasses and insects rapidly spoiling in the sun, Anyu hunted bats and pangolins and shared her food with Rain, who was recovering slowly, but still unable to walk.

One day, Anyu heard a thunderous boom coming from the lighthouse on Hong Kong Island. Days later, a fleet with British flags sailed across the ocean toward Mt. Davis. Fishermen's blue junk boats, trawlers, and sailboats also appeared on the horizon.

She waved. "Here! Here!"

I'm coming, Matthew, I'm coming!

CHAPTER 46

September 1945

Standing in front of the building that used to be her apartment, Anyu felt lightheaded. It was hardly recognizable, a heap of broken windows and fallen walls, and the roof where she had said goodbye to Matthew had caved in. The building looked like it had been bombed months ago, and all over the streets were emaciated men and women, sick or starving, signs of how difficult life had been in Hong Kong.

Three and a half years had passed. So much time had been lost. Matthew must be taller than her. He would rush out. *Let's go to the beach!*

But where was he? Had he followed her instructions? Had he made his way to the monastery?

Anyu slumped on the street, short of breath, debilitated by the hike uphill. Blackness cloaked her vision, and her ears rang strangely. Rain pulled her up, asking if she was all right. They should go to her home on Lantau Island, Rain was saying, but Anyu didn't want to leave. This was her apartment, the only place where Matthew could find her, and she would have liked to sit there and wait for him for as long as it took.

Rain was sighing, her eyes filled with pity.

"He's alive," Anyu said.

"You come with me, Anyu. All right? It's not that far."

"I know he's alive." Rain didn't know about the Diamond of Life.

"Then you must get better. When you're healthy, you'll go find him."

Oh yes. She would find him, and she knew how.

CHAPTER 47

October 1956

Finally. A necklace with a horseshoe-crab pendant—a whimsical piece that evoked childhood dreams and longing. It shined brilliantly, showcasing a hexagonal body composed of six cabochon rubies mounted on a twenty-four karat pure gold shell etched with sleek chevrons. The triangular spines were encrusted with pearls, and the marquise-shaped eyes were intricately carved from rare emerald-green jade. A delicate whiplike telson, crafted from rose-colored amethyst, swept upward to convey movement, while ten enameled legs, all in primrose pink, complemented the sweet pastel color scheme, highlighting the pendant's playfulness and innocent charm.

The necklace had taken Anyu eleven years to craft. It was the most time-consuming piece she had ever made. And how slowly the needle of time had moved. On Lantau Island, people were either too poor to buy jewelry or too busy to wear it. For eleven years, Anyu had lived in a stilt house above mudflats near a canal, selling salted fish and woven ropes to the fishermen. Every coin she earned she saved so she could buy tools and solvents and degreaser. Then, on days when she was spared from dizzy spells, she took sampans covered with a canvas, traveled as far as her feeble legs would carry her, to bargain with families selling antiques at the roadside. It always energized her when her hand held a rare find such as a moonstone snuff bottle, or a jade tiger, or an old picture frame decorated with pearls. She bought them, took them apart, reshaped them, and used the gemstones for her necklace.

"I hope you'll win, Miss Anyu," Rain said, packing the necklace for the international jewelry competition that had attracted jewelers from around the world. It was one of the most influential international competitions in Hong Kong, and many renowned jewelers from Paris, New York, and London had flocked to the city, vying for the top prize. Newspapers, television, and radio had gone wild over the event, advertising the competition and eagerly promoting the participating jewelry pieces, an opportunity Anyu had anticipated.

She smiled. She was forty-seven years old. These days, she felt, in her gut, that the horseshoe necklace would be the last jewelry she would make. "I might win, I might not."

"Then how will you find the boy of yours?"

"We'll be lucky," she said.

A few days later, while Anyu was melting gold in the ring mold, she felt again the stabbing pain in her eyes. She took off the headlamp and dabbed her eyes with a handkerchief. Her eyes were bleeding. She blinked. Through the window, the boats and houses blended together in a haze of gray, and the distant mountains looked pale like water.

A draft swept through the stilt house, shaking it; the door squeaked.

But someone was at the door; she could make out . . . a tall shadow. She cocked her head. "Rain?"

"I'm here." Rain's voice came from near her. "Miss Anyu, are you taking a break? This man wants to see you."

"Who is it?" Rain knew too well that she didn't have customers, nor did she receive visitors.

Rain explained slowly. The man said he was an American artisan jeweler who had traveled to Hong Kong for the jewelry convention.

He had seen the segment about her horseshoe crab jewelry on TV by chance. He wanted to congratulate her on her design and ask why she carved IMAM on the necklace, along with a double-headed eagle.

"From America?" Anyu asked.

The figure walked toward her, the floorboards cracking in rhythm. The stilt house swayed.

Anyu reached out. A hand, big, dry, firm, held hers. She swallowed, and she felt him, the shape of his face, the jawline, the nose, the eyelids, and the soft hair.

"It's you, isn't it?" she whispered.

The shadow in front of her trembled. "It's me."

The voice of eternity, the voice of the past and the future, the voice of love. But it couldn't be. Still, she asked, "Isaac?"

A chuckle, or was it a sob? "It's me, Matthew. Matthew Dearborn, Auntie."

"Of course, of course." She smiled, happiness swelling in her heart. At last. As she had dreamed. She had found him. Only he would know who made a necklace with his favorite creature. Only he would know the meaning of the maker's marks and the double-headed eagle. "I'm so glad. You're here. How wonderful! How old are you now, Matthew?"

"Twenty-five years and two months."

She chuckled. How she wished she could see his face, his golden hair, his mischievous eyes. But this was good enough, holding his hand, feeling his skin and the strength of his fingers.

"I looked for you during the war, Auntie. I couldn't find you. Then, after the war, I heard many people were sent to Lamma Island, and I went to search for you. It was flattened by fire, and there was a mass grave. People said many prisoners died during the fire. I thought you were gone."

"Ah. Tell me what happened to you during the war."

"After you left, many children were caught by the Japanese soldiers and slaughtered, but the soldier who captured me gave me a piece of candy and told me to run away. Many people grew sick and starved in the hospital, but not me. Even when the Americans bombed the city, I was unscathed."

She had always known he would survive.

"It is true, isn't it? What you said about the stone?"

She patted his hand. "You must believe."

He was touching her face—wiping her tears. "Now I'm an artisan jeweler of my own house in New York, the House of Dearborn, Auntie. I make jewelry, I create memories, I evaluate gemstones and treasures."

"Your mother would be so proud. You remember her, do you?"

"Of course. I have two mothers."

"Ah, didn't I tell you? You're the most precious treasure of all."

And her boy, the boy she had been waiting for these fourteen years, the boy she had protected, the boy who had the Diamond of Life, laughed. "How can I forget? I remember everything you told me."

"So did you pay your respects to Confucius?"

"I did, and guess what I found."

He guided her hands around something smooth, something oval, and then, as she'd expected, it opened.

Anyu smiled. She couldn't see the delicately carved eggshells, the diamond-threaded rivulets, the rock-crystal base, the fine features of the priceless ornament that had captivated her when she was fifteen years old, the ornament that had changed her life, the ornament that had beguiled a mad princess, but she always did believe her boy would find it.

AUTHOR'S NOTE

This is a work of fiction. All the major characters in this novel were created from my imagination, except the character Yoshiko Kawashima, loosely based on the real historical figure, who was born Aisin Gioro Xianyu in 1906. She was the fourteenth daughter of Prince Su of the Manchu's Qing Dynasty in China and a cousin of Puyi, the last emperor of the Qing Dynasty. After the fall of the dynasty, she was given away by her father to his friend Kawashima Naniwa, who raised her in Japanese culture in Japan. The Manchu princess, known for her beauty and erratic personality, was the topic of much gossip because of her unusual life: she was born as a princess, raised as an adoptee, and married as a woman, but in her adult years, she chose to wear a crew cut and cross-dressed as a man, and kept many lovers, all male. It was said she was a spy for the Japanese and an abettor of their invasion of China; she was executed in 1948.

Several minor characters are also loosely, very loosely based on real people, such as Mr. Du and the warlord Zhang. However, it is not known that warlord Zhang Zuolin had an illegitimate daughter called Zhang Anyu, the main character in this novel.

Regarding the Fabergé eggs, I relied on Toby Faber's incredible book *Fabergé Eggs: The Extraordinary Story of the Masterpieces That Outlived an Empire*. In his book, Faber states that a total of fifty-two imperial Fabergé eggs were created for Dowager Empress Maria Feodorovna and Empress Alexandra Feodorovna from 1885 to 1917, including the last two eggs crafted in 1917 that were never delivered. This priceless collection was inventoried and ordered to be taken to the Kremlin Armoury after the Bolshevik Revolution in 1917. However, it was revealed later that about ten eggs never made it to the Armoury's storerooms.

Among the missing eggs were the Cherub with Chariot Egg, the Mauve Egg, the Alexander III Commemorative Egg, and the Third Imperial Easter Egg, mentioned in the novel. The whereabouts of these eggs remained a mystery for many years. In 2014, Reuters reported that a scrap-metal dealer from the US Midwest had discovered the Third Imperial Easter Egg, one of the missing eggs. It was valued at 20 million pounds.

It's important to clarify that the Winter Egg mentioned in this novel was designed by Alma Theresia Pihl, and its workmaster was Albert Holmström, not Isaac Mandelburg, a fictional character. The ornament was not missing after the revolution, but it also had a tortuous history. According to Faber, it was "sold to Emanuel Snowman in the 1920s, missing for a number of years before reemergence in 1994," when it was sold to the emir of Qatar. I chose to center on the Winter Egg for its unparalleled aesthetic beauty.

Regarding the *tzohar*, I was inspired by *The Encyclopedia of Jewish Myth, Magic & Mysticism* written by Geoffrey W. Dennis. In his book, he acknowledges the ambiguity and the various interpretations of the word *tzohar*. He describes that the stone, a gift from God to Noah, was "a luminous gemstone holding the primordial light of Creation" and those who possessed it "not only had illumination" but access to many secrets and extraordinary powers.

The surname Bellefeuille came from a discussion I had with a writer whom I met at a Historical Novel Society conference. A French Canadian, she told me about the surname de Bellefeuille and instructed that it needed to be de Bellefeuille to indicate the Canadian roots. But I decided to use Bellefeuille instead to create a relatively more American impression. My apologies to the writer.

Sharp-eyed readers will notice *dollar* instead of *yuan* was used in the novel to describe the currency. This refers to silver dollars that were in circulation from the 1920s to 1935, when the Republic of China adopted the silver standard.

ACKNOWLEDGMENTS

This book would not have been possible without the kindness and generosity of the extraordinary people who have been part of my writing journey. I'm amazingly fortunate to be able to have them to work with.

To my agent, Alexa Stark, for your extremely helpful comments on the first draft of the novel, and your professional experience and guidance in bringing this novel to the world. And to my film agent, Tom Ishizuka, and his colleagues at Writers House, for all your help and for working tirelessly behind the scenes.

To Danielle Marshall, Melissa Valentine, Carissa Bluestone, Tegan Tigani, Chantelle Aimée Osman, the sensitivity reader, the copyeditor, the proofreaders, the production manager, the designer, the marketing team, and the entire team at Lake Union, thank you for your dedication and invaluable insight. Once again, it's been an honor and a pleasure to work with you.

I'm amazingly blessed to have my relative Mike Leibling, whose criticism and feedback were essential to giving birth to the idea of this novel. Thank you, Mike, for brainstorming with me when I was looking for a bright, shining diamond of a story, for listening to me moan about the plot in writing and the plight in life, and for always being a text away, even though we live a continent apart.

I'm also indebted to my dear friend Dianna Rostad, a talented writer, the most compassionate friend I lean on, whose writerly perceptions, encouragement, and friendship remain the nectar of my life.

I would not have had this idea of writing about a jeweler had it not been for David Fredrick, my husband's great-uncle, whose life story astounded me no matter how many times I heard it. A Jew and a jeweler, he was sent to a series of concentration camps in Germany during World War II, and he, along with two of his brothers, survived the Holocaust by making jewelry for the Nazi guards. Later, he immigrated to the US and opened Fredrick's Jewelry in Metro Detroit, which is still in business, though under different ownership. I was hoping to write a book about David Fredrick's survival, which would have been most appropriate, but I was unable to hammer it out. My deepest gratitude to Gail Posner and Paula Ceresnie, Uncle David's daughters, and Ken Posner and Mike Ceresnie, for sharing their memories with me.

I would like to take this opportunity to express my deepest gratitude to Toby Faber for providing valuable information on the workmasters and the Fabergé eggs in his book and for patiently answering my emails. Thank you!

I am extremely grateful to Rabbi Geoffrey W. Dennis. Thank you for your prompt emails, your steadfast support, and for opening my eyes about Jewish mysticism.

Sometimes, life throws you a nugget that's stranger than fiction, and if you're a writer, you can't help but pick it up—thank you so much to Liliana Kondracki, whom I met at a book club, for telling me the story of how her grandfather was poisoned by arsenic in his spicy soup and giving me permission to use it in my novel. More information about the scheme can be found in *A Murder in Lemberg: Politics, Religion, and Violence in Modern Jewish History*.

As always, I'm immensely grateful to my family and friends, whose love and support are the foundation of my life. Thank you to my friends who check on me, knowing my phone only works one-way because I am often marooned in another universe; to my husband for making sure I wouldn't run out of blueberries for breakfast; to my son for reading the first two pages and giving me a thumbs-up; and to my daughter for editing the first fifty pages of the novel's early draft—yes, I lowballed you, but that was the best twenty dollars I've ever spent!

SELECTED BIBLIOGRAPHY

The Art & Craft of Making Jewelry: A Complete Guide to Essential Techniques by Joanna Gollberg

Beautiful Creatures: Jewelry Inspired by the Animal Kingdom by Marion Fasel

The Complete Photo Guide to Making Metal Jewelry by John Sartin

The Encyclopedia of Jewish Myth, Magic & Mysticism by Geoffrey W. Dennis

Fabergé: Court Jeweler to the Tsars by G. von Habsburg-Lothringen and A. von Solodkoff

Fabergé's Eggs: The Extraordinary Story of the Masterpieces That Outlived an Empire by Toby Faber

The Fall of Hong Kong: Britain, China, and the Japanese Occupation by Philip Snow

Gem: The Definitive Visual Guide by Smithsonian Institution

Gemstones: A Jewelry Maker's Guide to Identifying & Using Beautiful Rocks by Judith Crowe

Harbin: A Cross-Cultural Biography by Mark Gamsa

Hong Kong Holiday by Emily Hahn

The Jeweler's Directory of Gemstones by Judith Crowe

Jewelry: Fundamentals of Metalsmithing by Tim McCreight

Metalsmithing for Jewelry Makers by Jinks McGrath

Mitya's Harbin: Majesty and Menace by Lenore Lamont Zissermann

Shanghai: The Rise and Fall of a Decadent City by Stella Dong

Verdura: The Life and Work of a Master Jeweler by Patricia Corbett

Zhang Xueliang Oral History, Chinese Edition (张学良口述历史), by Tang Degang (唐德刚)

ABOUT THE AUTHOR

Photo © 2024 Benjamin Cheung Photography

Weina Dai Randel is the acclaimed author of five historical novels, including the *Wall Street Journal* bestseller *The Last Rose of Shanghai*; *Night Angels*, long-listed for the Massachusetts Book Awards; and the Empress of Bright Moon duology. She is the winner of the RWA RITA Award, a National Jewish Book Awards finalist, and a two-time Goodreads Choice Awards Best Historical Fiction nominee. Her novels have been translated into seventeen languages, including German, French, Spanish, Portuguese, Russian, Italian, and Hebrew. Weina was born in China and now lives in Boston with her family. For more information, visit weinarandel.com.